THE TRAITOR'S STORY

ALSO BY KEVIN WIGNALL

Individual Works

People Die

Among the Dead

Who is Conrad Hirst?

The Hunter's Prayer

Dark Flag

A Death in Sweden

Short Stories

"The Window"

"Retrospective"

"A Death"

"Hal Checks Out"

THE TRAITOR'S STORY

KEVIN WIGNALL

THOMAS & MERCER

This is a work of fiction. Names, characters, organizations, places, events, and incidents are either products of the author's imagination or are used fictitiously.

Published by Thomas & Mercer, Seattle

www.apub.com

ISBN-13: 9781503933125
ISBN-10: 1503933121

Cover design by Lisa Horton

Printed in the United States of America

To Iain and Pip

King's Road

September 2010

History

Kaliningrad—early March

Harry Simons was dying—there was no question about it. The medics kept working, but even a brief look at that stricken face was enough to know it was pointless. He'd always been so easy-going, a young guy full of laughter, smiling eyes, and yet now his features were waxy and unresponsive, registering no pain or discomfort, his eyes flickering about but fixing on nothing.

Harry Simons was dying. And still the medics kept working, and Perry wished they'd stop and let Harry die with some dignity, because there was nothing more unsettling than the violence done to a man to keep him alive when he'd been critically wounded.

Johnson walked up and waited until he'd got Perry's attention before saying, "Jack Trelawney wants a word when you've got a second."

"I've got a second now. Where is he?"

Johnson pointed across the darkened dockyard to the ambulance where Trelawney was being treated.

Perry nodded, relieved to have a reason to walk away, but crouched down, ignoring the medics, and put a hand on Harry's cheek, which was cold and wet with sleet. He wished he could say something, but there were no words, and Harry looked too far away to hear them anyway, alone in some quiet descent.

He stood again and Johnson said, "Do you think he'll make it?"

"No."

Perry walked from the shelter of the warehouse, briefly exposed to the squall that was still blowing in across the docks—this small part of the Baltic refusing to acknowledge the early arrival of spring. He glanced up at the floodlights as he walked; the illuminated sleet looked like the grain in an old film.

Trelawney had taken a bullet to the hand. Not bad considering the complete bloodbath that had taken place here—not only Harry but two FSB men down, three of the local police, half a dozen of Karasek's men. Of course, Karasek hadn't been among them, and there was nothing to prove they were his men or that he had any connection to the shipment that had been intercepted. To that extent, this joint operation, the much-vaunted Sparrowhawk, had been a complete failure.

Perry looked at Trelawney. "What have you got for me, Jack?"

Trelawney shook his head, unable to form an answer, then said, "What about Harry?"

"They think the bullet bounced around inside his ribs, hit an artery." Trelawney looked devastated. Everyone liked Harry, but it was important they stayed professional, so Perry repeated, "What have you got for me?"

"If Harry dies, someone should take Finn Harrington and blow his brains out."

Trelawney used the hand that wasn't being bandaged to reach inside his coat. The medic continued working on the other hand, not giving way. Trelawney pulled a sheaf of papers free and thrust it out.

"Ed, this was in their truck. Take a look. Harrington's rotten—he's been working for Karasek all along."

Perry looked at the top sheet—a printed email—tipping it out of his own shadow and trying to protect it from the sleet at the same time, struggling to take in the information printed there. It wasn't so much that he hadn't known about Harrington, but that he hadn't even suspected, and he was technically Harrington's superior, so this would inevitably look bad on him.

He heard a voice—Louisa Whitman saying, "Let me see that." He turned. She was dressed as if going on a shoot at a country house: waxed jacket, matching hat. She also seemed unfazed by the cold and the wet. He handed the paperwork over, and as she took it she smiled at Trelawney and said, "How are you feeling, Jack?"

"Like crap."

"Good." She turned to Perry. "The FSB are less than happy, and it is just a little embarrassing for us, particularly as it seems half the shipment is missing. Now, what have we got here?"

"I've only just seen it, but it looks like what Jack says is true—Harrington's been working for Karasek, probably tipped him off about us being here tonight."

She studied the papers, shaking her head in ever-greater disbelief, then looked up and said, "But he and Harry Simons are best friends."

"In Harrington's defense, I very much doubt he thought it would end like this." Trelawney let out a single derisive laugh. Perry looked at him, then back to Louisa as he said, "He'll have to be dealt with, of course. By the letter of the law he's a traitor."

"He's a bastard," said Trelawney. Louisa looked at him in admonishment but he wasn't about to back down. "I don't care. If he was here right now I'd shoot him myself, but he isn't here right now, is he? How convenient is that?"

Perry said, "That's enough, Trelawney."

"Oh, Ed—Jack's only venting his feelings." She brandished the papers. "This will have to be investigated, as will the entire operation and the parts we've all played in it, and people rather more senior than me will decide upon the most judicious course of action. Either way, I suspect Harrington's life is about to become rather uncomfortable."

Trelawney, frustrated by Louisa's relaxed tone, said, "It's obvious, isn't it? It's why he resigned before all this—because he got paid off. All these bogus rumors about one of our team working for Naumenko, and it turns out Harrington was working for Karasek right under our noses. He's betrayed his country, but he's betrayed all of us, too. Even you, Louisa."

Louisa nodded, apparently accepting the unshakable truth of it, then said, "Shame—I rather liked him."

"Me too," said Perry, though in reality he'd never really warmed to him. Harrington hadn't been much of a team player—affable enough, but always a little distant, a little cold, at least with everyone except Harry, who he'd inadvertently sacrificed here tonight. But whether or not Harrington got the bullet in the head that Trelawney wanted, Louisa was certainly right about the way things would pan out for him now.

To be a traitor was one thing; to be stupid enough to get caught, and in such a careless way, that was another. To be a traitor and bring about the death of someone like Harry Simons raised it to another level. The future would be grim for Harrington, and the contempt and vengefulness he'd face would be nothing less than he deserved.

Perry glanced over his shoulder but couldn't see whether the two medics were still struggling to keep Harry alive. They were lost in shadow, ominously still.

He looked at Louisa again and said, "I suppose this is the end of Sparrowhawk."

"Take a look around you, Ed. What do you think?"

She turned and walked away, and he stood there in the sleet in the middle of the night, the dead and injured littering the dockyard. Yes, with absolute certainty he could say that this was the end of Sparrowhawk, the end of Harry Simons, and in one way or another, the end of Finn Harrington, too—no less than if he'd been here and taken a bullet himself.

Chapter One

Lausanne—six years later

Finn took a taxi from the station, and as it approached his building he spotted the concierge standing outside staring up at the sky, which even this early in the year had the promise of spring in it.

Finn paid the driver and said, "Bonjour, Monsieur Grasset."

Grasset looked as if he hadn't expected Finn to return, and smiled as he said, "Monsieur Harrington, it's nice to see you back. A research trip?"

"That's right. Béziers, mainly. I stopped in Paris for a night on the way home."

"Ah, so you're writing about the Cathars." Finn nodded. "Very interesting."

"I hope so."

Finn made to move on, but Grasset stopped him with a regretful look. "Monsieur Harrington—your wife . . . she left."

Finn heard the words as if they were a skillfully constructed riddle. Did he mean she'd left, or gone away? Finn had only been traveling for eleven days and she'd sounded fine the last time he'd spoken to her . . . seven days ago.

Unsure how to respond, and irritated by Grasset's kindly invasion of his privacy, he said, "She isn't my wife."

Grasset nodded, looking a little embarrassed, and in turn Finn felt he'd been churlish, that the old man had meant no harm. Finn searched for something mollifying to say, perhaps a suggestion of where she might have gone, but he could think of nothing.

"Do you know where she went?"

Grasset shrugged. "To the station. She looked upset, but . . ." More hopefully, he added, "Perhaps someone in her family is sick?"

"Could be. Thanks for letting me know."

Finn left Grasset outside, took the elevator, and let himself into the empty apartment. He left his case in the hall and walked into the kitchen and then the study, the two places she might have left a note. There was nothing in either room. He put his laptop case on the desk, then took his suitcase into the bedroom and hoisted it onto the bed but didn't open it.

For a few moments, he studied the rails of clothes in her closet, trying to estimate how much was missing. Apart from her current favorite coat, he wasn't sure, and he struggled even to remember what she'd been wearing when he last saw her.

Anyway, he supposed the things she'd taken wouldn't tell him much about how long she intended to stay away—for all he knew, the clothes in front of him might be those she was willing to abandon forever, things she'd bought on a whim, or loved once but no longer.

He tried her phone, but it went straight to voicemail and he hung up without leaving a message. She'd left him. He stood in the middle of the bedroom, uncertain what to do next. He called her again, and when the voicemail kicked in he said, "Adrienne, it's me. Grasset tells me you've left. Call me. If you want to." As he hung up, he regretted the final four words, knowing how she'd interpret them.

But there was nothing more he could do. He stood for a moment longer, then walked back into the study, knowing that the book needed to be written no matter what happened to his relationship.

He took the laptop from its case and opened it up, arranged his notebooks, and started to transcribe, all the while thinking his way through the Albigensian Crusade. He had enough material, but now it was a question of illuminating it for his readers in a style that was fresh and original and compelling.

He'd already decided it would need multiple viewpoints. There would be Pope Innocent III, struggling to keep his Church intact in the face of Cathar heretics. The Abbot of Cîteaux, of course—the leader of the crusade. Perhaps he would imagine the perspective of a regular soldier in that army, too. And then, as a counterpoint, one of the townspeople of Béziers itself, believing that the good intentions of twenty thousand people could save the lives of two hundred, a misjudgment like no other in history.

But Arnaud Amaury, the Abbot of Cîteaux, a Cistercian monk with a military vision, he had to be the key . . .

There was a knock on the door. He ignored it, but struggled to reconnect with his thoughts, his concentration already brittle. The knock came again, and he went to the door and opened it.

It was Adrienne's friend from the floor below, the preppy Debbie Portman, who looked like she might be a lawyer or a junior congresswoman, but who actually did nothing. Adrienne occasionally wrote features for a French art magazine but essentially lived off family money, so the two of them were natural companions.

Finn didn't even know what Ethan Portman did except that it was something in finance. They were American and had a daughter, which was about the sum of his knowledge—they were Adrienne's friends, and his only by default.

She smiled but it looked strained, and even though he picked up the signals in her expression, he said, "Debbie, good morning.

I'm afraid Adrienne isn't here." He realized Grasset hadn't told him when she'd left, though he presumed it had been recent. "I imagine she's just gone away for a day or two."

Debbie looked momentarily at a loss, as if she wanted to say one thing but felt obliged to respond to his opening comment. With the air of someone wanting to dismiss a subject quickly, she said, "Adrienne left nearly a week ago. Haven't you spoken to her since then?"

"Where's she gone?" She hesitated, not wanting to say. It galled Finn that he had to discuss this with someone else. "Debbie, I'm only asking where she's gone."

"To her brother's."

"In Paris?" That irritated him. He'd almost called Mathieu while he was in Paris, but had somehow failed to get around to it. "Okay. Well, thanks for letting me know."

He searched for something in her expression or body language that acknowledged the conversation was over, but she remained still, like someone held on pause. And now that he looked at her, he could see how drawn she looked, how lacking in sleep. For a sickening moment he wondered if Adrienne's departure somehow involved Ethan Portman.

"Might I come in for a moment?"

"Is it something that can wait? You see, I'm working . . . right in the middle of something, in fact."

He realized she must have seen him come in, and had to know he'd only been working for ten minutes or so, but she caught him out by saying, "On the Cathars. I know." He'd always asked Adrienne not to discuss his works in progress with friends, but before he could say anything, Debbie caught him off guard a second time. "My daughter's missing."

"Er . . ." She looked on the verge of tears, as if her entire unshakable, preppy edifice was about to crumble. "I see. Please, come in, come and sit down," he said, hoping movement would help her to pull herself together.

She walked through into the living room and sat down on the edge of one of the sofas. Now that she was inside, she looked eager to leave, perhaps wanting to be back in her own apartment in case there was news.

"Can I get you a drink or something?" She shook her head, looking into the middle distance. "Okay . . . er . . . so you say Hailey's missing?"

"Three days, and the police aren't helping, and I know something's happened to her, I know it. That's why I'm here, Finn. I just need someone who can do more than—"

Finn saw where she was heading and couldn't believe it. He jumped in quickly, saying, "Hold on, Debbie. I'm sympathetic, really I am, but I'm not sure what you want of me."

She fixed her gaze on him, her eyes rimmed with tears now. "Help to find her. I know about your career, about who you are . . . Adrienne told me."

"Told you what? I write popular history books."

"Before that, Finn. She told me—you were a spy or an agent or whatever it is they call them now."

He was briefly angry with Adrienne, not so much because she'd refused to let the whole spying business drop—if anything, he admired that she'd always seen through his denials—but because she'd shared those thoughts with Debbie Portman. It proved that he'd been right never to be completely open with her, that it was best never to be completely open with anyone.

"No, no, no. Adrienne likes to believe I was a spy, but she shouldn't have told you that because it's ridiculous, and now it's given you false hope. I'm not a spy, I never was. I write popular history books—"

She sprung up from the sofa. "Jesus, Finn, my daughter is missing! You're the only person we know who might have the contacts, who might know how to help, and I'm asking you to help find her, that's all."

He felt hemmed in, the startling sense of exposure less oppressive than the urgent realization that he had to deny it, that he couldn't admit to a past of any kind, no matter what the emergency.

He shook his head. "I wish I could, I really do, but I'm not who you think I am. Even if I were, I'm not sure how that would help me find a missing schoolgirl."

"You could help. There must be something you could do, someone—"

"Debbie, I can help you as a neighbor . . . as a friend. But what you're talking about, it's just Adrienne's fantasy. You know, not everyone with a gap in their CV is a spy."

She didn't believe him, perhaps believed him even less than before, and said with utter conviction, "You could help."

"No, I couldn't. Not in the way you think."

Her eyes didn't leave his, but instead stared hard—accusing, calculating. Adrienne's word meant more than his, and as a result Debbie saw only a man who didn't want to help, not a man who couldn't. If he was honest with himself, she was partly right in that assumption, because both of those things were true.

"Bastard." It was said with quiet hatred, and then she turned and walked out. He expected to hear the door slam, but she left with a composure and a dignity that made him feel less of a man.

He walked through to the bedroom, opened his suitcase but didn't empty it. Instead he went back to the study, to his notes, settling back into his chair, into history, struggling to put the unpleasantness of Debbie Portman's visit out of his mind.

He forced himself to focus, because Debbie Portman's daughter wasn't his problem. How to make the Abbot of Cîteaux sympathetic—that was his real problem, and the key to his book. The Pope, the crusader, the citizen of Béziers . . . he could see a way of making all of them sympathetic, but none of them was the key.

How could he make his reader empathize with a man who'd ordered the deaths of twenty thousand people, a man who'd brought such destruction on the city that it had taken two hundred years to put right—and all in the name of God?

For Finn, his understanding of the abbot's ruthlessness lay in the simple and brutal beauty of knowing it had worked. All the other towns had capitulated willingly in the knowledge of what had happened to Béziers, and surrendered the Cathars to their fate. That was enough to fill Finn with a sneaking admiration for the Abbot of Cîteaux, but he doubted it would be enough for his readers.

He heard an ambulance siren somewhere in the distance and his thoughts found their way stubbornly back to his neighbors and their domestic drama. He guessed the girl was around fourteen, and his mind reeled unwillingly through the possibilities of what might have happened to her, a backdrop against which running away was the fragile best-case scenario.

But Debbie hadn't talked of Hailey running away; she'd said she was missing. There was an implication there—one strengthened by her trenchant belief that someone with an intelligence background might be able to help in a way the police couldn't. It made him curious. What exactly did she think had happened to her daughter? Was it just a woman refusing to believe that her precious little girl had become sick of living with her parents?

His brain quickly discounted the second question. He was reassembling all his memories of the Portmans now, as well as all the things Adrienne had told him, engaging with the everyday details of his life in a way he probably hadn't for six years. Ethan and Debbie Portman were smart, decent people, and if they thought something had happened to their daughter, it probably had.

Finn closed his laptop and walked through to the living room again. He stood looking over the lake, reluctantly giving way to his curiosity, to his innate desire to solve any puzzle put before him. She'd been a pleasant kid, polite, wry. Then he felt a slight nauseous lurch as he realized he was thinking about her in the past tense.

He couldn't admit his background to them—that was beyond question. Besides, even if he did, how could he explain why he had no contacts, why that world was as closed to him as if he'd never been a part of it?

He'd offer his help as it was, without credentials, because he supposed that's what people did for their neighbors, for their friends. And a critical internal voice questioned why he even needed to think about it, questioned what had happened to him over these last years. When had doing the right thing stopped being the automatic option and become something that had to be worked at instead? He hadn't always been this person, but he was no longer even sure of when the transformation had taken place.

Chapter Two

He stood at the door and went through a mental checklist. Hailey was about fourteen, her parents around forty. They were from Connecticut. No, they'd met at Yale. Ethan was from Chicago, Debbie from Philadelphia. He worked in finance. And that was it. How could Finn have met them so many times, spent a reasonable amount of the last two years in their company, and yet learned so little about them?

They undoubtedly knew a great deal about his books, and that had been an intentional ploy on his part, to hide his past behind an obsession with history and his own literary reputation, but it was as if he'd actually become his own cover story.

He pressed the buzzer and waited, wondering as he stood there not about why Adrienne had left him, but what she had ever seen in him to begin with. Debbie was quick to open the door and his thoughts crashed into each other at the sight of her desperate, hopeful face—the expectation dying as she saw him.

"May I come in?"

She stepped aside and closed the door behind him. "I don't know why I thought you'd be able to help. You'll try anything, I guess."

"Of course." He became distracted by the silence of the apartment and said, "Where's Ethan?"

"He's gone to the embassy in Bern. I don't think it'll help but we're trying everything we can. Sorry, come on through."

He followed her through to the living room and said, "Does Adrienne know?"

Debbie shook her head, and looked worried as she said, "Should I have told her? She and Hailey get along so well together—she'd want to know."

Were Adrienne and Hailey that close? Most of the time, Adrienne went to the Portmans' apartment for coffee and glasses of wine and chats—so as not to disturb him while he was working—so he guessed it was possible.

"Probably best not to tell her for now, unless she'd be a comfort to you. From an entirely selfish point of view, I don't want her coming back to me for the wrong— What I mean is, she clearly needs time away from me."

Even in the midst of her distress, he thought Debbie might offer him some reassuring words, but she looked uncomfortable instead, as if not wanting to reveal bitter truths that he still hadn't imagined—probably that it was too late, that Adrienne wouldn't be coming back at all.

"Okay, look, we're not here to discuss what a lousy boyfriend I am. You said the police were no good, that you doubted the embassy would help. Why? Why aren't the police taking it seriously?"

"They're taking it seriously, it's just . . . they're treating her as a runaway."

"But you're convinced she hasn't run away." He couldn't understand why the police would so readily dismiss the disappearance of a child. And then the pieces fell into place—the obvious reason for the police treating the case in this way. "Debbie, did she leave a note?"

"Yes. Yes, she left a note, but it doesn't mean anything." She spoke rapidly, eager to get her reasoning out in the open, and put her hand on his arm, too, desperate for him not to walk out. "The note doesn't make sense, not for someone just running away, and she wasn't unhappy. She left of her own accord, Finn, but something's wrong. You have to believe a mother's instinct. I just know."

"Do you have the note?"

She left the room and came back a moment later with a sheet of paper.

"It's a copy. Ethan took the original with him."

He nodded, took the sheet, and sat down—then started reading aloud. "*Dear Mom and Dad . . .*" Debbie seemed to grow weak and lowered herself into a nearby armchair. "I'm sorry, would you rather I read it to myself?"

"No, read it out. I know the words by heart, anyway."

"*I have to go away for a while, but please don't worry about me. I'm with friends and I'll be safe. I can't explain more than that, not yet, but I don't think it's a good idea for me to stay here right now. Please don't worry, and I'm sorry.*" She ended by saying she loved them, but he didn't read that aloud, not wanting to tip Debbie over the edge. "You've checked with friends, of course?"

"Everyone we could think of."

"Which means it's someone you don't know about."

"But you see what I mean? She felt she wasn't safe here, that she was in danger."

Finn looked at the note again, struggling to see how Debbie had drawn those conclusions. He also understood why the police saw Hailey as a straightforward runaway.

"Actually, Debbie, she doesn't say that. She says it isn't a good idea to stay here right now—that could be because she wasn't getting on with you, or because there was bad news from school that she didn't want you to find out about."

"Our relationship with Hailey is . . . it's great. I know I'm her mother but she's a perfect kid, and a first-class student. The school has no idea why she might have run away, and if you knew her better nor would you." Finn nodded, looking at the note again, and as much as he felt for what they must be going through, he felt worse for their self-delusion, because for whatever reason, their daughter *had* run away. It looked to him like the act of a selfish kid, not a perfect one. "Finn, I realize you and I don't know each other too well, but I'm not an hysterical woman, and I want to assure you that if Hailey did run away it's because she was afraid. I don't know what of, but something frightened her into this."

For the first time, he noticed the picture facing him on a side table. It was a close-up of Hailey taken out on the lake: long mousy hair slightly windswept, big eyes, a big American smile. She was an attractive girl.

"How old is Hailey?"

"She turned fifteen last month—but Finn, she's not a streetwise kid, you know. She's had a privileged existence." He nodded, but could feel his interest waning and was already beginning to wish he hadn't intervened. "There's something else I want to show you. Please, follow me."

Finn stood and followed Debbie through the apartment to Hailey's bedroom. There were stuffed toys on the bed, posters on the wall, books everywhere, a laptop on the desk, an iPod in its dock—maybe the computer was dispensable, but what kind of kid went anywhere today without their iPod?

Debbie opened the doors of the closet and said, "Nothing's missing. Only what she was wearing, but if she'd planned to run away she would have taken extra clothes and she's taken nothing. Nothing at all."

He looked at the rails packed with clothes, and at the racks of shoes on the floor underneath. It was amazing that Debbie could tell nothing was missing, but he believed her. It didn't stop her opening drawers full of underwear and T-shirts. Adrienne had taken more than Hailey had—he was sure of that.

Debbie was still looking expectantly at him, so he said, "Did she take her passport?"

"No, we keep her passport with ours, it's in the desk in the—I'll be back in just a moment." She walked out of the room.

Finn looked idly through the rails of clothes while he waited, though they were crammed too tight to move them very much. Then he stood back, and noticed a shoebox on the floor of the closet—it was so full that the lid had come off.

He crouched down and removed the lid completely. The box was full of shopping bags, most of them plastic, scrunched up and put inside another bag, but also some folded paper bags. He opened a couple and looked at the receipts and the discarded tags still inside, and he became intrigued again, sensing that the rails full of clothes weren't the whole story here, that there was more to it.

Realizing Debbie hadn't come back, he went looking for her and found her sitting at the desk in the study, holding a passport. She was crying quietly, and when she saw him she waved him away, embarrassed, and took a tissue and dried her eyes.

"I'm sorry," he said.

She held up the passport—Finn guessed it was Debbie's, that Ethan had taken his with him to the embassy—and she struggled through a tight throat to say, "She took it. Why would she take her passport?"

It was a question that hardly needed an answer, and he was astonished that they were naive enough not to have checked for her passport before now, so instead he said, "Debbie, there's something in her room that I want you to take a look at."

She nodded, then looked at the passport again and put it back in the desk drawer. Her faith looked as if it had faltered, as if she no longer believed the beautiful and haunting lie that she'd been telling herself, that her precious daughter wouldn't do this to them of her own free will.

Slowly, fatigued by emotion, she stood and followed him. He lifted the shoebox out of the closet and placed it on the bed. He took the paper bags out, all from the same store, then emptied the plastic bags, which were mostly from just a couple of places.

Debbie's bewildered expression answered his question in advance, but for the sake of form he said, "Are these the kind of places Hailey usually shops at?"

She shook her head and pointed at the paper bags. "I've never even heard of that place."

The paper bags were from a store called Fate.

"What access does she have to money?"

"We trust her entirely . . ." She ground to a halt, perhaps realizing the redundancy of the statement. "She has a pre-paid credit card, but apart from some extra cash withdrawals there's nothing suspicious on it. I guess she gets a lot of cash from us, too, but . . . you know how it is with kids nowadays."

He took a few of the receipts and looked at them.

"It looks like she bought all this stuff over the last week or so. I suspect that's why none of her clothes are missing."

"But why? I mean, she chooses her own clothes anyway—she loves the things she has."

If Debbie's world had fallen apart with Hailey's disappearance, it appeared to collapse in on itself further as each of these truths hit home—that her daughter had chosen to run away, that rather than being in so much of a hurry as to leave her clothes behind, she'd been planning her disappearance for a week or more. All of Debbie's past certainties were as nothing now.

Perhaps this was the moment at which she expected Finn to make his excuses and leave. Yet the very things that had shaken

Debbie's faith had piqued Finn's interest. For the first time, he saw how this might be something more interesting than a straightforward runaway.

"You checked her computer, of course?"

She nodded absentmindedly. "That's how much she trusts us—we even know her password. But the computer's clean: no browsing history, nothing."

"Nothing at all?"

"No," she said, apparently unable to see the implication, that Hailey had wiped it, presumably because she didn't trust them as much as Debbie imagined.

He could also have told her that a computer was never clean, but as he no longer knew anyone who could look at it for him, there hardly seemed to be any point. Besides, even if he was here helping, he still hadn't admitted anything about his past, and he knew that it was best to maintain that stance.

He crossed the room, saying, "Is this her only iPod?"

Debbie nodded, not sure what he was doing. He picked it up and scrolled through the songs. A lot of them were things he didn't recognize, but there was a lot of middling pop on there, too—the kind of thing beloved by girls of a certain age.

He put it back in its dock, the pieces coming together. He picked up some of the bags, then turned and looked at a confused Debbie.

"I'll need to take these. I'll also need a good recent photograph." He looked at the laptop, but taking it would only hint at a level of sophistication above and beyond what he was bringing to the table. "I'm not promising anything. Adrienne was wrong in what she told you. I don't have any contacts, but I can help as a friend."

She shook her head, and he wondered if it was because his description of himself as a friend was incongruous, but then she said, "I don't understand—what's changed your mind? I'm grateful, of course, but you seem more keen to help now that it looks . . ." She gestured at the bags on the bed.

"Debbie, I don't know a great deal about the psychology of runaways, but I know what I see here. She created a new identity for herself, and she thought it through, even down to leaving her old music behind. She created a new identity."

"But why would she do that?"

"I don't know, but if we can find out, it might tell us where she's gone."

Even as he spoke, he thought of a dozen locations in Europe, hoping for Hailey's and her family's sakes that she hadn't headed to any of them. But wherever she'd gone, a new identity was as likely to get a girl like her into trouble as it was to keep her out of it.

And another even more troubling thought was lurking at the back of his mind. Because he'd found himself in a similar situation to this once before—in those weeks before Kaliningrad, when he had done the right thing without thinking, and had lost everything in the process.

History

Tallinn—late February

Finn was done for the afternoon, and was making his way out of the office as Perry came in. Perry gave him a knowing, exasperated look, as if they were both working in the middle ranks of some ramshackle multinational, his expression meant to represent their collective response to the latest mess-up.

"You quit at the right time, Finn."

A few people had expressed sentiments along those lines to him in the last ten days, but there was something more weighted in Perry's tone.

"What do you mean, Ed?"

"You haven't heard?" Perry looked around, although the corridor was empty, the building silent. "Just pop into my office for a minute—I won't keep you long."

Finn followed him to his office and shut the door behind them, but remained standing even as Perry sat down behind his desk.

"It's all over the media. A highly placed source in the Kremlin claims that, and I quote, 'a senior British intelligence officer in the Baltic has been selling sensitive information to Aleksandr Naumenko.'"

Finn offered little more than a shrug, because although this allegation was more serious than usual, it had the familiarity of a common irritant about it.

"Are we giving any credence to it?"

"Officially, no—but we think it's genuine."

"The Baltic won't mean us, though. Someone in St. Petersburg?"

Perry shook his head. "The media don't know this, but our contacts are pointing to us." Finn offered an appropriately surprised expression. "Exactly. Which begs the question . . . I mean, I know it can't be either of us, but who else does that leave? They'll wonder—who has the kind of information Naumenko would pay for?"

Finn saw where Perry was going with this and started to shake his head.

"No."

"I'm not saying it's him, Finn. I realize he's your friend and I like Harry as much as you do, but I guarantee he'll be their prime suspect."

"Friendship has nothing to do with it. Harry Simons is *not* selling secrets to Aleksandr Naumenko."

"I'm sure you're right. Trouble is, even a hint of suspicion can blight a person's career." He looked genuinely conflicted about Harry, as if he did suspect him but didn't want to. Then he said again, "I'm sure you're right."

"I am, and I'm willing to bet, too, that this Kremlin source is a phony." Finn opened the door with the relaxed air of someone who didn't have to concern himself with these things anymore, and said as he was leaving, "Don't lose sleep over it, Ed. These things never come to anything."

He made his way out of the building, relieved that he'd seen the news on the wires earlier in the day, happier still that Naumenko had told him about it three weeks ago. That's when the real shock had come, but the early warning had provided enough notice for him to be unfazed by it now.

It had given Finn the opportunity to practice his disillusionment, and to announce his resignation a full ten days before the news leaked out. It had given him time to develop a surface calm, and the discipline not to correct the inaccuracies, the worst of which concerned the nature of the crime—he'd been working with Naumenko but had never sold information to him, not least because Finn doubted they knew anything that Naumenko needed to pay for.

He'd still been a fool, throwing away a promising career at the age of thirty, with little idea of what he'd do next. Technically he was a traitor, too, though he didn't think of himself in those terms. In a sense, it was worse, because he hadn't acted on a point of principle or out of greed. He'd been drawn by the intrigue of it alone—but then he supposed that wasn't so very unusual in their profession.

He still hadn't told his parents that he'd resigned, or that he'd have to stay with them until he decided where to go. He had money, of course, but he'd have to be careful about how he used it, for the first few years at least.

No, he hadn't told his parents, and that notion seemed to sum up the immaturity of his behavior—it was as if he'd been sent down from college.

It had been a cold day, and the air already held the promise of it turning into a fiercely cold night, but the sky was blue and with the sun lowering in the west, the buildings were full of light. The pale-brown church on the square, a church he'd walked past nearly every day for the last eighteen months, was luminous now, more so than he'd seen it even in summer.

He'd never been in there, but he saw someone walk out of it now and Finn changed course, heading for the door. He'd probably only be in this city for another couple of weeks, and if he came back it would be to visit Sofi's parents rather than as a tourist, so he guessed it was now or never for this church.

He stepped inside, immediately lulled by the respite from the cold, and by the peacefulness. It was Lutheran—light and airy, its pale vaulted interior almost completely unadorned. He walked a little way up the aisle and sat in one of the white wooden pews.

There was no one else in there, and quite unexpectedly he found everything falling away from him: the storm that had been rumbling away in his thoughts, the questions, the self-recrimination, the low-level fear of being exposed even now. It all fell away, and when he did think again it was unencumbered, wondering only how old this church was, what its history might have been.

He'd look to see if there was a leaflet in English before he left, but right now he didn't want to move. He sat, only vaguely conscious of the city noise beyond. And he'd been there for ten minutes, maybe more, when the door opened behind him and someone else came in.

He turned briefly to check, but it was a young woman walking with her head down, up the aisle to a pew four rows in front of him. She walked along the pew until she was almost obscured from Finn's view by the pillar that was between them.

She sat with her head bowed, and Finn wasn't sure if she was crying quietly or perhaps just shivering from the cold. He'd got a glimpse of her face—pretty, pale skin, high cheekbones—but it was obscured now by her hair, which was long and reddish-blonde, worn loose.

She was hardly dressed for the weather, so maybe she was cold rather than upset. She was wearing Converse, which had made hardly any sound as she walked, skinny jeans, and a thin sweatshirt, but nothing else—no sweater, no coat or scarf.

He wondered briefly if she was a junkie, but he doubted even a down-and-out would be walking around the city dressed so lightly.

And from the little he'd seen of her, she looked too healthy, too well maintained. But whatever her story, and whether or not those were tears falling, it was none of his concern.

The door opened again. He noticed the woman flinch at the sound, then become rigid and silent, almost as if she were holding her breath. Finn glanced around and saw a heavy-set man walking up the aisle. The guy had already spotted the woman and was smiling with what looked like a mixture of relief and playfulness. He'd seen Finn, too, but without paying him any attention.

The guy reached the pew where the woman was sitting and stepped into it before saying a few words. She answered him without looking up, her words barely audible, and it was clear now that she had been crying because Finn could hear it in her voice. But they'd spoken in Russian, not Estonian—an even better reason for him to pay them no attention.

A flash of anger crossed the guy's face and he walked along the pew and pulled the woman up by her arm, not in a way that hurt her, but forcefully enough that there was no question of this game being over. He pulled her back along the pew and out into the aisle, and as a last desperate gambit she looked at Finn, her eyes pleading, and said a few words, tremulous, earnest.

Finn didn't understand, but the guy looked at her with a threat and tapped her on the nose with his finger. The guy still didn't look at Finn, as if utterly confident that no one would choose to intervene in his business.

He was right about that, and it was none of Finn's concern that she was quite possibly being trafficked, that unimaginable things had probably been done to her, that more would follow, that a lifetime of misery was probably the best she could hope for. It was even less of a concern to him now than it might have been two weeks ago.

It simply wasn't his problem, but she had looked at him, and the surprise of seeing her face clearly, her eyes, had taken him aback.

She was tall and slender, and it had been an easy mistake to make without seeing her face properly, but now he could be in no doubt that this was not a young woman but a girl, maybe only thirteen or fourteen, and she was pleading to be saved from this man.

Finn stood up, and for the first time the guy acknowledged his presence, pointing at him, a warning, followed by a couple of words in Estonian that Finn didn't get, even after eighteen months of hearing the language daily—it was just as well he hadn't been hired for his linguistic skills.

The girl also spoke again, imploring, even as the man's grip tightened on her arm.

Finn stepped out of the pew into the aisle, and looked at the guy as he said, "Do you speak English, because I'm about to call the police."

"You big man, huh?" He put his finger on Finn's chest, prodding him as he said, "Sit down! And keep your nose *out*!"

Finn hit him.

The guy reeled back awkwardly, falling against the end of the pew across the aisle, his head hitting it with a dull crack. He'd released the girl, and she stepped back, toward the altar. Finn glanced at her, wanting reassurance that he'd just done the right thing, that he'd read this situation correctly. She was still looking at the guy in fear, though, as if dreading what his response would be.

The guy himself laughed, struggling to get back on his feet, then cursed Finn in Estonian, spitting the words out. Finn waited until he was halfway up, both of his arms occupied with the effort, his balance off, then planted a kick on the side of his head.

It sent him crumpling back down again. Something fell out of his jacket onto the floor, a small hunting knife, and Finn wondered how it had come loose. The guy was wearing a shoulder holster, too, but he saw the knife and tried to reach for it. Finn kicked it clear, then powered another swift kick to the guy's ribs, reached down, and pulled the gun free before taking a quick backward step. He slipped the gun into his overcoat, showing that he meant no more harm.

The guy was beat, and knew that he was hurt now. He reached up, feeling the back of his head, cursing again, but under his breath this time. Finn glanced at the pew the guy had collided with—there was no blood on it.

When he looked back, the guy was staring up at him, but in recognition now, and with a sickening jolt the guy found a place in Finn's own mind. One of Karasek's men—no one he'd ever spoken to, but he'd seen him a few times. He was angry with himself for not identifying him earlier.

"I know you," said the guy, pointing. "Big mistake, asshole."

Finn wondered if these people learned English by watching cheap gangster films. But, language aside, Finn also knew the guy was right. There were just too many ways in which this was a mistake—number one being that he had no way of keeping this girl safe, not now.

"The girl didn't want to go with you."

"Not your girl. Karasek's girl." He tried to push himself up but was still unsteady, and settled for pushing himself farther along the aisle, away from Finn. "You're dead man now. Dead man."

Finn looked back at the girl, although he wasn't sure why. Perhaps he was hoping that she would offer a way out of this. She looked terrified, though—aghast that he was even having a conversation with the man. There was no question of Finn letting him take her—as much of a mistake as this was, he just couldn't let that happen.

He turned back, trying to think of a conciliatory note, but the guy was struggling to his feet. Sensing Finn's gaze back on him, he repeated, "Yeah, big mistake, asshole."

They were still alone in the church. And alarming as it was, Finn saw there was only one solution, only one way out. He moved forward, scooping the knife off the floor before knocking the guy back off his feet. He followed through with the movement, dropping a knee onto his chest, putting his free hand over the guy's mouth and forcing his head back onto the floor.

He said something urgent, hot, and garbled against Finn's palm. He tried to swing a punch, too, but Finn slid the blade quickly and forcefully across the side of his neck, a smooth movement until the end, when the blade snagged on something gristly. The blood pulsed out in gulps rather than spurting, and the guy seemed to realize too late what had been done to him. His eyes had a look of astonishment, and his body twitched with an odd rhythm beneath Finn's weight.

Finn waited, watching the pool of blood grow, the stillness and peace of the church feeling ominous now, as if they were about to be disturbed. The guy was dead, or as near as made little difference. Finn stood, dropping the knife onto the body.

He turned and looked at the girl then, expecting her to be in shock at what she'd just witnessed. But, far from looking horrified, she gave a nervous little nod as she stared at the body, and looked at Finn with moist eyes and a weak smile that seemed nothing less than gratitude.

He beckoned for her to follow, and walked back to the door of the church. When he reached it, he turned and found her right behind him. His coat would look ridiculous on her, but he took his scarf and handed it to her, then his gloves.

As she put them on he said, "I've never killed anyone before."

She smiled again and said something back to him in Russian, and it hardly seemed to matter that neither understood the other.

Using hand gestures to back up his words, he said, "You, come with me."

She nodded and they walked out of the church. Across the square he could see a car by the side of the road, its doors open. A police car had stopped behind it, and the policemen were inspecting the empty vehicle. He noticed that the girl recoiled slightly from the sight.

"Don't worry, we're not going that way."

He couldn't take her home, though. He didn't know how Sofi would react, and it was best for her not to be involved in this—whatever this was. He needed to get the girl somewhere safe, with someone he could trust, someone who could speak Russian. Harry was the only option, and it helped, too, that he was in the business.

Finn pointed and said, "This way," and they started walking. Almost immediately, the girl put her hand in his. She was tall enough that from a distance she might have passed as his girlfriend, but there was no mistaking the nature of that hand in his—it was that of a child to an adult, a yielding of responsibility. She was entrusting herself to him, and he only wished he could be as confident as she was that he was worthy of that trust.

Chapter Three

Fate was a small, crammed place that specialized in a certain kind of student fashion—he could imagine plenty of young wannabe poets and indie folk-rock kids wearing the stripy Breton sweaters and disheveled blazers and other overpriced jumble.

A couple of them were working in the store, including a girl who wore a flowery summer dress over a T-shirt, the outfit finished off with a cardigan that looked on the verge of falling apart. She was pretty, but looked at Finn with a smile that was borderline patronizing.

He smiled back. He was too old to be shopping here, that was for sure, but he guessed he wasn't quite old enough to have a daughter who'd shop here. A younger girlfriend, perhaps?

Adrienne was a few years younger than him but he looked at the rails of clothes and could imagine her turning her nose up, at the quality rather than the style. Adrienne had that French thing for quality, for wearing it well—even as he prepared to speak, his thoughts raced off like an outrider toward her.

He put the photograph of Hailey on the counter and said, "I wonder if you could help. Have you seen this girl shopping in here recently?"

The assistant looked suspicious, her smile falling away into unfriendliness as she said, "I couldn't tell you if she had. It would be a breach of privacy for us to talk about our customers. And, anyway, you could be anyone."

She hadn't even looked at the photograph, but she glanced down at it now. It was subliminal, but he could tell she recognized Hailey—hardly surprising given that she'd been in here nearly every day for over a week.

"I'll tell you who I am—I'm working for her parents. See, the girl in that picture is fifteen and she's disappeared. So I understand what you're saying about privacy, but we know she was shopping here—and if I don't ask you, it'll be the police calling in."

"When you say she's disappeared . . ." The assistant's colleague, a tall, thin guy with the beginnings of a beard and a striped blazer that looked two sizes too small for him, had been hovering nearby but he stepped closer now. "I think we can tell him. She's American, right?"

Finn nodded.

The guy picked up the photograph. "She looked a little older in person. She wasn't a regular customer but the last . . . ten days, maybe, she's been in here nearly every day, if not every day."

"Okay." Finn took the tags from his pocket and said, "These are some of the things she bought—could you show me what they are?"

The female assistant looked to her colleague for approval and then said, "Of course, let's see what we have here."

She showed him half a dozen items—a pair of jeans, a few long-sleeved T-shirts, a cardigan, a threadbare knitted sweater—and couldn't resist saying how great or how popular the various pieces were. Even without the clothes Hailey had bought in other stores, he could see the beginnings of a look here, a kind of capsule wardrobe that was just a few vital notches more bohemian, more lived-in, than the way Finn remembered her.

Finally, the assistant said, "I'm not sure if that helps—I mean, you said she disappeared, right?"

"Yeah. She ran away, but the circumstances are odd, and trust me, this tells me a lot." He looked at the girl, who seemed to have been won over somehow, as if the act of showing him the clothes had helped her understand the seriousness of what he was doing. "If she was here every day for a week or more, she must have talked."

The girl nodded. "But only about the clothes—what she liked, what she didn't, that kind of thing."

The male assistant said, "How did the clothes tell you something?"

Finn looked around the shop. "They confirmed something I already suspected. She wanted to look older. I guess with these clothes she'd look like a student, not a schoolgirl."

The guy said, "You know, now that you've told us, I can see she did look like a schoolkid, especially when she first came in. I didn't see it at the time, but yeah, with these clothes and the haircut."

"What haircut?"

"Oh, she'd cut her hair, man—like, the last time she was in here, maybe two days ago?"

Finn looked through the receipts and said, "Four days ago."

"No, she came in after that. Friday. *Three* days ago. I can't remember what she bought, but she bought something, and I mentioned her hair, how cool it looked. She said she'd just had it done."

"What was it like?"

"Short, like a boy's, and she'd had it lightened—you know, the way some of these actresses are wearing it now. I guess it should have made her look younger, but thinking back, it didn't, it kind of made her . . ." His words dried up, as if he'd realized he was about to say something he shouldn't. Finally, he added, "She didn't seem unhappy. I mean, she didn't act like someone who needed to run away."

Finn picked up the photo. "I know. Thanks for your help."

As he walked out of the shop, the female assistant said, "I hope you find her!"

He raised his hand in an acknowledging wave but didn't turn, and nor did he visit any of the other stores.

Hailey's new identity had been planned carefully. She was at that fluid age anyway, when girls could morph into women with a change of clothes and the wrong make-up, but she'd judged it perfectly in only seeking to make herself a few years older: a student, a recognizable type. Like the assistants in the store, people would see the clothes, the hairstyle, the attitude, and it would never occur to them that they were looking at someone who was fifteen.

Fifteen no longer even seemed so very young. He'd been thinking of the Hailey he knew—albeit less well than perhaps he should have—a girl who still seemed like a child in his memory. No doubt her parents thought of her the same way, and yet Finn's visit to Fate had made him see that she was on the cusp of adulthood. Maybe she wasn't streetwise, something Debbie had insisted upon, but even if that were true, it wouldn't stop her from *acting* streetwise.

He walked back, letting the chill and the late-afternoon sun work through him. He thought of Adrienne a couple of times and took his phone out, but put it back without calling her. It was pointless trying to speak to her when he still didn't know why she'd left.

It didn't help that he'd thought everything had been okay between them—routine, perhaps, which was understandable after four years, but still okay. Now, looking back, he felt how Debbie and Ethan Portman had to be increasingly feeling about their own lives, that he'd completely failed to see the warning signs, that he'd taken her love and her very presence for granted.

In a sense, though, Finn had more in common with Hailey than her parents, because he knew at some instinctive level that it was he who'd run away, not Adrienne. He'd been running away from his own past—that was the clichéd and comforting lie he told himself—but he'd run from her in the process.

As he neared home, he started to think about Hailey again, about the news he had to pass on to her parents. Superficially it was less than encouraging, and he could see that it would come as another blow to them. Not only had their daughter planned to run away, she'd made herself older.

The most innocent explanation was that she'd wanted to avoid suspicion as she traveled alone across Europe. More likely, she'd done it because the "friends" she claimed to be staying with were older themselves and she wanted to fit in with them, to match the persona she'd probably created online. For all the talk in the media of grooming and child exploitation, it was probably that simple.

Yet, strangely, even as his interest in the disappearance of Hailey Portman should have been waning, even as he should have been dismissing her as a spoiled and selfish kid, he actually found himself more intrigued. It was almost like the frisson he felt when he started working on a new book, the sense that this familiar story contained some deeper mystery, if only he could peel back the layers and find it.

Chapter Four

He stood outside their apartment for a moment, listening. It was so quiet he assumed Ethan wasn't back, but when Finn knocked, it was Ethan who opened the door. For a moment there was a look of hostile confusion on Ethan's face, so much so that Finn wondered if Debbie had told her husband about his involvement.

His expression uncoiled, though, and he stood back as he said, "Hey, Finn, we really appreciate this. Come in."

Finn stepped into the apartment, but wondered now if Debbie had oversold the help he was offering.

"Any luck with the embassy?"

Ethan shook his head as he closed the door, saying quietly, "Not really, but Debbie called me about the passport while I was there and they said something about putting a watch on it."

"Good—well, that's something." He didn't want to say what he was really thinking, that it meant nothing, that Hailey was most likely still in Europe, that she'd taken the passport in the full knowledge that she'd almost certainly never have it checked.

"Come through to the living room. Debbie's just lying down for a little while."

Finn nodded and followed him, but no sooner had he sat down on one of the small sofas than Debbie came into the room. Her eyes were a little reddened but she didn't look as if she'd been sleeping.

Their earlier awkwardness seemed to be forgotten, and she looked at him now as if he was one of the family, rallying around in a crisis, and said, "Can I get you a drink?"

"I'm fine, thanks. Why don't you both sit down?" Debbie sat down immediately, urgently, but Ethan hesitated, with the look of someone who wished he could put off what he was about to hear. Finn said, "It's nothing bad, I just found out quite a bit."

Debbie nodded, as if she felt this justified her decision to approach Finn in the first place. Yet he'd done no more than anyone else could have done. Ethan sat, too, not quite relaxing.

"Okay, I went to Fate, the store where the paper bags came from. As we knew, she'd been in there nearly every day for over a week. It's clear from what she bought that she was creating a new wardrobe—what I could only describe as a kind of student look. I also learned that three days ago, presumably between the last time she saw you and disappearing, she had her hair lightened, and cut short like a boy's."

Ethan looked more shocked by the final revelation than Finn had anticipated, and sounded devastated as he said, "She cut her hair?" Finn wondered if it was a typical paternal response—the cutting of the hair symbolizing that he'd lost his little girl, no matter what happened now, that she was growing up and becoming her own person.

Debbie said, "Do you have any idea why?"

"Yeah. I'm pretty certain she did it to make herself look older, just by a few years—that's backed up by what the people in the store said. Maybe she just thought it would be easier to travel that way, or maybe . . ." He looked at both faces, making sure they were still with him. "Was she very active online? I mean, did she generally talk about online friends?"

Finn hardly expected she would have mentioned the kind of online friend she might run away to meet, but he thought she might have spoken about other virtual friends, giving him an idea of how active she was when it came to social networks and forums.

Debbie looked horrified as she thought through the implications and said, "Oh my God, you don't think she's been . . ."

"I don't think anything—not yet."

Actually, what he thought was that Hailey might have been the instigator in whatever had happened. He had no reason for thinking that, and even her intricate planning might have been a response to someone with a very sophisticated grooming technique.

It was instinct alone that convinced him she hadn't been the victim of some wily and predatory man, but his instincts had been wrong in the past—sometimes spectacularly wrong.

Ethan said, "I don't think she really has many online friends. She uses the Internet, naturally, but if she contacts people it tends to be her friends here."

"And you've spoken to all of them."

He nodded. "Even Jonas didn't know anything."

Finn hadn't even had time to respond when Debbie offered up an explanation, saying, "He's not a boyfriend—they're just the closest of friends, almost inseparable. You've probably seen him with her."

"I'm not sure. Possibly."

"They're both very strong academically. They often work on projects together, that kind of thing, and they do a lot of the same classes."

Ethan nodded in agreement and said, "He's a lovely kid. He's pretty cut up about it, too."

For some reason, Finn latched on to the tone Ethan had used for the words "lovely kid"—it was the way someone might talk about a child if they were disabled in some way, fighting a battle against life.

"Jonas? Swiss . . . ?"

"Half-Austrian, half-Australian—he finds that pretty funny."

"Is there something wrong with him?" They looked confused, as if they thought the question was a response to the statement about his nationality. "Just something in the way you spoke about him a moment ago. It suggested—I don't know, that there's something . . ."

Debbie looked like someone venturing into dangerous territory as she said, "Jonas is exceptionally intelligent."

"Off the scale," said Ethan.

"This is strictly between the three of us, of course, because he hasn't been diagnosed and his parents don't seem to think there's any cause for concern, but Ethan and I . . . we suspect he might be mildly autistic."

"Or more specifically Asperger's. But Finn, we know him well enough to know that he's in the dark on this. He looked seriously put out when he heard she was missing."

"Maybe because he thought he was going with her." He caught their expressions and added, "I'm not suggesting that—I'm just trying to make clear that things aren't always as they seem." He stood up. "Let me have a think about my next move, but in the meantime, let me know if you hear anything from the police or the embassy."

Ethan stood, looking full of gratitude as he said, "Finn . . . both Debbie and I—"

Finn put his hand up to stop him.

"Don't. If I find your daughter you can thank me then. But I doubt it'll come to that—I'm sure she'll get in touch first, or the police will find her. You know, they might act like they're not doing much, but they will be, behind the scenes."

Debbie stood, too, and said, "She's such a good girl."

He wanted to tell her how pointless that phrase was, how ridiculous, particularly under the circumstances.

Instead, he said, "Debbie, we all do stupid things. And for all the news stories you hear, there actually aren't that many bad people in the world."

She looked reassured and yet Finn was lying, because he knew there were more than enough bad people to do for Hailey Portman. There were so many varieties of bad that it really didn't bear thinking about, and he knew that better than most, because he had been one of them.

History

By the time they reached Harry's building they'd been walking for ten minutes. The girl seemed fine but, once inside, she started to shiver violently. Her teeth were chattering, which appeared to amuse her, as if she couldn't believe how cold she was.

Finn removed his coat now, and put it around her. He felt the weight of the gun in the left-hand pocket and took it out, slipping it into his waistband—something he'd promised himself he would never do.

They took the stairs, and as soon as Finn rang the bell Harry opened the door. He had his coat on and looked ready to make his excuses, but then spotted the girl and did a double take.

"Are you going out?"

Harry was still distracted by the girl as he said, "Jack and a couple of the others are meeting up for an early drink. I said I'd join them if I could." It was the kind of invite Finn had received for the first six months, but once he'd become serious with Sofi the offers had slowly dropped off.

Harry stepped back as he started to take his coat off. "They won't miss me. Come in."

Finn ushered the girl in and closed the door. "She could use some coffee or something to warm her up."

"Sure, I'll put some on."

He disappeared into the kitchen. Finn showed the girl into the living room and gestured toward the sofa. She took Finn's gloves and scarf off before sitting down, but kept the coat on.

Harry popped his head around the corner, but before he could speak, Finn said, "Do you have a sweater that might fit her?"

"Er, sure." He looked at the girl, then threw Finn a look, making clear he was intrigued, that he was eager to hear what this was all about. But he went into his bedroom and came back a minute later with a heavy red sweater, which he threw across to Finn before diving back into the kitchen.

Finn caught it, and held it out for the girl. She smiled, standing to remove the coat, the two items swapped like prisoners. Finn took the gun out of his waistband and put it back in the coat, which he hung up in the hall.

The girl was still standing when Finn went back in, the sleeves of the sweater hanging down. She held them up for him to see how big it was on her, and smiled shyly before sitting down again. The color suited her, and now that he looked at her properly, he saw that she was incredibly beautiful—big blue eyes, high cheekbones, flawless skin.

Harry came in carrying a tray and said, "Here we go." He put it on the coffee table, and Finn sat down in the armchair facing the girl. Harry sat at the opposite end of the sofa to her, but she tensed up and looked at Finn as if wanting reassurance. He nodded and smiled, and she seemed satisfied with that—it almost made Finn fearful that she should be so trusting so soon after what had just happened to her.

"So, you gonna introduce me?"

"I don't know her name. She's Russian." Harry had been about to reach for the coffee pot but stopped, his eyebrows raised. "I went into that church on the square, she came in a little while later. She'd escaped from some guy—I'm guessing she's being trafficked. I intervened, but . . ."

"But?"

"The guy recognized me. One of Karasek's." He glanced at her briefly. She was looking on, mesmerized by their conversation though she clearly understood none of it. "I killed him, Harry. I didn't even think about it. I knew she was in trouble, and look at her, she's a kid. It would have got back to Karasek that it was me."

"Witnesses?" Finn shook his head. Harry turned to the girl and spoke a few words. She looked astonished, her eyes lighting up as she asked him if he spoke Russian. Harry nodded and she told him her name: Katerina.

Harry introduced himself and Finn, and she said, "Finn," and smiled, shy again as she said something else in Russian.

As Harry poured the coffee he said, "She thanked you for saving her life."

"You're welcome," Finn said to her, then turned back to Harry. "Ask her what happened."

The story spilled out of her without much need for encouragement, her voice wavering occasionally, a pause to wipe a tear from her cheek—but the whole thing was retold with a remarkable stoicism.

She was an orphan from some provincial Russian city, southeast of Moscow. She'd been offered the chance to become a model, a plausible offer given her looks, but she'd been drugged and brought to Estonia. It wasn't such an unusual story for Finn or Harry, given that their job was dealing with organized crime.

But after one brief exchange, Harry looked momentarily lost and said to Finn, "I asked her if she'd been attacked by the people who took her."

"And?"

Harry shook his head.

"But the guy you killed, he told her Karasek wanted her for himself—that's the only reason she hasn't been raped. Karasek wanted her."

"How old is she?"

There was another brief exchange, but this time Harry was so shocked that he asked the question again and she laughed as she repeated her answer.

"She's thirteen. Can you believe that?"

"I thought thirteen or fourteen, but you're right, she could pass for older."

"When you first brought her in I thought eighteen or nineteen."

"She's a child. If you'd seen her afraid, you wouldn't have doubted it. Thank God I was there, thank God . . ." He paused, trying to think what it was that he was grateful for. "You know, two weeks ago I wouldn't have intervened."

"Yes, you would. It's who you are." Harry smiled. "It would have been wrong, probably, but you still would have done it. Anyway, at least now you know you were right to kill the guy."

Finn hadn't given it any thought. He'd killed a man half an hour earlier, had sliced through the side of his neck and watched him bleed to death. But for the time being at least, it carried no weight whatsoever within his thoughts. He was too busy wondering what to do now.

Harry was clearly thinking along the same lines because he said, "Whatever Karasek had in mind, he'll be peeved as hell about losing her, and peeved that someone killed one of his guys, too. Of course, he could think the girl had done it herself."

Finn thought back to the dead guy. The knife wound could have been inflicted by a determined girl of her age, but Finn had given him a beating beforehand.

"No, he'll know it was someone else."

"And you're sure no one saw you in the church?"

"Absolutely." Now that he said it, he realized he should have checked the church before leaving, not that there was much he could have done, short of killing any witnesses. He supposed he would find out soon enough if he had been spotted. "Anyway, that's less of a concern than what I do with her now."

The girl asked Harry something. He answered and she poured herself more coffee, and held the mug between her hands as if still trying to get warm.

"There's the authorities of course, but Lord only knows where she'd end up." Harry looked preoccupied for a moment, as if mentally going through his address book before saying, "None of my old Russian contacts would be much use. I did know one or two who might have been able to help, but . . ."

The solution leapt out at Finn—a hundred attendant questions coming with it, but a solution all the same. And it hardly mattered that he didn't know how it would work, because he knew immediately that it was the girl's only real hope.

"I know one. A Russian."

Harry laughed. "We all know Russians, Finn, but that's—"

"I mean a Russian who could help." He looked at Katerina, gave her an encouraging smile. "Could she stay here a while? I can't take her home with me. Even if we could understand each other, how would I explain it to Sofi?"

"How long for? I mean, yeah, of course she can stay. But how long? What's your thinking?"

Finn nodded, realizing that one way or another he was about to test his friendship with Harry to the limit. They'd known each other eighteen months, had bonded from the start, had been through a lot in that time, but this was the point at which Harry might begin to doubt he knew Finn at all.

"The Russian I know, he'll be in Stockholm, I think a week from now. We could go on the overnight ferry, no need to get her a passport. He'd be able to deal with everything from there."

Harry made a show of accepting that much, or of at least deferring acceptance for the time being, but said, "Can you trust him? You know, the girl just escaped who knows what, we don't wanna hand her over to someone who'll sell her to the highest bidder."

There was no question in Finn's mind. "I trust him completely, Harry. I trust him as much as I trust you. Maybe even more."

Harry laughed at the slight. "Do you trust him more than Jerry de Borg?"

Finn smiled. It was one of their private jokes—"Jerry de Borg", their stock invented explanation for everything that went wrong.

"Maybe not, but Jerry de Borg isn't a powerful Russian."

Harry laughed again, but then stopped abruptly and stared at Finn in shock.

"You sly bugger!" Finn hadn't expected him to take even this long to work it out. "It's you! Jesus, I thought they'd suspect me . . . I suspected Perry, but it's you." There was an implicit acceptance in the tone of Harry's response, the suggestion that the crime had been stripped of all seriousness by Finn's involvement, but the shock was still there and he shook his head. "You're the least likely."

"Because?"

"You don't speak Russian. You've only been here eighteen months, flitting around the Med for five years before that."

"Which is, of course, where I met him, and he speaks pretty good English." Finn sat forward in his chair, put his coffee mug back on the tray and said, "Look, Harry, I never sold him anything. We've been in business together, and yes, I made things happen, things I'm not going into now, but I never betrayed my country—never, you have to take my word on that. Now, if you want to hand me in, fine, you're my friend and I'll accept that, but let me get this girl safe first."

"I am your friend, so why on earth would I wanna hand you in? If you say you didn't do anything to damage our country, then I believe you. Just swear to me you didn't compromise anyone and that's enough."

"I swear."

Harry seemed to accept that, but asked almost as an afterthought, "Why did you do it?"

"Boredom, I suppose." Harry laughed. "I'm serious, you know. Flitting around the Med, as you described it, all very nice, but I felt like the big game was somewhere else. I met Alex, we had a shared interest in history, he's a nice guy . . ."

"A *nice guy*."

"Actually, yeah. I know his background, I know he's been ruthless and could be again, but he is a nice guy. And, as embarrassing as it sounds, it was exciting, you know?"

Harry took it all in and sighed. Katerina had been watching them avidly and she looked at Harry now, knowing it was his time to respond, waiting for his words as readily as if she'd understand them.

"So he tipped you off? That's why you quit?"

"Yeah. The timing could've been better. Me and Sofi and all that, but I have to admit, I'd been starting to worry it was bound to catch up with me." Finn laughed at a reality that still seemed out of kilter with his own view of his actions. "I could go to prison."

"I doubt that very much." Harry smiled, his alternate theory not needing to be voiced. Then he looked suddenly decisive, as if it had all been settled. "We'll sit down and talk about this one day, properly, but our priority now is getting Katerina to safety." She watched more attentively at the sound of her name. "She can stay here. But the quicker you sort things with Naumenko, the better for all of us."

"I'll do my best." Finn took his wallet out and emptied all the notes onto the table. "Buy her some clothes—she's got nothing."

"Put your money away, I can buy—"

"Just in case they're watching your accounts. I give cash to Sofi all the time, so they'd think nothing of me drawing a few thousand extra krooni here and there."

"Okay, fair point."

"Katerina." She looked at him and he said, "You'll stay with Harry for a few days." Harry translated and she nodded as if being given important instructions. "You'll be safe here, but you mustn't leave the apartment. Soon, I'll take you to a Russian friend, a good man who'll help you. If you want to go home he'll help you do that."

Her reply came back, simply put and all the more mournful for it, and Harry translated, "She says she has no home."

"Then he'll find a good family for you to go to, or—he'll help."

Finn stood up, gesturing for her to stay sitting, but as Harry stood too she said hesitantly, "Finn. Thank . . . Thank you."

Finn nodded, but at the door he said to Harry, "If there's a problem, or if you think they're looking like investigating you— "

"I'll just point them in your direction." Harry laughed. "I know, if there's a problem, I'll call. But there won't be. We can do this."

Finn nodded and thought back to the body in the church, to the blood gulping out onto the floor. He'd seen people killed before, but that made it no less mystifying to contemplate the life he'd ended himself.

"I killed someone, Harry. How about that?"

"Well, you could say you killed someone, could say you saved someone—depends which way you look at it. Just a shame it wasn't Karasek himself."

"I'll leave that job for you." Finn started to walk along the corridor. "See you tomorrow."

"Usual place, usual time," said Harry, and closed the door.

Finn started down the stairs, at a loss as to what he'd just done. He'd guarded that secret so carefully for so long and yet he'd just given it up, albeit to someone he could trust—someone he thought, or hoped, he could trust—and all because of a girl he didn't know, a girl for whom he had also killed a man. But she needed help, it was as simple as that, and those two acts had been the only way he'd seen of giving it. What else could he have done?

Chapter Five

For the last half an hour he'd been thinking about Arnaud Amaury. More specifically, he'd been wondering if he could make a case for Arnaud suffering from Asperger's. Here was a man who'd struggled to connect with the people, who'd been ridiculed and humiliated but who, when faced with an intractable religious problem, had hit upon a chillingly logical solution without any recourse to human emotion.

The Cathars had been a small but growing heretical minority, dispersed among the wider population, indistinguishable from them. And that wider population had been unwilling to surrender people they'd probably known their whole lives.

That had been Amaury's problem: how to identify the Cathars. To a man who believed that true Christians had nothing to fear in death, the solution was simple—put the entire city to the sword and let God identify the heretics. Was that an autistic response, or just that of a committed believer in an extreme age?

Realistically, and for a modern readership, it was probably easier to paint him as a psychopath. Finn supposed he could portray Amaury as a magnificent, Kurtz-like character—and Béziers had not been his only atrocity—but that hardly squared with a man who'd also been a figure of fun.

Perhaps he had to accept that there was no humanizing Arnaud, not in the modern understanding of humanity. He would be able to paint the Pope sympathetically enough, and the two fictionalized figures on either side of the Béziers massacre, but not Arnaud.

Finn considered a different approach. He imagined his various human figures, all of them with hopes and fears and preoccupations that would be recognizable to his readers, and all of them engaged in a dance of death around the monstrous enigma of Arnaud Amaury himself—cold, murderous, unknowable.

That was the solution. He scribbled "monstrous enigma" in his notebook. He hesitated for a moment and then wrote another note, instructing himself not to use "dance of death" anywhere in the manuscript—it was too flowery, too clichéd, much too likely to be picked up on and ridiculed by reviewers.

He pushed himself away from his desk and strolled through into the living room. He didn't bother turning on the lights, but stood looking out over the lake as dusk fell. Lights were already on here and there—a peaceful evening at the end of a peaceful day.

He smiled at the strange trajectory of his thoughts, seeing them as a passive observer might, because his day had hardly been peaceful. The Portmans' daughter was missing, his own girlfriend had left him, and yet at some level he did feel at peace. He'd enjoyed making inquiries, had enjoyed exploring a mystery that was not of his own making, a reminder in some way of the life that might have been his.

Maybe his enjoyment of that process had encouraged him to see Hailey Portman's disappearance as something more than it was. He didn't doubt that she might be in more danger than she'd ever imagined when she'd set out, but it was unlikely there was anything more sinister at play here than the whims and desires of a willful fifteen-year-old girl.

Finn glanced down as someone came into view on the street below, then did a double take because the figure looked familiar. He was wearing a kind of multicolored, felt bobble hat, with flaps hanging down over his ears and ending in tassels. Was it South American in design? He wasn't sure, but he recognized it and the memories clicked into place now as he realized he *had* seen Jonas before.

He was on the opposite side of the street, but he was moving about and he came a little closer and then out of sight. Finn opened the door carefully and stepped out onto the balcony, bringing Jonas back into full view. The kid looked agitated, walking up and down as if he expected something to happen.

For some reason, when Finn had listened to the Portmans describing Jonas, he hadn't thought of this boy. He couldn't see him clearly in the dusk, but he remembered him well enough—taller than Hailey, wide-shouldered but slim, a good-looking kid with bone structure and lively eyes, someone he imagined hitting the slopes every weekend in the winter, though it had probably just been the hat feeding that impression. Finn had only met him briefly, a couple of times at most, but even if it was just his own prejudice at work, he wouldn't have had him down as someone in the outer reaches of the autism spectrum.

Jonas looked at the entrance to the building as if he'd seen movement, but looked away again and resumed his pacing. Finn had vaguely registered him and Hailey as boyfriend and girlfriend, and he wondered now if Ethan and Debbie had been blind at even that fundamental level to their daughter's private world.

Certainly, the boy in the street below looked like the stereotypical lovelorn youth. Jonas knew Hailey was missing, so Finn couldn't quite make out what he was doing here. Did he expect her to show up, or was he engaged in his own private search for her? For all Finn knew, the little vigil below was the kid's way of focusing his thoughts.

Finn didn't want to move, but he became suddenly aware of how cold an evening had pursued the spring-like day. A chill breeze was pushing in off the lake, needling him through the thin material of his shirt.

He thought about stepping inside to get a sweater, but Jonas stopped moving below, checked his watch then appeared to check his phone, and looked up at the building, not at the Portmans' apartment but at the one next to it, immediately below where Finn was standing. He looked at his watch again, then back at the same apartment, an air of confusion about him.

Finn tried to think who lived in that apartment but had no idea—in truth, he knew only the Portmans, and that was through Adrienne. He knew a few others by sight or to say hello to, but had no notion of which apartments they occupied.

His thoughts stuttered as he realized he'd been spotted. Jonas had looked at his watch again, briefly gone a floor too high when he'd returned his gaze to the building, and spotted Finn standing there. The kid took a step backward and looked both ways along the street, apparently deciding what he should do.

Finn stepped farther out onto the balcony and called down, "Hey, Jonas, wait there a second." He ignored him and started to walk. Finn wondered if it had been a mistake to use his name. But he'd used it now—too late. "Jonas!" The kid stopped and turned, looking up at him. "Just a second . . ."

He ran through the apartment, the sudden rush of warmth spurring him to grab his coat on the way out. He didn't wait for the elevator, but tore down the stairs and put his coat on as he ran through the lobby. It didn't surprise him that Jonas was no longer outside the front of the building.

Finn headed quickly in the same direction, breaking into a run, and got to the end of the street before he gave up. Jonas was nowhere in sight—he'd obviously broken into a run himself as soon as Finn had disappeared from the balcony.

He crossed the street and walked back on the far side, letting his breathing and his heartbeat level out again. His throat and lungs felt spiked by the sudden influx of cold air, a feeling that was at once both refreshing and queasily redolent of his time in the north—anything that reminded him of his former life had a way of making the ground feel unsteady beneath his feet.

When he reached the spot where Jonas had been standing, he looked up at the building. He was drawn first to the Portmans' apartment. The lights were on, the blinds open, and Finn recognized their living room even from the street, so he had no doubt that Jonas would have done.

It confirmed what Finn had already suspected, that Jonas hadn't been looking at the apartment below his by mistake. But it didn't tell him what exactly the boy *had* been looking at, because the apartment in question was in darkness. He glanced up a floor to his own, also dark.

Jonas had checked his watch a few times, with what looked like agitation or impatience. He'd expected to see something in that apartment, something that he believed was connected in some way to Hailey's disappearance, or that would perhaps help him to find her.

Finn doubted Ethan and Debbie would hold much store in what Jonas thought about this, and for all Finn knew, he was indeed borderline dysfunctional, prone to delusions. But he was following a trail of some sort, so whether he was reliable or not, he clearly knew more about Hailey's disappearance than her parents realized.

Finn took one more look at the building, then checked his own watch and went inside to find Monsieur Grasset.

Chapter Six

Grasset invited him in and offered him a drink. He'd been watching the news, but left Finn in the hall as he went in and turned off the TV. As he came back he said, "Bombs in Iraq, bombs in Pakistan—none of it makes any sense."

"Religion, Monsieur Grasset. We did it here in Europe too, remember."

"And it didn't make any sense then, either." Grasset smiled. "Now, how about that drink?"

"How about it," said Finn, and they walked through and sat at the kitchen table. Grasset seemed to have a predilection for industrial-strength schnapps and grappa, but with some relief Finn saw that there was an open bottle of red wine, probably left over from his lunch—the old man always drank good Swiss wine.

After Grasset handed him his glass and they drank and Finn nodded his approval, Grasset said, "I apologize, Monsieur Harrington, if I was intrusive when you arrived back this morning. It was not for me to say, and actually none of my business."

The apology was hollow because Grasset loved to know what was going on in people's lives. This in itself was probably an attempt to get Finn talking about Adrienne leaving.

"Don't worry about it. Anyway, Adrienne leaving isn't the worst thing that happened while I was away." Grasset looked blank for a moment, so Finn said, "The Portmans?"

"Of course, their daughter! She's a beautiful girl." He shrugged as if dismissing his failure to bring up the topic himself. "I forgot that you were a friend of theirs."

"Well, they're Adrienne's friends, really. But I'll do what I can for them."

Grasset nodded and waved his hand at a family photograph of himself and his late wife and their three grown-up children, two boys and a girl.

"They say boys are more likely to die or be in an accident, but one always worries more about a daughter—of course, my children all have families of their own now, so the worry is theirs." He laughed to himself as if sharing a family joke.

Finn smiled, too, and allowed a suitable pause to insinuate itself before saying, "Monsieur Grasset, I wanted to ask you about the apartment beneath mine. Who lives there?"

Grasset looked confused, perhaps suspecting this was a complaint about noise, and said, "Nobody. The man who lived there was Gibson, but he left . . . four days ago."

"Four days ago? The day before Hailey Portman disappeared?"

The question hung there for a moment.

"*Oui, mais . . .*" The implication had shocked him into French, and then into a further silence.

"Who was he?"

Grasset shrugged. "I don't know. The apartment is owned by a company."

"Called?"

"BGS, that's all. I think probably financial—Monsieur Gibson I could imagine in finance, or hedge funds perhaps. Today, everyone is in hedge funds."

"What did Gibson look like? Was he friendly, did he have family?"

"He was average height. Quite a young man, but he was losing his hair already. He wore a suit when he went out . . . he was friendly. One day he was wearing glasses and he stopped to tell me he had no more contact lens fluid."

"When you say 'young'?"

"Thirty? Maybe younger."

"Good-looking?"

Grasset looked bemused, as if asking how Finn expected him to judge that. The real question for Finn was whether Gibson was young or attractive enough to appeal to a fifteen-year-old girl. He'd have to speak to Ethan and Debbie again, find out how much they'd had to do with their neighbor.

And Jonas—*he* clearly thought Gibson had something to do with it, or that the apartment did. Finn was briefly struck by the thought that Hailey might not have run very far, that the clothes and the passport might be a distraction from a less glaring truth.

"I imagine you have a key to that apartment, Monsieur Grasset. Would it be possible to take a look inside?"

"I have a key to your apartment, Monsieur Harrington, but I would not have allowed anyone to go in there while you were away."

Finn smiled. "Of course, I respect that, but this is a corporate owner, not a private one. Last week Mr. Gibson—next week someone else living there. If there was a complaint, you could say one of the neighbors had a concern about the apartment."

"But they don't."

"Actually, they do. See, I think I can hear water running down below."

Grasset laughed politely, but then grew serious. "Monsieur Harrington, I know you wouldn't ask if you didn't think it was important, and as the apartment is empty . . ." He finished the wine in his glass. "But you don't think this Gibson has something to do with Hailey's disappearance?"

"I hope not. What I was actually thinking was that Hailey might be using the apartment—that she might have run no farther than across the hall."

"Ah!" Grasset was impressed.

Finn drained his glass while Grasset went and got the key, and they took the elevator up to the floor where the Portmans lived. Grasset remained silent until they were inside the apartment, perhaps worrying about being seen. Finn was relieved, having feared that the sound of a conversation might have drawn Ethan and Debbie out.

"The removal people came the same day as Monsieur Gibson left, and I checked the apartment—it was as you see now, quite empty."

Finn walked through into one of the bedrooms, then the other, then a procession through all the rooms with Grasset behind him. The apartment was the same layout as Finn's, and he ended up in the living room. The entire place was empty, with nothing to indicate someone might have been bedding down here for a few nights.

The rooms were almost more than empty, without even the telltale shadows and fittings on the walls to suggest that pictures had once hung there. The polished wooden floorboards completed the effect, giving the apartment a desolate acoustic.

"Isn't this odd, Monsieur Grasset? When a company owns an apartment, there's usually some furniture left in place—or at least pictures? Isn't it quite unusual for a company to give their employee a completely unfurnished flat?"

"No," said Grasset, unimpressed by the theory. "Perhaps he wanted no furnishings from them."

Finn pointed at the walls. "He didn't appear to have a single picture hanging on his walls—not a mark in here."

"So he didn't like art, or he was a minimalist. There is nothing suspicious in that."

"True." He didn't want to tell Grasset about Jonas, but the boy's interest in this apartment had convinced Finn that there was a link, even if only tangential, between Gibson and this apartment and Hailey's disappearance. "Did the company . . . BGS . . . Did BGS have anyone in here before Gibson?"

"Yes, Gibson was here for a year. Before that, a woman—I can't remember her name. She was also here for a year. Not very friendly."

"And before her?"

"No, BGS bought the apartment then. Before that was Madame Schafer . . . you must remember her—such a lovely old lady, but fierce!"

"Yes, I think so." Finn had no memory at all of Madame Schafer, nor of any old ladies at all—it wasn't really that kind of building. "There's nothing suspicious here, I suppose. But I'll speak to the Portmans again tomorrow, find out how much they had to do with Gibson. Hopefully we can rule him out."

Except for Jonas, he thought to himself—unless the kid was completely unhinged, his behavior seemed to suggest there was a connection.

"If there is a link, at least we know how to find him." Finn looked at Grasset, who said, as if stating the obvious, "Through his company, through BGS."

"Of course."

They parted in near-silence at the elevator. Grasset descended, and Finn took the stairs back to his apartment. He tried to work but couldn't, his mind flashing back again and again to the memory of Jonas standing out there in the cold, of his loyal and lonely vigil.

Nor did he sleep well. Having toured Gibson's empty apartment, he kept hearing noises. At one point, as he slipped into sleep for the first time, he thought he heard footsteps on the wooden floors below, the sound so realistic that he got up to look over the edge of his balcony, to make sure there was no light coming from Gibson's living room.

He stood for a moment then, braced against the cold, shocked and exhilarated by it, and looked out across the dark lake to the mountains beyond, with their snowy peaks standing out like a painted glass backdrop.

He couldn't help thinking of Hailey Portman. She should hardly matter to him, because he hadn't really known the girl, and the family were Adrienne's friends, not his—and, anyway, nothing much had mattered to him for a long time. But he thought of her all the same.

If she was still alive, then she was out there somewhere. Was she traveling, sleeping rough or in a cheap hotel? Had she reached the place and person she was aiming for? Was she scared and alone—or happy, liberated from a life she'd come to resent or simply tired of?

They were compelling questions, appealing to his natural intellectual curiosity. It was as if, in becoming a mystery, Hailey Portman had become interesting to him in a way she had never been as the lively girl who lived on the floor below. He was intrigued, but also aware that the questions only applied if the first part of it were true—*if* she was still alive.

Chapter Seven

Finn called on the Portmans the next morning, and could hear voices even as Ethan let him in. He was introduced to a sympathetic-looking policeman, who was just on his way out. The officer assured them before leaving that the police were as keen as anyone to find Hailey.

Once Finn was on his own with Ethan and Debbie, he looked at them properly and felt an ever more urgent need to find their daughter. They seemed to have aged a few years during the course of the night, a decline so rapid that he wondered how long they could go on like this.

For want of anything better, he said, "Well, at least the police are taking it seriously now."

Debbie's expression didn't so much as flicker.

Ethan gave a sardonic smile. "I think the embassy probably put some pressure on them, that's why we got the visit—the message was still pretty much the same."

"Oh, I see."

Debbie emerged out of her torpor and said, "Have you heard from Adrienne?"

Ethan looked at her as if at someone he suspected might be an impostor, so odd did he find the change of subject.

"No. I left her a message yesterday morning, but let's keep focused on finding Hailey. Me and Adrienne can sort our problems out after that."

"Of course," said Ethan, looking a little embarrassed.

Debbie appeared to sink away again, and Finn wondered if she was medicated. They both needed medication by the look of them, but he supposed the last thing they wanted when their daughter was missing was to take sleeping pills.

Wanting to get out of there as quickly as possible, he cut straight to it: "How well did you know your neighbor . . . Gibson?"

"Not particularly well. Not at all, really. We would say good morning to him, that sort of thing, but we hardly ever saw him. You know how this building is."

Finn nodded, feeling vindicated somehow by Ethan suggesting it wasn't the kind of place where neighbors became friends.

"He moved," said Debbie. "I think it was the day before Hailey disappeared."

She didn't appear to grasp the meaning of what she'd said, but Ethan looked and sounded sickened as he said, "Oh my God, you don't think he had anything to do with it?"

Finn was quick to respond. "No, not necessarily. It's more than likely just a coincidence. But I wanted to know what he was like, whether he ever had visitors, whether Hailey ever spoke to him. From what I've heard already, Gibson doesn't square with the image Hailey was building for herself, but I'd still like to rule him out."

"Sure," said Ethan, still looking very much in doubt. He visibly assembled his thoughts before saying, "He was English—no, I mean, he was a Scot. Single. I'd guess in his late twenties. His hair was receding at the temples but he had it cropped short so it wasn't that noticeable. Don't remember him having any visitors, ever. I'd see him leaving in workout clothes a few evenings a week, but don't recall him going out much beyond that."

"And Hailey?"

It was Debbie who answered, as her orbit crossed briefly into theirs again. "I don't believe she ever spoke a word to him. She would laugh sometimes . . ."

Ethan smiled at the recollection and said, "Yes, a couple of times she was standing by the window and saw him go out. He had a road bike—I'd forgotten that, he'd carry it up and down in the elevator—and Hailey found his cycle clothing amusing. You know what kids are like."

Debbie said, "I found it quite amusing, too. All that spandex—it wasn't a flattering look for him," She seemed almost back to herself, but then sounded oddly insistent as she said, "Hailey has a great sense of humor."

Finn found a response running around in his thoughts, but kept it to himself and said instead, "You said Jonas was spoken to and didn't know anything? It seems odd that they were such close friends and he didn't have any inkling."

"We thought the same," said Ethan. "When we first realized she was missing, Jonas was the person we called. He didn't know where she was, didn't know she'd run away. Then once it was clear she'd disappeared, the police spoke to her closest friends, including Jonas."

"You don't think he might have been lying, maybe because she'd asked him to?"

"I doubt it. You know we talked about the possibility of him being, or rather—"

"Having Asperger's, yes, I remember."

Ethan looked uncomfortable, as if he was now doubting their casual diagnosis, and certainly regretting that they'd mentioned it to someone else.

"Yes, well, one of the things that makes it seem . . . You see, he doesn't hold back, he can't help but say what he's thinking. He's just not the kind of kid who lies, and Hailey wouldn't have asked him to lie because she knows that."

"So as close as they are, Hailey probably wouldn't have told him anything about her plans?"

Ethan shook his head, acknowledging what he presumably thought was a roadblock. Finn thought it was anything but—Jonas knew something, or suspected something, about the "how" and the "why" of Hailey's disappearance. The fact that he'd been staring at an empty apartment suggested he didn't know the "where," but he still knew more than anyone else.

Finn stood and said, "Okay, I have a few things I have to do this afternoon, and some things to check out this evening. As ever, if you learn anything in the meantime, please let me know."

Debbie looked up at him. "It's only when things are bad that you learn the truth about people, and who your friends are."

He wanted to tell her the real truth, that he didn't even know why he was doing this, that if Adrienne had still been here he almost certainly wouldn't have been helping them—he'd have been criticizing Adrienne for getting too involved herself. Perhaps it was simply that his curiosity had filled the gap left by Adrienne, rushing into the vacuum caused by the rather mundane collapse of his own domestic certainties.

"I'm sure anyone else would have done the same."

Ethan showed him out, and Finn drifted back to his apartment. He had nothing to do except wait for the evening and, he hoped, the return of Jonas. He spent a couple of hours reading a densely written book on Pope Innocent III, making notes, knowing he'd use almost none of it.

After lunch he phoned Mathieu, but Adrienne's sister-in-law answered.

"Hello, Cecile—it's Finn."

Cecile's English wasn't great, but it was better than she pretended and Finn was certain she used it as an excuse to avoid talking to him. In his present mood of self-reappraisal, he could hardly hold that against her.

Even so, it rankled slightly when she said, "Hello, Finn, a moment please." And she was gone, the phone placed down heavily.

A few moments later, Finn heard footsteps approaching, a labored sigh, the phone being picked up again, and Mathieu saying, "Hello, Finn, what can I do for you?"

His tone was disarming, and Finn briefly wondered if Debbie had been mistaken about Adrienne's whereabouts, given everything else that was going on in her life, but even with a missing daughter it was the kind of detail Debbie Portman wouldn't get wrong.

"Mathieu, I know she's with you—her friend told me."

There was silence, then another sigh—Mathieu was thirty-four, nearly two years younger than Finn, yet he had a way of sounding like a weary parent—and he said, "Yes, Adrienne is here, but she doesn't want to speak to you."

"Okay. Am I at least allowed to know what I'm supposed to have done, why she left without a word?"

"That's none of my business," said Mathieu, his tone ambiguous, suggesting an extra level of meaning that Finn couldn't quite decipher. "But you know, Finn, when a man has a problem with his wife and he thinks he's done nothing wrong, sometimes what he's done wrong is nothing."

"Well, thanks, I'll give that some thought. But let her know I called, and that I would like to hear from her."

He didn't get any more effusive than that, in part because he refused to pour his heart out to a man who wasn't even his brother-in-law, in part because there wasn't a great deal to pour out. Far from asking her to come back, he had to resist the urge to ask what he should do with the rest of her stuff.

But something about his response seemed to mollify Mathieu, and he sounded sympathetic as he said, "Just give her some time."

It seemed as if he was about to go on, but he stopped abruptly, and Finn knew that Adrienne was standing there listening. He could imagine the look she was giving her brother right now.

"She can take as long as she needs," said Finn, unable to stop himself, despite knowing how those words would be interpreted. He ended the call and took both phones through to the living room, doubting that she'd call back or send a message, but not wanting to miss it if she did.

And he fell asleep there on the sofa, deep and fast, as if finally making up for the research trip and the confusion since. When he woke, it was already growing dark and he was disoriented, unsure of the day or time. He went to the bathroom, washed his face, brushed his teeth, trying to shake the grogginess out of himself.

Before making coffee, he decided to close the curtains in the living room, making it easier for him to spy on the street below without being seen. But he stopped short of closing them fully, and stood back to one side, because there Jonas was again, walking up and down on the opposite side of the street, occasionally looking up at Gibson's apartment.

Finn took another step back, completely out of sight. The coffee could wait, he supposed—it was time to find out what Jonas thought he knew.

Chapter Eight

Jonas was wearing a different hat. It was the same design, but from this distance Finn could see that it was knitted, a more traditional alpine pattern. It was the only thing that would have differentiated surveillance footage from the two nights, because his behavior was identical: the walking, the checking his watch, the looking up at the empty apartment.

Finn had slipped out of the building and moved a little farther along the street. Now, having watched Jonas for a few minutes, and having once more looked up at the lit windows of the Portmans' apartment, he crossed the street and started walking casually toward the kid.

He thought it was odd that Jonas didn't seem to look at the Portmans' place himself. Presumably, he knew Hailey wasn't there and wouldn't be there. He probably wasn't much interested, either, in what her parents were going through, whether because of autism or adolescence.

Finn had his head bowed slightly as he walked, as if against the cold. He was certain that Jonas would run again if he recognized him or suspected anything amiss. Finn tensed slightly as he realized

Jonas was looking at him, but the kid clearly discounted him as a threat, because he turned back to the apartment block.

By the time Jonas turned a second time, Finn was more relaxed—he was only a few feet away and knew he'd catch him even if he did bolt. Finn raised his head and, noting the kid's look of alarm, smiled at him as he spoke.

"Hi Jonas, don't worry, I just want to—"

The kid ran.

Finn set off after him, and almost immediately doubted he'd catch him. Jonas was fast, and apparently determined that this conversation wouldn't take place. Finn wondered if Jonas hadn't recognized him, if perhaps he suspected Finn of being connected in some way with Gibson.

Either way, Finn was regretting not having that coffee. He seemed to be lumbering, unable to find a rhythm, in his legs, his breathing, his heartbeat, his footsteps falling heavy on the pavement, jarring through him. Jonas was increasing the distance between them with each of his steps—steps that Finn couldn't help notice made no sound at all.

He hadn't wanted to do this, but Finn guessed he would have to ask Ethan and Debbie for the kid's address, to visit him at home, with all the potential problems that would raise. And just as he was resigned to it, the distance growing to the point of losing sight of him in the dusk, Jonas stopped as suddenly as he'd taken off.

Finn kept running. The kid had reached a junction with another street and was now staring up it at something that had caught his attention. It had really caught his attention, too, because he completely ignored Finn's approach.

As Finn reached him, he took a glance in the same direction and saw someone on a bike, dressed in proper cycling gear, lights blinking as he disappeared up the street. The kid thought it might be Gibson, that much was clear.

"It's not him," Finn said. "He left."

Jonas turned, as if shocked by his sudden appearance, and looked ready to set off again, but Finn reached out and grabbed his arm, only lightly, but enough of a contact that he knew he'd be able to stop him running. It was just as well—Finn had no more running in him.

"You must remember me? I'm Finn, Hailey's neighbor from upstairs. Adrienne's boyfriend." For the first time in his life, "boyfriend" felt ridiculous, and he half expected Jonas to tell him he was too old to be anyone's boyfriend.

"Adrienne left."

Had Finn heard him speak before? For some reason, he'd imagined him talking with a slightly Germanic accent. He was half-Austrian, half-Australian, that's what they'd told him, but his accent, if anything, sounded vaguely mid-Atlantic.

"Yeah, she did. Everyone seems to be leaving right now. First Adrienne, then Gibson . . ." Jonas looked confused at the mention of the name. "That's the name of the guy who lived in the apartment next to Hailey. Which brings us to the final disappearance."

"She didn't tell me where she was going."

"I know. Now promise me you won't run again. I need to talk to you, Jonas, and if you run away from me I'll just have to come to your house, speak with your parents."

Jonas laughed. At first Finn thought it was just at the plea for him not to run again, but then he realized it had been the implied threat of involving his parents—this was clearly a kid who didn't fear such things.

"How do you know she didn't tell me?"

Finn let go of his arm. "Ethan and Debbie have asked me to help find her. They told me you'd been asked and said you didn't know, and they said you don't lie."

"Everyone lies." Jonas looked back up the street, but the cyclist had long since disappeared. "Why would they ask you to help find her? Don't you write books about history?"

"Yes, I do, but—"

"It's because you used to be a spy. Hailey told me."

"I didn't used to be a spy—that's just what they think, what Adrienne thinks. You know, it's quite hard to prove that you weren't a spy."

"You're not doing a very good job right now." Jonas smiled, not needing to spell it out, then appeared to dismiss the subject and move on. "Mr. and Mrs. Portman think I have Asperger's—I expect they told you that. It's a pet theory of theirs, and you needn't deny it, because that's why they think I don't lie."

"Do you? Lie, that is."

Jonas laughed. "No, but not because of any moral position or intellectual incapacity—I just have very little about which I need to lie. I don't have Asperger's, either."

"I didn't say you did."

Still, it seemed to be something that irked the kid, because he couldn't resist saying, "Mr. and Mrs. Portman are good people of above average but not exceptional intelligence. They've succeeded through a combination of nature, nurture, and hard work, and most of the people they mix with are the same. So if they meet someone who deviates from that norm, it unsettles them. They'd prefer to think of me as an idiot savant than someone whose brain simply happens to work in a freer and more complex way than theirs."

Finn assumed Jonas hadn't spoken to the police like this, because if he had they'd probably have put him on a suspect list and taken him in for questioning—for all the reasons Jonas had just suggested.

"And what about Hailey—how does she do on the intelligence scale?"

"Different, from them and from me. She doesn't have ideas the way I do, and she can stare at a puzzle and have absolutely no interest in solving it, but she thinks deeply about things. You know, she's truly profound. It blows me away sometimes. She'll recommend a book and I read it, but then she talks about it and I see it in a completely different light. She's amazing."

There it was: Jonas was in love with Hailey Portman. His eyes were sparkling now, his face animated, as if it wasn't enough to be in love with her, he also had to communicate that love, to help a relative stranger understand how incredible she was.

That explained his vigil, too, his need to find her, to ensure that no harm came to her. Finn noticed him shiver as a cold wind found the junction on which they stood.

"It's cold, Jonas. Let's go and grab a coffee somewhere and then you can tell me what you know, and why you're watching Gibson's apartment."

"Okay." Jonas started walking. Finn fell in with him, guessing he knew a coffee shop and was heading for it. "You can tell me about Gibson, too."

"Maybe. I don't know much."

"He's the reason she left." Finn looked at him questioningly. "She was scared. I was scared, too." He pointed ahead, and Finn stared for a moment before spotting the coffee shop, which wasn't one that he'd ever noticed before, but then Jonas looked at him earnestly and said, "Actually, I'm still a bit scared."

Chapter Nine

Jonas took his hat off as he walked in. Again, Finn was sure he must have seen him without a hat before, but he was surprised somehow to see the brown, tousled hair. The kid was disturbingly good-looking, and as they sat down Finn noticed one of the waitresses and two young women at a nearby table giving him intrigued glances.

But if Jonas knew he was intelligent, he either didn't know or didn't care that he was good-looking. His whole view of that probably came down to whether Hailey found him attractive, and Finn suspected this wasn't the time to be asking about the nature of their relationship.

Jonas ordered a hot chocolate, Finn a black coffee.

"Okay, Jonas, let's start from the beginning. What's your history with Gibson?" Jonas looked confused, so for the second time Finn explained, "That's the name of Hailey's neighbor."

"I know that, you already told me. But we don't have any *history* with Gibson. We've never even spoken to him, we just accidentally spied on him."

"Okay, so tell me about that."

Jonas nodded, apparently acknowledging that it was a fair request, and said, "Hailey and me, we do a lot of the same classes, so we often work together at her apartment or mine." He glanced across at the waitress, who smiled back at him, a smile that was interested. She looked in her late teens herself, and Jonas probably looked more than fifteen. "I think we should split the bill, if you don't mind. I think it would be inappropriate for you to pay for me. After all, I don't really know you that well."

Finn took a moment to catch up with the sudden change of subject. "I hadn't given it much thought, but since when did buying someone a hot chocolate count as inappropriate? Actually, for something like this I think it's stranger to split the bill. What would you and Hailey do if you were out having coffee?"

"That's a very different scenario, you can't compare the two—but you do make a good point." Jonas thought about it, as if Gibson had been forgotten, and added, "As I chose the venue, on this occasion I'll pay."

"Okay." Oddly, Finn still accepted the kid's earlier assertion that he didn't have Asperger's, but there was something out of the ordinary about him—the words "different drummer" spun through his mind.

Satisfied, and without registering that there had been a break in his story, Jonas said, "More often than not hers, because I have a younger sister, who's pretty cool, but she thinks Hailey is amazing so she never leaves us alone."

"Do you hang out together when you're not studying?"

Jonas looked suspicious, but said, "Of course. Anyway, about three weeks ago I was explaining to Hailey about how networks aren't always secure, and I used her computer—I installed Linux onto it last year—and picked up a network that I now know was Mr. Gibson's. I don't understand why he needed a network at all, except for desktop to laptop maybe, but I would do it wired if I cared about privacy, and the guy was using WPA but with a PSK, so it was easy. The guy was sharing files between his computers, and within an hour we were sharing them with him."

"Jonas, I write history books. I have no idea what you just said."

Their drinks came and Jonas sipped his immediately. He had froth on his top lip as he started talking again.

"I didn't explain it very well."

"You have froth on your lip."

He wiped it off and said, "Thanks. Basically, and I only did this to prove a point, I hacked into Mr. Gibson's network. Over a couple of days, I just dug around, and we copied a whole load of information."

"*We*?"

"We. Hailey knows her stuff. I mean, software and computers aren't really her thing—they're not even mine—but she still knows her way around."

"Okay." Neither of them struck him as archetypal geeks, but then as Jonas had said, this wasn't an obsession for them, just something they considered normal for a wired teenager. "Presumably, Gibson found out."

"First thing we knew was when all activity ceased. I thought he'd gone away. But then his network went live again, this time with the kind of security he should have had in place to begin with."

"So you couldn't hack into it?"

"I doubt even a hacker would have been able to hack into it, but like I said, it's not really my thing. I mean, that's what's crazy about what happened—we weren't even interested in his stuff. We just did it to prove to ourselves that we could." He took another sip of his drink and said, "Do I have froth on my lip?"

"No." Finn stifled a laugh and took a gulp of his coffee, too hot, before saying, "Go on."

"With what?"

"What happened next?"

"He spoke to Mr. and Mrs. Portman. He just knocked on their door and was all friendly, like it was just a misunderstanding, wondering if their daughter had accidentally accessed his network. He made some joke about not understanding how it worked but his technician had told him that's what had happened. Only it wasn't a joke if you think about it, because he actually didn't understand it—if he did he would have had the right security to begin with."

Finn nodded, but he was wondering why Ethan and Debbie hadn't mentioned this. He'd specifically asked about Gibson, about the possibility of his departure being linked with Hailey's disappearance, and they hadn't mentioned that he'd spoken to them. It might just have slipped their minds, he supposed, but it was odd that they'd remembered other unimportant things and forgotten that.

Finn said, "Hailey said she hadn't, of course."

"She was clever. She said she didn't think so, then asked if she'd know about it or if it was possible to do it by accident."

"Smart reply." *Devious,* he thought to himself. Hailey Portman was devious, a fact that filled him with a little more optimism.

But Jonas said, "Not smart enough. A few times, she noticed him staring at her from his window as she came in, then one night a car followed her when she was walking home from my house, then someone broke into their apartment."

"Into the Portmans' apartment?" Jonas nodded, and Finn was once again knocked back, wondering why they hadn't mentioned this to him, wondering if they'd mentioned it to the police.

Then he came to the obvious—perhaps too obvious—conclusion, that these were just kids with overactive imaginations. How many teenage girls haven't thought they were being followed at some point or other? And by a car? It suggested a kid who'd seen too many made-for-TV thrillers.

"They didn't take anything, but Hailey knew they'd searched her room. Of course, they'd tried to access her laptop, too, but thanks to Linux, they didn't stand a chance."

Finn thought again about how devious Hailey was, and hit upon another explanation, one that depressed him, because it made a fool of Jonas and he was already taking to the kid. But he had to admit, it seemed a lot more likely than a psychotic hedge fund manager.

Hailey had changed her image, which his instinct told him was a response to a boy—or a man. She'd wanted to go and meet him, had wanted a reason for doing so, and had fabricated these various threats: the pursuing car, the searched room. If she was really smart, she might even have cajoled Jonas into hacking Gibson's network in the first place, setting up the scenario in advance.

"What do you think they were searching for?"

Jonas shrugged. "The material we collected, I guess."

"They could have just taken the laptop."

"True." Jonas thought about it and said, "It wouldn't have helped them, but they weren't to know that. Of course, it would have made Hailey's room a crime scene, instead of the location for a teenager's paranoid fancies."

Finn laughed, impressed on some level—it was as if Jonas had read his thoughts and sought to counter them.

"What's funny, Mr. Harrington?"

"Please, call me Finn, and what's funny is that I *was* wondering how much of a break-in there had been." He didn't spell out that it wasn't paranoia he suspected, for fear of hurting the kid's feelings. Besides, he wasn't certain yet, about any of it.

"It's a natural conclusion, one her parents also came to, though perhaps for different reasons."

"You said it wouldn't have helped them if they'd stolen the computer. What did you mean by that?"

The two girls who'd been at a neighboring table got up and left, one of them looking back at Jonas two or three times, trying to make eye contact. At the very last, Jonas noticed her and threw a shy and slightly lost smile back at her. Seeing it made Finn feel like a ghost.

Jonas turned back to him. "We put it on a memory stick. Hailey has it."

"She could have left it in her room."

"No, she would've taken it with her."

"You don't have a copy?"

The kid shook his head and took a deep draft of his hot chocolate.

"I made some notes, but I didn't have a copy of the files. I don't have my notebook with me. It's a Moleskine, which is what Hemingway used, though really it's just a brand now. I don't much like Hemingway, anyway."

"*The Old Man and the Sea* was pretty good."

"True. But don't you think it's the idea of Hemingway that people like, rather than the writing?"

Finn nodded, smiling. "That's an interesting theory. I like that."

Jonas smiled, too—flattered, even a little embarrassed.

"But, tell me, the information you hacked, did it seem sensitive?" Thinking of Gibson's possible careers, he added, "Did it deal with stock information, perhaps, or sensitive industrial data?"

"It didn't seem to relate to anything that we could make sense of. If I showed you my notebook it might give you an idea of how random it was."

"You can't remember any of it now?"

"Little bits." He thought for a moment. "It mentioned Helsinki. I remember that because I've been to Helsinki."

Finn looked at him expectantly.

"It mentioned . . . let me get this right. It mentioned 'Albigensian,' but then another note said he should disregard that comment."

Finn could almost feel his thoughts tumbling away into an abyss, could feel his body tightening.

"Albigensian?"

"Yeah. I checked it out because I'd never heard of it—it's from the Albigensian Crusade, which wasn't against Islam, it was against—"

"The Cathars. It's what my new book is about."

Jonas looked lost for words momentarily, then said, "Hold on, you don't have a network in your apartment?" Finn shook his head. Jonas was ahead of him, though, saying, "But no, it was Mr. Gibson's network, I know it was. Do you think he was spying on you?"

"Could be a coincidence," said Finn, but he knew that it wasn't, looking instead for the least troubling explanation for why he might be under surveillance again after all this time.

Jonas checked his watch, then attracted the attention of the waitress and said, "I have to go now, but if we meet tomorrow, I'll bring my notebook."

"I'd appreciate that," said Finn, then watched as Jonas settled the bill with the smitten waitress.

His mind was racing. They'd left him alone for the best part of six years, the terms of his departure agreed upon, a line drawn under it. So why would they be showing an interest again now? Unless the mention of "Albigensian" really had been a coincidence, something that seemed too unlikely but that he still wanted to hold on to as a possibility.

They walked out into the cold together and arranged a time to meet—Jonas had the following afternoon free, which made it easier—and a place: the same coffee shop. And then Finn thanked him and Jonas walked away.

Only after Finn had started walking did he hear Jonas call him. He turned and looked, and Jonas shouted, "I remember something else. Something he talked about a lot."

"What was it?"

"Sparrowhawk," said Jonas. "You know, like the bird of prey? Sparrowhawk!" He shrugged, as if to suggest how absurd it was. And he waved and walked along the street and left Finn standing there, knowing that it was over, that Adrienne had left at the right time, because the life he'd constructed over the last six years, already insubstantial, had just evaporated.

History

Harry called in sick the following morning. Perry seemed preoccupied for most of the day, like a man awaiting bad news, but he saw Finn after lunch and said, "Doesn't look good, Harry taking a day off just after the news breaks."

"Ed, he could just be ill. I'll call in on him later and see how he is."

"Even if he's ill, tell him it's better if he drags himself in here. Don't give them anything to latch on to."

"Okay, I'll tell him."

"Good. I've seen careers destroyed by this kind of question mark, and I don't want it happening to anyone on my watch."

"Don't worry, I'll see to it."

Ed nodded absently and walked up the corridor. It made Finn realize he'd never really been cut out for this line of work anyway. It had always been too much of a game for him, and seeing the genuine concern Perry had for his team only reinforced how reckless and immature Finn had been.

Finn took a different route home to call in on Harry, conscious at the same time that he didn't want to pass the church again. Stray flakes of snow were falling from the overcast sky, but it didn't look as if they'd come to anything.

When he reached Harry's place and rang the bell, there was a weighted silence before Harry finally answered. He looked perfectly healthy, of course, and ushered Finn inside.

"It's okay, Katerina."

She came out of the bedroom, smiling broadly when she saw Finn. She was wearing a new sweatshirt, but Harry had done a pretty good job of matching the style of the previous one.

"Hello, Finn," she said, shy—either around him or around the language.

"Hello, Katerina, how are you today?"

"Good. Thank you."

Harry smiled as if he'd performed a magic trick and said, "Actually, her English is pretty good. I think she was just so shocked and afraid when you found her." Katerina said something in Russian and Harry smiled. "And we speak too quickly."

Finn nodded, smiling at her but saying to Harry, "So you took the day off."

"I couldn't leave her. She was nervous about being left on her own— understandably so at the moment. Maybe tomorrow."

Finn glanced at Katerina. "You went out to buy her clothes."

"While she was still asleep." He gestured to the sofa. "I didn't have the best of nights."

Finn looked at the sofa, and at the pillow and folded blankets on a chair in the corner.

He pointed and said, "You should have hidden those just now."

"Oh wow, yeah, of course." Harry went and picked them up immediately, taking them into the bedroom. "I can't believe I left them there." He sounded distraught at what, after all, was an easy enough slip to make.

Katerina looked at Finn, concerned. He smiled dismissively. "It's okay."

"Okay," she said.

As Harry came back in, he said, "Sorry, Finn, do you want a drink?"

"No, I'm good thanks, I'm gonna head home. But look, I think it'll be this time next week—is that okay?"

Harry shrugged, as if the question hardly needed asking. "Yeah, don't worry about us, we'll be fine."

"Okay. I'll call again, but don't take any more time off. Don't do anything to raise suspicions." He got a nod from Harry and raised his hand, saying, "Bye, Katerina."

"Goodbye, Finn."

Her voice had that mournful, musical quality he so often found in Russians when they spoke English—it made her seem simultaneously fragile and much wiser than her years. He wanted to say something else, offer some further reassurance, but held back, guessing he was reading too much into it, and that for all that had happened in the last few days, it was nothing more than a matter of inflection.

He made his way home, and as he opened the door to the apartment he caught the smell of meat cooking, onions, and herbs. He'd forgotten Sofi had said she'd be earlier today, that she'd cook, and the combination of the aromas and the gentle clatter filled him with calm.

He saw his summer coat hanging on the rack in the corner of the hallway. He'd dropped the gun into the pocket when he got home the night before, and he reminded himself now that he had to get rid of it. For the time being, though, he didn't even take off his overcoat, just walked on through.

She hadn't heard him come in, and he stood in the kitchen doorway for a moment watching her. She was in her stocking feet, wearing her beige woolen dress; he didn't know what it was called—a sweater dress, perhaps—but he liked the way it looked, the way it hugged her curves. Her hair was pulled back into a simple ponytail, something she only did when she cooked.

There had been some tension between them this last week or so, never spilling over, never descending into blame, but it was still there, the knowledge that he'd quit, that he'd soon have no job to keep him in Tallinn. Standing there watching her, he knew they had to find a solution, because he didn't want to be without this woman, couldn't be without her.

Throughout his twenties, he'd feared the prospect of "settling down," a term that had always seemed possessed of its own claustrophobic menace. He'd been in love before, but in retrospect it seemed that one small part of his psyche had always held back, counting down the days, looking to the horizon.

Perhaps he'd even been like that with Sofi, treating it like a game. And only now did he see the folly of it, because only now did he fully understand that he wanted to spend his life with her, have a family with her, to become middle-aged and dependable.

As if hearing his thoughts, she finally realized he was behind her and she looked over her shoulder and smiled and said, "How long have you been standing there?"

"Oh, a little while."

"I made a casserole." She opened the oven and put the dish in, and as she wiped her hands he walked over and kissed her, then again, and put his hands on her hips and pulled her close.

She laughed a little and said, "Okay, I had intended on a bath, but . . ."

He pulled away so that he could look her in the eye and said, "I've decided on a solution, to our problem." She looked at him quizzically. "I'll stay."

"In your job?"

"No, but I'll stay here, in Tallinn."

The quizzical stare turned to confusion. "But how? What about money?"

"I have a little money." The lie of it stung him. He wanted to tell her, was desperate to tell her. "I've saved some money over the years, maybe enough to start my own business, or tide me over while I write a book—"

She was about to interrupt, but the doorbell beat her to it. They both hesitated and then Finn said, "Do you want me to stay?"

"Of course. I want us to be together." She laughed, as if seeing that the problem really could disappear so easily. The doorbell sounded again, and she pulled away from him, releasing her hair from its ponytail at the same time.

"Don't answer it," he said quietly.

She smiled, shaking her head. "Easy for you to say—you know it won't be for you."

She made for the door, and he walked over and looked at the bottle of wine she'd taken out. Automatically, he resented whichever friend or relative or colleague had come calling, but after a barely audible exchange there was silence, and then Sofi appeared in the kitchen again.

She looked slightly bemused as she said, "It's for you."

He walked through into the hallway and took a second to identify the woman standing there, another second to appreciate the implications. He concentrated on staying relaxed as he said, "Louisa—I didn't hear you were in Tallinn."

He was annoyed with himself because they'd been waiting for him, because the car had clearly been on the street when he'd come in a short while before, and he should have spotted it.

"Hello, Finn." She smiled, but it veiled over a much graver expression. He wondered if this was it, if the Kremlin source had proved too reliable, if he'd pushed his luck a little too far. Would they prosecute him? Again, he thought of his parents. "I only arrived this afternoon."

Sofi came out of the kitchen and Finn said, "Er, this is Sofi, my girlfriend. This is Louisa from our head office in London." They shook hands, exchanged greetings.

Then Louisa looked at Sofi apologetically and said, "I feel awful doing this but I wonder if I could borrow Finn, just for half an hour or so? Something smells delicious, so if you're ready to eat I can come back later."

"It's a casserole," said Sofi, only a hint of suspicion in her voice. "I'll leave you alone."

"No, not at all. We'll go out, if you don't mind, but I promise I'll bring him back before supper's ready."

Sofi shrugged. "Okay. Would you like to join us?"

"That's very sweet of you, but I won't."

Without being sure why, Finn wanted to stall, even made to say something, but he realized he still had his coat on, that there was no reason for him to delay going with Louisa.

He gestured toward the door and said, "Okay, after you."

Louisa said goodbye to Sofi, and Finn turned himself before heading out. Sofi gave him a concerned look and he smiled reassurance, an echo of his parting with Katerina, given with even less confidence.

They took the stairs, and as they descended Louisa said, "She seems nice. Terribly attractive. Journalist, isn't she?"

He didn't bother answering what hadn't really been a question, but said, "So what brings you—"

"Let's wait until we're outside."

"Of course."

He didn't like her tone, and could feel his heart beating a little faster now. He could feel a muscle fluttering under his left eye, too, though he knew from experience it probably wasn't visible. Still, he had to control himself, in case this was still at the level of suspicion rather than accusation.

He thought of Katerina again. He'd promised he would help her and wasn't sure how he could if they carted him off to London. He could rely on Harry, though, he was sure of that. If anyone else could get the girl to safety, it was Harry.

Once they were on the street, the sudden blast of cold relaxed him—the temperature had dropped dramatically even in the short time he'd been inside. He spotted the car now, too, and Louisa waved at the driver but set off along the street.

"There's a little bar just around the corner—I thought we'd go there."

"Sure," said Finn a little too gratefully, sensing they didn't have anything concrete on him yet. She might be trying to trap him, to get him to confirm their suspicions, but for the time being it was no more than that. "So, can you tell me now what you're doing here, why I didn't know you were coming?"

"Ed's the only person who knew I was coming. And officially, I'm here to sort out this whole bloody mess with the Kremlin mole and Aleksandr Naumenko. Tiresome. I'm having dinner tonight with the people at the embassy, just trying to calm them down, reassure them that our operations aren't going to compromise theirs." She pointed as she headed off across the street, as if Finn were the visitor. "This way."

Finn laughed a little, and noticed as he crossed that the driver was following some way behind, on foot. More importantly, Finn had latched on to one crucial word in what Louisa had said, and he held on to it now with a little too much hope—he could feel his heartbeat skipping along again.

"You said that's why you're here *officially*. What did you mean by that?"

"You're a smart young chap, Finn, what do you think? Kremlin moles! My only interest in that story is that it gave me a reasonably plausible cover for this visit."

"So you don't believe it?"

"Do you?"

Finn shrugged. "Point taken." He was regaining control, his mind slipping into gear, responding as if there really was no truth to the story.

"No, the unofficial but primary reason for my visit is to offer you an opportunity—one last hurrah."

"A chance to go out in a blaze of glory?"

They'd reached the bar, but she hesitated at the door as she said, "Not quite, but a chance to do a very great service for your country."

She smiled, perhaps at how arch that line had sounded, then pushed open the door to the warmth and the hubbub of voices inside. Finn had been in here a couple of times—once with Sofi, once with Harry—but no more than that. It was a traditional place, but with a youngish crowd of students, creative types. It was half empty this early in the evening, and they were able to choose a table in the corner with clear views. As they ordered their drinks, the driver came in and strolled to the bar.

"Charming place," said Louisa, then looked at Finn. "You'll know the Russians arrested Demidov last week."

"Of course."

"And they've done a pretty good job on dismantling his little fiefdom. But in the process it's given us the chance to collaborate and wrap up several different pieces of business."

Their drinks arrived and they raised glasses, but Louisa didn't drink from hers. Finn took a small sip and put his glass back on the table.

"We alerted the Russians that there was a small cargo ship bound for St. Petersburg with a ton or so of cocaine onboard. It's due to arrive next weekend. The Russians decided to monitor it, use it as a chance to round up any of Demidov's people who might have escaped the net. But then we picked up on something very interesting—it seems one of his men has decided to go it alone, because the ship is now going to make an unscheduled stop at a disused dock in Kaliningrad. So we suggested this might provide an opportunity to remove a thorn in their sides and ours. Hence this operation—Sparrowhawk."

"I'm following, Louisa, but if you're expecting me to second guess, I have no idea where this is going."

"Don't worry, you're not losing your touch. This *is* complicated. But this part of the plan is quite simple, and it involves Karasek. We'll talk through the cover story and the details later, but in short, you go to Karasek, tell him you're leaving, that you want a retirement plan. You tell him about the ship docking in Kaliningrad—no one else knows about it, only you—giving him the opportunity to go in there and steal a nice big container full of marching powder."

Finn laughed at her use of slang—he always imagined Louisa as the headmistress of a girls' boarding school—but his thoughts were tumbling over each other. He wasn't sure how he could decline her offer without arousing suspicion, but the parallels were frightening.

They wanted Finn to deal with Karasek, who was currently raging because a girl he'd wanted had gone missing—a girl Finn had spirited away. They wanted Finn to pretend he was corrupt, that he was looking for a payoff, when he'd already had his payoff because, of course, he was corrupt.

"So the Russians get to intercept the shipment and take Karasek out in the process—assuming Karasek falls for it."

"You're persuasive, I'm sure he'll fall for it."

"But apart from taking Karasek out, I'm not sure what *we* get out of it."

"Before I say any more, I need to know whether you're in. Chances are, you'll be seen as a traitor by your colleagues, you'll leave under a cloud, and only a small number of people will know the service you'll have rendered."

"And if I say no?"

"Then, presumably, you'll leave without blemish."

Was that a threat? Was it an implicit warning that they did know about him and Naumenko, and that this was the price for them turning a blind eye? He had to assume it wasn't, that it was actually Louisa's subtle way of suggesting there were nobler things than a clean but undistinguished record.

He thought back to some of the things he'd learned about Karasek in the last year or so, and to the thing he'd learned about him in the past couple of days, and said, "If it gives us a chance of removing Karasek from the face of the earth, I'll take the fall."

She smiled and raised her glass again, but this time she drank. Was she surprised? Pleased with herself? It was hard to tell. Then she became more somber and put the glass back down.

"For some time, we've suspected one of our people might be working with Karasek. It barely registered to begin with, only the slightest indications that something was amiss. Even now, we don't have anything concrete, which is why we want you to help build a case. If all goes well, you'll tell Karasek about the need for secrecy and you'll get him to acknowledge the name of his man on our team. Acknowledge, no more than that—we don't need to prosecute this person, just pin him down."

Finn thought back to the face-to-face meetings he'd had with Karasek and said, "I wouldn't be able to go in there wearing a wire. I presume we'd be meeting at his club? His guys are scrupulous—electronic scan, pat down."

"That's all being taken care of as we speak, and you won't be wearing a wire. It'll all be explained, but all you really need to do is get him to respond to one name."

For some reason, Finn had been assuming it was someone from the embassy, but he realized now it was more likely one of their own, and his mind made a sudden and unexpected leap. It was based on instinct alone, but he felt it so strongly that he said, "It's Ed Perry, isn't it?"

"You see, you *were* cut out for this line of work. How did you know?"

Even though he'd guessed, he was shocked by her tacit confirmation. But he saw it clearly now, and was impressed at some level, that the touching concern for Harry and the others was all a sham. It even made him feel better about himself and his own foolishness.

"I'm not sure. Just the way he's been acting the last few days."

Finn noticed the driver become more alert then, and a moment later he heard voices himself, and a small party of red-faced and leery English guys piled through the door. One of them was wearing a sequined tutu and a wig. They were already drunk but harmless enough, and the driver relaxed again.

"Oh dear, I'd heard it wasn't good at the weekend out here."

Finn laughed and said, "Actually, they're off the beaten track—some streets really are no-go zones come the weekend."

Louisa pushed her drink toward the center of the table. "We do ruin everything, don't we? Come on, let's go."

He stood, his mind still reeling—with what seemed like his own narrow escape, with the revelation that Perry was rotten, the realization that he'd signed up not only to ignominy but also to danger in the week ahead, and underpinning it all, with the knowledge that there was a girl in Harry's apartment, a girl Finn had vowed to get to safety.

They stepped out into the cold, the English stag party raucously singing behind them. It was the sort of jolly rowdiness Finn usually viewed with contempt, but right now he envied those men, envied both them and everything they represented.

Chapter Ten

Sparrowhawk—a name that brought all its attendant ghosts with it. He walked back like a man tranquilized, only dimly aware of his body and its progress along the street, his thoughts flitting around without settling on anything in particular. The only thought that registered with any certainty was the realization that his new life was over, that the rebuilding effort had been in vain.

Like the message Gibson had apparently received, Finn too could forget about the Albigensian Crusade, because he doubted he would get to write that book. He immediately countered, asking himself what was to stop him—they wouldn't kill him, or at least, they would have killed him already if that had been the plan, and they couldn't try to pin anything on him now, not unless there had been some seismic shift in the hierarchy.

So why were they interested in him again? Either they'd found out that his activities had stretched beyond what had happened at Kaliningrad, crimes for which they *could* still prosecute, or he was misreading the situation completely and it wasn't even his own people watching him.

His own people! He didn't have any people, not anymore. There was no one he could contact, no one who could help him find out what was going on. He could hardly put in a call to Louisa Whitman to ask if they'd had him under surveillance for the last year.

He neared his building and saw Ethan Portman standing in the window of their apartment. He seemed to respond to Finn's appearance, and walked rapidly away. Finn hoped he wasn't about to be intercepted. He needed time on his own, space to think through his own problems, not theirs, and only as he stepped into the elevator did he acknowledge to himself that the two were related.

How did he tell the Portmans about that? How did he tell them that their daughter's disappearance might be linked to his own past? The simple answer was that he wouldn't, that for the time being he would deploy the truth the same way he always had—to his own ends.

The elevator reached the floor below his and stopped. The door opened and, as he'd suspected, Ethan Portman was standing there.

"Hey, Finn, sorry to trouble you, but you did say to tell you if we found out anything."

Ethan kept his finger on the button but stepped aside, suggesting it wasn't a piece of information that could be quickly exchanged before allowing Finn on his way.

"Of course," said Finn. He stepped out and followed Ethan back to the Portmans' apartment.

Debbie Portman was sitting exactly as he'd last seen her, as if she hadn't moved at all in the intervening period. She'd merely eroded a little more, become less herself. She struggled to find a smile for him.

Ethan said, "Sit down, Finn." He reached into his pocket and took out a small piece of paper. "I spotted this in Hailey's room earlier. It had fallen between the bed and the bedside table, and I guess she didn't notice it."

He held out the piece of paper, and Finn took it and studied it. She'd bought a hundred euros. He looked at Debbie, then up at

Ethan, trying to gauge what this meant to them—a source of new hopes or of new fears.

Ethan sat down, and sounded like someone who'd found a big lead as he said, "It means she isn't in Switzerland, but it's not a lot of cash, so maybe she's close by—France or Italy, Germany . . ."

"She could be anywhere," said Debbie in a defeated tone.

She was right, too, though Finn wasn't sure how even the three countries already mentioned could fill Ethan with any hope—he was talking about three large countries, all of which had their seedy corners.

"This is one receipt. There could be another five that she didn't drop. Even if it's the only one, she could be anywhere in the euro area—if she got a bus or a train from here, she wouldn't need to use a lot of money until she got to where she was going."

Ethan looked deflated.

They looked as though they needed to be left alone, but now that Finn was here he was eager to move things on. "I spoke to Jonas this evening—it seems there are a few things you didn't tell me."

They both looked at him, even Debbie appearing more alert in response.

Ethan said, "I don't understand—what things?"

"I asked about your involvement with Gibson. Jonas says that a couple of weeks ago Gibson knocked on your door and asked if Hailey might have accidentally accessed his network."

It was immediately obvious that it was true. Debbie looked horrified, seeing the incident in a new light, perhaps wondering if it should have been mentioned to the police. Ethan looked dismissive, but it was a veneer, not quite masking his nervous lack of certainty.

"It slipped our minds, I guess, no more than that. But Finn, it was nothing, he just knocked on the door one night, mentioned it, and that was it. He didn't come in, didn't seem unduly upset or concerned."

"Did you ask Hailey if it was true?"

"Of course! It wasn't."

"It was," said Finn. They looked shocked, defensive, and fearful. "Don't worry about it—it's the kind of thing kids do. Hailey and Jonas hacked into Gibson's network, just to prove to themselves that they could." Ethan looked ready to respond but Finn said, "You didn't tell me that Hailey thought someone had searched her room."

Debbie laughed, suddenly animated. "Finn, it was just some random comment she made—said and then forgotten. If you had children you'd soon learn to pay little attention to such things."

"True, until that child disappears, leaving a note that you believe suggested she was in danger. As it happens, I don't agree with that interpretation of the note, but given that you do, I'm amazed that you wouldn't mention either of these things."

He thought of bringing up the third omission, but didn't, because he was certain they would have told him and the police if their daughter had claimed she'd been followed by a car. In truth, his instinct told him that both the curb-crawling car and the break-in had been fabricated by Hailey to justify her disappearance.

Debbie's eyes were glistening now and Ethan shook his head slowly, as if they were both struggling to come to terms with their own petty failings.

"We should tell the police," said Debbie.

Ethan looked at her, though Finn couldn't see what passed between them.

"I don't think that's necessary." Finn had their attention again. "I just need a day or two more to piece things together. Besides, I don't think the police will take seriously anything you say about Gibson now, and for what it's worth, I don't think he's directly connected to her disappearance."

Ethan said, "On what basis?"

"Instinct, which is fallible, of course." Finn stood up. "Give me another day or two. I'll find her."

For the first time in the last two days, they looked as if they doubted him, perhaps only because he was making promises that seemed without foundation. And yet, also for the first time, he was determined he would find her, because the girl was carrying a memory stick that had the details of his past on it—and, in one way or another, the key to his future.

Ethan saw him to the door and Finn walked away toward the stairs, but once he heard the Portmans' door closing, he strolled back along the corridor. He put his ear to Gibson's door and stood for a while. It was silent.

Had they cleared out after all this time because they'd been rumbled by a couple of curious teenagers? Or was that just coincidence? For all Finn knew, they'd wound up the surveillance because they had whatever they wanted, or because they were moving into the next phase.

Finn briefly entertained the idea that they'd given up on him, but he doubted that. He'd witnessed plenty of waste and incompetence in his time, but they wouldn't commit to a surveillance operation of at least a year—maybe two—unless they were after someone or something specific.

Whatever this was, he suspected it was only the beginning as far as he was concerned. Beyond that, the only thing he knew for certain was what he'd learned from Jonas's notebook, that they weren't interested in his skills as a popular historian.

Chapter Eleven

The next morning, he started training again. He rescued his weights from the closet they'd been stored in for the last couple of years, then went for a run. Perhaps he would have done it anyway, shocked into action by his failure to keep up with Jonas the night before, but there was no question that he had to be in shape now.

The run proved less of a trial than he'd feared, and once he'd relaxed into it he found his old pace coming back to him. He'd let things slide over the last six years, but the memory of the fitter person he'd been was still there, and wouldn't take long to be reactivated.

He knew, though, that reactivating the other part of his life would be tougher. He hoped the kid's notebook would provide some clues, but he needed to get his hands on the memory stick if he was to have a real chance of finding out why they were interested in him again. Even then, he wasn't sure how he could go about responding to that interest.

He went early to the coffee shop, but before he walked in he saw that Jonas was already there, one of the few customers during this hollow part of the afternoon. The waitress from the previous night was standing at his table, talking shyly, making lots of eye contact—she was pretty, Italian-looking, dark-haired.

Jonas waved at him as he walked in, even though they were only feet apart. He had a tall glass of some sort of fruit tea in front of him, and Finn smiled at the waitress and said, "I'll have one of those, please."

She smiled back and threw a glance at Jonas before walking off.

As he sat down he said, "How's it going, Jonas?"

Jonas stared at him for a second, then said, "Hello."

"Hello."

Quietly, Jonas said, "She's a university student, studying business law."

"She's very pretty. Does she know how old you are?"

Jonas looked at him askance. "Why would she need to know that?"

Finn looked across at the waitress as she put his fruit tea together, a more complex process than he'd anticipated.

"Jonas, she's crazy about you."

Jonas laughed a little, embarrassed, not so much for his own part but as if it was Finn making a fool of himself.

"No she isn't! She was just telling me about her life—she doesn't think she wants to do law anymore. I think she's confused, that's all."

"Jonas, since I became a writer I've met a hell of a lot of women who just wanted to tell me about their lives and their problems, and I've met a much smaller number who were crazy about me—you'll just have to trust that I've learned to spot the difference."

"What about before you were a writer?"

He smiled at the way Jonas picked up on even the ballast of a sentence, and said, "The same, I suppose—I just meant that if you're a writer, people want to tell you their life stories."

"I'm not a writer."

"No—she's crazy about you."

The waitress approached and placed his tea in front of him. He thanked her, and noticed that Jonas was on edge the whole time, perhaps fearing that Finn was about to say something to her, ask her outright, the kind of social death that only adults could handle flippantly.

Once she'd walked away, he visibly relaxed and said, "It's quite awkward if she does think like that. Surely she can see that I'm a lot younger than her?"

Finn looked at him, sympathizing with the waitress, because Jonas could probably pass for eighteen, maybe even twenty. And within those shifting sands lay the secret of Hailey's reinvention. At their age, nearly everyone looked either older or younger than they really were. Briefly, his memory flitted back to Katerina, but he banished it quickly, the attendant thoughts too troubling.

"What about you and Hailey?"

"What about us?"

"Are you a couple?"

"*No*." He feigned confusion, as if it were an outlandish suggestion, then sipped at his tea to avoid scrutiny. "We're just friends."

"Okay," said Finn, not wanting to make him uncomfortable, particularly when it wasn't something that mattered.

"You know . . ." Jonas hesitated and sipped at his tea again. Finn wondered if the kid had decided to share his feelings anyway, a thought that filled him with a certain dread, but Jonas took him by surprise yet again. "I think everyone's trying to find this point in time where they fit, where everything's right, where they fit into the universe. Me and Hailey, that girl"—he gestured toward the waitress—"we're young, so we keep thinking it's in the future and we're running toward it. I guess people who are older, like you or like our parents, you keep thinking you missed it and it's some place back in your past but you can't pin it down. You know, we're all looking for this same point of time and it always seems just out of reach—when we were happy, when things felt right, when we'll fit into the universe, but maybe it's out of reach because it's not a point in time at all, it's something else, something inside us. Like déjà vu."

"Er, sure, you might be on to something." Finn had forgotten what it was like to be that age, and even now he wasn't certain that his thoughts had ever been that far out there. "But, do you have a reason for saying all that? I mean, does it relate to anything that we've been discussing?"

Jonas sounded hesitant, testing the question against his thoughts as he said, "I don't think so. But it could. It's just an idea I've been playing around with—I haven't worked it out yet."

Even as he spoke, Finn realized Jonas's navel-gazing theory was possessed of something relevant. It probably summed up the real reasons for Hailey's disappearance. She'd reached the apogee of teenage restlessness and had tried to escape into the future she was no longer willing to wait for.

"Jonas, I want to look at your notebook, but let me ask you something first. You said you didn't know where Hailey had gone, and that's all people have asked so you haven't said more. But now I'm asking you—do you have any ideas about where she might have gone?"

"I have ideas about how she got there." Finn looked at him questioningly and he added, "I think she went by train."

"Because?"

"One day, a few weeks ago, I walked into her room and we were talking, and then I noticed she had the page up for InterRail on her computer. It's like a pass you can use to travel anywhere in Europe for a month or something."

"Yeah, they had them when I was . . . a student."

"Really? Did you ever go on one?"

"Yeah, I did. It was okay, although kind of like your theory, probably better in the memory than it was in the moment."

Jonas smiled, liking Finn's last comment, and said, "She looked pretty embarrassed when I noticed it, but she covered up really well, said she was wondering if we should do it together between school and college, which is years away, but then Hailey's a dreamer."

A dreamer.

"Was this before or after you hacked Gibson's network?"

Jonas thought for a moment. "After, but before all the other things that happened. Yes, in fact, that was also the day we tried and his network had been taken down."

It backed up what Finn had been thinking more and more. There was no doubt that they'd felt threatened by Gibson, but Hailey had used that fear or concern as an excuse for organizing her own longed-for escape.

"So she went somewhere far away."

"I didn't say that. I really have no idea where she went."

"No, I said it. I doubt she would have just planned to tour the rails for a month, and she mentioned in her note that she was with friends, which suggests she was going somewhere in particular. If it were somewhere close, she'd have bought a ticket to that place. Say she was going to Munich, she would have bought a ticket to Munich. The InterRail pass only makes sense financially if she had a long way to travel."

Jonas stared at him for a moment, impressed at some level, but then, as if wanting to remind Finn of a crucial underlying fact, he said, "She left because she was scared of Gibson."

"Maybe. But there are two separate issues here—why she left and where she went. Now, for the sake of her parents, the latter is the most crucial. I have to admit that, for my own purposes, the former is perhaps more interesting."

"So you do think Gibson was spying on you!"

"I'm not sure—that's why I want to find out what you put in your notebook."

Jonas reached down into his jacket pocket, but looked doubtful as he said, "I didn't make quite as many notes as I remembered, and I'm not sure how useful any of it will be."

He produced the small Moleskine, opened it on a certain page and handed it across the table. Finn looked at the tiny scrawled notes and handed it back.

"You'll have to read it to me—I can't make out your writing."

Jonas laughed, suggesting this was an accusation made quite often, and pored over the notes himself. "Okay, like I told you, Albigensian got mentioned once but then discounted. Sparrowhawk was mentioned six times, and on two of those occasions it was mentioned alongside someone called Karasek. He's also mentioned separately in relation to Helsinki."

"Are you sure about that?"

Jonas looked intrigued. "I'm certain—why is that strange?"

Finn wasn't sure there was anything strange about it. He wondered if Karasek had relocated from Tallinn—it made sense in a way, just a short hop across the water, and things had been getting tougher for him in Estonia.

"It's not strange. I knew a Karasek, that's all, and I don't connect him with Helsinki."

Jonas took in that information, looked at his notes again, and said, "I'm curious. If Gibson works for an intelligence agency and they were spying on you, why were they talking so openly? Shouldn't they have been using code names or something?"

"One would think so. Of course, all of these words *could* be code. Sparrowhawk is the most obvious, but even Helsinki could be code for something else."

"So, Sparrowhawk doesn't mean anything to you?"

"No. Does it mean anything to you?"

"It's a bird of prey." Jonas stared at Finn for a second, then back at his notebook. "There were lots of sequences of numbers, which could be code, I guess, and then this sentence: *Imperative to identify Jerry de Borg.* Does that name mean anything to you?"

Finn reached out and took the book again. Jerry de Borg—even in the kid's crabby handwriting the name was quite visible. Finn kept looking at it, not because the scribbled words could tell him anything more, but because he didn't know what to say, was struggling even to think what it meant to see that name there.

Only one other person had ever known about Jerry de Borg—and, joke that it was, it made no sense for either one of them to have ever spoken of it. Finn never had, which made it stranger still that the name should reappear, because the other person had been Harry Simons.

"What's wrong?"

Finn shook his head, doubtful, and said, "I don't know, and I couldn't say if I did, but seeing that name makes me think someone I've long believed dead is actually still alive."

"Wow." Jonas took the notebook and sat in silence, apparently stunned by the realization that what everyone had said about Finn was true. Finally he said, "What kind of spy were you?"

Finn looked at him, guessing it was pointless to deny it now, and said, "Not a very good one." Jonas laughed. "I'm serious. I wasn't incompetent, but I was . . . corrupt, for want of a better word."

Jonas still looked bemused. "No, I mean, who did you work for?"

"Oh. Well, I can't answer that, even now, even after everything that's happened."

Jonas nodded and looked at his watch. "I'll have to go quite soon."

"Okay." Finn's mind leapt back to the other side of the equation they were dealing with, reminded again that as well as *wanting* to find Hailey Portman, he also *needed* to find her if he was to stand any chance of getting to the truth of why they were watching him.

Thinking back to a question he'd asked Ethan and Debbie, he said, "Are you and Hailey on any of the social networking sites?"

"Officially, we think they're lame. For older people, you know."

"Unofficially?"

"I think Hailey's on Facebook." Jonas looked at the dregs of his tea, but decided against drinking it. "She was talking one day about some really stupid game on Facebook, and when I asked her how she'd seen it, she said she was just browsing, but you know, it's a closed site—you can't browse properly unless you're a member."

Finn smiled. He wasn't sure if it was the kid's intelligence or his infatuation with Hailey that gave him this attention to detail, but he couldn't help but admire it. And it undoubtedly offered the key, because there weren't many reasons why Hailey would join a social networking site without telling her best friend about it.

"Okay, I need to find and access her Facebook page."

Jonas nodded vigorously and wrote something on a page in his notebook, then tore it out and put it on the table.

"I think I can do that. Meet me at that Internet café at eight o'clock." Before Finn could answer he added, "We can't use your computer—if they're monitoring you, we don't want to give Hailey's location away. And we can't use mine. I mean, my parents are pretty cool, but they'd be freaked out if I brought you home with me."

"I suppose they would," said Finn, and took the piece of paper. Jonas had written in block capitals for Finn's benefit. "Thanks for your help."

Jonas smiled crookedly, as if he thought the thanks were inappropriate, then glanced toward the waitress.

Finn said, "No, I'll get this—you paid last night, remember?"

Jonas stood and said, "Eight o'clock."

"See you then."

Finn sat for a moment after Jonas had left, then looked at the waitress. She came over and handed him the bill, then said, "Could

I ask you something?" Finn looked up at her, offering encouragement. She looked uneasy, though, not wanting to hear the answer even before she'd put the question. "How old is your friend?"

"He's fifteen."

It didn't seem to surprise her, but rather confirm her suspicions. Perhaps she'd watched him as they'd talked, lopping years off him as the conversation had gone on. She shrugged, looking a little embarrassed.

He wanted to say something to comfort her, because she was pretty and seemed desperate to find someone, to be in love. But he could think of nothing to say that wouldn't sound cynical or jaded. Instead, he thought of Adrienne, who had perhaps wanted only the same, to be in love, and he thought of the reasons why he'd made that so hard for her. They were good reasons, perhaps, but he felt ashamed nevertheless.

History

In bed that night, Sofi lay on her side, idly running her fingers across his chest, a habit she'd developed, something he usually liked, but tonight he wished she'd stop. He stared up at the ceiling, and the soft trace of her fingertips was a distraction from what really preoccupied him.

He should have been thinking about what Louisa had proposed to him, but instead he was thinking about what it would mean to the girl who was in another bedroom not far away, probably sleeping, her trust placed entirely in Finn's ability to rescue her.

He almost resented Katerina for that trustfulness. In the context of her life thus far, the fact that he'd killed a man to protect her, had found her a place to stay, and had promised to get her to safety shouldn't have counted for much. Perhaps it was simply that she was still a child, or that she'd seen something within Finn that was different.

Because he *would* get her to safety, no matter what it took. He wouldn't get more accurate timings for Sparrowhawk until tomorrow, but it was already looking tight in terms of getting the girl to Stockholm next weekend. Still, he wouldn't be deterred, whatever the obstacles.

"What are you thinking about?"

"Sorry, nothing important." He raised his hand and put it on hers, as much to stop its gentle progress around his chest as a sign of affection and reassurance. "Just thinking through the business we were discussing this evening."

Sofi knew, more or less. She was a journalist, a canny one at that, but she'd never pushed at the edges of his cover story, had never asked questions, had never even mentioned stories from the paper that might touch on the world she imagined he inhabited.

Now, though, she said, "It's odd, that she should give important work to you, when she knows you're leaving. Odd that she doesn't give the work to your colleagues."

"Ours is not to reason why."

"What?"

"Nothing, it's an old saying. She asked me, anyway."

For a moment Sofi didn't respond and then, curious, she said, "Will you keep in touch with your friends from work, when you leave?"

It was the closest she'd ever come to hinting at his real job. He could tell what she was really asking, if the clandestine nature of his work would make it possible to stay in touch, even though he'd still be living in Tallinn. But she'd inadvertently hit on something more serious, something he hadn't considered until now.

How could he stay in Tallinn, the thing he'd suggested to her only that evening, if his former colleagues were under the impression he was a traitor? And why hadn't Louisa considered that, knowing his domestic setup? The answer to the second question was easy enough—for all Louisa's jolly-headmistress warmth and informality, she was ruthless when it came to getting results.

"I'll stay in touch with Harry, probably." Perry, of course, wouldn't be around if it all worked out.

"Good," said Sofi. "I like Harry."

She'd met him twice. Everyone liked Harry.

They picked Finn up the next morning, Saturday, and took him to the office. It wasn't always the case that the office was empty at weekends, but it was today. Crucially, Perry had been sent to Moscow on the early flight, to soothe concerns about the Kremlin mole story.

He wouldn't have liked that, but when Louisa arrived to fight fires, no one questioned her methods. If she'd been in a generous mood, she'd have assured Ed that it was a job requiring someone with experience, someone who was respected.

Louisa and Finn headed into the small conference room, and then a moment or two later a guy came in who Finn hadn't seen before. He was wearing a pale-gray suit, scarf, city overcoat, and he had an oddly bouffant mass of gray hair.

"Finn, this is John Castle."

No introduction was needed in the other direction—Castle undoubtedly knew everything about Finn. They shook hands, but then Castle sat and didn't say another word. Finn waited for Louisa to sit before taking a seat himself, and she smiled and threw a look of teasing admonishment at the older man. Castle looked unimpressed.

"Okay, Finn. Time really is short on this, and it's going to take considerable nerve to pull it off. I hasten to add, if you don't get the evidence we need on Perry, it's not a disaster—that's just one strand of this operation."

"For you, perhaps, but if I'm about to make myself look like a traitor, I intend to take Perry down."

He looked for a change in either expression, but there was none.

"Admirable," said Louisa. "Now, the ship is called the *Maria Nuovo.* Our current intelligence is that it's due to arrive in Kaliningrad next Saturday, just after dark. However, smarter people than I have suggested this is unlikely, and that Friday night or the early hours of Saturday morning is a better guess. Naturally, we'll know more nearer the time. Demidov's lieutenant will be there to meet it, but we think he may have as few as three other men with him, primarily because most of the others have been arrested."

"So it should be a tempting target for Karasek."

"And for anyone else who found out about it, I shouldn't wonder. But the important thing is this—we have less than a week for you to get in to see Karasek, convince him that you're looking for a final payday, get him to trust you enough that he'll spill about Perry, and lead him into the trap in Kaliningrad."

It sounded a ridiculously ambitious task when put like that, and Castle grimaced slightly, as if he wanted to voice concerns to that effect.

Louisa ignored him, suggesting that this was an argument they'd already had, and looked at Finn as she said, "Do you envisage any problems?"

"I envisage only problems."

"Good," she said, and laughed. "Anything I might not have accounted for?"

Finn shook his head, then said almost absentmindedly, "I was planning to go away next Friday for a long weekend."

"Can't it wait? You're about to have one very long weekend."

"It could, but it might arouse suspicions, particularly as I'm winding down."

Louisa nodded, thinking it over. "We wouldn't want you in Kaliningrad anyway, but Karasek might." She tapped out a short little rhythm on the table, and finally said, "We'll have to play it by ear. You may have no choice but to cancel."

He didn't push it for now, but he knew that his plan depended on convincing Karasek that he didn't want him in Kaliningrad. That was assuming they could get Karasek to show an interest in the first place.

"What's my reason for going to Karasek? If I just go in and offer him this, he'll know it's a phony."

Castle reached down to his briefcase, took out an envelope, and passed it across to Louisa.

"You know one of Karasek's men was killed here the other day. Turns out he was escorting a young girl Karasek had a particular interest in, and the girl disappeared. Karasek's furious. I think one could even say *incandescent.*" She patted the envelope. "You're going to pay him a visit, tell him we might be able to help each other, that we have a surveillance picture of a man leaving the church just after the murder. If he can help us identify the man, we might be able to help him get his property back. We don't need to give him any more information than that—indeed, any more and he'll be suspicious. I think this will get his attention."

It had certainly managed to grab Finn's attention. His body had flooded with adrenaline, to the extent that it was taking all his concentration to keep still. For a moment, he couldn't even think how to respond without giving something away. Then he hit on it.

"Just a second. I'm assuming this is an underage girl, and we're going to hand him a photo that could help him find her?"

With a strange sense of liberation, he realized he obviously couldn't be identified from the surveillance photo. But his heart kept beating hard, even as Louisa said, "The photo's a fake. Take a look."

She slid the envelope across to him and he pulled the picture out and looked at it. It had been well done. The guy walking away hurriedly from the church was wearing a winter coat, no hat, his fair hair caught in the wind and looking ruffled—a lot of detail, but nothing that made him easy to identify.

Hardly visible at first, there was a girl on the far side of him, her head obscured by a protective arm. With some relief, Finn couldn't see anything to convince Karasek it wasn't Katerina, and he presumed Karasek had never actually seen her in the flesh.

"Who is he?"

"Doesn't matter—he's not in Tallinn now." She paused, pleased with herself. "And I can see from your face that you think it'll be enough to interest him, maybe even enough to get his guard down."

Finn nodded, but from his few meetings with Karasek and his greater knowledge of the man, he also knew how volatile he would be right now. For whatever reason, Karasek had invested a lot of energy in Katerina, and his rage at losing her would make him even more unpredictable than usual.

"It'll get his attention, but I'll have to judge on the day whether to put the other matter to him."

"Of course. You'll have received an email—it's in your inbox now, in fact—outlining the intelligence on the *Maria Nuovo*. Realizing that you're the only person to have been sent it, you'll have spotted the opportunity to make a little business deal of your own."

Once again, Castle pulled an awkward face. It made Finn wonder what his job usually entailed, because this didn't sound a great deal more wing-and-prayer than many of the other operations he'd been involved with. And with more detail it would seem less ramshackle.

But then Louisa said, "As for judging on the day—that day is today."

It shouldn't have been a surprise, given the narrow window within which they were working. Even so, Finn found himself veering toward Castle's position now, doubting whether this had been thought through clearly enough, wondering if Louisa was sending him on a near-suicide mission, with only the slightest hope that it might yield a result.

"That's quite short notice."

"It is, but you'll have all the information you need. This is high risk, Finn, I won't deny it—high risk in terms of whether it'll work, rather than regarding your own safety— but sometimes that's what it takes."

"Trust me, Louisa—with Karasek, this is high risk in every sense. It's not as if I can go in there armed. I presume I'll be going to his club."

"You presume correctly, on both counts. And although we'll be aware of what's going on, there'll be no close support, so if you get into trouble, it's unlikely anyone will get there in time to help you. For obvious reasons, this has to be, to all intents and purposes, a lone wolf operation."

"I understand that."

"Good. Now, in some senses I'm rather glad we don't have much time, because it won't allow you to overanalyze things before going in. But we do have a great deal of ground to cover, so let's get on with it. John?"

Castle reached into his briefcase again and pulled out two folders, sliding one across the table to Finn, the other to Louisa. They opened them simultaneously, and Louisa started talking. But as important as it was for him to listen, a part of Finn was distracted, wishing for more time, to think through the consequences of this operation for the other things he'd planned, for Sofi, for Katerina.

Most of all, he wished he had more time to think through whether this stacked up in any way that was good for him. Just as he had one foot out of the door, he was being asked to step back inside, to put himself on the line in a complex and potentially dangerous operation, and he couldn't help but wonder if maybe his resignation had suddenly made him expendable in Louisa's eyes—expendable in every sense.

Chapter Twelve

Finn had often wondered who still used Internet cafés. The answer seemed to be predominantly a mix of backpackers and immigrants. The place was busy, with a friendly coffeehouse vibe to it. Jonas wasn't there but came in just as Finn was deciding whether or not to go ahead and book a session.

Once they were sitting down in front of a screen—Jonas on the keyboard, Finn just off to one side like a late learner—Jonas brought up the Facebook homepage and started typing. Finn looked closer; it was Hailey's email address. Jonas clicked in the password box, then turned to Finn.

"Let's hope she's as much a creature of habit as I think she is."

He smiled, and typed *Patch22*. He hit the "Enter" button and Hailey Portman's Facebook homepage appeared before them.

"That's amazing. How did you know that—Patch22?"

"Hailey's wanted a dog for as long as I've known her, so much that she's always known exactly what it would look like and what she'd call it. So some time when she had to make a password for a site she tried to use 'Patch,' but she needed to use numbers, too, so she used 'Patch22'—you know, kind of like the novel. She's used it ever since, for almost everything." As if he'd completely forgotten the Facebook page in front of him, he said, "Have you read *Catch-22*?"

Finn shook his head. "Friend of mine at college recommended it to me, but I couldn't get on with it. I've seen the film." He pointed at the screen and said, "I do have one question. You're a smart guy—so why didn't you think of doing this before? You know, you were wandering up and down outside the apartment, but you didn't think of checking Facebook?"

Jonas glanced at the screen, Finn sensing he almost didn't want to look at it, perhaps fearing what it might reveal, then said, "I thought about it after we met this afternoon. I guess she made a fool of me because we were meant to be best friends and I didn't get what was going on, not at all. See, I had an idea she had a Facebook page but I didn't think it'd tell me anything because I thought she was on the run. I never realized it might be her choice to run away. I was wrong about that. I think maybe I've been wrong about a lot of things to do with Hailey."

The look of resignation on his face was total, as if he couldn't understand why he'd ever expected any more from her.

Finn nodded. "For what it's worth, she probably didn't think it through. People let you down in life, but they don't usually mean anything by it, it's just that they're fallible—weak."

"Is that why you became corrupt?"

A burst of laughter sounded across the room—three Africans laughing at something on the screen in front of them, full of a joy that struck Finn as nostalgic, tinged with sadness.

Finn smiled. "I shouldn't have used the word *corrupt*, but yeah, I suppose it's why I went off the rails—I was curious, I got off on the machinations of it all, like it was a puzzle or a game, not real life." He looked at the kid, feeling for him, and said, "I'm sure Hailey will come to her senses sooner or later."

"We're just friends."

"I know."

Jonas looked at the screen, scrolling down as he said, "I think these are updates by her Facebook friends."

"Do you know any of them?" Jonas shook his head. Finn noticed the text in a number of the updates, and said, "Quite a few of these are in Swedish or Danish."

It filled him with a certain degree of hope for her—it was fanciful, perhaps, but he imagined there was less chance of her coming to harm in a Scandinavian country. It also filled him with a strange sense of nostalgia and sadness of his own.

Jonas scrolled back up and said, "I think we need to go to her profile page."

He hit a button and another page opened, with a picture of Hailey in a hat and sunglasses, skillfully obscuring enough of her face that she could have been any age. There was some information along the top of the page: a line saying she was studying at the University of Geneva; then, after a small heart, another saying she was in a relationship with Anders Tilberg.

Finn didn't get it. Assuming Anders Tilberg was in Scandinavia, she couldn't have met him until a few days ago. Finn was fully conversant with the online world, but couldn't understand how an entirely digital exchange could be described in that way—perhaps it was the twee little heart that troubled him most.

Jonas had clearly seen it at the same time and seemed to tense up like someone braced against a blow, but he sounded oddly casual as he said, "So now we find out who Anders Tilberg is."

He clicked on a link and another page opened. With some relief, Finn saw that he was a young guy, looking not much older than Jonas. He was studying at Uppsala University, and he was in a relationship with Hailey Portman, a declaration that was in some way still astonishing to Finn.

"So I guess she's in Uppsala," said Jonas. He stared at the screen, his hand poised over the mouse, then turned to Finn and asked, as if it were the only thing that intrigued him, "How would you get there on an InterRail pass?"

"I don't know. Through Germany, naturally, Copenhagen maybe? Then Stockholm. Uppsala's north of Stockholm."

"Have you ever been there?"

"Not to Uppsala. But how can they be in a relationship? Allowing for the journey, she could only have been there a day or two."

Jonas smiled at him. "People of your generation are doing it all the time. So is Hailey, apparently, even though we used to joke about people having virtual friends. I'm sure we could find the whole history of it on here if we wanted to, but that's not what we're looking for, is it?"

Finn wondered if Jonas would be able to resist looking at the page again later, in the privacy of his own room. It was hard to know. The only sure thing was that he was an extraordinary kid trapped in that most ordinary of youthful traps: an unrequited love.

Jonas scrolled down the profile page of Anders Tilberg, copied a block of text from a friend, opened a new page and brought up Google Translate, then converted it from Swedish into English. He took his notebook out and scribbled something in it, then repeated the process with another couple of blocks of text. Then he copied a single word and searched for it on Google, making notes the whole time.

Finn looked at the text as it appeared and was highlighted and disappeared, taking in snippets even though Jonas worked remarkably quickly. He understood immediately that Jonas had allowed the puzzle-solving instinct to take over, perhaps as a way of pushing her betrayal to the back of his mind.

Finally, Jonas tore a piece of paper out of his notebook, the contents once again capitalized, and said, "A group of them are meeting for dinner at Domtrappkällaren—a restaurant next to the cathedral. Someone asked him when they'd get to meet Hailey. He said they'd meet her Thursday at the dinner. Sounds like quite a few of them are going. Their table's booked for eight thirty."

"That's tomorrow night."

"Is it too soon? I could look for something else, maybe an address, though I don't think most people list their addresses." He looked back at the screen.

"No, I'm sure I'll be able to get a flight out tomorrow."

Jonas started tapping away at the keyboard as he said, "Of course, it would make more sense for Mr. and Mrs. Portman to go, or for them to alert the police, but I guess you want to go because you want the memory stick."

"And because we haven't found her yet. We have an idea where she might be tomorrow, but not where she's staying." Jonas was looking at him with a knowing smile. "But yes, I want the memory stick."

Jonas pointed at the screen. "There's a flight out of Geneva just after midday tomorrow."

"You're good at this."

He smiled, then asked, "What will you do with it? The memory stick, I mean?"

Finn shrugged. "Try to find out why they're watching me, what they want, who they are. But I don't want you thinking I've only searched for Hailey because of the memory stick. I could have looked into who these people are just by using the notes you gave me—running an information trail on BGS."

"What's BGS?"

"The company that rented Gibson's apartment."

Jonas tapped the keys without even looking, then glanced at the screen and did a double take. "British Geological Survey?"

Finn laughed. "No, some things aren't quite as easy as doing a Google search. But anyway, don't worry, I'll find out what's going on, and in truth it's probably nothing."

Jonas looked thoughtful for a moment, and stared at the screen as if expecting something new to appear there. He shut down some of the pages, then logged out of Facebook.

"Are you a bit disappointed?"

Finn said, "What do you mean?"

"It was like a mystery, wasn't it? I was worried about her, of course, but it was a mystery, too. That's how it looked, anyway, but I guess it wasn't a mystery at all. She just met a guy on the Internet and went to visit him."

That last sentence summed up everything Finn had feared for Hailey, and yet now it did seem as mundane and innocuous as Jonas was suggesting. Okay, she was somewhere she wasn't meant to be, no doubt doing things her parents wouldn't want her to be doing, but she was almost certainly safe and, for a few delirious days at least, happy.

"No, I'm not disappointed. I'm relieved for her and her family. Because it could've been so much worse."

"Have you seen an old film called *Picnic at Hanging Rock*?"

"Yes, I have. I've read the book, too—by an Australian."

"Joan Lindsay."

"That's correct. And you know what, she made it up. In real life, girls don't just vanish into thin air—they run away or they're taken, and there's no mystery about what happens to them. It's nearly always bad."

Jonas nodded. "I'm glad she'll be coming back, despite everything."

Despite everything. Those two words summed up how hurt he was. Finn felt the urge to comfort him, as little as they knew each other. But he had no doubt he'd bounce back, if not with Hailey then with someone else.

"I have to go and see the Portmans." He stopped short of thanking him, remembering the way it had been received earlier, but said, "Hopefully we'll be back in a day or so—maybe I'll see you then."

Jonas laughed. "Okay, but it's not like we're gonna start hanging out together."

Finn laughed, too, and they left. They stopped briefly outside in the bracing cold, and Jonas put his hat on. It was similar to the others but yet another design.

"You have a lot of hats."

"I have six."

Finn nodded and pointed as he said, "I'm going this way."

"Me too." So they set off walking together, and after a few paces Jonas said, "You probably think I'm pretty lame."

It was the closest he'd come to an admission of how he really felt, perhaps emboldened because they were both facing forward as they walked along the night-lit street.

"I don't think you're lame at all." Finn thought back across the messiness of his own life and added, "Thinking you have a special connection with someone and then finding out it's not actually reciprocated, it's the toughest thing."

They walked in silence for a few seconds, long enough that Finn wondered if he'd talk again, but then Jonas said, "You've been there?"

"Yes, I have."

"You think it's why she left? Adrienne, I mean."

Finn's thoughts stumbled, because he hadn't been thinking of Adrienne, but he could only say, "What are you talking about?"

"Oh—only, Hailey said she saw her crying a couple of times, when she was talking to Mrs. Portman. And once we heard her saying it was like you were never really there."

And now Finn's confusion crystallized into shock and shame and an urgent desire to call her, so injured was he by the thought that he'd ever reduced her to tears.

"I didn't know that. I've been a pretty crummy boyfriend."

"I thought that, too, so did Hailey, but actually, you're okay. You should be more like this with Adrienne." They reached a corner, and Jonas stopped before Finn could answer and said, "I turn here, you carry on."

"Okay. Well, thanks for the help, and maybe I'll see you when we get back."

"Okay. Bye."

He raised his hand and walked away, but just as Finn prepared to cross the street, Jonas called to him.

Finn looked in his direction and Jonas said, "Actually, I have seven hats, but one's too small for me now. That's why I said I have six."

He really didn't lie. Finn waved and watched him walking off with his easy stride, feeling an odd affection for this kid who'd seemed so strange, but who no longer seemed strange at all.

Chapter Thirteen

He stopped before he got home and used a phone booth to book a seat on the next day's flight. He was either being too careful or not careful enough, though he doubted Gibson and his superiors were searching for Hailey Portman, not least because they knew nothing about the memory stick.

When he knocked on the Portmans' door, there was a short delay before it opened to reveal them both standing there, the same mixture of expectation and dread followed by disappointment.

Ethan said, "Oh, we thought because of the hour, it might be the police."

Or Hailey were the unspoken words at the end of that sentence.

"I've found her—I know where she is."

Debbie's mouth opened, but whatever she'd thought of saying remained unformed. Her legs buckled and Ethan, his arm already around her, caught her and helped her away. Finn followed them through to the living room as Ethan helped her into a chair.

"I'll get some water."

"I'm fine, really."

She didn't look it. The color had drained from her face. Finn and Ethan sat down, too.

"She's in Uppsala, in Sweden. Jonas helped me find her."

Ethan said, "But he was adamant—"

"He didn't know where she was, but with the right prompting he knew where to look."

Debbie looked more confused than he'd ever seen her as she said, "Why would she go to Sweden? It's such a long way."

"There are two separate issues here. I do believe that Hailey thought she was in danger. They hacked into Gibson's network and they were convinced that they were being watched, and even followed, as a result."

"I said it all along," said Debbie. "The note. She said it wasn't a good idea to stay here."

Finn took a deep breath. "True, but it also has to be said that the perceived threat did play into Hailey's hands, and gave her the excuse to do something she'd been thinking about anyway. You see, at some point in the past weeks or months, Hailey struck up a friendship online with a boy in Uppsala."

Finn had already lied to them a couple of times, but now Ethan picked up the danger signals and said, "When you say a boy, do you know how old he is?"

Finn shook his head. "He's a university student, but I'm afraid Hailey, in her online profile, also claims to be a university student. It explains the change of image, and whilst I know it won't make you any less uncomfortable, it looks like the young man in question has no idea that Hailey is only fifteen."

Ethan jumped up. "We have to call the police. Or the Stockholm police." He looked at his watch, his thought processes painfully visible.

"Ethan, please." He gestured with his hand for Ethan to sit again, which he did. "Hailey has been there for at least a couple of days, so calling the police now isn't . . . it isn't going to prevent anything happening. I'm not sure what the law is in Sweden, but you could also get this young guy into a whole load of trouble."

"Good. The bastard deserves everything he gets."

"The bastard has a name—Anders Tilberg—and chances are he's been duped by your daughter." Ethan looked ready to object, but Finn took on a different tone. "Which is something else to consider. Again, I don't know the law in Sweden, so I don't know if getting the police involved would lead to them taking action against Hailey."

"She'd never forgive us, anyway," said Debbie, suddenly coming back to herself, composed. "I think it best that this be done discreetly and with dignity. We have to bring her back, but that will be fraught enough without turning it into a public spectacle."

"I've booked myself on a lunchtime flight tomorrow."

Debbie accepted the fact without question, saying only, "We'll reimburse all your expenses, naturally."

"No, that won't be necessary."

As if the husband and wife had swapped roles, it was Ethan who was struggling now, saying, "Just a minute, Finn, we really appreciate your help but I don't get this. Why would you fly to Sweden? She's our daughter—we'll go get her."

Finn nodded, accepting his point. Debbie looked between the two men, and Finn sensed she preferred his own plan, but he would still play safe, still tell them the truth.

"You could. I don't know where Anders lives but I know where they're all going for dinner tomorrow night. I could argue that it would be less of an ordeal for her if an intermediary turned up, but I'll be straight with you—I have an ulterior motive. Apparently, Hailey has a memory stick with her, containing all the information they copied from Gibson's network." They both looked at him intently now. "Jonas didn't have a copy but he made a few notes, which he showed me. It seems Gibson was running a surveillance operation and the subject was me."

They stared in silence for so long that he wondered if either of them would speak, but then Ethan said, "I don't . . . Gibson . . . He lived here for a year."

"I know, and possibly the woman who was here before him, too."

Debbie said, "So Adrienne was right—you were a spy."

"That's a rather emotive word, and Adrienne was guessing, as it happens. But yes, I worked in intelligence."

"Doing what? Why would they have you under surveillance all these years later?"

"I'm hoping the memory stick will give me the answer to that question. But you have to understand that I can't tell you any more than that. I've already told you more than I should have done."

Once again, he was reminded how pointlessly he'd played the hollow man these last six years. Adrienne, to her credit, had seen through his backstory from the start, and yet he'd continued to lie even to her, perhaps in part so that he could avoid having to tell her bigger lies about his reasons for leaving.

Ethan looked emotionally washed up but said, "Will you come back tomorrow?"

"No, I think Friday's the earliest I'm likely to be back. As soon as I've got her, I'll make sure she calls you." He checked his watch. "It might help if you put together a quick letter saying that you're authorizing me to escort her back here. And while we're at it, could I use your computer to book a hotel for myself?"

"Of course," said Debbie. "I guess yours is still being monitored."

"Honestly, I have no idea, but it's always better to err on the side of caution." As he said it, he wondered if the same principle was behind this entire surveillance operation, but he doubted it—they were after something specific.

"You don't think Hailey's in danger?" It was Ethan who asked the question and Finn looked at him now. "If you're worried about them finding out where you're going— why? You think if they find out they'll go after Hailey?"

Finn shook his head. "No, I'm just being cautious, for my own sake. Until I know what's behind this surveillance operation, I'd rather have them know as little as possible about my movements."

They seemed to accept that, and over the next ten minutes they produced and signed a letter and Finn booked his hotel. Then they showed him to the door and he said goodnight.

Debbie said, "Will we see you before you go in the morning?"

"Possibly not."

She hugged him. To his surprise, so did Ethan. Finn didn't do hugs, and that was nothing to do with the life he'd been play-acting, but he was bemused just as much by his transformation in their eyes.

Until a few days ago, the Portmans had probably considered him a distant figure, or an opaque one. Perhaps they'd thought Adrienne would be better off without him, perhaps they'd even looked upon him with contempt. And now, even before he'd brought their daughter back to them, they were hugging him with gratitude.

Once they'd shut the door, he looked again at the door of Gibson's silent apartment, and walked along the corridor to the stairs. If only it were that simple—bringing the Portmans' daughter back—for everything to return to normal. If only.

Chapter Fourteen

He ran for longer the next morning, going out early, getting such a rush off it that he couldn't remember why or how he'd stopped. And every time he thought of Adrienne, he ran faster. He guessed that complacency had played its part in the demise of both his fitness and his relationship. One of them, at least, could still be restored easily enough.

When he got back to the apartment, there was a note pushed under the door, a piece of paper folded in half. He opened it and knew instantly from the block capitals that it was from Jonas. Finn checked his watch—he'd probably called in on his way to school.

BGS = BRAC GLOBAL SYSTEMS, BASED IN THE CAYMAN ISLANDS. NOTHING ELSE YET BUT MORE SOON. JONAS.

Finn smiled, at the way it resembled a telegram, at the fact that Jonas had gone after BGS like a terrier, digging up information that Finn doubted he'd have found himself so easily. In his experience, though, knowing that Gibson's apartment had been rented by Brac Global Systems would lead to a handful of cul-de-sacs and not much else.

Even so, when he got back he'd tell Jonas to forget about BGS, that it wasn't smart for him to keep hacking in that particular direction. Finn wasn't even certain he wanted to find out any more himself. It would depend on what was on the memory stick, but sometimes he knew it was better just to let things stand, and he had a fragile hope that this would be one of those cases.

He took the train to Geneva Airport. A couple of girls were sitting a few seats away from him with backpacks and suitcases, both American, probably on a study year at the University of Lausanne. No one paid them any attention, and he wondered if Hailey had aroused as little interest as she'd traveled across the continent.

These girls looked noticeably older than he remembered Hailey looking, but then, she'd changed her hair since, and his view of her was informed by the knowledge of her age, by having known her first as a child proper. The two girls on the train were much more conservatively dressed than the threadbare, bohemian look she'd developed for herself, but that would have probably worked in her favor, too.

He wondered if she'd been scared at all. She'd had to have taken at least one night train, and he doubted she would have spent her limited funds on a compartment. He imagined her sitting all night in a regular seat, afraid to fall asleep.

For some reason, he wanted to think that this girl, who'd so coldly planned her escape, so badly used Jonas and hurt her parents, had been beset with fears and doubts once she'd set off, her emotions in turmoil even now. Sadly for all concerned, he suspected instead that she was breezily happy with her new boyfriend in Uppsala, giving little thought to the people she'd left behind.

Not that he felt in any position to judge Hailey Portman for her human failings. She would at least stand a chance of growing out of hers, this whole episode put down to a moment of youthful madness. His own youthful madness had been rather more prolonged, and had left its marks on him to this day.

He checked in at the airport and made for the business lounge. There were a dozen or so other people there, and Finn studied them casually as he grabbed a coffee and a paper and sat down—a classic selection of business travelers, none of them standing out.

Once he'd started reading, though, he sensed that he was drawing someone's attention. There was a guy across the lounge from him, overweight in a robust foodie kind of way, checked shirt, yellow tie, red cheeks, and fair curly hair. He looked like a wealthy farmer, and was more likely a hedge fund manager.

Or rather, Finn would have labeled him like that, except for the fact that he kept glancing over. It wasn't blatant or even obvious to most eyes. He was eating a sandwich and casually looking around the room, but every time he reached Finn the progress of his gaze would stutter for a fraction of a second, as if in response to some gravitational pull.

Finn didn't think the guy was professional enough somehow, not least because of the very fact that Finn had picked him out. Still, he thought through the ways and means by which he might have been followed to the airport, his movements tracked.

That in turn set him wondering why they might think any of this was worth their time. He'd been completely dormant for six years, so what on earth could make them think it made sense to keep him under constant surveillance for at least two of those years? What were they expecting him to do?

The guy finished his sandwich and put the plate down on the table in front of him. He wiped his hands and mouth on a napkin and threw it on the plate. Finally, he stood and walked toward Finn, and only in the last few feet did Finn notice the book in his hand.

"Excuse me." He was English. Finn looked up from his paper. "I'm sorry to bother you, and I know you must get this all the time, but are you Charles Harrington?"

"Yes, I am," said Finn.

The guy smiled. "I'm such a fan of your books. I don't suppose you'd mind?"

He held out the book, *The Hand of Death* in hardback. Finn noticed a bookmark about halfway through.

He took the book and said, "I'd be more than happy. Do you have a pen?"

"Of course, sorry. Just a second." He hurried back to where he'd been sitting and then said from there, "Of course, I haven't—they always leak, don't they?" He pointed toward the business lounge's front desk and set off to ask for a pen.

He seemed genuine, but Finn looked through the book anyway, the marker at the beginning of chapter nine, the pages before that smudged here and there with fingerprints.

The guy came back, saying as he approached, "Sorry about that. I have to be honest, I didn't think the Black Death would be my thing, but I'm riveted, absolutely riveted."

"Thank you," said Finn, taking the pen and opening the cover. "Who's it to?"

"David. Actually, no, could you sign it for my wife, Georgina—she's a fan, too. Actually, it was George got me on to you in the first place."

Finn signed, noting the date and location—people seemed to like that, he'd found—and handed the book back.

"Well, thanks again, and I hope you enjoy the rest of it."

"I'm sure I will." He hesitated, as if fearing, correctly, that he was outstaying his welcome. "Do you mind me asking what the next one's about, or is it top secret?"

"Not at all. There's a book on the Hundred Years' War coming out in September. I'm working on something else now, but I'm afraid I can't tell you what that's about."

"Of course." The guy looked a little embarrassed now as he said, "Thanks ever so much."

He walked back to his seat. He was genuine, and Finn hoped they weren't on the same flight. At the same time, now that he'd been put on alert, he took in the other people in the lounge, searching for anyone who might be a less obvious observer.

No one else set alarm bells ringing. But his mind was locked stubbornly back into that mode. He thought of the words from Jonas's note: *BGS = BRAC GLOBAL SYSTEMS.* He would still tell Jonas to forget about it when he got back, but he realized now, and had perhaps known all along, that it was fanciful to think that he could do the same.

BGS represented real people, presumably from his own past, perhaps people he'd crossed in some way, and if they'd pursued him this doggedly for two years or more, they were unlikely to give up now.

History

There was a side door, but Finn and his colleagues almost always called in on business visits when the club was open, using the main door. It was mid-afternoon, but Finn did the same now, ringing the bell insistently until he heard someone approaching, an ever-louder stream of Estonian expletives.

The guy who opened the door was young and sinewy. Finn wasn't sure if he'd seen him before, but the guy recognized him and simply nodded grudgingly as he stepped aside. He closed the door behind him, and escorted Finn through the club to the stairs that led up to Karasek's office suite.

It had been cleaned since the previous night, but Klub X was the kind of place that smelled and felt sordid even when empty. But then, he thought, maybe all nightclubs were like that in the daytime, maybe he was allowing his knowledge of Karasek to color his thoughts.

At the top of the stairs the young guy stopped, realizing he'd made a mistake, and gestured for Finn to strike a pose. He patted him down, then opened the door into the green room where Karasek's guys seemed to spend most of their time.

They were sitting around a table now, smoking, drinking coffee, playing cards, like a cliché they were aping from American TV shows. Karasek was with them, but looked up as Finn was ushered into the room.

Very few people, asked to pick the boss out of that group, would have included Karasek in their first three choices. He looked like a hanger-on. He was average height, average build—Jack had once told Finn of Karasek's constant but futile attempts to bulk up—with nondescript looks. He wore his hair cropped, but even that backfired, the odd shape of his head and the babyish face combining to make the style completely unthreatening. He was older than Finn but looked in his mid-twenties at most.

But if Karasek's looks had robbed him of the natural gravitas he craved, marking him out not as an alpha male but as someone to be patronized, his actions made up for those shortcomings. Finn had never known him to throw a punch, but he also knew that some people didn't need to.

Finn raised the brown envelope in his hand, as if that explained the reason for his visit. Karasek responded by asking the young guy a question: whether Finn was armed. He nodded to one of the men at the table, who reluctantly got up, crossed the room, and came back with a scanner. Finn submitted again, and even stood patiently as the guy double-checked, pulling Finn's shirt up to look for wires.

Once satisfied, the guy took his seat again, and Karasek got up and came over. The young guy melted away, back out of the door.

"What can I do for you?" He knew Finn's name, but it was a typical ploy of Karasek's not to use it.

Finn played him back, saying, "We were hoping we might be able to do something for each other. We understand you mislaid something a couple of days ago."

One of the guys called over, asking in Estonian if he wanted to be dealt in. Karasek waved his hand dismissively. He looked at Finn, suspicious, brimming with an anger that played out on his face like teenage petulance.

"What about it?"

"Mr. Karasek, we don't approve of trafficking, and we have every reason to distrust your motives with regard to this girl." Karasek's jaw was clenched shut. "But we have some information, and on this occasion, we might be able to help with the return of the girl if you can fill in some of the details for us." Finn allowed a slight pause to creep in before holding up the envelope again and saying, "This is a surveillance photo, taken outside the church just after your man was murdered."

Karasek's expression changed from anger to one of desperation and longing—it made Finn want to hit him.

"Let's go through to my office."

Finn smiled. One of his men called out something again and Karasek answered, the sentences too quick and too complex for Finn to understand with his basic Estonian, but he guessed it was about the card game. One of the guys said something else and they laughed among themselves, then one said in English, "Relax, we get you a hundred girls."

There was no laughter this time. Maybe if he hadn't spoken in English—showing off for Finn's benefit—it would have been different, but the guy had chipped away a little too much at Karasek's authority, and everyone else at the table knew it.

Karasek turned on his heel and took three or four quick steps back to the table. Finn didn't see him pull his gun, heard only the guy shouting out some plea, the deafening report of the shot. The guy's face burst open and those around him cried out, not in shock or in anger at their boss, just in irritation at having been soiled with the blood and viscera that sprayed out of their unfortunate colleague, as if Karasek had done no more than spill a drink across the card table.

For a moment, the body looked as if it might topple over backward, but the chair held in place and he fell to the side. The guy next to him pushed back, and the bloodied face fell onto the table with a soft thud. A couple of the guys stood now, but one was quick to reassure Karasek, perhaps telling him that they'd clean up the mess.

Karasek turned back to Finn, gun arm swinging wildly, as if he didn't know what to do with the weapon now. He used it to gesture toward his office with the look of someone who'd just had to reprimand a secretary in front of a visiting client.

Finn took one last look at the subdued hive of activity around the table, and followed Karasek into the trashy opulence of his office—white leather, gold, mirrors. He dropped the envelope onto the desk in front of him and sat down.

Karasek still seemed unsure what to do with the gun, but the sight of the envelope focused his attention and he slipped it back beneath his jacket. He pulled the photograph free and studied it for a long time in silence, a slight smile creeping onto his lips as he spotted the girl's legs, almost but not quite hidden as she walked alongside the man.

He looked up. "You're sure this is him?"

Finn nodded. "Look at the time and date. I assume that tallies with when your man was killed? Besides, we're certain. What we don't know is his identity—that's what we were hoping you might be able to help with."

Karasek didn't look down, saying instead, "Why do you need to know?"

Finn smiled but didn't answer. Karasek shrugged and looked at the photo again, holding it up to the light, studying the figure of the man in it.

"I don't know him." He looked more closely still, and Finn knew he was focusing on the tiny visible details of the girl, either to reassure himself it was her, or perhaps out of that same longing Finn had spotted earlier.

"This girl means a lot to you, doesn't she?"

He looked up at Finn. "It's not what you think."

"It's not really my job to think anything. I was ordered to help you get her back if you could help us to identify the man in the picture."

"You know where she is?"

"We have a lead. But you don't know who he is so—"

"I can ask around." It was odd seeing him this compliant. From what Finn understood, Karasek had never had any direct contact with the girl, and yet he'd clearly seen enough of her to become completely smitten. That didn't mean it would be any easier to work him over, though.

Finn stood up. "Well, you know where I am."

Karasek stood, too, and walked with him to the door, but instead of showing him back into the green room, he led him along the corridor, heading for the side door.

Finn said, "If it's not in the next couple of weeks, it might be better to contact Harry Simons—you know Harry."

Karasek nodded, uneasy in some way with this new spirit of collaboration, then something clicked and he said, "Of course, you're leaving. I heard you were leaving."

"Did you?"

Karasek smiled, trying to look superior, coming across as a precocious but unpopular schoolboy.

"What will you do?"

Finn shook his head, making a show of looking at a loss. They took a couple of steps and Finn stopped, his expression betraying the desperate calculations he wanted Karasek to believe he was making.

"What is it?"

"There might be something else I want to discuss with you. Something unofficial."

There was a pause—Karasek reading him, Finn making a show of being on the verge of changing his mind.

"Okay," said Karasek with a shrug. "We go back into my office."

"No." Karasek was surprised by the urgency of Finn's response. "Is there another office? I'll explain."

Karasek looked him in the eye, making calculations of his own, then said, "Okay. This way."

They walked through to the general office, less ostentatious than Karasek's private space, but still plush by most standards. Finn sat down and waited for him to do the same.

Karasek made a show of finding the office chair uncomfortable, then looked Finn in the eye again and said, "Why not my office?"

"What I have to say is private and unofficial."

There was that fragile, superior smile again as he said, "My office is clean—the whole club is clean."

"No," said Finn, enjoying seeing the smile crumble. "You found what we wanted you to find. Don't make a big thing of it—maybe in a couple of days you can decide to redecorate your office. In the process, you'll find a total of five devices, including two cameras. They've been there for over a year."

Karasek was staring at him hard now, his face full of questions, and Finn guessed that chief among them was the question of why Perry hadn't told him about this. The answer was that Perry didn't know, because they'd actually been there less than a week.

"The rest of the club?"

"No, just your office. We did have one in the green room which was accidentally removed by your odd-job man—I don't think he even realized he'd done it—but the intelligence had been so poor we didn't bother replacing it." He could tell Karasek was rocked, all the more so because of the complete confidence he'd held until a few moments before. "My advice would be to do a thorough sweep of your office once a week, strip it down once a month."

Karasek nodded, lost in thought, then concentrated again. "Why are you telling me?"

"You needed to know why I didn't want to talk in there, and given what I'm about to discuss with you, I don't think it makes much difference for me to tell you about the bugs."

Karasek looked smug, his calm restored as he sensed the power balance moving back in his favor. This was one of the things Finn liked about Naumenko, because Naumenko, in the same situation, would have assumed he was being double-bluffed and that the room they were in now was also bugged. Karasek didn't think that fast.

"What do you want to discuss?"

"I'll tell you in a moment, and I'm going to place my trust in you, because I can give you something you want, but before I speak, I want an assurance from you that this will not be shared."

"I share with my closest people, no one else."

"Mr. Karasek, we know one of our people is working with you. I know who he is, you know who he is, we don't have to mention his name, but under no circumstances can you tell him that we've had this conversation. If you do, it's all off. And I have to say something else—before you have any more conversations with him, ask yourself why he never told you about the bugs in your office." Karasek didn't respond. "Likewise, I'm sure he always had a plausible explanation, but he never met you here at the club, did he, not when it was private business?"

"I'll make my own decision on that, but thank you for pointing it out."

"It's nothing," said Finn. "I won't ask you to give your word, I'll just reinforce to you that if you repeat any of this to Perry, none of it will happen and we'll both be the losers."

Karasek thought about it for a second before nodding his assent. Crucially, he hadn't been surprised by the casual dropping of Perry's name. It probably wasn't enough on its own, but it was a start, something to work on over the coming days.

"Good. You know Demidov was arrested. I received some intelligence just this morning from somebody who only deals with me. Usually, I would pass this up the chain, but I'm leaving and I know a retirement fund when I see one."

Karasek laughed and said, "Why are you leaving if you have no money?"

Finn ignored the question.

"A ship is due into St. Petersburg next week, and a reception committee will be waiting for it, but the ship will have made a stop beforehand. One of Demidov's men and a couple of associates will meet it. Some cargo will be off-loaded, around enough to fill one shipping container—just over a ton of uncut cocaine, worth almost half a billion dollars on the street, and there'll be no one there to fight you for it, just three guys, four at most. I want a quarter of a million dollars in exchange for the exact information."

"Let me guess, you want half up front."

"No. You'd be a fool to trust me, and you're no fool. This is a onetime deal. If you want in, I'll give you the details as soon as I get them. You pay me once you pick up the shipment."

Karasek stared at him, a noncommittal smile playing on his lips. He knew something was wrong, but it was taking him a while to work it out. It was taking him so long, Finn was almost tempted to give him a clue.

Finally, though, he said, "You're no fool either, Mr. Harrington, so why would you trust me to give you the money afterward?"

"Because you're a man of honor, Mr. Karasek." He didn't like that, didn't like the fact that Finn was teasing him with something

Karasek probably believed to be true. "And because when the deal is done and I have my money, I'll tell you where the girl is."

"You know where she is?" He sounded frantic. "How do I know you're telling the truth?"

"What if I'm lying? You get a ton of cocaine for a quarter of a million dollars. But think about it—why would I lie? This is just a neat way of us all getting what we want, and all getting out safe."

Karasek was only half listening, his mind snagged by the final part of this deal, and he sounded distracted as he said, "So you must also know the man in the photograph—why did you ask me?"

Finn shook his head, saying, "What I know and what we know are two different things, and for the sake of our private arrangement, should you decide to take me up on my offer, it's best if you still ask around about the guy in the photograph."

"Why are you doing this?"

"I have reasons. Why does anyone do it? Why does Perry?"

Karasek didn't answer, but he was focusing on the details now. "You mention three or four people, but what about on the ship?"

"The guys on the ship won't be armed, but here's the really good thing—you can wait until the ship leaves if you like. See, they won't hang around because they don't want the authorities in St. Petersburg to know they stopped somewhere."

"When?"

"Probably late Friday. You should have your people ready from Thursday onward."

Karasek thought about it, probably realizing there was a drive involved, imagining the various places along the Baltic coast where a ship could be docked without anyone knowing about it, maybe even finding his way mentally to Kaliningrad.

He stared at Finn then, his eyes flitting about as if he was wired on something.

"A quarter of a million dollars—you could have asked me for that just for the girl."

"True, but you're putting things the wrong way around. I don't care if a ton of cocaine goes up the collective noses of you and your class, so it's a good payoff for me. I'm reluctant to give you the girl, and frankly I think you're sick in the head, but I see it's a way of guaranteeing my safety, and sometimes sacrifices have to be made."

Karasek produced a brief contemptuous laugh, more high-pitched than he probably would have liked, and said, "That's typical of you English—so principled, so full of morals, but you're happy to turn blind if it's good for you. Anyway, I told you, it's not what you think."

"What really concerns me, Mr. Karasek, is the possibility of it being worse than what I think, but you're right. If we conclude this business successfully, I will turn a blind eye."

"Then we have a deal. When will I hear more from you?"

"Monday or Tuesday. I'll call in to get an update on the photograph. I won't have anything before then anyway."

Karasek stood, and Finn followed suit.

"And, if you please, some evidence. For my own peace of mind, so I know this isn't some sting operation."

"Evidence shouldn't reassure you of that—we can fake the evidence—but sure, I'll print up the emails and bring them along." Karasek had walked around the table but Finn didn't move, close to him now and staring into his eyes as he said, "You have to believe in me—not always, but as far as this is concerned. If you don't, then you'd be a fool to go through with it, and like I said, you're no fool. So if you don't believe me, just walk away."

Karasek smiled, superior again as he said, "Relax, Mr. Harrington, all I want is accurate information."

"I'll leave through the club. If anyone's watching they might think it suspicious, me leaving by the side door."

The body was gone from the green room and so had most of the men. One was mopping the floor, another was sitting at a different table playing solitaire. He looked up at Karasek and shrugged, dismissing the earlier bloodshed as one of those things, which Finn guessed it was for people working for Karasek.

He left through the club and was surprised to find himself emerging into daylight, his mind tricked after being in that resolutely nocturnal atmosphere. And as the winter sunlight hit his skin he felt nauseous, not because of the tightrope he'd just walked on Louisa's behalf, but because in some intangible way he felt his own aims for the week ahead had slipped further away from him—and with them, Katerina's safety.

Chapter Fifteen

Winter still had a hold on Uppsala. There was snow on the ground and a fierceness in the air. It reminded him of his former career more than the winters in Switzerland did, perhaps simply because he knew he was back in the north again for the first time in six years.

That in turn made him think of Harry Simons, a name which had been a certainty all this time, and one of his biggest sources of regret, but which was now causing more confusion than anything else that had happened these last few days. It was a simple enough question, whether Harry was dead or alive, but neither answer made complete sense.

Harry had died in Kaliningrad—he'd been told that as a fact, by more than one person, including Louisa Whitman. But if Harry was dead, how had they heard about Jerry de Borg? Had Finn and Harry been under surveillance by their own people long before Sparrowhawk? It didn't seem feasible, not from what he remembered of the events and meetings and conversations that had preceded the operation.

So maybe Harry had survived, a fact they'd kept from Finn for whatever reason. But, no, he couldn't have lived. Harry was the only other person who knew about Jerry de Borg, but he also knew that there could never be anything imperative about identifying him—with some relief, Finn realized Harry couldn't be part of this, even if he was still alive.

He reached the river, the water wild and dark below. He'd glimpsed the cathedral a few times, but seeing it now, rising up above him, somehow made the whole town feel familiar. He knew he hadn't been to Uppsala before, and wondered if it reminded him of somewhere else in the Baltic. Maybe he'd just seen it in a Bergman film.

He crossed the bridge and found his way to Domtrappkällaren, a salmon-pink building that was under the cathedral as much as it was beside it. The snow was banked up against the railings at the front, with only the steps to the door cleared.

The lights were on inside, and now that the sun was low and the afternoon was fading, the snow developed a blue tinge in the shadows and the temperature seemed to drop another couple of notches. He stepped inside. There was no one in the small reception area, so he walked through into the white-domed cellar of the dining room, where even this late in the afternoon there were still people eating.

A waiter was standing chatting with the people on one table, but he saw Finn and left them, smiling and talking as he came over.

Finn said, "Hi, I was wondering if I could book a table for tonight."

"Sure," said the waiter, slipping seamlessly into English. "We're pretty busy tonight, but if you can be flexible . . . How many people is it for?"

They had made their way back to the reception desk and Finn said, "Just one. I'm here on business and had this place recommended."

"Yes, it's very good." The waiter smiled then, saying, "One person is good, too—what time?"

"Eight o'clock?"

"That's not a problem. Your name?"

"Harrington."

He scribbled it down and said, "We'll see you at eight o'clock."

"Good. And if I could, a table back in the corner." He pointed through the arch, spotting a place that had a good view over the dining room whilst allowing him to blend into the background.

"Of course."

"Okay, thanks." Finn turned and headed to the door, and the waiter looked set to walk back into the dining room. But then Finn said, "Oh, one more thing. You might be able to help me." The waiter stopped and turned, though he didn't look inclined to continue the conversation. "I was just curious. I see all these students about, but there doesn't seem to be a campus as such—where do they all live?"

"Most of them live in Student Town." The waiter caught Finn's quizzical expression and added, "You were probably at Ekonomikum—if you keep going in that direction you'll come to Student Town."

"Thanks." Finn thought of adding something to make his inquiry sound less suspicious, but it was obvious the waiter didn't care, so Finn smiled and left.

The sun had gone even from the upper reaches of the buildings now, and a sharp wind kicked along the street. Finn walked quickly, up to the cathedral, making his way around to the entrance. It was warm inside, and he immediately felt at peace in there.

Again, he was surprised that even this late in the afternoon and at this time of year there were still a few tourists wandering around, some of them taking pictures—it was one of his pet hates, each camera flash like a little piece of carelessness.

He sat for a while, a few pews behind a middle-aged woman who appeared deep in prayer. Religion fared badly in so much of the history he wrote about, and yet he was constantly surprised by how much solace he gained from places of worship. It wasn't redemptive, nothing to do with conscience—more the strange sense of meaningful emptiness he found in these places, a quality that allowed him to disappear effortlessly.

The woman stood up and left, nodding to him as she passed, as if sensing a fellow pilgrim rather than just another trigger-happy tourist. He stood himself, and walked around the cathedral, stopping to look at the tomb of Gustav Vasa and two of his wives.

He left then, finding night had set in while he'd been in the cathedral, though now that the darkness above was total, the combination of lights and snow gave the city a picturesque, illuminated look. He would come back here, when he was finished with the Cathars—if he ever finished with the Cathars.

He'd avoided writing about the north until now, wanting in some way to keep his past at bay. But that past had followed him to Switzerland, and now he was drawn to Vasa and all the other stories he'd been ignoring unnecessarily, as if the ghost had been exorcised by coming here.

He asked for directions to the Ekonomikum, and once he was there he stopped a couple of young female students and asked them for directions to Student Town. They pointed the way for him, and as he walked he noticed he was part of a small migration, students with ruddy faces, more vigorously wrapped up against the cold than he was, most of them wearing gloves and woolen hats. A couple of times he saw a hat bobbing along that reminded him of Jonas, and he couldn't help but smile.

Apart from the snow, the accommodation blocks could have been part of any university, anywhere in the world. He looked at the lights appearing in windows, people here and there sitting at their desks or moving about their rooms, preparing for the evening ahead, some of them perhaps preparing for the meal at Domtrappkällaren.

He guessed the blocks would have some sort of security to prevent strangers getting in. He didn't want to check—there were plenty of students moving about in the shadows as they headed back to their rooms, and he didn't want to stand out any more than he probably already did.

But if Anders Tilberg was in one of those blocks, then Finn's original thought, which had been to pay him and Hailey a visit first thing in the morning, might not be practical. He'd probably have to intercept them between leaving the restaurant and arriving back here, a simple plan that would leave him with a big headache—what did he do with Hailey overnight?

He'd deal with that when the time came, he supposed, but he thought of her now and appreciated how exciting it all probably seemed, to be immersed in this student world. She was probably a little nervous, too, that she might be out of her depth, that she'd be found out, but this would be a story she'd tell for years to come, how she once ran away and lived for a while with a boy at Uppsala University.

She was out there right now, perhaps in one of the blocks in front of him, perhaps elsewhere in the city, living life. And though she was living life a few years too early, and though he disliked the way she'd treated her parents and Jonas, in some way he envied her, for doing what he had neglected to do for too many years.

Chapter Sixteen

It was eight fifteen by the time Finn got back to the restaurant, but he could see immediately that Hailey's party wasn't there yet. On the other hand, although there were a few tables empty, they were all set for four people, not the large student party he was expecting.

A waitress showed him to his own table, the room lively enough with cheesy music and people chatting over each other that no one paid him any attention. She left him, and he stood again and walked down the small arched tunnel to look into the back room, full but also with small parties.

He'd no sooner got back to his table than the waiter from earlier in the day came down some stairs and directly across to him.

"Hello again. Are you ready to order?"

"No, I've only just arrived."

"Oh, okay. I'll give you a little while. Something to drink while you're waiting?"

"Just some water for now—I'll look at the wine list." He looked around the room and said, "I thought it would be busier."

The waiter glanced at the room, a little confused as he said, "Well, it's busy enough. Those tables are reserved, but we had a party cancel so that made it easier." He smiled awkwardly. "I'll get your water."

The waiter made off, exchanging chatty comments with some of the diners as he went. With one group those comments were in English, so the slightly standoffish air Finn was picking up from him was nothing to do with Finn being foreign. He wondered if he was acting suspiciously, if his casual questions were coming out as forced or strange, whether in the last six years he'd lost the knack for this.

Of course, that was possibly the least of his problems. "Remember Isandlwana," one of his old history tutors had been fond of saying. "Never forget to laager your camp." It had been a catchall piece of advice, essentially boiling down to: "Prepare for all eventualities."

And Finn had spectacularly failed to laager his camp. If the party that had canceled was that of Hailey and Anders Tilberg, he'd be left without a lead. He didn't even have a number on which he could contact Jonas. He'd be able to dip back into their Facebook pages, but beyond that he'd be left with the even more suspicion-inducing option of asking the university office for Tilberg's address.

The waiter headed back with a jug of water, and Finn looked quickly at the menu and ordered while he was there. He seemed better disposed now and said, "You'll enjoy the reindeer—it's great."

"Good, and I'll have a bottle of the Côtes du Rhône to go with it." He pointed at the wine menu.

The waiter nodded, smiling in appreciation. In some way, ordering good food and a decent bottle of wine had brought Finn back on side. He wouldn't ask any more questions, not for now, but the change in mood was so marked that he probably could have asked the waiter outright for Tilberg's phone number.

The wine came first, and during the small ceremony of approving it, the clock reached the half-hour and a small party came in and occupied one of the vacant tables. It was two couples of about Finn's age. No one else came in during the fifteen minutes it took for his first course to arrive.

The room was still lively, but it was looking increasingly as if the party he was there to observe was the party that had canceled. With some dread, Finn imagined the next call to Ethan and Debbie, but at least that could wait until tomorrow. When he got back to the hotel he'd check Tilberg's Facebook page. And if necessary, he could go to the university administration office early enough in the morning that the Portmans wouldn't be wondering at his failure to call. It wasn't a disaster, just a setback.

He noticed a couple of people heading up the stairs at different points and realized that was where the bathrooms were situated. He got used to seeing people coming and going during the meal, but then as he finished the reindeer loin, he glanced up because someone was coming down the stairs, someone he hadn't seen going up.

The guy was smiling as he walked around to the reception area. He spent a while chatting there, then came back in and went up the stairs again, still smiling as he folded a long receipt and put it into his wallet. He had floppy fair hair, longer than in his picture, but there was no doubting that it was Anders Tilberg.

There were tables upstairs, something Finn should have checked earlier in the day, and Tilberg and his friends hadn't canceled, they'd been early. Now that he was aware of them, his hearing separated out the noise and he realized a fair amount of it was coming from up those stairs.

The waitress who'd shown him to his table had just finished seating a party at one of the other vacant tables. Before she could leave, Finn gestured to her and she nodded and came over.

She picked up his plate and said, "Everything was good?"

"Really good."

"The dessert menu?"

"No, thank you. I'll just finish my wine, but could I have the bill now please."

"Of course."

She walked off and he listened for signs of movement upstairs. Their bill was paid, so they could leave at any moment. The waitress was quick and he could still hear settled laughter from up above, but he paid in cash to ensure he didn't get caught out by a slow credit card transaction. He counted out notes and told her to keep the change, then settled back with his wine.

It was another ten minutes before he heard a collective movement of chairs being pushed back, and a few minutes more before the first person came down the stairs. He was followed by a girl, but it wasn't Hailey.

A second girl emerged, her hair short and blonde, throwing Finn for a moment. He was no longer even confident he'd be able to pick Hailey Portman out of a group. But the girl with the short hair spoke to the others in Swedish, jolting Finn's memory into seeing she looked nothing like Hailey.

And when Hailey did come into view, almost at the back of the group, he realized he should never have doubted himself. She looked older, it was true—very much a young woman, fashionable, the short hair giving her face character—but easily recognizable.

She didn't see Finn, didn't see anybody in the dining room, and as soon as she reached the bottom step she turned to say something to the last person in the group of ten, Anders Tilberg. He smiled, said something back and gave her a fleeting kiss, and as they moved toward the reception he rested his hand on the small of her back as if they'd been a couple forever.

Finn had to admit to himself that they looked good together—two attractive people who also formed what seemed an obvious and natural unit. It was clear, too, that Anders Tilberg had no idea of her true age. Even more surprisingly, as briefly as he'd seen her, Finn had seen nothing in Hailey's manner or expression to suggest guilt or confusion or uncertainty—if anything, he'd never seen her looking so at ease, perhaps only because he was now seeing her not around adults but living as one.

They were slow to get themselves together, and once they'd left he gave it another thirty seconds before leaving himself. They were moving quicker once outside in the cold but they were still within sight. They were in high spirits, too, so it was easy to stay on them, the voices and laughter telling Finn where they were even when he let them disappear from view.

Only once did he hear Hailey's voice, clearly saying, "Oh my God, you have to come to New York." Again, it was very much a student talking, not a schoolgirl. Finn wondered if she was claiming to come from New York City or just talking in general terms—as far as he knew she'd never lived there, and hadn't lived in America at all since infancy.

Finn turned a corner and stopped. Ahead of him, only twenty yards off, they'd reached an impressive-looking townhouse and were piling inside. Tilberg was clearly a wealthy young man, given that he'd just bought dinner for ten people, so it made sense that he might live somewhere like this instead of in regular student accommodation, but Finn wanted to be sure.

Once the door was closed and the lights came on inside, he walked along and stood on the corner of a narrow side street facing the house. As it did at home, the snow gave everywhere a deceptive look of coziness, but he didn't need to stand for long before the cold started to bite.

He heard a burst of laughter from within the house, then music, but only faintly. He looked up and down the street, checking there wasn't a bar or coffee shop that might provide a better surveillance post, but he was drawn back to the house by another light coming on.

It was on the second floor, what looked like a large bedroom. Hailey walked into the room, threw something that might have been a coat onto a bed or chair, then crouched down. When she stood again she was holding a cardigan that she put on, quickly checking her appearance in a mirror. Finn smiled, recognizing it as one of the items she'd bought at Fate.

She turned, in response to someone, and Anders Tilberg came into the room. They kissed, briefly at first but serving only as a trigger for something more passionate. Perhaps someone called from downstairs, because they broke apart then and laughed, and Tilberg called something over his shoulder. They kissed again, a promise, and left the room, turning out the light.

Finn returned the way he'd come, confident now that he would get Hailey back in the morning, and hopeful that in the process he'd find out why they'd had him under surveillance for two years.

Yet something about the evening had left him in surprisingly low spirits. His mind flitted about, trying to identify the cause, thinking of Sparrowhawk, the USB stick, his threatened career. The catalyst, though, had been something simultaneously more mundane and more profound, and he felt ludicrously forlorn when his memory landed on it again.

It had been nothing more than that simple act of intimacy between Hailey and Tilberg in the restaurant: the fleeting kiss, the two bodies moving seamlessly together toward the door, his hand finding the small of her back. It was just one more thing that made him want to call Adrienne, albeit with little idea of what he would say to her.

Perhaps they had once appeared like that to onlookers, a couple comfortably wrapped up in each other, but at some level he now felt that it hadn't been true, because he had been a fake. He'd held back more than he'd ever given to Adrienne, taking for granted that it would be enough—maybe it had for a while, but he supposed four years was a long time for anyone to live with a shadow.

Of course, despite appearances, Hailey was also holding something back, and though it was probably of little consequence in the grand scheme of things, he doubted her fledgling relationship would survive that revelation when it came. Finn imagined the kitsch little heart being removed from their Facebook pages, his immediately in horror and embarrassment, hers more reluctantly.

It was too bad. He'd had little sympathy for Hailey Portman so far, and at some level he knew he should still have none, but after seeing her tonight, after seeing the appeal of the lie she'd constructed for herself, he regretted that in the morning he would have to bring that idyll to an end.

Chapter Seventeen

It was just after seven when he had the taxi drop him at the end of the street. Fresh snow had fallen during the night, and the dawn light was muted by the blanket of cloud that still hung low and uniform over the city.

The house, as he'd expected, was shut up and full of sleep. He'd guessed all eight of their fellow diners probably didn't live there, and he saw now that one had dropped a beer bottle as they'd left—it had landed in the snow on the step and been partially covered by the fresh fall, left looking like some ancient, fossilized artifact.

Finn looked at the lock, refreshing his memory of the methods for opening various simple mechanisms. But the first method was successful as often as not, and so it was this time—he tried the door and found it open.

Stepping inside, he half expected the stale early morning atmosphere that followed any student party, but he guessed none of them smoked, and the only smell here was coffee. It was as if the place was on the market and they were expecting prospective buyers.

The coffee smelled fresh enough that he wondered if someone was already in the kitchen. He didn't wait to find out, moving quickly up the stairs, across the landing, stopping for a second outside the door before knocking. There was no reply and he knocked again, a little harder.

He heard Tilberg call out some sleepy response, then stepped inside and reached up to find the light switch as he closed the door behind him. Light flooded into the room, which was large and strewn with clothes and various student staples. The double mattress, like student places the world over, was on the floor.

Hailey was almost completely hidden under the duvet on the far side of the bed. Tilberg was sitting up, reaching for his watch, trying to adjust his vision to the sudden light. Then he saw Finn, realizing it was no one he knew, and he tensed and spoke angrily in Swedish and looked ready to jump out of bed.

Finn raised his hand and said calmly, "I wouldn't do that."

Tilberg responded to something in Finn's voice, easing back onto his elbow, briefly confused as to what his next move should be. He still sounded outraged as he said, "What are you doing, man? This is a private house—I'm calling the police."

He reached for his phone but stopped when Finn said, "No, you don't want to call the police."

Suddenly, Hailey's head emerged from the duvet, staring at Finn in horror as she said, "Oh God!" She fell back onto the pillow, pulling the duvet back over her face, repeating, "Oh God, oh God!"

Tilberg turned to look at her, staring at the relief of her face beneath the duvet as he said, "Hailey, what's up?" She was silent, but even under the covers it was clear that she was shaking her head.

"Hailey and I know each other, that's what's up."

Tilberg didn't get it and said, "What difference does that make? You know, man, you just can't come into someone's bedroom like this, and who let you into the house?"

"Anders, stop," came Hailey's muffled voice.

Finn hesitated, wondering if it was better to leave her to do the telling, but he guessed it was like removing a Band-Aid—and the very fact that she was hiding her face suggested she was desperate to avoid doing it herself.

"My name's Finn Harrington. I'm here because Hailey's parents asked me to find her and bring her home."

"Oh God." It was Tilberg this time, hit by dread at the thought of what those words meant. He sat up and covered his face with his hands.

"Hailey's fifteen years old, Mr. Tilberg."

Tilberg let his hands slip down his face, and looked visibly sick with worry as he said, "I had no idea, I . . ."

"It's okay, they're aware that you were tricked. They don't want any fuss and they don't want to take this any further. They just want their daughter back." Tilberg nodded, looking absurdly grateful, or perhaps not so absurdly given how this might have panned out for him. "I'll wait in the kitchen."

Finn left, closing the door behind him, and he heard nothing from the room as he descended the stairs and found his way to the kitchen by following the drug-like smell of coffee.

There was a girl sitting at the kitchen table in what looked like running gear, her hair pulled back in a ponytail. It took him a moment to place her as the first girl who'd come down the restaurant stairs the night before, her appearance transformed in these clothes. She looked remarkably fresh.

The girl looked at him, confused but unthreatened as she said, "*Hej!*"

"Hello. Anders knows I'm here."

"Okay. Coffee?"

"I'd love some, thank you."

She got up and filled a mug for him. He thanked her as he took it, and sat across the table from where she'd been sitting.

"I'm Camilla."

"I'm Finn. How do you do?" He reached across and shook her hand.

"I'm sorry, would you like something to eat?" She herself only had coffee, and he guessed she was running carb-free.

"No, I'm fine, thanks. Are you going for a run?"

She nodded, like someone admitting to a secret vice. He wished he could offer to go with her. The thought of setting out in that fresh snow, the cold air burning his lungs, blood prickling beneath his skin, it all held infinitely more appeal than the endurance test he had ahead of him.

Camilla finished her coffee, washed the mug and said, "Okay, nice to meet you, Phil."

"Likewise," he said, not bothering to correct her.

She left and there was a brief influx of cold air from the front door, then the house became silent again. He sipped at his coffee—not quite as good as the aroma had suggested, but still welcome. Through the silence, he picked up movement on the floor above, and one hushed voice—Tilberg's. There were pauses, too, filled by Hailey's responses, he imagined, though he couldn't hear her.

Someone went to the bathroom, then back to the room at the front. There was no conversation this time, no movement, a stillness that lasted a minute and seemed so potent that Finn found himself holding his breath. Finally, a door opened and closed, there were soft footsteps on the stairs, and Tilberg came into the kitchen wearing jeans and a T-shirt.

He looked grim-faced, and nodded at Finn as if they were both caught up in the same tragic situation. Finn had his own small collection of miniature tragedies to live with, but this wasn't one of them. He nodded back all the same.

"She's taking a shower, getting her stuff together."

"Of course. Camilla made coffee."

"Thanks." Tilberg got himself some coffee, and sat where Camilla had been until a few minutes before. He looked down at the coffee, then up at Finn, his eyes verging on pleading as he said, "I had no idea, I swear."

Finn shrugged. "It's nothing to me, but for what it's worth, maybe you should have been more careful, looked for the signs—they were there." Tilberg looked confused. "I saw your Facebook page, Anders. You have a lot of friends on there who are also at Uppsala University—does Hailey have any other friends at the University of Geneva?"

"But she explained that. She was having trouble making friends there—that's one of the reasons she came to visit." It was interesting to hear him speak, as if he still wanted to believe that her story was true.

"Any Facebook friends from back home in America?" He didn't wait for an answer this time. "Look, I'm just saying you should have been more careful. I don't know what the law is here, but in some countries you'd be in a whole load of trouble right now, and it wouldn't matter that she'd lied to you."

"Actually, it's legal here, but she just told me she only became fifteen last month. You know, she talked about coming here before Christmas, and then it would have been . . ." He shook his head, briefly repeating the gesture of covering his face with his hands, sighing through them and then saying, "I completely believed her."

"Well, if no law was broken and her parents don't want to take it further anyway, I'd just put it down to experience. And maybe choose your next girlfriend from among your fellow students. You know, I just had coffee with a very attractive young lady."

Tilberg laughed, as if the suggestion of Camilla as a girlfriend was clearly a joke, then looked downcast again as he said, "I should have known it was too good to be true."

Finn had nothing more for him, so he waited a couple of beats and said, "This is a pretty nice house by student standards."

Tilberg looked thrown for a second, but looked around the kitchen and said, "Oh, yes, it belongs to my family." He smiled. "And on the subject of family, the attractive lady you had coffee with is Camilla Tilberg, my cousin."

That explained the bemused response to Finn's comment.

"And is that legal here?"

Tilberg laughed properly, then looked curious. "Did you say your name was Harrington? Are you any relative of Charles Harrington, the historian?"

If nothing else, this trip had done wonders for Finn's ego as a writer.

"I am Charles Harrington—Finn is just what people call me."

Tilberg looked amazed, the whole situation forgotten as he said, "I read your book on the Black Death. It was really great. I'm a history student."

"Thanks. I didn't think my books would be considered academic enough to appear on university reading lists."

"No, they're not. I read it for myself. Actually, I bought it in London when I was there, in Foyles. But I really enjoyed it."

"I appreciate that."

"What are you working on now?"

"The Cathars, though I haven't done much this last week—what with trying to find Hailey and, you know . . ."

"Sorry."

"Don't be, I'll get back into it soon enough." Though not yet, he thought, because finding Hailey wasn't the end of his search.

There was a shuffling noise on the floor above—what sounded like a backpack being dragged. Tilberg looked ready to get up, but thought better of it and stayed in his seat, and the two of them listened to her progress down the stairs. She left the backpack in the hall and appeared in the kitchen doorway.

Even with the fashionably short hair and the student clothes, she looked very much a schoolgirl to Finn, and he couldn't understand how the people in Fate or Tilberg and his friends had been fooled by her. And that in turn reminded him of Katerina all those years before, and he realized that some people just wanted to be fooled.

Hailey looked at Tilberg, her eyes a little red, but he stared resolutely at his coffee and she gave up and turned her attention to Finn, meeting his gaze.

"Hello, Finn."

"Hello, Hailey." He turned to Tilberg. "Anders, could you call us a taxi?"

"Of course." He reached into his pocket for his phone, and crossed the kitchen as he searched for a number.

Hailey came across to the table, looking lost. Idly, she picked up Tilberg's mug and drank some of his coffee, and in that one simple action Finn saw how she'd fooled them all. There was something sophisticated and worldly about it, like a woman who'd seen life, and the best and worst of what it could throw at a person.

She sat down, the third person in that chair, as Tilberg got through and spoke a couple of sentences in Swedish. He stayed where he was, as if afraid to come back to the table, but said, "It'll be a few minutes."

"Thanks." Finn took the letter from his pocket and held it out for Tilberg. "For the sake of formality, a letter from the Portmans authorizing me to escort her home."

"I don't need to see that."

"Maybe not, but I'd rather you looked at it—make it the beginning of your new cautious approach to life."

Tilberg stepped forward and took the letter but then retreated again, leaning back against one of the kitchen counters. Hailey looked at him, stung by the change in him, as if she considered his behavior unreasonable.

"Have you got everything?" She looked back at Finn, nodding. "I'll explain later, but I have to ask if you have the USB stick with you, the one you and Jonas made?"

She looked vague for a second, the fabricated reasons for her disappearance long consigned to the back of her mind, but the pieces fell into place and a different confusion surfaced.

"Yeah, but why do you need to know that?"

"It's not important, but it's too complex to explain now. I'll explain later, maybe on the plane."

She looked put out as she said, "We're flying home right away?"

"What did you have in mind, a trip to the ice hotel?"

Tilberg handed the letter back, and Hailey looked up at him and said, "Can we stay friends?"

"Hailey, how can we be friends? I don't even know who you are."

"How can you say that, after the last few days?"

Tilberg shook his head and sighed heavily, not knowing how to get through to her how betrayed he was feeling. Finn should have felt as if he were intruding by being there, yet in fact, he wanted to tell Hailey that it was completely possible to be intimate whilst remaining strangers—it was an act he'd managed for four years.

Finn heard a car pull up. It didn't sound the horn, but sat outside with the engine running. He stood up and shook Tilberg's hand. "I'll let you say your goodbyes."

Tilberg looked uncomfortable even at the prospect of being left alone with Hailey again, but accepted it as a necessity and said, "Thanks, I mean . . . well, thanks."

Finn nodded and said to Hailey, "Don't take too long."

He picked up her backpack as he moved through the hall, reminded again of the students he'd seen on the train to Geneva.

He told the cab driver where they were headed, told him to wait for another person, and they both sat in silence for a few minutes.

Finn sensed some movement in the house and turned. Hailey was coming out alone, looking upset and angry. He expected her to slam the front door behind her, but she didn't, just as Debbie Portman had confounded his expectations by not slamming the door when she'd stormed out of his apartment at the beginning of all this.

Hailey got in the car and the driver looked at Finn. He nodded and they set off along the street. She sat motionless, without tears as far as he could tell—he didn't want to stare at her—and the only words she said were, "Where are we going?"

"To my hotel, then to the airport." He took the opportunity to look at her. Her eyes still looked a little puffy, but they were dry.

She didn't reply, and Finn was equally happy for silence to resume. The adventure was over, definitely for her, maybe for both of them, and silence seemed the appropriate way to mark it.

Chapter Eighteen

When they reached the hotel he paid the taxi driver and she finally spoke again, a hostile curiosity in her voice as she said, "Are my parents paying your expenses?"

He didn't like her tone and said, "What's it to you?"

He got out of the car. The driver got out, too, and retrieved her backpack, standing it on the dry floor of the lobby entrance. Finn walked into the hotel then, leaving Hailey to carry the backpack.

They reached the front desk together, and he asked for his bill and for someone to bring his bag down.

Hailey seemed to understand immediately why he'd done that, and said, "You could've gone up for it—it's not like I'm gonna run away." He looked at her, bemused, wondering if she saw the irony of what she'd just said. She did, and sounded petulant as she added, "I don't have anywhere to go, remember—not anymore."

"Maybe, but I've come a long way to risk losing you again."

"Are my parents paying your expenses?"

"No."

"Why would you do that?"

"As a friend?"

She raised her eyebrows, so arch an expression that he nearly laughed.

He turned back to the receptionist and said, "I wonder, could you call SAS and see if you can get us two business seats on the eleven o'clock flight to Geneva?"

"Of course, I'll do that for you right now."

"Business?" He turned back to Hailey as she said, "What I said earlier, you know? This is a nice hotel, and you're flying business, paying for me to fly business, and you're not taking any money off my parents. What's it all about, Finn? You're not that much of a friend. In fact, I can't even think why my parents would ask you in the first place."

"I found you, didn't I?"

The receptionist interrupted, saying, "Mr. Harrington, the eleven o'clock flight is fully booked."

"Really? Just business or the whole flight?"

"The whole flight. There are two seats available on the late-afternoon flight, but only one in business."

It wasn't something he'd allowed for, that he might need to travel back on a day when it seemed everyone else in Sweden wanted to get to Geneva.

"Okay, well I suppose—" A thought struck him, immediately beguiling. "No, wait, how about flights to Paris?"

"I'll check." Finn and Hailey watched as she negotiated with the SAS office. Then she covered the mouthpiece of the phone. "There's a flight to Paris at thirteen thirty-five, arriving sixteen ten, and they have two business-class seats available."

"Good. We'll take them." He could detect Hailey's gaze, trying to work out what was going on, but he ignored it, concentrating on the details of the booking. When that was finished he said, "We'll wait in the lounge for an hour before leaving for the airport. Could we have some coffee and pastries, please?"

"Of course, or would you rather go into the breakfast room?"

They left Hailey's backpack at reception and walked through to the breakfast room. He expected Hailey to tell him she wasn't hungry, but she assembled an ambitious breakfast and set about it with relish. Only when she'd finished her bacon and scrambled eggs, and sat stirring the muesli in the bowl in front of her, did she look up at Finn again.

"You didn't arrange a connecting flight from Paris."

"I know. We can take the train directly to Lausanne."

"Flight doesn't get in until after four—it's gonna be pretty late getting a train."

"We'll get a train in the morning. We'll stay with Adrienne's brother tonight. Adrienne's there, too."

She'd raised a spoon of muesli almost to her mouth but she hesitated now, the milk dripping off and back into the bowl in small splashes. "Will Adrienne be okay with that? Didn't she leave you or something?"

"Yeah, she left me or something. I'm sure she'll be fine."

She ate the spoonful of muesli, chewing for a while. She looked ready to ask him another question, but dug the spoon back into the bowl and kept eating. Finn leaned back, drinking his coffee as he looked around the room, taking in the other guests, mostly business people sitting singly at tables. When he turned back, it was because he heard her put the spoon into the empty bowl and push it away.

She got up and went and got more coffee, then came back. Once she was sitting again, she said, "How did you find me?"

Finn gave a small shrug. "I didn't buy that you'd run away because you were afraid. I found the shoebox full of receipts in your room, went to Fate, found out that you'd made a new identity for yourself. It suits you, by the way." She gave a little grimace, the kind she would have produced if her parents had tried to talk about sex or the latest music—apparently Finn was too old to have any worthwhile view on fashion. "Anyway, that convinced me you'd gone away to meet someone. Jonas helped me find out where."

At the mention of his name, Hailey looked dumbstruck—a mixture of betrayal and annoyance. She shook her head. "I can't believe he would do that. What a jerk."

"Did you ask him not to?" She didn't understand the question. "If you'd told Jonas where you were going and asked him not to say anything, he would've protected you."

"No, he wouldn't! You don't know him. He can't lie. I don't mean he's congenitally incapable of lying. I don't buy that whole Asperger's thing my parents are obsessed with, not at all, but he just doesn't lie. He's just too laid-back to believe that the truth could ever be really harmful."

"Well, you're right, I don't know him that well, but I think if you'd asked him he would have lied for you. And he helped me because he was worried."

She shook her head again and said, almost to herself, "Jerk."

"Jesus, I don't know you too well, either, but I'm beginning to see that you're a complete bitch." She looked as if she'd been slapped around the face, so unused was she to anyone talking to her like that. "Okay, let's just think about it for a second. Let's think about what you put your parents through—that's if you've given even a moment's thought to how distraught they've been this last week—"

"Of course I have!"

"Then your best friend—good God, am I glad I never had a best friend like you—you know full well the unique way his mind works, and you completely manipulated him—"

"How did I?"

"This is me you're talking to. You encouraged him to hack into Gibson's network. You got him to create the scenario that would allow you to run away. It was a lucky break that Gibson asked your parents about it, but the break-in, the car following you, none of that happened." He was guessing, but she stared down at her coffee and was silent. "So you used Jonas, too, and all of that so you could hoodwink some guy into being your boyfriend, with not a thought of the consequences. Anders told me you wanted to come here before Christmas, when you were still fourteen, a small difference that could have landed him with a few years in prison."

She looked up, her face red, but in what appeared to be anger rather than embarrassment, and said, "Why do you think I didn't come? I checked. I'm not stupid."

"Oh, I'm not accusing you of being stupid, Hailey. I have to admit, I even had some admiration for the way you planned it all, for how devious you've been. No, I'm not accusing you of being stupid, I'm accusing you of being cold and selfish and manipulative."

She pushed her chair away from the table and stood in one fluid movement. For a moment, it looked as if she might pick something up and throw it at him, but she sounded quite calm as she said, "I have to go to the bathroom." She approached one of the waitresses and asked her directions, then left the room.

Finn waited a moment, then followed, telling the waitress he'd be back. He walked only as far as the lobby, knowing she couldn't leave the hotel without him seeing her.

She was only five minutes or so, and when she came back her eyes were newly reddened. He'd gone too far, perhaps, forgetting she *was* still only fifteen, and that she would have to face worse from her parents. He felt a little hypocritical, too, in just about everything he'd said, and yet he simply hadn't been able to sit there and listen to her running Jonas down like that.

It was true, he hardly knew the kid, but he knew he deserved better than that. Maybe one day she'd see that, too, even if it was years after she and Jonas had gone their separate ways and lost touch with each other.

Hailey didn't look at him as she approached, offering no reaction to the fact that he still didn't trust her not to run. She walked past him and resumed her place at the table. He followed her in, and got himself another cup of coffee before sitting down again.

She sipped at her own coffee, but then pushed it aside and got up, coming back a moment later with a fresh cup. Once she'd sat down, she looked him straight in the face and said, "I'm not a bad person."

"If you were, I wouldn't have bothered saying those things."

She nodded a little, as if accepting that as a truce marker, then said, "How did he know where to look?"

"He knew you'd gone by train—the InterRail page you had up on your computer." She nodded again, like a master criminal looking back on the small mistakes she'd known about all along. "You also gave away one day that you were on Facebook—you told him you'd played a game on there, then tried to say you were just browsing, but—"

"You can't browse on Facebook."

"That's right. It says something for his loyalty to you that Jonas had never looked at your page until I asked him to. Naturally, he knew your email address, and he knew your password. From there it was easy. I was at the restaurant last night—I followed you back, found out where Anders lived."

She looked briefly transported back to Domtrappkällaren, and said quietly, "It was such a great night." Her voice was full of regret—that it was over rather than remorse for what she'd done. "It's been a great few days."

"I'm sure it has." She looked defensive, as if sensing another attack, but he smiled. "I doubt you'll ever look back and regret this. You might regret aspects of it, as you should, but it'll be one for the memory bank." She became glum, the bigger picture not something she wanted to contemplate right now. "Hailey, let me ask you, how did you imagine this panning out? How long did you think it could last?"

She gave a little twitch of her mouth—a gesture he'd seen before, her version of a shrug—and said, "Longer than this. If you hadn't gotten involved, or Jonas." Again, Jonas's name was said with a certain bitterness.

"You really have it in for Jonas, don't you?"

"Because he's maddening." She was about to drink from her coffee cup but was overtaken with thoughts and put it down. "You must've noticed the way his mind never settles on anything for more than, like, two minutes. He's just so random, it's untrue. It's partly his fault anyway, that all this—"

She stopped abruptly, gave the minimalist shrug again as if to suggest it wasn't worth saying, and finished her coffee.

"Why was it his fault?"

"I didn't say it was his fault, just partly."

"But why?"

"Why do you think?"

"I have no idea."

She looked more bashful than he'd so far seen her, looking down at the coffee cup as she spoke, turning it around as if searching for a maker's mark.

"Because if he'd shown any interest in me—proper interest—I wouldn't have gone on Facebook. I wouldn't have done any of this."

"Oh, I see. Maybe he didn't realize you liked him like that."

"Of course he did."

She looked up at him, and Finn made a show of accepting the point, then said, "He's certainly a very good-looking guy. We went to a coffee shop and the waitress couldn't take her eyes off him. Two girls at a neighboring table were the same."

"It's like that everywhere we go, and he's not interested. I don't think I've ever seen him look at a girl like that. I'm not saying I think he's gay, he's just . . ." Finn was smiling now, and she stopped, looking a little offended as she said, "What?"

"Hailey, Jonas doesn't look at other girls because he's in love with you." She looked as if he'd said something ridiculous. "I'm serious, I've known him a few days and I can assure you that he's crazy about you."

"I would know."

"Clearly not. But you would probably need to make the running on this one, although it might be an idea to let the dust settle. And I also think you need to make a full and frank apology first, telling him exactly the ways in which you lied to him, and why."

Even as he spoke, he realized his advice applied more urgently to him than it did to Hailey.

She shook her head, saying, "He'd never forgive me."

"He would."

"Anyway, it wouldn't work now even if he does like me. I'm in love with Anders."

She probably expected the usual adult response, that she was too young to know what she wanted, that Anders was a grown man, a grown man who almost certainly didn't want anything to do with her now. Instead, Finn nodded and stood up. She stood, too.

"Life is like comedy—it's all in the timing."

She stared at him for a second, taken with the thought, perhaps flattered because he hadn't given the adult-to-child speech, but then said sadly, "So what happened with you?"

With you and Adrienne, was what she meant.

"I suppose I'm not as funny as I thought I was."

She smiled.

"You're pretty funny," she said, encouraging. "I wouldn't give up writing the books . . ."

He laughed a little, and they walked out of the breakfast room and retrieved their bags. He'd warmed to her through that final part of their conversation, perhaps just because of the eternally innocent situation of two kids not realizing they were each in love with the other, misunderstanding all the signals, all the words spoken.

Of course, Finn wasn't a kid and nor was Adrienne, and she'd know exactly why he'd chosen to turn up at Mathieu's place with Hailey. He was using the girl as a convenient shield, someone he could hide behind while he tested the water and tried to find out how things stood between them.

It was cowardly, and he wished he could follow even a little of his own advice, and be open and truthful with her—about who he was, about how little she'd known of the real him this last four years. But how could that be a solution, when the truth was worse than what she had run away from?

History

On Sunday, they drove along the coast to Sofi's parents' house. Neither of them had a car, but Sofi had a long-standing arrangement to borrow a colleague's Saab now and then. It was ancient but in beautiful condition, which Sofi always cited as her reason for not letting Finn drive it—her stand was one of personal responsibility rather than based on any knowledge of his driving.

Once in the passenger seat, Finn wound down the window and slightly adjusted the wing mirror. She didn't say anything. The first time, he'd come up with some story or other and she'd laughed and made no more of it. She'd known pretty much from the beginning, he was certain of that.

Only once before had the precaution borne fruit. A car had followed them to her parents' house, but disappeared thereafter. He'd alerted Ed, but they'd already had an apology from the CIA who, for reasons they didn't share, had been keeping an eye on Sofi's colleague, the Saab's owner.

Today was the second time. A black BMW tailed them from the city, disappearing just before they reached her parents' house on the shore. The best-case scenario, discounting coincidence, was that Karasek was hoping Finn would lead him to the girl without needing to part with any money. After that came the Russians, Americans, or the Estonians themselves, wondering what was going on. Worst case was that he was being tailed by his own people—worst case because it suggested there was much more to this operation than he'd been given to believe.

Sofi's father didn't speak English but, as always, greeted Finn enthusiastically and talked to him in Estonian. Sofi translated in snatches—odd words and phrases rather than full sentences. She translated even less of Finn's replies, but her father didn't seem to mind.

Her mother was of Russian origin but was a translator, and spoke fluent English and French. She'd worked for the Estonian government but was a freelancer for publishing houses now, and loved talking to Finn about the latest British novels.

Lunch was inevitably relaxed and entertaining, and the house had a good family atmosphere, even though her parents had only moved there a few years earlier—Sofi had been brought up in the city. It was a house that had the feel and the smell of the sea about it, open and light even in the winter, and he couldn't help but imagine children running around here—their children maybe.

After lunch, Finn and Sofi walked on the beach and he said, "If I stay . . ."

"If you stay? I thought you'd decided."

He laughed and felt more confident, because he could see a way now.

"I am staying. I was just thinking, we could move out here."

"With my parents?"

As much as she loved them, the thought seemed alarming to her.

"Why not? We get along okay." He laughed, giving away that he was teasing her, then said, "I meant we could get a place out on the coast—somewhere like this, not necessarily right here."

"Don't you like Tallinn?"

"I love Tallinn, and we'd be within driving distance. It's just, I was thinking about what you said, about bumping into old colleagues. I'd rather be away from all that. And you know, if we were maybe, at some point, thinking about having a family." She smiled. "I'm not saying just yet, but if we were, this would be a great place, all this light and space, and the air."

She stopped and turned, kissing him then holding on to him, nestling her head against his shoulder. He put his arms around her, conscious of the biting cold now that he had the warmth of her body against his, wanting to be lost in that warmth, but at the same time he looked along the dunes for signs of someone watching them. There were two people farther along the beach with a dog, but that was all.

When Sofi pulled away, she looked up at him again and said, "Are you okay?"

"I'm fine. Why?"

"I just wondered—all this talk of getting out of Tallinn, families. And you think somebody followed us out here."

"How do you know?"

She frowned. "Because I know you too well. You're very discreet, but I still know you too well. And I saw it too, a black car."

He nodded, smiling as he said, "It's almost certainly nothing to worry about."

"The lady who came to see you—it has nothing to do with that?"

She was rattled, perhaps, because she'd never been so explicit before. He took hold of her arms and said, "No, and I'm not going to be working for them much longer anyway. Look, this week I'll be busy, I'll have a lot to do, but it's . . ." He still couldn't bring himself to be indiscreet, even with Sofi. "It's routine, and I don't want you imagining it's something else."

"A car followed us."

"Maybe. But it means nothing."

He held her again, his cheek against hers, the touch of her skin relaxing him like nothing else could, and then he turned and they kissed and he no longer cared who might be watching them.

It was late afternoon by the time they headed home. They hadn't been driving long before Finn spotted the BMW. He didn't react, but a few moments later Sofi glanced in her rearview mirror.

"How long have they been following us?"

"I noticed them a few minutes ago."

She looked at him, snatched glimpses whilst keeping her eyes on the road ahead, and said, "What do they want?"

"To see where I'm going, I imagine." He shrugged. "Don't worry about it. It's nothing unusual, and think of those poor guys, sitting in that car for the last few hours waiting for us to reappear."

"What if they're following *me*?" He didn't respond and she glanced at him again. "I've been working on some sensitive stories lately—so what if they're following me?"

"They're not."

"But how can you be sure?" She didn't give him time to reply, adding quickly, "Find out. I just need to know. I don't like them following you, either, but it's a bigger risk for me. I need to know, for defending of myself."

Her English was excellent, but when she was stressed or upset her phrasing went off a little, as it had just now. He put his hand on her leg to reassure her.

"I'll find out, but I'm certain they're following me. Don't worry about it."

"I am worried, Finn. That woman coming the way she did—"

"Sofi, you know . . . you've always known that I can't talk about this. You just have to take my word that it's nothing to worry about."

He felt like he was lying to her, and yet surely he was telling the truth. He was worried for Katerina, worried for how he would pull off all these disparate tasks in time—but he wasn't in any danger. He allowed his eyes to stray to the wing mirror, though, a reminder that there was never any real certainty in this business.

It was dark by the time they reached the city, and in the busier traffic he didn't notice when the BMW peeled away and left them. They dropped the car at her colleague's place and walked back through the dry, cold streets. They'd almost reached their building when a car door opened across the street and Louisa stepped out. She didn't approach, just stood, the message clear.

Sofi immediately looked at him with reinforced concern, but he smiled and said, "Listen, the main part of what I had to do was yesterday, and Louisa just wants my report on how it went, nothing more." She seemed desperate to believe him, but also afraid to believe. "Go inside and I'll be back soon."

She nodded, and he watched as she walked into the building, angry with himself for putting her through this. He walked across the street then and Louisa said, "Won't keep you long."

They got into the car—the same driver as last time—and set off, not heading anywhere in particular, just around the city.

"Excellent job yesterday."

"That's not why you're here."

"No. He has people tailing you."

"I noticed today—I'm glad it's him. I thought it might have been you."

"Is it that you don't trust us, or you think we don't trust you?"

"Both." She made a show of mock offense and he said, "Louisa, you once told me the key to this game is never trusting anyone. Make friends, make alliances, but take nothing on trust."

"One of my wiser moments." She paused. "He thinks you'll lead him to the girl, so you need to be careful."

He looked at her, wondering for a moment if she knew that it was Finn who'd saved the girl, that she was hidden away at Harry's place. The only way she could know was either real surveillance footage or from Harry, but despite what he'd said about trust, he knew Harry wouldn't have talked, not even to Louisa.

"What do you mean?"

"I mean his people may pay particular attention to anywhere you visit, so be careful where you visit—you don't want any of your friends to get unwanted attention from Karasek's men."

She was right about that, which meant he'd have to be careful about visiting Harry. Even though he called to see him often enough, he had to make any visits in the coming week look entirely natural. Then he thought of where he'd been this afternoon.

"Should I warn Sofi's parents?"

"I shouldn't think so. We could ask the local police to keep an eye on their place, but that might just convince Karasek all the more that it's where you're hiding her." Finn nodded, not responding. He looked out at the street, realizing the driver had carried out a large circuit and they were now heading back. "The mother's Russian, isn't she?"

"Yes—or she was. She translates for Estonian publishers. She's a nice old girl."

Louisa produced a single contemptuous laugh and said, "How very sweet of you to consider a woman of fifty-six as a nice old girl. You won't be thirty forever, you know, Finn."

"No, I'm sorry, I didn't mean it like that. I—"

"Yes, I'm not quite fifty-six myself, so don't apologize too hard or I'll really take offense." Finn noticed the driver laughing to himself. "Now, tomorrow you'll be office-bound—some drudge work to occupy you. Everyone else will know about Sparrowhawk tomorrow, and will know that you're not part of the operation because of your imminent departure. Ed Perry won't be in the office until Friday, so no need to worry about him. We think we'll have more accurate information by tomorrow afternoon, so Tuesday you'll go back to Karasek."

"How much more do you need on Perry?"

"If you can get him to mention Perry's name himself, that would be ideal. What we have is enough to derail Ed, but he has powerful supporters, so something more demonstrative from Karasek would be useful. However, don't chase to the extent where you'll risk the other objectives."

Finn nodded, and the car pulled up at the end of his street. He walked back to the apartment and found Sofi waiting for him just inside, her coat still on. He smiled, once more offering reassurance.

"They were following me, so you don't need to worry."

"She told you that?"

"Yes, and everything else is fine."

She started to undo the buttons on her coat, and he did the same. He couldn't understand why she'd suddenly become so apprehensive, and wondered if perhaps she was getting it from him, if the tension of everything that had happened these last few weeks was affecting his behavior, making her nervous.

And then, unexpectedly, his mind skipped back to something Louisa had said.

"How old is your mother?"

"Fifty-six. Why?"

He shook his head. "I don't know—I was thinking about it today. I thought she was younger."

Louisa knew how old Sofi's mother was. Why would she know that? Why would she want to know? That was the question troubling Finn. Not how she knew—that hardly deserved consideration—but *why* she knew, because Louisa did nothing and said nothing without a reason.

Chapter Nineteen

As soon as they got into the taxi, Hailey slid down in the seat and looked out of the window. He imagined she was committing the snowy city to her memory, dwelling on the last few days, but he realized after a short while that she'd fallen asleep. She woke only as they reached Arlanda.

They got out of the taxi, and he picked up her backpack and threw it over his shoulder.

She walked alongside him and said, "So we're friends now?" He looked at her. "You're carrying my backpack."

He nodded. "That was a little childish of me, not to carry it earlier. But I reserve the right to be childish again."

She smiled and they walked to check-in, but before he'd handed over the backpack Hailey said, "Wait there." She rooted in one of the side pockets, and took out a red memory stick and handed it to him. "Just in case they lose my bag."

"Thanks."

As they walked away from the desk she said, "You still have to tell me why you wanted it—the USB stick."

"And I will. But first let's find a phone box."

"Don't you have a cell?"

"I do. That's also part of the USB story."

She accepted that, and remained silent as he found a phone and made a call, a look of dismay freezing on her face only as the call was answered and he said, "Hi Debbie, it's Finn."

"Oh, thank God, Finn. Please, tell me—"

"I've found her, Debbie. She's fine and we're here at the airport. I'll put her on in a second."

Hailey stared at him open-mouthed, and gestured wildly with her arms to say she didn't want to speak to them.

Debbie said, "You're at Geneva Airport?"

"No—Arlanda. And listen, Debbie, there were no seats left for a Geneva flight today, so we're flying to Paris. We'll stay with Mathieu tonight, and get the train to Lausanne first thing tomorrow."

There was a pause, and then she said, "Oh, okay. I can hardly deny you that, I guess."

She'd also read him too well, but he said, "Debbie, it was either that or stay in Uppsala another night, which I didn't think would be a good idea. Anyway, this might be good—it'll give time for the dust to settle."

He was overusing that phrase. He wanted to write a note to himself, a reminder not to use it in the new book.

"Finn, I'm sorry. I didn't mean to imply . . . and yes, you're right, staying in Sweden wouldn't have been a good idea. But she's okay?"

"She's fine. I'll put her on now and we'll call again from Paris."

He didn't even wait for Debbie to reply, and despite giving him a look of consternation—an expression that asked him if he'd understood nothing of what she'd been trying to say to him—Hailey took the phone, breathed deeply, and held it to her ear.

"Hi, Mom."

He backed away, strolling some distance before turning to look at her again. She spoke for ten minutes or so, and stood for a minute longer after she'd put the phone down. Finally, she turned and scanned the people coming and going until she saw him.

She mustered a smile and raised her hand in a wave. He raised his hand in response. She'd been crying again, of course, and as if talking to her parents had robbed her of her newfound maturity, she looked small and vulnerable standing there.

He walked over and said, "Okay?"

She nodded, biting her lip.

"Let's head to the business lounge then."

They walked together in silence, and sat for a few minutes in the lounge without talking, either. She still looked fragile, only just holding it together as she processed the conversation with her parents, but he sensed she didn't want to discuss it now, not with him, anyway.

He looked at the other passengers and said, "In the business lounge in Geneva yesterday, a guy asked me to sign one of my books."

"Really?" She was being polite, but then something snagged her interest and she said, "Does that happen a lot?"

"No, not very much. People ask me to sign books when they know me, but I don't think I've ever seen anybody reading one on a plane or anything."

"Why did you call yourself Charles for the books?"

"Charles is my real name."

She laughed. "No it isn't!"

He took his passport and handed it to her. She opened it and said, "How come I didn't know that?" She handed it back. "So why are you called Finn?"

"I have a brother, five years older than me. When my mother was pregnant with me, my brother's best friend was called Finn and he kept insisting that the new baby should be called Finn, too. Naturally, my parents paid no attention and called me Charles. But my brother was a determined child and called me Finn anyway, so much so that pretty soon it was the only name I answered to. Even my parents ended up using it."

"That's so cool." She laughed, but then said, "Pretty wild, though, in a way—like being an impostor your whole life."

"I never thought about it quite like that," he said, wondering if she'd meant to imply something with those words.

She hadn't, and her mind made a link to something else in his story and she said, "Mom wants me to take a pregnancy test, and . . . other stuff. I tried to tell her we'd been careful."

"That's good, that you were careful. As for the pregnancy test and the health check, I'd say that's a pretty small price to pay for their peace of mind."

"I guess."

"How were they generally?"

"Forgiving. Relieved. I think it would've been easier to bear if they'd just yelled at me." She thought about it, quickly adding, "But then I guess you don't think it should be easier for me."

"I think you should be aware of the upset you've caused, and you should feel bad about it. Hurting people who love you should cause remorse, simple as that, whatever your reasons. But that's not the same as beating yourself up about it, and I'm glad your parents have reacted the way they have. They're cool people."

He didn't actually see them as cool people, but Hailey seemed to accept it, then drew a line under that part of the conversation and said, "Why did you want that USB stick? I hope Jonas didn't give you the wrong idea about what's on it."

"You hacked Gibson's network, that's what's on it."

"Yeah—but it's, like, random boring stuff. Most of it doesn't even make any sense."

"Welcome to my life." She looked confused. "For two years, it seems someone has been running a surveillance operation from the apartment next to yours—Gibson for the last year of it. The person they had under surveillance was me."

Slightly too loudly, she said, "So you *are* a spy—Adrienne always said you were!"

From the corner of his eye, he spotted a woman looking across at them in response to the comment. Finn burst out laughing, showing it up as a joke, and the woman lost interest. It *was* a joke, anyway—maybe he'd have concealed his past better if he'd claimed to be a spy all along, double-bluffing Adrienne and the others into thinking he was a fantasist.

"Adrienne was guessing, and I don't want you to get carried away—I worked for the British government, but not doing anything particularly clandestine."

"That's so obviously a lie."

"Because?"

"Because they've been watching you for two years—they wouldn't do that for someone who worked in the mail room. And all that stuff Jonas and me hacked into, they wouldn't collect all that." She stopped abruptly, surprised at herself for not seeing something obvious until now. "That's why you came to get me, and why you didn't mind paying all that money, because you weren't really coming to get me, you were coming to get the USB stick."

It was hard to tell whether she was annoyed by that realization.

"I agreed to help find you before I found out about Gibson and the USB stick. I came to Uppsala partly because I wanted to see through what I'd started, but mainly to get the information on the memory stick."

She thought about it for a second and said, "Actually, that's kind of a relief."

"How so?"

"Well, I thought it was pretty weird, you coming up here to get me when you don't know me that well. But it makes sense now." He could see her point. "What will you do . . . with the information?"

"Maybe nothing. I want to find out what they've been looking for, but it might be something and nothing."

"You clearly don't believe that!" He looked puzzled. "The cell phone? I've seen enough movies to know about stuff like this. You think they're tracing your phone. Who is Gibson anyway? Have you confronted him?"

"Gibson left, the day after you did."

"Oh." To her credit, she seemed to realize how this might have looked, how it might have added an extra layer of worry and confusion to her disappearance.

"Like I said, something and nothing, and it's never like it is in the films. Chances are, Gibson left because they decided to wind up the operation."

She either believed him this time, or had accepted that she wouldn't get anything more out of him, because she let the subject drop, saying only, "I can't believe it—Adrienne always said."

He briefly imagined himself having that conversation with Adrienne later today: *Adrienne, you guessed all along but you're the last to know, I was a spy and now the people I used to work for are coming after me, and I don't know why or what they plan to do with me.* Hopefully, it was a conversation she wouldn't want to have, not tonight—not until he at least had something resembling answers.

Chapter Twenty

Finn had wondered a few times about Hailey's journey across Europe, and now he had an idea what it had been like. She'd probably slept the whole way because, just as she'd slept in the taxi to Arlanda, so she did on the plane. It was a flight that was occasionally bumpy, but no sooner had they taken off than she fell asleep and didn't wake until just before they touched down.

He thought she might fall asleep in the taxi, too, particularly as it took longer than usual in the late-afternoon traffic. But she didn't, seeming excited, asking about Mathieu: where he lived (a big apartment), which *arrondissement* (Finn wasn't sure, but it was nice), did he have kids (two boys, eight and six), what were their names (Pablo and Henri).

As they got there, one of the neighbors was just coming out of the street door, but Finn let it go and buzzed up to the apartment. Mathieu answered.

"Hi, Mathieu, it's Finn."

There was a pause, lasting a few seconds, and then the line died and the door opened. Finn pushed it, and stood aside for Hailey to walk in first. She looked at him in mock alarm at the frostiness of the reception.

Finn smiled. "If it comes to the worst, we'll book into a hotel."

Now she looked genuinely alarmed. "You don't think it'll come to that?"

It was touching, after all that had happened, that she was still enough of a teenager to be disturbed by the possibility of social embarrassment.

"No."

He could have qualified his response—he was certain they'd take Hailey in for the night, but wasn't so sure of his own welcome.

When they reached the apartment, he pressed the buzzer and was immediately left in no doubt. The door flew open, Adrienne in full fury.

Her eyes fixed on him, and in little more than a whisper, but one that only served to reinforce her rage, she said, "What the hell do you think—" Then she saw Hailey. Her face swam with confusion, which softened it again, her mouth almost forming a smile as she said, "Hailey?"

Finn looked at Hailey, realizing that Adrienne's questioning voice might well have been based on uncertainty, because the girl standing before her now, with her gamine blonde hair and student clothes, was not the girl she'd seen a week or so ago.

"Hi, Adrienne," said Hailey, sounding a little apologetic.

"But I don't understand . . ." Adrienne stepped forward, kissed her on both cheeks, and hugged her.

She stepped back again then, as if remembering the more important matter of blocking the doorway.

Before she could speak, Finn said, "We're on our way back from Sweden, but there was a problem with the flights. I was hoping Mathieu might put Hailey up for the night. I can check into a hotel."

She looked full of hostility and suspicion, and he was struggling to understand how things had become so poisoned between them. He thought back to his departure for Béziers, to his last phone conversation with her, unable to detect anything within them that might have predicted this.

"What are you talking about? You've been in Sweden? Both of you?"

"It's my fault," said Hailey. They both turned to look at her, but she looked back only at Adrienne. "I did something stupid, Adrienne. I ran away, to Uppsala, to stay with a boy I met online. Mom and Dad didn't know where I'd gone. Finn tracked me down and came and got me."

He could have hugged her himself, because he could see exactly what she was doing. Even if Hailey hadn't known it before—and he hadn't thought to ask her how much she'd known about the precise reasons for Adrienne's departure—it was clear from Adrienne's body language and the way she'd spoken that she wasn't in a forgiving mood. Yet everything in Hailey's little admission—the tone, the words used—had been designed to weaken Adrienne's resolve, to cast Finn in a different light. It was no less fraudulent than he'd been himself, but he was grateful all the same for the effort.

"You ran away? But why would you do that?" Adrienne put her hand to her mouth and said, "Of all the times for me not to be there."

"Finn was there," said Hailey, pushing home her message.

Reluctantly, Adrienne looked at him, as if still suspecting some sleight of hand on his part, and said, "You should come in. For now."

Finn nodded, and moved aside so Hailey could go in ahead of him.

As they stepped into the hall and Adrienne closed the door behind them, Mathieu came in from the kitchen and looked at Finn with that odd parental expression of his, as if welcoming back a prodigal son for a second time.

"Hello, Mathieu."

"Finn."

Cecile, as if responding to the sound of Finn's voice, also came out of the kitchen, but she saw Hailey first and Adrienne introduced them, Cecile becoming excitable, all three of them jabbering away in French. Finn spoke a little French, but not enough to keep up when they were talking fast and over the top of each other.

Pablo and Henri came tearing in from some other part of the apartment, jumping excitedly at Finn, asking to be picked up, though they were both getting too big for that now. For some reason, at Christmas they'd insisted on pronouncing his name like the French "*fin*," but fortunately, and somewhat ironically, they'd forgotten about that and reverted to saying it properly, speaking slowly in French to him and mixing in bits of English.

After struggling to hold them aloft for a few seconds, he put them down and said, "Boys, this is our friend from Lausanne. She's called Hailey, she speaks French."

They noticed her for the first time, and as young as they were, became instantly magnetized by her, grabbing her by the hands, dragging her away to look at their bedrooms, still speaking slowly even though there was no need with her.

The chatter ebbed away, and the four adults were left standing there. For the first time, Finn noticed the smell of food coming from the kitchen. They were good cooks.

Mathieu said, "I overheard a little. The boys have their own rooms now, since the new year, but the guest room has two beds, so Hailey can stay with Adrienne. If you don't mind the couch, Finn."

Finn looked at Adrienne. "Do you mind me staying on the couch?"

"It's not my apartment."

He nodded and turned back to Mathieu, saying, "It'd be good for Hailey to be with other people tonight. I'll come back and get her in the morning."

He picked up his bag, but Adrienne, once again searching for that sleight of hand, said, "No, absolutely not, you don't get to be so reasonable. Stay on the couch." She said something in French, rapid and outside of his vocabulary, and marched into the kitchen.

Cecile gave Finn a surprisingly sympathetic smile, making him wonder all the more what Adrienne had just said or called him, then followed her in.

Mathieu said, "Go on through, Finn, and I'll bring you some wine."

"Thanks."

Mathieu followed the women into the kitchen and Finn took his bag through, dropping it behind the sofa that would be his bed for the night. He sat down then, listening to the distant musical chatter of the boys as they vied with each other for Hailey's attention.

From the kitchen, he could hear only the gentle percussion of food being prepared. Nothing was being said out there as far as he could tell. Then he caught a little movement in his peripheral vision, and Adrienne walked in carrying a glass of wine.

She handed the glass to him and then sat on the sofa opposite. Her face looked as if his very presence was an assault to her. He thought back to what Jonas had told him, about her tears, her complaints of his absence, and he could see it all in her face now, how much he'd hurt her without even knowing it, and he was afraid that he would never be able to fix it.

"I can stay in a hotel if you want me to. It's not about being reasonable, it's about not making anyone uncomfortable, and about not being uncomfortable myself."

She shook her head, saying, "I'm sure we can all manage to get on for one night, at least."

"I honestly thought we'd been getting on okay anyway."

Even as he said it, he realized it was a mistake, not so much because it clearly wasn't true, but because it seemed the biggest part of the problem had been his apparent ignorance of it.

She said only, "We're not doing this now."

"Okay. Thanks for the wine, by the way." He sipped at it.

"Please explain to me what happened." His spirits lifted for a moment, thinking she'd had a change of heart, but then she said, "Why did Hailey leave home? She didn't have an argument with Ethan and Debbie?"

He put the glass on the coffee table in front of him, shaking his head, then listened briefly to check that Hailey was still busily engaged with the boys.

"It's a mess. Essentially, she met a guy online, a student at Uppsala University. She claimed she was a student in Geneva, and they developed some sort of virtual relationship. Then Hailey and Jonas, her friend, hacked into Gibson's computer or something . . ."

"Who is Gibson?"

"The guy who lived below us."

"Cycling guy?"

"That's the one. Anyway, they hacked his network. Gibson duly obliged by asking Debbie if Hailey had accidentally hacked it. Then Hailey claimed someone had followed her and that someone had broken into her room. Next thing, she disappears, leaving a note implying it wasn't safe for her to stay. But it was all a ploy—she wasn't being followed, she'd secretly bought new clothes to change her image, had her hair cut the day she was leaving."

"She looks so much older all of a sudden."

Finn nodded, accepting the point. "Jonas and I tracked her down to Uppsala. I went to the boyfriend's house early this morning, and here we are."

"Boyfriend? You mean she was sleeping with this guy?" He looked at her as if to ask if he needed to answer that question, then she said, "How old was he?"

"I'm not sure—nineteen, twenty—but remember, he was completely convinced by her story. I felt sorry for the guy."

"That's a very male response."

"Yeah, I didn't feel sorry for him because he's a guy. I felt sorry for him because he's the one who was deceived." The sentence hung there heavily, bearing too much meaning, particularly for Finn.

Adrienne stared at him, her gaze piercing, and deceit was apparently on her mind, too, because she said, "What's going on, Finn? It's not like you to help, even to be involved. I can't even understand why they would ask you to help."

"Yeah, well, that was your fault. The police weren't interested, figuring correctly that Hailey was just a runaway, and because you've apparently told them on many occasions that you think I'm a spy, they came to me."

She looked momentarily embarrassed, but she regrouped and said, "And you found her, so they did the right thing. But why . . . why did you get involved?"

The truth was, he couldn't quite remember. The business with Gibson had made his involvement imperative, but he'd committed himself well before that. Had it been the mystery alone, or the opportunity to cast himself in a different light for Adrienne? Or perhaps, at some subconscious level, he'd spotted his chance to rediscover the person he'd once been.

"I don't know. I got back and Grasset told me you'd gone." She grimaced, acknowledging that he shouldn't have found out like that. "Just as well he did tell me, because there was no note."

"But I did leave a note, on your desk."

His mind reeled. Had they been into the apartment while he was away? And if they had, why had they been so unprofessional as to take the note with them?

He recovered his composure quickly. "I don't understand. Maybe I knocked it onto the floor when I put my laptop case down—I didn't see it, and I've hardly been in the study since." He waited a second and said, "What did it say?"

She shook her head, reminding him what she'd already said, that they weren't doing this now.

"So you got back to the empty apartment . . ."

"I called you twice, left a message." Another frown. "And within ten minutes, Debbie was at the door and told me about Hailey being missing. I didn't want to help at first—all that business about me being a spy."

"I'm surprised you helped at all, because . . . you don't really care about other people very much, not unless they've been dead for a very long time."

"That's true. Or at least, it has been true. And even when I decided to help, I think it was more the challenge than anything else. I don't know Ethan and Debbie, not really, and I don't know Hailey."

"Do you know me?"

"I thought we weren't doing this now?"

"True."

"Jesus, Adrienne. I don't know what your reasons for leaving were, but if it's something to do with me being cold and out of reach then you'd be wrong to read too much into this business. I helped to find Hailey, now I'm taking her home and then I intend to get back to my book." Again, he was lying through omission, not wanting to tell her that there was one other piece of business to be dealt with first. "I'd like you to come back, to see if we can sort this out, but that's your choice."

"It's not that simple. I need some time to think."

"Take as long as you need."

She'd been softening toward him for the last few minutes, even her retaliatory responses laced with a slight smile, but he knew immediately from her expression that his last comment had been the wrong one. He wasn't sure why, or what she wanted him to say, but her face visibly hardened again, and it was worse because he could see the fragility and sadness beneath that anger.

He was saved from any further deterioration by Mathieu, who appeared in the doorway and said, "Would you like to eat?"

Dinner was lively and chaotic, conducted in a mixture of English and French, sometimes within single sentences, and with little in the atmosphere to suggest that two of the diners were in a disintegrating relationship and that another had recently run away from home.

The boys were probably the saviors in that regard. They'd always been excitable around Finn, certainly more than he merited, but they were doubly so with Hailey. A couple of times Cecile tried to calm them down, but in the end everyone rolled with their good humor.

If the atmosphere stumbled at all, it was when they were discussing Sweden, as if Finn and Hailey had just been on a long-planned break there, and Adrienne said, "But I don't understand, Hailey, I thought Jonas was your boyfriend?"

There was a tense pause. Hailey looked at Finn, who gave a minimal response, making clear he didn't know where the comment had come from, and then she laughed.

She shook her head and said only, "Adrienne!"

Adrienne laughed, too, and shrugged, looking almost envious as she told Cecile in French about Jonas. Finn didn't catch it all but something earned another "Adrienne!" from Hailey. Adrienne laughed all the more, and then the boys both mimicked the outraged "*Adrienne! Adrienne!*"

Finn had often dreaded coming here, no doubt rather less than Mathieu and Cecile had dreaded him coming, yet as the evening unfolded he realized he was more relaxed than he'd ever been in this apartment. It was late in the day to see that they were a good family, just as he was in danger of no longer being a part of it.

Hailey saw it, too, and before going to bed, she said to Finn, "Thank you so much for bringing me here." It was as if the events of earlier in the day had been forgotten, as if Paris had been their sole objective.

"You're welcome. Sleep well."

Adrienne looked on, suspecting some ulterior motive even after the good humor of the evening, not believing the details of the Finn Harrington who'd turned up here. She didn't bid him goodnight, simply made eye contact, her gaze lingering for a second before she turned and walked away with Hailey.

Mathieu was the last to leave him alone with his bedding and his sofa, but just before he left, Finn said, "Mathieu, do you still have that old laptop you had at Christmas?"

Mathieu nodded but said, "It's no good. The battery. You have to plug it in the whole time."

"That's fine, it's only to go through a memory stick—I don't want to take it away with me."

"Oh, I see." He smiled. "I'll get it for you."

A few minutes later, he'd left Finn again. Finn plugged in the laptop, opening it up on the coffee table in front of him. As it booted up, he retrieved the memory stick from his bag and stopped briefly to listen, making sure the rest of the apartment was done for the evening. Adrienne was one thing, but this was where he'd really find out, he supposed, what the future had in store for him.

Chapter Twenty-One

Much of what Hailey and Jonas had intercepted was effectively gibberish—discreetly crafted messages, the same words often repeated, a catalog of boredom as Gibson reported daily on the absolute lack of activity by their target. Finn could only guess as much, without knowing the exact meaning of the coded words, but he was convinced that was what he was looking at.

One of these missives mentioned the Albigensian Crusade, Gibson perhaps hoping that he'd finally stumbled on something, that Finn had inadvertently broken cover. In response, he'd received a quiet rebuke telling him to ignore any such references in the future.

The messages received by Gibson were by far the most interesting. There were no names, but the tone suggested they'd all been sent by one person. It was in these that Sparrowhawk was mentioned, in these that Helsinki came up more than once, and Karasek, and in these that the puzzling line appeared: *Imperative to identify Jerry de Borg.*

The messages sent to Gibson seemed ridiculously indiscreet, almost as if the person sending them was intentionally spilling information. Finn toyed with the idea that he'd been meant to see this, that they were throwing out bait for him, but there was no way they could have anticipated him getting his hands on it.

The tone reminded him of someone, but he couldn't quite pin it down. He tried to think back. It might have sounded like Ed Perry, but his career had ended with Sparrowhawk. Unless, of course, Perry was out on his own, but that didn't square with financing a two-year surveillance operation.

Finn found a Word document that Gibson had transferred from one computer to another. It contained the number codes Jonas had mentioned—about twenty of them in a row, with just one name at the top—and more than anything else he'd seen, this set Finn's heart beating a little faster.

The name at the top was Aleksandr Naumenko, and Finn knew that the numbers were not code, but the identifiers for Swiss bank accounts. He knew this, because one of them was his own.

They knew about the money; they knew about his links to Naumenko. This was what he'd been looking for and had hoped not to find, a suggestion that the surveillance had been part of some retrospective examination of his record, that they were coming after him because they'd finally uncovered his business relationship with a Russian oligarch.

He heard a noise somewhere in the apartment, and automatically shut the laptop and pulled the memory stick out of the USB port, slipping it into his pocket. He looked at the time, realizing he'd been poring over the files for an hour.

He heard the soft pad of footsteps, and Adrienne came in wearing a long white flannel nightshirt. He didn't think he'd seen it before, but she looked great in it, the material showing off her curves, teasing around the movement of her breasts.

The part of him that was always at a step's remove noted how clichéd it was to be newly attracted to a partner after an enforced separation, but he couldn't help himself. He'd seen her beauty afresh since the moment she'd opened the door earlier that evening, and now that beauty was magnified further by being stripped down to the simplest of garments.

For the briefest of hopeful moments, he imagined her putting a finger to her lips, pulling the nightshirt over her head. But even if Finn had succumbed to cliché, Adrienne had not. She sat on the edge of the coffee table, close enough to whisper but still at a distance. He simultaneously admired and resented her for it.

She'd had something in mind, but looked down at the laptop and said, "That's Mathieu's old computer—what are you doing with it?"

"Not very much, as it happens. Mathieu did warn me."

"I have mine here—you could have borrowed it."

"It doesn't matter now. Couldn't you sleep?"

It was the most innocuous question but the response was flinty. "Yes, you told me a very nice story earlier this evening, about helping Debbie and Ethan, about going to find Hailey."

"Go on."

"Only, you did wish so much that I hadn't imagined things about your past, that it was really all my fault that Debbie came to you. Is that not so?"

He nodded, knowing what was coming, his expression one of capitulation as much as anything else, and he was amazed and frustrated by his inability to stop messing up.

"So, Hailey was talking to me in the bedroom, about how I'd been right all along, about you being a spy. I pretended it was nothing, of course, but I was so angry. I lay awake, waiting for her to fall asleep."

"I couldn't tell you this evening because everyone was milling around, and there was a lot to tell—other stuff, I mean."

Her whisper became rapid and angry. "Why could you not tell me a year ago—two years? Why could you not tell me when

I guessed? You were a spy, maybe you're still a spy for all I know, because I know nothing about you, it seems. I know less than this Gibson who I also find out has been watching our apartment." She stopped, but almost instantly struck another seam. "And how do you think *that* makes me feel, that everything of our life might have been recorded, people watching us?"

"It wasn't that kind of surveillance—just my computer, probably phone calls, maybe my movements about the city."

"How can you be so sure?"

It was an accusation he couldn't counter.

She looked up at the ceiling with a hint of frustration. "All this time, and you give me nothing. I learn what I suspected all along from a girl. I'm the last to know."

He shook his head, saying, "You're not the last to know. They don't know anything, only that I have a background in intelligence. It's something I never told you about because—well, hey, despite my form over the last few days, it's something you're not really meant to talk about. And I didn't tell you because it ended badly, because it's not a chapter of my life that I'm particularly proud of."

She looked skeptical. "Is there a part of your life that does fill you with pride?"

"When you put it like that—I don't know. I had a few good years in my late teens."

Despite everything, she laughed a little, and he was absurdly grateful for that, suggestive as it was that there was still something to hold on to.

"I'm sorry, that was unfair."

"No, Adrienne, it wasn't. I've been a lousy boyfriend. I've held back with you and not been straight, and I didn't realize how much I loved you until I got back and found you gone. If I'm honest, it even took me a while to realize it then."

"I'm flattered."

"But I am in love with you, Adrienne. That has to count for something. Okay, not very much if you're not in love with me anymore."

"Of course I am!" The words came out almost as a gasp, and she looked hurt and emotional that he could have even doubted her love. He thought again of the tears Jonas had told him about, wishing he could undo them.

He moved closer, putting his hand up to her cheek, her skin soft and hot to the touch.

"You're hot—are you okay?"

She smiled. "I'm fine. But thank you for saying I'm hot."

He smiled, too, and said, "Oh, I don't even need to say that you're *hot*."

He let his hand slip down across her shoulder, then traced his fingers across her breast. Her body seemed to respond to his touch, but almost instantly she reached up, grabbing his hand and holding it firm over her heart.

"No more secrets."

"No more secrets," he said.

"Then tell me what's going on. Why are they watching you? What's on the USB stick?" He looked surprised. "Yes, she told me about that too, so you don't fool me—it's why you have Mathieu's laptop."

He looked at her, earnest as he said, "I can't tell you." She pulled his hand away from her and let it drop. "Not yet, because I'm not even sure myself what it's about. I left under a cloud six years ago, but I thought it was done, finished with."

"And it isn't?"

"Maybe not." She looked frustrated again, and he said, "I'm not being evasive, Adrienne, I just don't know what's going on. They appear to be raking over the past, but I don't know why. I don't even know if I need to do anything about it."

"How can you do nothing? People are spying on you. I can't come back to an apartment like that."

"So you might be coming back?"

Almost involuntarily, she shook her head. "I don't know. I don't know if I can believe you anymore. I don't know how much of the person I've known is a lie."

"Most of it." She looked shocked, as if she might have misheard. "I only thought about it the other day . . . I don't know how you stayed with me for so long. I'm cold, distant, I keep secrets—and I don't know if I'll ever be able to not keep secrets. I know it must seem like I'm not even there most of the time."

"You're too hard on yourself." Then she thought about it and said, "But all those things are true, most of the time, and I've loved you in spite of them. I've loved you in spite of them but I can't anymore. It's not even about secrets, although if I *were* to come back there could be no more—it's about living, about the way we never discuss . . . getting married, having a family."

"Is that what you want?"

She laughed, perhaps at the hopelessness of it all, and after a moment she said, "You know, there's a quote from Antoine de Saint-Exupéry, about love not being a matter of staring into each other's eyes, but both staring out together in the same direction. With you, it feels like we're both looking in different directions."

She stood up abruptly. He tried to reach out for her again, desperate for her not to go. Even being admonished by her, in ways and for things he did not fully comprehend, he still wanted just to be with her. But she moved away too quickly, and how could he explain that, despite his continuing need for secrecy, he would be different, that something about this last week had changed him.

"Adrienne—" She stopped and put a finger to her lips. Quieter, he said, "Will you be back?"

"I don't know. Will you?" He smiled, acknowledging the point, finally reduced to its most concentrated form. She hesitated then, near the door, and said, "Do you remember the last time we spoke, when you called from Béziers?"

"Of course."

"Do you remember what I said to you?"

"No. No, I don't."

She smiled—a smile tinged with sadness—as she said, "Because I said almost nothing at all. I had things I wanted to talk to you about, but you didn't ask me anything, just told me about your research and your hotel and the journey and the hire car. It was the final thing, to make me decide, so I came here, where people would want to talk with me about the things I wanted to talk about."

"We could talk about them now."

"But I don't want to, not anymore. Goodnight, Finn."

He watched her glide away, then turned and looked at the laptop. He took the memory stick out of his pocket, but decided against looking at the material again tonight, doubting there was anything more he could learn, not even wanting to think about it.

That memory stick now seemed to represent the final, perhaps insurmountable, obstacle to Adrienne's return. She still loved him, a revelation of beauty in itself, one that amazed him—and there had been something there, an understanding that he wanted to be more open with her.

But the memory stick remained, its cryptic contents speaking of secrets he couldn't share with her, not yet and maybe not ever. It represented an obstacle in another way, too, because until he found out what they wanted from him, he wouldn't want her to return. How could he, when he had no idea how safe either of them would be?

History

Monday was a long day for him, and Louisa hadn't been exaggerating when she'd told him he'd have drudge work to do. For most of the morning, the rest of the office was conspicuously quiet.

At lunchtime, six extra bodies arrived from London, including one, Rachel Rose, who'd worked with him before.

She popped her head around his door and said, "Hello, stranger."

He got up, and she came into the room and kissed him on both cheeks, reverting to their old Mediterranean routine. She was one of those people who had a slightly crumpled, just-woken-up face; he always imagined she'd age badly, but the effect for the time being was to make her all the more attractive somehow.

"You're looking good, Rachel."

"You're looking . . . okay. Better than when we were married."

He laughed. They'd never been married, but had acted it a couple of times for work purposes.

"You here for this Sparrowhawk business?"

She nodded and said, "You not in on it?"

"Long story, but no, I'm leaving." She did a double take and he added, "Longer story. I have a girlfriend, too, local journalist . . ."

"Good for you. But even so—" Someone called her from along the corridor, and she smiled and said, "Let's catch up, if we can, before the weekend."

"Sure. Good to see you, Rachel."

"You too, Finn."

She walked out and he went back to his desk. Both of them knew they were unlikely to have a longer conversation in the coming week, and not just because the operation would use up all her waking hours and eat into her sleep.

Finn was on the outside now, and over the next few days, as the team's ties strengthened, his exclusion would become all the greater. It was the culmination of a process that had begun years before, when he'd started working with Naumenko—and there was some irony in Rachel being here now, because she'd been with him the first time he'd met Alex.

Very soon, this would no longer be his world, and he felt that keenly now, a passive observer as the preparations for Sparrowhawk ebbed and flowed around him.

Louisa wasn't around, but Castle had reappeared and seemed to be running things at an operational level. He didn't once acknowledge Finn's presence, even when passing him in the corridor, although Finn sensed this wasn't just for the sake of preserving his cover. For whatever reason, Castle didn't like him—maybe just because he was quitting.

Midway through the afternoon, Finn received an email. It was from a Gmail account in the name of "Brodsky1051" and was phrased as if he was one of Finn's regular contacts, with the message signed off "BB." Finn had never heard from him before, and doubted he even existed.

The email confirmed that the *Maria Nuovo* would arrive in Kaliningrad sometime after midnight in the early hours of Saturday morning, gave the precise location of the dock that would be used, even the license-plate number of the truck that would be meeting it. A couple of supporting documents were attached.

He'd find out tomorrow how keen Karasek was to believe it, a decision he guessed would be more about his desire for the girl than about getting his hands on a ton of cocaine. Finn doubted even Louisa appreciated how deranged Karasek was over Katerina.

He was getting ready to leave just before five, when Harry stopped by, his coat already on.

"You leaving?"

"Yeah, I am," said Finn. "You're not, though, surely?"

"Just for a few hours." He looked out into the corridor before saying, "I'm going home to eat, but I'll be back later. Walk with me?"

"Sure."

They walked casually enough as they left the building, and Finn didn't bother to look for a tail because he was certain there would be one. As ever, the temperature had crashed with the onset of evening, and Harry looked all the happier for it—Finn had never known anyone to like the cold more than Harry.

Finn said, "What do you make of Rachel?"

"She's okay. You used to work with her, didn't you?" Harry glanced at Finn, who gave him a nod in response. "Must be weird for you, something like this kicking off and you're sitting on the sidelines."

"Yeah, I guess it's hitting home. But then I can afford to be sanguine—can't imagine Ed taking it so easily."

"As far as I know, Ed doesn't even know this is happening, and he's been held up in Moscow, won't be back until Friday. It'll almost be over by the time he gets back."

"Won't stop him claiming the glory."

"If there is any. I have a feeling Jerry de Borg's likely to make an appearance before this week's over. It just has that . . . smell about it."

"Harry—"

"Finn, there's something I need to say." He looked over his shoulder, checking the street behind them, and Finn wished he hadn't because it would have immediately raised the suspicions of whoever was tailing them. "I put the spare key for my apartment in your inside overcoat pocket earlier, while you were out of the office. Obviously, I'm heading back now because she'll be worried, but I'm not gonna be around much for most of this week, probably not until late at night."

Finn couldn't feel the key, hadn't been aware it was there, but he could suddenly sense it in his pocket, resting against his chest, and all the danger it represented. Harry wanted him to call in on Katerina, something he could hardly do without putting her in danger.

"I can't."

"I don't mean stay with her, I just mean call in on her, check she's okay."

They walked a few paces without speaking, and in that time Finn decided Harry already knew too much to hold back now.

"I'm being tailed, Harry. Less I tell you the better. You know how intense it'll be this week—I don't want you to know anything that might slip out."

Harry didn't respond physically, keeping his gait natural, his face fixed ahead, but he said, "You can at least tell me who's tailing you."

"Karasek's people. The bait Louisa used to draw him in, it's complex, but Karasek's under the impression I could lead him to the girl."

Harry laughed, finding some tainted humor in the situation, and said, "Don't tell me, Louisa doesn't have a clue how close to the truth she is on that?"

"You're the only other person who knows. Even Alex doesn't know who the girl is."

That revelation seemed to fill Harry with doubt and he said, "Promise me she'll be safe with him, Finn." His tone was oddly possessive, making Finn uneasy in some way.

"I trust him completely." As he said it, he thought back to the conversation he'd had with Louisa, about trusting no one.

"Well that'll have to do, I suppose. But look, if you can shake the tail off—I mean, if you're sure of it—try to call in and see her. She'd really appreciate it. So would I."

Again, Finn felt a little uncomfortable with his tone.

"Sure." They'd been walking toward Harry's place, but now Finn realized it wasn't wise to walk all the way there. "But listen, I should leave you in a minute, head off home, not give the tail any ideas."

Harry nodded but didn't respond, looking deep in thought, then finally he looked at him as he said, "I'm falling for her, Finn."

"What?"

"I know it's crazy, but—"

"Crazy? She's thirteen years old. She's a child!" Harry looked ready to stop walking, all the better to explain himself, but Finn, even with anger and fear building up inside him, remained casual as he said, "Keep walking. Keep it natural."

Harry nodded, like a drunk, not fully comprehending but going along with the order.

"Finn, I haven't done anything. I wouldn't, obviously."

"Oh, well, that's a relief, to know that my best friend isn't a pedophile."

"Jesus! Why do you have to talk like that? I don't mean anything sexual. Oh, what's the point? You wouldn't understand."

"Tell me, Harry, because I have to understand. It has to be something that I can understand."

"I don't know. I love being around her. She's smart, she's interesting, she's just . . . a beautiful person. And yeah, if she were six years older, it'd be different, but . . . I just hate the thought of not seeing her again after the end of this week."

"You know that's how it has to be."

Finn looked at him, and Harry turned and said, “I know. And Finn, I haven’t touched her. I wouldn’t. That’s not what I’m talking about.”

“I know.” But he thought of the way everyone liked Harry, of how young he looked, of the stability he’d given this girl over the last few days and how she might view it. “Promise me though, even if she says something or—she’s a kid, Harry, a kid who’s had a tough run, you have to remember that.”

“I do. I do. And I promise, you have nothing to worry about. I just needed to tell someone.”

“I know,” said Finn. And though he wished he hadn’t been told, he said, “I’m glad you told me. Okay, you gave me a bit of a scare for a minute there, but I’m still glad you told me. Now I’m taking a right—keep it casual.”

He veered into the street and Harry raised his arm and said, “See you tomorrow.” Finn waved back but he was struggling to keep his cool.

The one thing Finn couldn’t change about the coming week was the timetable, and yet he was overpowered by a growing sense of urgency. Without being any closer in real terms, it felt as if Karasek was homing in on the girl. And now Harry was going to pieces on him, and Finn felt responsible in some way, feeling he should have picked up on the signals.

He took a left and went into the Hotel Regent, a sleek business hotel that had good public phones in the lobby. The receptionist was checking someone in, and there were a couple of businessmen sitting on the minimalist sofas, their luggage beside them.

Finn made his way to one of the phones, but turned to face the entrance before making the call. It would be hard for the tail to follow him in without being conspicuous, particularly if he wasn’t in business clothes. No one came in.

When Alex came to the phone, he said, "It sounds like people are having fun in Tallinn."

"You heard?" Someone came into view outside in the street, peered into the lobby but almost immediately backed away when he saw Finn looking out. It had only been a glimpse, but Finn thought it was one of the guys who'd been playing cards on Saturday. "It doesn't involve me, anyway."

"Of course it doesn't. But you still want to meet?"

"I still want to meet. I'll be in Stockholm early on Saturday morning."

"Good, then we can indulge in our favorite subject. I'll be in the Vasa Museum all morning, so come and find me there."

"You'll let me know if anything changes."

Alex laughed. "I'm in good health, Finn. See you on Saturday."

"I'll look forward to it."

Alex's comment said it all. Only a health issue, or death, could force Aleksandr Naumenko to change his plans. He'd already reached that point of being almost untouchable—none of his former rivals powerful enough to take him on, governments going out of their way to court him.

Finn felt more confident as he walked the final stretch home through the busy streets, no longer concerned by the tail now that he knew he was only leading him home. Speaking to Alex, even just to confirm the details, had made Katerina's escape seem within reach again.

There were still plenty of things that could go wrong, but he was determined they'd be on the Friday-night ferry from Tallinn, even if it meant risking his own position. Because he'd talked a couple of times about trust these last few days, but now, for the first time in the eighteen months they'd known each other, he was wondering if he could really trust Harry.

Chapter Twenty-Two

Pablo and Henri woke him in the morning, finding it hysterical that he was sleeping on the sofa, clambering all over him, jumping up and down until Cecile came in and upbraided them with good humor and apologized to Finn.

The thaw between Cecile and Finn seemed to be lasting, and he wondered if it was because of what he'd done for Hailey, casting him in a different light. Perhaps he'd make a habit of rescuing runaways.

The mood was once more good over breakfast. Mathieu was having fun with the boys, appearing less parental with them than he did with Finn most of the time. Adrienne and Cecile were talking to Hailey, apparently making plans for an imaginary return trip to Paris—imaginary, he thought, because he couldn't foresee Ethan and Debbie allowing her to go off on tour any time soon.

If anything, during pauses in the conversation, he thought he noticed Hailey looking a little lost or sad. Was she thinking about the boy she'd left behind in Uppsala, the brief taste of a more exciting adult life she'd had there—or was it that she knew they would be home later that day, the reunion with her parents beginning to weigh heavily on her thoughts?

Finn had hoped he'd find another chance to speak to Adrienne, to reinforce what he sensed was the progress they'd made, albeit intangible, the previous night. She had other ideas, and appeared determined that they wouldn't be left alone together, that the lively atmosphere of the morning would not be sacrificed for things that had already been said.

So almost the only time she spoke to him directly was as he and Hailey readied themselves to go downstairs and get the taxi to Gare de Lyon.

"Bye, Finn."

"I'll call."

She nodded, only to say, "Do what you have to do first."

Finn noticed Hailey look at him, as if she also knew what that meant. Finn resented both of them for it in some way.

"Okay, if that's what you want," he said, sounding conciliatory rather than defiant. "But it may be some time. Take care."

The rest of them said their goodbyes. Mathieu and the boys came down to the street to wave them off, and Hailey waved excitedly back from the taxi. Finn noticed she had tears in her eyes as she finally faced forward again.

She smiled, wiping the tears away as she said, "It's silly, I know, but I'm so glad we came here. They're such a beautiful family."

"I suppose they are." He glanced behind, but of course they'd already driven too far and Mathieu had probably taken the boys back inside by now. "We forgot to call your parents."

"No, I called them last night. I called from the kitchen."

"Oh." He wasn't sure why he should feel put out by that—it wasn't as if he had some sort of ownership over her return—but he did feel put out, and couldn't remember her being missing and on her own at any point in the evening. The thought that Adrienne might have been there as she'd made the call left him feeling more dislocated. "Who did you speak to?"

"Dad."

"Was he okay? I mean, how did it go?"

"Okay, I guess. Mom was more hysterical the other day. Dad was kind of teasing about it, joking about how he hoped I'd got it out of my system. That was almost worse in a way, because it sounded like he was hurt but he didn't want me to know it."

Finn didn't bother to tell her that when she talked about "the other day," that had also been yesterday—the day had no doubt been so momentous to her that it felt like a week.

He said, "I think they're both hurt. It's hard for them not to see some kind of rejection in this."

"But that's not what it was about at all. They know how much I love them. They're great parents." He grimaced slightly, saying no more, and she relented. "I know. I know what I did was pretty crappy."

The taxi driver blasted his horn at someone on a bike who cut in front of them. The cyclist gave a couple of hand gestures in response and hurled a few specialized words in French that Finn didn't understand but that made Hailey laugh.

The two of them looked out at the streets and the traffic then, and when they got to Gare de Lyon they talked only of platforms and trains and other necessities. On the train, Hailey looked out of the window, her head resting against the side of the seat, and he thought she might fall asleep again.

But half an hour into the journey, she looked across at him as if only just remembering he was there, and said, "Do you mind if I say something to you—something personal?"

He did, alarms immediately sounding, but he could hardly admit to being intimidated by a fifteen-year-old girl.

"Go ahead."

"Okay. I think you'd be really dumb to let Adrienne go."

He smiled, almost laughed.

"I don't intend to let her go. We spoke last night. We have a few things we need to sort out, that's all."

"I just thought . . ." She stopped, uncertain, but he looked expectantly and she said, "I just thought things didn't seem great between you this morning."

"Yeah, well, if I'm completely frank, it probably didn't help that you told her about my past in intelligence and about the USB stick before I'd had the chance to tell her myself."

Hailey came back at him, surprisingly combative, as she said, "When would you have told her?"

"I don't know. When would you have told Anders that you're fifteen?"

"That's so unfair."

"Is it? I've lied for all these years about my past because that's the nature of clandestine work—you keep it secret." Even as he spoke, he was editing himself, a reminder that his real reason for keeping the secret from Adrienne was not the clandestine nature of his work but the darker truths that lay within his past, truths he didn't even want to revisit himself. "Maybe I should have been open, particularly with her, but it's a balancing act, one that's hard to get right."

"What was on the USB stick?"

"No, Hailey, we're not doing this. I appreciate you giving me the stick, and you and Jonas probably helped me out by hacking that network in the first place, but you're not involved in this, not anymore."

"Could it be dangerous?"

"Not dangerous enough to run away." She was ready to respond angrily, but realized he was teasing and smiled halfheartedly, as if at some corny joke from an uncle. "I don't know, probably not. But it deals with sensitive material and serious people, so the safest way to proceed is without getting anyone else involved."

"But Gibson definitely left, right?"

"He definitely left. The apartment's empty. And your part in this is over."

She looked offended by his final comment and said, "Okay, I only asked a question. He knew we hacked his network so I think I have every right to ask if we might actually be in danger."

"Maybe, but you're not. I doubt they have any interest in what you or Jonas did. But Hailey, don't ever ask me about any of this again, because I won't answer you."

As if he were a nagging parent, she gave a grudging "Okay!" And that was it, though she didn't fall asleep, she rested her head against the side of the seat again and looked out of the window for most of the journey. Only occasionally, as if to demonstrate that she wasn't sulking, she'd point to something or other and say, "Beautiful church," or, "The snow's almost gone off some of the upper slopes." She seemed disinclined for any further conversation than that.

It suited Finn, too, and he also looked out of the window for much of the journey. There had been rain, because he could see puddles here and there on roads and in fields, but the spring-like weather he'd left behind a couple of days ago was back in control, very few clouds in the sky, the landscape sun-drenched.

It created a false sense that he was returning to an idyll, but one that was now in danger. An idyllic country, perhaps, and his life had been as ordered as the place he'd chosen to live, but there had been little idyllic about it in retrospect.

It wasn't even the way he'd lived, the way he'd slowly starved his relationship of oxygen. The clue to the real problem was in the way he'd left the money in that numbered account, untouched for all these years. Because at some level, he had always expected his past to finally catch up with him.

Maybe that was the sole reason for him starting to open up this last week. Adrienne leaving him, Hailey disappearing—both counted for nothing against the cathartic realization that he no longer had to look over his shoulder. The thing that he'd secretly dreaded all this time was something he no longer needed to dread, it was now something he had to tackle head-on.

Chapter Twenty-Three

Hailey's nerves became more visible the closer they got to home, and by the time they were in the taxi from the station, she looked fragile enough that she might shatter if touched. She didn't speak, and nor did he.

When they got out of the cab, she looked up at her apartment and said, "Oh well, here goes."

"It'll be fine."

He looked up at the apartment himself, expecting to see one of them standing there looking out, but the windows were reflecting sky and he could see no movement beyond them.

They took the elevator, and when it opened on her floor he put his hand on the button to hold the door open.

She looked at him, nervous, as she said, "Aren't you coming with me?"

"You don't need me there."

"I guess not. So . . . Well, thanks, for everything." She looked ready to hug him but thought better of it, perhaps taking her cue from his body language. She picked up her backpack and walked along the corridor.

As she reached the door, she looked back at him and crossed her fingers, then pressed the buzzer. He was certain she had a key of her own, and he thought it summed up the momentous shift in her life this last week, that she temporarily felt unable to enter her parents' apartment uninvited.

He heard the door open and let his finger move from the button. The elevator doors closed and he went back to his own apartment. It felt too empty, more so than when he'd arrived back from Béziers. He wondered if Adrienne would press the buzzer when she came back—if she came back.

Thinking of her, he went into the study, and there, sure enough, he found her note where it had fallen on the floor. He opened it but it told him nothing new, only that she needed some time away, to think through what she wanted—in fact, reading it, Finn was glad he hadn't found it at the time because he wasn't sure he would have understood from it that she'd left him.

He did a quick search of the apartment while his laptop booted up, looking for telltale signs that anyone had been in there while he was away. Then he went back to the laptop and plugged in the memory stick. He took a new notebook and started scribbling down the information he'd glanced at the previous night.

He should have scanned the computer first, he knew that, searching for key-logging software or any other spyware. Of course, six years on, he might not have known what to look for or how to find it, but that wasn't why he didn't look. At some bloody-minded level, he wanted them to know that he was on to them.

He'd filled a couple of pages with notes when the buzzer sounded. He got up and went to the door, dreading that it was Debbie or Ethan coming to thank him, realizing now that he should have gone with Hailey to their apartment and got this done and out of the way.

But when he opened the door, it was Hailey standing there. It was unexpected, but part of the same problem, and he was ready to tell her that they needed to get some things straight, that their relationship might have changed, but not to the extent where he could be disturbed whenever she felt like it.

Within a moment he'd abandoned those thoughts, seeing how pale she looked, as if she might be in danger of fainting.

"What's wrong?"

She looked at him like someone who'd been hit over the head and was being asked to count fingers—an expression of confusion and wonder, not sure where she was or how she'd got there.

And her voiced was laced with that same confusion and wonder as she said, "Jonas killed himself."

"What are you talking about?" He'd said the words before realizing what an absurd question it was. The thing she'd said was completely rational—simplicity itself—she was telling him that a young man he'd last seen a few days ago had since committed suicide.

"Yesterday, he did it yesterday. Don't you get it? While we were having fun in Paris . . . If only we'd got a connecting flight."

She started to cry, and though he had seen her in tears or upset several times over the last day and a half, there was something shocking and pitiful about her distress now, perhaps because he no longer saw it as the self-indulgent sorrow of youth but as something more adult.

He stepped forward and tentatively put his hand on her shoulder, realizing that until now he had not had any physical contact with her. Her response was immediate, throwing her arms around him, great heaving sobs issued directly into his chest, a release so great that he wondered if she had not sought the comfort of her parents first. Perhaps she had come to him only because of what he'd told her about Jonas, because he was in on the secret of her attraction to him and had revealed the reciprocation that neither teenager had imagined.

He felt no emotion himself, only a sort of curious anger. Why would he kill himself? There had been no signs of him being suicidal on Wednesday evening, nor in the note he'd left on Thursday morning. Finn didn't know him, it was true, had spent only a few hours with him in total, and yet he had never struck Finn as the kind of kid who would take that way out.

And yet, and yet . . . on Wednesday evening, for Finn's benefit, they had looked at Hailey's Facebook page, at Anders Tilberg's page, and learned about their relationship. Finn believed that Jonas hadn't looked at her page until that point, but he might well have looked at it many times since, drawn back by a sickening curiosity, particularly after they'd failed to return on Friday.

Jonas had been in love with Hailey, there was no question of that, and he had appeared sanguine about that love not being returned, had almost appeared to expect nothing more than her friendship. But perhaps witnessing her love for someone else had been enough to undermine his calm acceptance.

Yet it still didn't make sense to Finn. He may have known him for only a few days, but it was still well enough to know that Jonas would not have killed himself.

Finn held Hailey by the shoulders, and looked down at her, saying, "Was he on any medication at all?"

He realized that he knew the answer already, that it was only Hailey's parents who'd believed him to be in need of a prescription.

Still, she shook her head. "Nothing at all. He didn't believe in . . . what I mean is, there's a guy in school who's on medication for acne and Jonas even tried to talk him out of taking it. He thought it . . ." She started crying again.

"When did this happen? How?"

She looked up, oddly hopeful through the tears, as if just by asking questions he would come up with some solution or prove it all to be a mistake.

"Last night, they think, in the basement of his building. He . . . he hung himself."

"Okay, let me get my keys and I'll come back down to your apartment."

She nodded and let him go, and until now he hadn't realized that she was still hanging on to him. He grabbed his keys, then almost without thinking about it, he pulled the memory stick from his laptop and slipped it into his pocket, and they walked back down the stairs.

It had been little more than a subconscious action, but his retrieval of the memory stick summed up the worst of his fears about what was happening now. The thought of Jonas killing himself was bad enough, particularly if it had been induced by his exploration of Hailey's Facebook page, but the other possibility was even more sickening—that someone had killed him, either to get at Finn or because Jonas had delved too deep.

Finn thought back to the note he'd received on Thursday morning, trying to remember what he'd done with it, because although he could remember the two sentences that had been written there, he wanted to check.

The first had been simple enough—*BGS = BRAC GLOBAL SYSTEMS, BASED IN THE CAYMAN ISLANDS*—and he'd made a mental note to himself at the time, to tell Jonas that he shouldn't look any further into BGS, that it could be a dangerous thing to do.

But that had been only two days ago, probably thirty-six hours before Jonas had been found dead. It seemed impossible to believe that he could have dug far enough for them to silence him—a teenager—within such a short time frame. It seemed impossible, except for the fact that this was Jonas, and that the other sentence he'd written had made his intent clear: *NOTHING ELSE YET BUT MORE SOON.*

Chapter Twenty-Four

Debbie and Ethan looked as numb as they had earlier in the week, one crisis replacing the other. Finn couldn't help but think, though, that their crisis had been resolved, and this one they would be able to leave behind—as upsetting as it might be, it was not their child.

Hailey sat on the sofa next to Debbie and nestled up against her, dropping her head onto Debbie's shoulder, as if she wanted to undo her identity change and recast herself as a little girl. Finn sat on one of the armchairs.

Ethan paced up and down for a few moments, finally sitting on the other side of Hailey and taking her hand, which she gave willingly, as he said, "I always feared something like this would happen. Whether or not we were right about his condition, Jonas was—I don't know—too special for the world."

Hailey raised her head and looked at him. Finn thought she might challenge Ethan's comment, but she stared hard at her father for a second and said, "That's so right. He was too special, or the world was too ordinary for him."

"What nonsense." All three of them looked at Finn. "How special is too special? Einstein? Hawking? People kill themselves all the time, and you don't help anyone by mythologizing them."

Ethan looked confused and hurt as he said, "But Finn, we can't help Jonas now, whatever we do. I certainly don't see what good it does to disrespect his memory."

Hailey and Debbie's expressions suggested a solidarity with Ethan, a wall of unease that was accusatory in some way. It was as if they had suddenly been reminded who Finn really was, the person they'd known all along rather than the aberration of this last week.

He tried to look conciliatory as he said, "I'm not trying to disrespect him, and I know we can't do anything to help him now, but . . ." He was reluctant to say any more of what he was thinking, and said finally, "What do we know?"

At first it didn't look as if anyone would reply, but then Debbie cleared her throat and said, "Sam called this morning, that's his father, because he thought Hailey would want to know—he knew about Hailey going missing but he knew she was due back. He was distraught, naturally." Her voice caught a little and Finn noticed Hailey squeezing her mother's hand. "Theirs is an old building and there are several rooms in the basement, one used as a laundry room. Jonas hadn't come home for dinner. Then, last night, one of the residents went down to the laundry room and she had her dog with her, one of those little toy things. The dog ran off into one of the empty rooms, and when she went to look for it, she found Jonas hanging from one of the beams."

Hailey started to sob quietly, burying her face farther into her mother's shoulder.

"When was he last seen?"

"Not since getting out of school."

"He didn't leave a note?"

"Not that we know of. We didn't ask." Debbie thought about it and added, "But Sam said they couldn't understand it, that there'd been nothing to suggest he was unhappy."

Ethan said, "I guess all parents think that."

Finn was once again aware of the parallels with the Portmans' own situation a few days earlier, but he didn't think Ethan had meant to make a comparison, and the other two didn't appear to pick up on it.

Hailey said, "Mr. and Mrs. Frost are such cool people."

"That's Jonas's surname," said Debbie.

"He knows that, Mom." Finn hadn't known it, but then Hailey's thoughts touched on something else and she looked newly upset as she said, "His poor sister! She's so cute, how terrible for her." Finn remembered Jonas saying how his little sister idolized Hailey.

"You should go and see them," said Finn.

Hailey took a moment to realize he was talking to her and then said, "Oh, I couldn't, and they wouldn't want to see me, not now."

"I have to go and see them," said Finn. "Ethan, Debbie, I wonder if one of you could call them, ask them if it's okay for me to go over there, tell them who I am."

Before they could answer, Hailey said, "I don't get it, why would you want to go see them? You hardly knew him."

"I don't want to go and see them, but I feel I have to, just to satisfy myself that he really did kill himself."

Debbie said, "Finn, he hanged himself."

Finn nodded, but Ethan joined up the dots rapidly and said, "Oh God, you think this might have something to do with you, with Gibson and the whole thing."

"I don't know. I hope not. But Jonas left a note under my door early on Thursday morning, saying he'd found out who Gibson worked for. I'd intended to tell him to forget about it as soon as I got back. It's probably nothing more than a coincidence, but for my own peace of mind, and perhaps for his family's, I'd rather be certain."

Though he wasn't sure what peace of mind would come to the family from finding out that Jonas had been a murder victim rather than a suicide. And if it proved to be the former, he didn't expect them to feel too well-disposed to the person who'd inadvertently set Jonas on that path, but he still had to go.

He hadn't voiced it, but there was another family's peace of mind at stake here, and again it was Ethan who immediately saw the tangential but very real risk to his own daughter's safety if Jonas had been murdered.

He stood up urgently and said, "I'll make the call." And he left the room.

Hailey looked astounded by her father's sudden capitulation, but then the reality of the situation hit her, too, and she said, "If he was killed, then I could be in danger, too."

Debbie looked from her daughter to Finn with increasing levels of fearfulness.

Finn shook his head. "I don't think so, and I hope I can rule it out even for Jonas."

Debbie didn't like his response and said, "But what will you do, Finn, if he was killed and it was these associates of yours? We can't just go from day to day wondering if they might come after Hailey. If he was murdered, it would be the result of your mess—"

Hailey interrupted, full of self-reproach as she said, "No, it wouldn't be Finn's fault. It would be mine. If I hadn't encouraged Jonas to hack Gibson's network, if I hadn't run away, none of this would have come out. Jonas wouldn't have gone searching. I'd never have done it like this if I'd known, but we thought Gibson was just a nobody."

Gibson *was* a nobody, thought Finn—that was the whole point.

"Look, I don't think it helps anyone to start apportioning blame. Chances are, he killed himself, and that's no less tragic, but I want to be sure."

Ethan came back into the room and sighed heavily before saying, "You can go over whenever you want." Debbie looked up at her husband, surprised. He looked back at her and said, "Sam thinks it's suspicious, too." Ethan glanced at Finn then, a look that seemed to warn him to tread carefully, to appreciate the fragile state of the people he was dealing with.

Finn said, "I'll go over right away, if you could give me the address."

"You won't need it," said Hailey. "I'll come with you."

Debbie looked disturbed by the change of heart and said tentatively, "Honey, I'm not sure that's a wise thing to do."

Hailey looked at her mother and said with conviction, "Mom, it's the wisest thing I've done in a long time. I have to go."

There was no further objection, just a lost look in Debbie's eyes, as if she were wondering if their daughter had really returned, if that little girl of memory would ever truly return to them, or if this headstrong young woman was who they'd have to deal with from now on.

Finn stood up, glad that Hailey was coming along. It would offer a distraction from his business there. And Hailey might have as much of an idea on how to access Jonas's computer as he'd had about cracking her virtual world. That was what it all came down to for Finn—what Jonas had been doing with his computer these last two days, and what that might suggest about the way he had died.

Chapter Twenty-Five

Once they were in the taxi, Hailey said, "I'll never forgive myself. It was my fault."

She sounded overly dramatic but he knew it was a front, a way of concentrating on some hypothetical tragedy as a way of not thinking about the simpler truth of Jonas being dead.

It occurred to him, too, that Hailey might well be able to blame herself whatever the truth of Jonas's death. She'd already outlined her culpability if he'd been killed, but if they got into his computer and found that he'd looked at her Facebook page a hundred times in the hours before his death, she would feel equally responsible.

And she would be wrong on both counts, so Finn said, "Whatever happens, it's not your fault and it's not mine. If it was . . ." He hesitated, conscious of the taxi driver. "If it was suspicious, then the only people responsible are those who thought they had to silence a fifteen-year-old boy. We all make mistakes, we overlook things that could have prevented this or that, but that doesn't make us responsible—other people have to take that guilt."

Involuntarily, his mind skipped back to Tallinn, to Kaliningrad, Sparrowhawk, Harry Simons, to all the things he could never quite leave behind.

"What will you do?" He looked across at her as she spoke. "If you find out it was someone else, what will you do?"

He realized now that, in some way, too many loose threads had been left hanging six years ago, in the debacle of Sparrowhawk, in his own affairs. But what could really be done? In the real world, lone operators did occasionally try to run up against organizations like that, but they never achieved anything, except perhaps an anonymous death for themselves.

"Let's just find out what happened first."

"But . . ."

He looked at her and could see the desperation in her eyes, as if Finn's actions could somehow undo all of this.

"Hailey, I don't know what I'll do, and it's best you don't ask, but you can give me some information. What do his parents do?"

"His dad's a professor at the university, his mom's a physicist."

"Names?"

"Sam and Maria. His sister's called Alice."

"I don't think I'll need to talk to the sister."

Her voice was laced with contempt as she said, "I just thought you might be interested in knowing her name, as they've just had a death in the family."

"Of course, I'm sorry." He looked at her. He felt uneasy with himself, fearing that not very much had changed in the last week after all. "Jonas said she was younger."

"Eleven," Hailey said, grudgingly allowing him back in. "I can't imagine what they must be going through."

Finn nodded. "What would be worse—knowing your son killed himself, or that he'd been murdered?"

She stared at him, helpless, and after a moment she said, "Each has to be devastating in its own way, I guess, but I think murder is worse." Finn nodded and she added quickly, "But more than anything, I think you would want to know. Wouldn't you?"

"I think I would."

She looked at a loss, as if there were too many things here to contemplate, not only the death of Jonas but the question of how he'd died, the equally intractable puzzle of what his family had to be going through. Finn sympathized—it was a puzzle even Jonas might have struggled with.

The car pulled to the side of the road, and he paid and they got out. It was an old building, grand, and inside it had the feel of discreet money, even by Swiss standards.

Sam Frost was quick to open the door when they reached the apartment. Finn had never seen him before, not quite as striking as his son, though there was a resemblance, and a look in his eyes that suggested the life had gone out of them.

Hailey hugged him immediately and then stepped back, grinding her words through a clenched throat as she said, "This is Finn."

"Thanks for coming over, Finn." Even though he'd known it in advance, he was surprised by the easy Australian accent.

Finn shook his hand and said, "I'm sorry for your loss—he was an amazing boy."

Sam nodded, holding the muscles of his face rigid, as if he feared what might happen if he lost control of them.

"Come in." They stepped into a large entrance hall. It looked like a big apartment. "Maria's sedated. Her mother came in from Salzburg first thing this morning—she's looking after Alice."

Hailey said, "How is she?"

Sam shook his head.

"Go in and see her if you want—she's in the living room."

Finn said, "Sam, we're here—"

"I know, Ethan told me. You don't think he killed himself."

"I think that's a possibility."

"So do I. I know Jonas was different, the way he thought and all that, but he wouldn't kill himself. Someone did this to him. It's the only explanation."

Finn felt queasy. Far from having to persuade Sam Frost, he sensed how impossible it would be to convince him if it looked as if Jonas *had* killed himself.

"I need to see his room."

"This way." They followed him to a bedroom that once again was large when compared with the apartments Finn and the Portmans lived in. The walls were covered with posters of Escher prints, startling optical illusions that somehow seemed to sum up the boy and the riddle in front of them now. Sam saw him looking and said, "He loved Escher. They're mostly copies, of course, but some of them are original."

"Originals?"

"I mean he thought them up himself." Then, understanding Finn's confusion, he said, "Jonas drew all of these. He copied most from prints in books, but some are his own designs."

"That's amazing," said Finn, and stepped closer to look at some of the drawings, seeing afresh what a remarkable kid had been lost to the world here.

The room was scrupulously tidy, but he noticed one of his distinctive hats on a chair and was caught unawares by the memory of Jonas's last words to him, about how he had seven hats but one didn't fit anymore. The thought of him standing there in the street, calling out an explanation of the hats, ambushed him with emotion.

He put it quickly out of his mind, and turned to a large desktop computer on the other side of the room.

"We need to turn this on."

Sam switched it on as he said, "It's not as if we haven't tried, but it's password protected."

Finn noticed Hailey, staring across the room and yet into space, her thoughts elsewhere, and he needed her to hold it together for the time being, so he said, "Hailey, do you have any idea what his password might have been?"

She jumped a little, her attention focused again. "He changed it all the time . . . random things, the kind of stuff I'd never remember."

Sam had taken a step back and was looking at the screen, which was already asking for a password. Finn sat down in the chair in front of the desk and looked up at the monitor, and at a yellow Post-it note stuck to the side of it:

DISREGARD

Sam saw him looking and said, "We've tried that, and been through the thesaurus—nothing."

Finn studied the note, understanding immediately that Jonas hadn't written it to himself. It was in block capitals, and Finn felt a slight chill as he realized it had perhaps been written specifically for him. A word came to mind, the thing that Gibson had been told to disregard, and he typed *Albigensian* into the box, hoping for some reason that it proved incorrect.

The password was accepted, the computer completing its boot-up, and Sam Frost said, "I don't get it, what did you type?"

"Albigensian. It's just something the note brought to mind."

Sam's voice was a dangerous mix of hope and confusion as he said, "So he wrote that note for you—he knew you'd look at it."

"Clearly he hoped I would."

Hailey said, "Albigensian? That was something we found on Gibson's network. Something about a crusade."

Sam looked from Finn to Hailey, and with a hint of dread, Finn realized before he spoke what he was about to say.

"Whose network? Gibson? Who's Gibson?"

"We hacked my neighbor's network, or at least Jonas did, on my computer, just to prove to me that it could be done." She stopped there, for which Finn was grateful.

Finn opened the Internet browser and clicked to look at the history, hoping that Jonas hadn't deleted it, a hope based on the fact that Jonas wouldn't have given him a clue to the password if there was nothing of interest on here.

At the same time, he hoped there would be nothing in that history that the boy's father or the girl Jonas had loved wouldn't want to see. He needn't have worried, and nor should he have feared that Jonas might have spent the last day of his life looking at Hailey's Facebook page.

His browsing history still didn't provide any comfort, though. There were pages on Cayman Island government websites, company searches, links to news sites, and others on varying subjects, including Karasek and Helsinki. Most disturbingly, he'd searched on incidents in Estonia and Kaliningrad, suggesting he'd dug further in twenty-four hours than Finn could ever have imagined. A smart intelligence organization would have recruited him, not killed him.

Not that Finn believed his old outfit could have been involved in something like this. Part of it might have been, in the way that parts of it had always operated outside the rules and without official sanction. Louisa Whitman would never have been part of something like this, but there were plenty of others who would.

He turned to Hailey and said, "Which word-processing software did he use?"

"Word—it was about the only Microsoft program he could tolerate."

Finn nodded and searched for documents, but found none. He looked around the desk and opened a drawer, hoping to find disks or memory sticks, then stopped, remembering in a startling moment of clarity that Jonas liked to write things down.

Sam was looking over Finn's shoulder at the history still visible on the browser, and said, "I don't understand—what is all this?"

"He was researching." Finn pushed the chair back and stood up. "The network Hailey mentioned, it belonged to a guy called Gibson who was spying on me."

Hailey looked uneasy and said, "I'll go see Alice."

Finn turned to look at her, but she was already heading out of the door.

He turned back to Sam and said, "When he found out, he seemed keen to find out more. I tried to warn him off. It goes without saying that I didn't think it would lead to this, and I certainly didn't think he'd dig as far as he seems to have done."

"What are you talking about? Someone was *spying* on you? Why? Who are you?" He didn't leave time for Finn to answer, saying, "And you let Jonas get involved? Why would you do that?"

"I didn't let him get involved. If they hadn't hacked Gibson's network, if Hailey hadn't run away, I never would have known about it. Jonas helped me to find Hailey—the very nature of that help meant that he learned about the surveillance operation." Finn thought about it and said, "If I'd known him better, or even a little longer . . . but you're right, I should have realized."

Sam Frost put his hands to his bowed head and stood like that for a second, then let them drop again and said, "Let me get this straight, you're saying this proves that he was murdered?"

"I think so. I'll need to look into it in more detail, but it seems plausible, even likely."

Sam's anger was shifting visibly, from an amorphous sense of suspicion that his son hadn't killed himself, to something more specific, a single person he could blame—Finn.

"You're saying he was murdered by people who had you under surveillance—and, mate, now that I think about it, I don't even wanna know why you're under surveillance—and that's because, what, you told him stuff and got him curious?"

"No, it was information he—"

Sam swung for him, his fist flying up hard toward Finn's face. Finn surprised both of them by deflecting Sam's arm and grabbing it by the wrist, putting his other hand against Sam's throat. They made eye contact, expressing that mutual surprise, Sam wondering who Finn really was, Finn wondering how those instincts had stayed so fresh, and then Finn let go.

Sam let his hand drop and looked from left to right, as if looking for a way out, the thoughts and the anger stacking up again behind his eyes. Finn saw it coming again even before Sam himself knew he would throw another punch. This time he didn't deflect it, knowing he had to let Sam land that punch, knowing that he probably deserved it.

He felt the fist meet his cheek with a dull thud, was knocked back a step. Sam hurt his hand in the process and shook it afterward, wincing, and swiveled the chair around and fell into it, his head sunk onto his chest.

He was silent through a few deep breaths, then said, "Sorry."

Finn looked down at him. "You don't owe me an apology. I owe you one, but I swear I had no idea this would happen. I wouldn't have let it happen if I had."

At first it looked as though Sam might not respond, but then, without looking up, he said, "He was murdered." Though he'd suspected it all along, he seemed hollowed out by even a partial confirmation of that possibility.

"I think so."

"So we should call the police . . ." He sounded doubtful.

Finn thought through that process, adding it up in seconds—the difficulty in persuading them of what had happened, the way their investigation would be hampered at every turn, the certainty that no one would ever be charged with the crime.

And he knew instantly what he needed to do, not only for Jonas, but for himself. Because this was about him first and foremost, and now that these people had broken cover he doubted they would ever leave him alone, not until they'd got whatever it was they were after.

"We could go to the police. It's one of your options, Sam. I think your son was murdered, I'm certain of it, his death made to look like suicide. I'd have to give the police information about myself, which I'm more than willing to do, to convince them that this was indeed a murder. They'll investigate, but I can tell you now that they won't find anybody." Sam looked up, tears in his eyes. "They won't find anybody, or if they do, strings will be pulled, and for diplomatic reasons no one will be brought to justice, not in any way that would satisfy you."

"I don't understand, how . . ." Sam stopped, his thoughts shifting. "You said going to the police was one of the options?"

Finn nodded. "The other is that you don't go to the police, and the verdict will be suicide, though you'll know differently. You don't go to the police, and you accept my promise that I'll track down the people who did this and I'll kill them, every one of them."

Sam stared at him, open-mouthed. Perhaps because of that single intercepted punch, he didn't seem to doubt that Finn was serious, or that he could do it.

"I can't make a decision like that. And you don't have any real evidence, not yet."

"I'll get the evidence, and you don't have to make a decision as such. Just tell me you won't be going to the police. Answer from the heart, Sam, and tell me if you want to make that call."

Sam nodded, certain of the kind of justice he wanted, but still said, "I don't know, I . . . you know, if you were certain . . . but Maria—she couldn't know—"

"What are you saying, Sam?" They both looked to the door. Hailey was standing there with a woman who Finn presumed was Maria, Jonas's mother. It was Maria who'd spoken, with sorrow and pity and love. She looked at Finn now and said, "Mr. Harrington, I've just overheard your exchange. My husband is upset, as you can imagine, but the reason he doesn't want me to know is that we do not believe in an eye for an eye, just as we do not believe in capital or even corporal punishment."

She stepped into the room. Once again, there was a slight resemblance to her son, most notably in the striking eyes, but it seemed that two averagely attractive people had combined to produce a beautiful child. Maria Frost looked less battered than her husband, no doubt thanks to the sedation.

Finn noticed that Hailey stayed in the doorway, looking on with a mixture of concern and awkwardness.

When Maria reached them, she looked down at her husband and smiled, then back to Finn as she said, "So you think Sam has been right all along, that our son was murdered?"

"I'm afraid I do."

"You're basing this on the result of some Internet searches he made?"

She sounded skeptical but he said, "Yes, and I'm also aware of how flimsy that sounds, but I'm still certain of it."

She nodded, accepting his certainty if nothing else. "And you could do these things that you talked of to my husband?"

"I could and I would, but not without your approval, and not until I know the truth of what happened."

"The truth? The truth is that our son died, and nothing we do will ever bring him back."

She rested her hand on Sam's shoulder and gave it a light squeeze. He looked up at her and smiled.

"I made our beliefs clear, but a belief is nothing until it's tested. I wish we could have remained high-minded our whole lives, I wish it so much, but this is where we are. We won't be going to the police, Mr. Harrington." She turned and looked at him, and gave him a faint smile, something that looked like gratitude. And then she left the room.

Hailey remained still in the doorway, looking at Finn as if he'd transformed into a new person before her eyes. Finn gave her a reassuring smile, but she continued to stare blankly. He turned back to Sam.

"Sam, did you find Jonas's Moleskine notebook? In his pockets or his jacket, maybe in his bag?"

Sam shook his head. "We searched everywhere, just for a note. It didn't occur to me that the Moleskine was missing, but now that you mention it . . ."

"Maybe they took it." Finn looked around the room, wondering where they'd picked him up. The Post-it note suggested he thought something might happen, but Finn couldn't imagine them coming to the apartment. It was more likely that they'd waited for him as he got back from school. "Can I see where it happened?"

Sam nodded and stood, looking like an old man getting to his feet.

"And do you have a flashlight?"

"There are lights down there."

"Even so." Sam nodded and walked out of the room.

Hailey was still staring at Finn and he said, "You don't have to come down to the basement. In fact, maybe you shouldn't."

"I'd like to."

"Okay."

"Did you mean what you said?"

"You weren't meant to hear that."

"But I did."

He took a step toward her and noticed that she couldn't help but brace herself, as if she no longer felt entirely safe with him. He stopped a few feet from her.

"The people I think did this, I have unfinished business with them, but even if I didn't, and even though I only met Jonas a couple of times, I meant every word of what I said—I will find them and I will kill them."

"Have you killed anyone before?"

He smiled a little and shook his head, and she seemed to understand and accept that it was a question he wouldn't answer.

Sam appeared, holding out a flashlight, and Finn nodded and reached out for it.

And as they left the apartment, he realized that Jonas had not only played a part in helping Finn to see where he'd gone wrong these last years, he was now, inadvertently, helping him go back further still, to complete what should have been done in Kaliningrad.

Chapter Twenty-Six

When they got down to the basement, Sam pointed to an open doorway and said, "It's through there. The light's just inside. If you don't mind, I'll leave you here."

"Thanks," said Finn.

Hailey looked for a moment as if she'd changed her mind about seeing it herself, but she smiled sympathetically at Sam and said, "We'll come up before we go."

Sam nodded sadly and left.

Finn waited for Sam's steps to reach the top of the stairs, then walked through the door and turned on the light. It was a big room, and though the central floor space was extensive, it was far from empty, with various wooden boxes and other old items stacked around the edges of the room, some of them under sheets.

There were wooden beams in the ceiling, and he guessed that Jonas had been tied up to one of them. There was a smell of disinfectant, and a patch on the stone floor that had been washed down and still looked damp, even now.

Hailey spotted it and said, "They washed the floor. But there wouldn't have been any blood, would there?"

"Maybe they were just being cautious, not knowing how long the body had been there, but chances are there was urine on the floor."

She stared at him in disbelief, as if the violence of what had taken place here was only just becoming apparent to her. She'd probably imagined Jonas being drugged, his body hanging serenely as the rope starved his brain of oxygen. Perhaps she was only now beginning to imagine that he had struggled, that he had probably soiled himself, that his face would have been disfigured.

If she hadn't come down to this basement, she might have held on to all kinds of romantic notions about Jonas and the way he'd died, but any such dreams were shattered now. Jonas had died a miserable and frantic death, and even if he'd realized he was courting danger, he'd almost certainly failed to anticipate the violence that would be done to him here.

Finn turned on the flashlight, aiming the beam along the passageway that linked the basement stairs to this room. Then he moved into the center of the room and pointed the beam at ground level, among the boxes and crates that had been stored there.

Hailey watched him, her attention finally drawn from the trauma of that disinfected patch of floor, and said, "What are you looking for?"

"His Moleskine notebook."

"Why would it be down here?"

He made a mental note of the point he'd reached with the flashlight, and turned to her, saying, "It wasn't anywhere else. I think he was too smart to let them take it. But I think once he was in here, once he knew what they intended to do, he might have tried to hide it, throw it aside, in the hope that someone else would find it."

"You mean you?"

"Not necessarily."

"He left the note for you on his computer. It's like he knew he was in trouble, maybe even that they'd kill him, and he left all these clues for you to follow."

Finn doubted that even Jonas had foreseen his own death. She had a point about the messages, though, because since leaving that note under Finn's door it seemed that Jonas had been working exclusively as his agent.

He said, "I wish I'd been here, or that I'd seen him again before I left, because I would have told him to stop."

"It wouldn't have made any difference—once he got something into his head he couldn't let it go."

Finn remembered what Jonas had said about puzzles, and about Hailey not having the same kind of mind, how she could just leave a puzzle unsolved. Then he looked at her and realized she was resentful in some way, perhaps because Jonas had been her best friend, that secretly they had been in love with each other, and yet in his final days and hours Jonas had thought of leaving messages only for Finn, whom he had hardly known.

"Hailey, he left things for me because mine was the puzzle occupying him at the time. For days before that, he'd been obsessing about you and where you'd gone. For all I know, he thought this was part of the same thing. The simple fact is, he didn't plan on dying here—if he had, I'd have been the last person he'd have thought about contacting."

She nodded. "I guess you think I'm being selfish."

"In a good way." She smiled a little. "When I was leaving, I told Jonas I'd probably see him when I got back, and he looked slightly freaked out and said, 'It's not like we're gonna be hanging out.'" She laughed now, crying at the same time, wiping away the tears.

Then, quite abruptly, she stopped and pointed to a corner. "There's something on the floor over there." He aimed the flashlight in that direction, seeing nothing, but she said, "No, move over here. It's between those two crates."

He moved toward the middle of the room, standing almost where the floor had been cleaned, and now he saw it, what looked like a small black notebook. He moved closer, keeping the beam on it, as if he feared the darkness might swallow it up.

And he only turned off the flashlight once he'd picked it up—the Moleskine. He could imagine Jonas waiting for his moment, throwing the book toward this corner. The thought of that simple little act of bravery only reinforced the cowardice of the crime committed here.

"Is that it?"

He nodded and opened the book, turning through the pages of dense script before finding the last page Jonas had written on, in block capitals—a code in itself, Finn now sensed. At the top of the page was the name *GIBSON*, and below it were two addresses in Geneva. Next to one address he'd written *BGS OFFICE*, next to the other: *APARTMENT WHERE GIBSON IS STAYING*.

Finn tore the page out, then looked at the previous pages, but could decipher nothing of interest. There were a handful of comments about the Cayman Islands, which Finn knew would be a false lead—he doubted anyone from BGS had ever set foot there—and a line in which he'd written *Karasek—mafia?*, but the barely legible script didn't offer Finn anything he didn't know.

Possibly, Jonas had understood that, too. That was why he'd written only the final two pieces of information in capitals. By the time he'd done that, he might well have suspected they were on to him, so much so that he'd had time to share only the bare facts.

"Well?"

Finn looked up at her and nodded, and held up the torn page, saying, "If this is right, it gives me the first step." She looked ready to ask another question, but he cut her off. "I'm not teasing anymore, Hailey. I don't believe for a minute that you're in any danger right now, but these people are so tightly wound that they killed a teenager for digging into their whereabouts. People that afraid are unpredictable, so I just don't want you being involved any more than you already are."

She still looked ready to object, but backed down and said, "Okay. Do you think I could keep the notebook, just as something to remember him by?"

He held it out. "I don't see why not, as long as his parents don't mind."

She took the Moleskine and Finn turned out the light, and they went back up to the Frosts' apartment. Sam opened the door, looking expectant, and it was Hailey who said, "We found it. He'd thrown it into a corner." She handed the book over to Sam, who looked at it sadly, perhaps seeing its discovery as the final proof that Jonas really had been murdered.

He looked back up at Finn and said, "Did it have anything useful?"

"I've torn one page out, something that should help me a lot. I won't say more than that for now."

Sam nodded. "How's the face?"

"Stings a little, might have a bruise in the morning. Nothing serious."

Hailey glanced between the two of them, trying to make sense of the exchange, studying Finn's face and seeing nothing. If nothing was visible now, maybe it wouldn't bruise.

She appeared ready to speak, but before she could, Sam held out the book again and said, "Hailey, I know you bought this for Jonas for Christmas, and he loved it. Would you like to keep it? You know you can have something else from his room, any keepsake you want."

She nodded and took the book back, and now Finn understood why she'd asked for it. She appeared unable to speak, but kissed Sam on the cheek and walked through into the apartment, presumably to say her goodbyes. Finn realized he hadn't seen Alice at all.

"Would you like to come in, Finn?"

"No, thanks all the same. And you won't see me again for a while, but that doesn't mean I'm not doing anything."

The words felt like an echo of what he'd said to Debbie and Ethan at some point in the week, except it was too late to do anything for the Frosts. There would be some retribution, but this problem would not be solved.

"Yeah, I get that." He looked into Finn's eyes for a moment, searching, and said, "Why are you doing this, Finn?"

Finn looked to the side, making sure that Hailey wasn't on her way back, then said, "Honestly? A lot of reasons. I do feel angry about your son, and I do feel it was my fault in some way, but if I'm being straight, the fact that they killed Jonas makes me think they'll never leave me alone unless I get to them first."

He thought Sam might object to that admission, but he merely nodded. Perhaps an unsatisfactory explanation was better than none at all. And Finn had probably undersold himself—he was acting out of self-preservation, out of revenge for everything that had gone wrong in the past, but he was also acting out of conscience and a sense of moral outrage, traits that until that moment he'd believed he no longer possessed.

History

Karasek stared across the desk at him and said, "You have evidence, of course?"

"Of course." But Finn didn't move, just stared back. "I'm not sure that this is going to work though, Mr. Karasek, because you're not being entirely professional."

Karasek looked stung, and was clearly desperate to make a sharp reply, one that would no doubt come to him an hour or so from now.

In the absence of a decent comeback, he said, "Don't screw around with me."

"I know where the girl is, but I don't know the place myself. I've never been there, I have no plans to go there. So your guys who are tailing me are doing it for no reason, but if my people spot them, then we're both screwed."

Karasek seemed more comfortable now that he knew what the problem was, and said, "Don't get so rattled, Harrington. I thought people like you were used to being followed."

"I'll bring you the evidence you need by this time tomorrow. But if I see any of your guys following me, the whole thing's off."

"Relax, I'll make sure you're not followed any longer."

Karasek was looking superior again, but Finn was playing the paranoid card to his own advantage. He made a point of still appearing on edge, suspicious, as if convinced he was missing something.

"You've kept your promise? Not to mention it to your contact?"

"Naturally," said Karasek, bemused now. "He's not here, anyway. He's in Moscow until Friday."

"How do you know that?"

"How do you think I know? I kept my promise, that's all that matters to you." He looked at his watch. "I think we're done for today, but I look forward to seeing you tomorrow." He stood up, but leaned across the table and said, "Mr. Harrington, we both have promises to keep. If for one moment I think this is a plan to—"

Finn knew he'd get nothing else from him now, so he reverted to type and said, "I'm starting a new life, Mr. Karasek, and hard as it may be for you to believe, I've got bigger things to think about than taking you off the street. You're not important to me."

Karasek stared at him, full of hatred, and Finn had no doubt that if it weren't for the promise of Katerina at the end of all this, he'd have pulled his gun by now.

"You should be careful with that mouth of yours—one day you get killed for it."

Finn stood up. "This time tomorrow, I'll bring you the paperwork."

He left, stepping out into sunshine and a clear sky, deceptive because it was forecast to turn wet and cold by the end of the week. His phone didn't have a signal in the club, but it started to ring almost as soon as he was on the street. It was Sofi.

"I've been trying to call you."

"I didn't have a signal—is everything okay?"

"Somebody broke into my mom and dad's house this morning."

He stopped and turned, a natural movement but one that allowed him to check behind him and take anyone following by surprise. There were quite a few people on the street, none of them suspicious.

"Were they hurt?"

"No, they'd gone out."

"Was anything taken?"

"A little money, a few small things, nothing important. But I'm going out there. I'll spend the night."

"Do you want me to come?" Even as he said it, he knew he couldn't go.

Sofi produced a sharp little laugh and said, "Isn't that what caused the problem in the first place?"

"You don't know that. It could have been anyone."

"What were they looking for, Finn?"

It was pointless to argue it further, so he said, "I can't say, but whatever it is, they know it's not there now. What time will you be back tomorrow?"

"Probably in the morning. I'll go straight to work."

"Okay. I'm sorry if this was connected to me. A few more days and it'll be done with."

"I hope so." She ended the call, and only then did he appreciate quite how angry she was—no affectionate signing off, not even a cursory goodbye.

She'd never ended a call like that before, but then, they'd never argued as far as he could remember, not properly. It made him realize all the more that he needed out of this job, because they were good together, but they needed the space and time and freedom to be with each other fully.

He took a circuitous route home, stopping on the way for a coffee, behaving oddly enough that anyone following from a distance would have been forced to close in. He still couldn't see anyone, so it appeared that for the time being at least, Karasek had called his people off.

He cooked for himself, and realized it was another first. Although he'd been away plenty of times since Sofi had moved in, she'd never spent a night away when he was there. It wasn't a particularly big apartment, but he walked around it after washing the dishes, looking into each of the rooms, and it felt like he was rattling around inside it now.

He'd just gone back into the kitchen, ready to pour himself another glass of wine, when there was a knock at the door. He checked the spy hole and let her in.

"I was just about to have a glass of wine—would you like one?"

"Are you on your own?"

He smiled. "Louisa—enough."

She backed down, smiling herself as she said, "I'd love a glass, thank you, and I was sorry to hear about the break-in. It's not worth us getting involved, not now that Karasek knows the girl isn't there."

She followed him as far as the kitchen door and watched as he poured two glasses of wine, then stood back for him to lead the way into the living room. Once they were sitting, she raised the glass to him and took a sip.

Finn said, "Was it enough?"

"Not sure. He didn't mention Ed by name, of course. But it's persuasive nonetheless. Don't try to get any more out of him tomorrow, though—I thought I detected a hint of suspicion in his voice today."

Finn sipped at his wine, then put the glass on the table and said, "He's spoken to Ed since he went to Moscow."

She nodded, following suit with her own wine glass.

"Yes, and we're not entirely sure how he's done that, because Ed's being carefully monitored out there. But what's your take? Do you think he's talked to Ed about the *Maria Nuovo*—about you?"

Finn thought of Karasek's obsessive desire to get Katerina back, that thought mixed up now with the memory of Harry telling him that he was falling for her. It was a madness he couldn't quite comprehend, but he knew the way people acted around obsessions like that—obsessions of any kind.

"He won't tell Ed, and even the cocaine's a sideshow. This girl, whoever she is, this girl is all he's thinking about."

"All we really know about the girl is that she was in an orphanage, thirteen years old, that she was lured away and trafficked out here. I shudder to think what a man like Karasek would do to her."

"Presumably he knows the girl? I mean, if she was just a random girl he could replace her easily enough, whatever he wants her for."

Louisa smiled, leaned forward, and picked up her glass, taking a sip before putting it down again.

"We wondered about that, but we caught a couple of his men talking about it. The girl comes from some provincial city. Karasek was there on business and just happened to see her walking down the street. And that was all it took, he fell head over heels in love with her, and told his men to set about enticing her away."

It's not what you think—that was what Karasek had said.

"At least he doesn't want her for a snuff movie."

"That's a very male response."

He wasn't sure what she meant by that, but he said, "Louisa, I'm not suggesting being kidnapped and forced into a relationship with a man in his thirties is a happy outcome, but who knows where she is now, what danger she might be in."

Louisa nodded, accepting the point, the clearest suggestion yet that she didn't know what had really happened, and she looked vaguely hopeful as she said, "Someone rescued her from his man—a girl of her age couldn't have inflicted those injuries on her own—so we just have to hope that her rescuer is just that. And, beyond that, I'm afraid it's not really our problem."

"So what happens now?"

"Very simple. Take the documents to him tomorrow. Go away on your long weekend . . ."

"I can do that?"

"Yes, I think so. Actually, might be better for you to be away Friday and Saturday, let the air clear."

"You know I'm planning to stay here, so is there any reason, once it's all done, that I can't be exonerated?"

She sounded hesitant, and less than convincing, as she said, "No, I don't think so. *If* it all goes entirely to plan. If we don't achieve everything, you may have to keep that black mark—that's the nature of deep cover, I'm afraid."

Until now, he'd thought the only way the plan could fail was by not finding enough evidence against Perry. Karasek had been so firmly on the hook from the start that Finn had developed a certain complacency, and yet past experience told him there was every chance of the operation going wrong, of Karasek walking. And if it did, how could he stay in Tallinn then, or even in Estonia?

Louisa had known that from the start, of course she had, and he wouldn't give her the satisfaction now of knowing that he'd overlooked it. Instead, he said, "And Ed, what happens with him?"

"He arrives back Friday, we parachute him into Sparrowhawk as a glorified observer. And then, in the inquest, the comments you've elicited from Karasek will rise to the fore. All very low-key, the way we like it."

"Of course," said Finn, and he was glad he hadn't been privy to much of the detail for this operation, because the more he heard, the more doubtful he was about all of it.

Louisa looked at her watch and said, "Goodness, I'll have to fly, but well done, Finn, a good job so far. When will you be back?"

"Sunday morning."

"Good, well, let's catch up then."

He showed her to the door, and wondered once she'd gone why she hadn't asked him where he was going. But that was simply paranoia, because he knew the most plausible explanation was that Louisa simply wasn't interested.

He spent the next morning in the internal exile of the office, speaking to no one, hardly seeing anyone. He didn't see Rachel, or Harry, though in the latter case he was almost relieved. He was no longer sure he'd quite know how to look Harry in the face.

After lunch, he printed the documents and took them to Klub X. Karasek was overlooking the redecoration of his office, but immediately showed Finn into the other office. A woman was working in there, but she stood without needing to be told and left.

Karasek flicked through the papers once he was sitting, then settled back on the top sheet with a smile as he said, "This has your email address on it."

"That's correct. You could use that to get me in a lot of trouble. I thought about removing it, but I see it as a symbol of our mutual trust—if we're partners in this, we're partners, simple as that."

Absurdly, Karasek looked touched and had to restrain himself, saying only, "Good. I like that."

Finn stood and said, "I'll call on Sunday if that's okay—give you time to get back. We can arrange a drop for the money, and then I can tell you where she is."

Karasek stood, too, and shook his hand. "Until Sunday."

Despite the newfound air of friendship, Finn was still cautious as he walked away, and went back to his own apartment before leaving again and making for Harry's place.

When he opened the door, the apartment seemed empty. He walked into the living room. There was the bedding on a chair in the corner, and Finn was less forgiving of Harry's sloppiness this time.

"Katerina? It's me, Finn."

He heard soft footsteps and the bedroom door opened. She smiled broadly, but put her hand over her heart and said, "You scared me."

"I'm sorry."

"It's okay. I'm happy now." She came over and hugged him before stepping back, looking almost apologetic.

"So, you're speaking English?"

"Better than before. Harry teaches me." She put her finger up, stopping any reply he might make. "Would you like a cup of coffee?"

He nodded, impressed, and said, "Yes, I would, thank you."

"Please, sit down." She gestured to a chair, her tone full of the joy of having unlocked the mystery of another language, one she'd known in the classroom perhaps, but that was coming into its own now that she had an English-speaker for company.

She went into the kitchen, and Finn took his coat off and sat down. He noticed there were some English books on the table—novels, but also language-study books that Harry had bought for her. A short while later, she came back in with the coffees and sat on the sofa, a reminder of the first time they'd sat there together.

"So, do you like it here?" He was aware of speaking slowly, and wasn't sure he needed to anymore, because her English had leapt forward in just a few days.

"Yes, but Harry is busy now. I read the books." She pointed at the table.

He nodded, made a show of leaning forward to look at the books, even though he'd already done so.

"And you like Harry?" He felt guilty asking the question, innocuous as it was, as if he were betraying his friend's trust, when in truth he was just desperate to know that Harry hadn't betrayed his.

She nodded and said, "He's kind, and . . . funny. He makes me laugh."

"Good."

In some intangible way, he was reassured, because she didn't sound like a girl who was besotted. She sounded like a child describing a favorite uncle, not a potential boyfriend. He looked at her, and though she was beautiful, though she looked superficially older than her years, she so obviously still had the spirit of a child that he wondered at both Harry and Karasek, at how they could not see it, too.

"On Friday I'll come for you . . . Friday afternoon."

"Where may I go?"

"You'll be okay. A good friend of mine will help you. He's Russian. He'll help you."

"I believe you, Finn. I . . ." She had a momentary lapse and reached over for a Russian–English dictionary, flicking through the pages before smiling and saying, "I trust you."

Trust. There was too much trust around at the moment, but she was right to trust him, he knew that—in his intentions, at least. And it seemed within reach now, the end of his involvement in Sparrowhawk, the way clear to get her to Stockholm, everyone else wrapped up in other concerns. If he was anxious, and he was, it was perhaps because it had all come together a little too nicely, and because nothing in this business ever concluded that neatly.

Chapter Twenty-Seven

They didn't speak on the journey home. Hailey sat looking at the closed Moleskine, tears streaming down her cheeks, though she was still and silent. Finn looked out at the city streets and thought of nothing.

As they entered their building, he noticed that Grasset's door was slightly ajar, and at the sound of their steps, Grasset looked out and said, "Ah, Monsieur Harrington . . ." Then he saw Hailey and stopped. "But it's nothing, a matter I wanted to discuss with you in private."

"Okay. I'll just see Hailey home and I'll come back down."

Grasset nodded, but to Finn's eyes the old man looked troubled.

Hailey said, "Go now. I traveled right across Europe on my own, I'm sure I can manage the elevator in my own building."

Finn smiled, but though he had no reason for it, he didn't want her to go up on her own. He'd said she wasn't in danger and he believed that, but something, perhaps just the fact that Grasset wanted to speak to him, had put him on edge.

"I know that. I was thinking of your parents. I think if we put on a show of being extra-vigilant, at least for the next few days, it'll make them sleep easier."

She knew she didn't have a response to that, having only returned from her unsanctioned road trip a few hours earlier, so she shrugged and headed to the elevator.

Finn saw her almost to the door and then headed back down. Grasset's door was still ajar, and he knocked lightly on the woodwork.

"Come in, Monsieur Harrington."

Finn stepped inside, and Grasset came out of his living room and gestured toward the kitchen. Now that he thought of it, he'd been in Grasset's apartment a dozen or so times and he didn't think he'd ever seen the living room. He was curious about it, and realized that what he had seen of the apartment was too old-fashioned for the building it was in, as if in some way it predated the current construction.

"Please, sit down." There was already a bottle on the table with two shot glasses. "A drink?"

Finn tried to see what the bottle was, some sort of grappa, and said as he always did, "That'd be great, thanks."

Grasset sat and poured two glasses of clear liquid. It had an odd viscosity about it that Finn mistrusted. They raised their glasses and drank, and Finn felt the fire lingering in his mouth and throat long after he'd swallowed.

"Good, no?"

"Yeah, it's powerful stuff." He showed a cursory interest in the bottle, as if he wanted to memorize the label for the next time he was out shopping, then said, "What did you want to speak to me about, Monsieur Grasset?"

"Ah yes, Monsieur Gibson's apartment. Yesterday evening, I came in and noticed a light was on. I thought maybe we had left it on so I took the spare key, but when I got there I could hear footsteps inside. I knocked. And a man from the company, from BGS, was in there."

"You mean he'd moved into the apartment?"

"No, he said he was inspecting it. I asked if someone new would come soon but he said he wasn't sure."

"What did he look like, how old?"

"Your age, perhaps. He looked average. Dark hair and, er, a suntan."

"He wasn't foreign? I mean, Arabic or—"

"No, and I mentioned it and he said he'd been on vacation, to the Caribbean." Grasset shrugged nonchalantly, as if he and Finn shared a dim view of people who holidayed in the Caribbean. Finn wasn't sure what the view was, but as if countering the disapproval, Grasset said, "But he was friendly, very much wanting to talk and ask questions about the building."

"You hadn't seen him before?"

"Never."

"Okay, what kind of questions?"

Grasset topped up both glasses, even though Finn had drunk hardly any of his, then said, "That is what I wanted to talk to you about. He asked about the kind of people who lived here, but then—it was strange the way he changed the subject—he said he'd heard the neighbor's daughter had run away and he hoped she would be found. I asked him if he had spoken to the neighbors, and he said Monsieur Gibson had told him about it."

"Gibson left the day after, so he might have heard about it before he went."

"It's possible." Unspoken was Grasset's suspicion, even based on the little knowledge he possessed, that the visitor to Gibson's apartment had a specific interest in Hailey's disappearance. "Monsieur Harrington, people talk to me all the time, and so often they talk about one thing when they want to know another. What a beautiful day, Monsieur Grasset . . . oh, and I haven't seen Madame Harrington lately. Or they ask directions and then suddenly they wonder if any apartments might be available." Finn smiled, because it was the truth, and because Grasset was a master at it himself. But Grasset grew serious as he said, "This man last night, he humored me, but he wanted to know only about Hailey Portman."

"What did you tell him?"

"I told him everything I know—that the police are not involved, that Hailey ran away, as teenagers sometimes do, and God willing she will come back when she realizes it's not nice to be alone in the world."

"That's good," said Finn.

Grasset was dismissive of the comment, but said, "When did she come back?"

"Only today."

"I almost didn't recognize her." He tipped the grappa in his glass, first one way, then the other, as if studying the meniscus. "I don't understand very much of . . . of anything anymore, but if Hailey was my daughter, I would be concerned. This man from BGS, he was very friendly, but why would he be so interested in a young girl like that?"

Finn nodded, appreciating Grasset's instincts, particularly as he probably didn't know yet that Hailey's friend was dead, a boy he'd probably seen here countless times. The real question was whether they were curious about Hailey, wondering how much she knew, or whether they were erring on the side of caution, intent on eliminating her no matter what.

It seemed inconceivable, but then it seemed inconceivable that they'd killed Jonas, a boy who wouldn't have known what to do with the information he'd found. It was something Finn had seen in the people he'd once contended with, and sometimes even among his own colleagues—a policy in which killing was the first option rather than the last, because lives counted for nothing against the security of guaranteed silence.

And now he had to rethink his position. He'd told Hailey several times that she was safe, but he no longer knew that. As if to reinforce that fact, he saw something that had eluded him at first—the timing of this visit to Gibson's apartment.

Jonas had most likely been killed shortly after arriving home from school, and then later the same evening, someone from BGS had turned up here. Had this been the person who'd killed Jonas, calling by in the hope of being able to finish the job?

Finn thought of how tall and rangy Jonas had been, how easily he'd outrun him that first night. He imagined that if the visitor to Gibson's place had been faking the suicide of a kid like that, he wouldn't have taken the risk of doing it alone.

"Was he alone, Monsieur Grasset?"

"In the apartment, yes." He opened the bottle again. Finn hadn't touched his drink since the last refill, so he obligingly drained the glass and watched as Grasset filled it again. "I saw him to the door and he waved. He walked away. But along the street there, he got into a car, in the passenger seat, and the car drove away."

"Did you see who was driving?"

"I couldn't be sure. You know, if I was talking to the police, I wouldn't like to say, but talking to you I can say it looked like Monsieur Gibson." He paused. "You think they mean harm?" Finn nodded, his thoughts settling into a greater clarity than he'd experienced for a long time.

"Yes, they do, but I'll deal with it."

Grasset smiled, as if Finn had just confirmed a long-held suspicion of his own. Maybe Adrienne had spoken to him, too. Finn knocked back the shot in one and stood.

"Thank you, Monsieur Grasset. This is a great help." He headed for the door, then stopped. The flow of information had diverted him from asking a key question, but he asked it now: "This man who called, did he give you a name?"

"*Mais oui!*" Grasset stood, embarrassed at having forgotten to mention it himself. He crossed the kitchen and picked something up, holding it out to Finn. "He gave me his card."

Finn took it and looked at the thick card, the glossily embossed black lettering: the BGS logo, an office phone number, and the name of the person who'd come calling. Finn looked at the grappa bottle, and if he'd still been sitting he would have poured himself another shot, because the name on the card was Harry Simons.

Chapter Twenty-Eight

Finn stood outside the Portmans' apartment but didn't press the buzzer. He could hear the soft muffle of voices somewhere inside, the family perhaps finally talking over Hailey's disappearance or the events that had overtaken it. There were no raised voices and it was a comforting sound somehow, none of the words distinct enough to make out.

But that wasn't why Finn had failed to press the buzzer. He was thinking about Harry Simons. Harry Simons, he reminded himself again, was dead. And if by some medical marvel they had managed to keep him alive, he would not have become the kind of person who killed fifteen-year-old boys, no matter who ordered it.

But Harry Simons was dead, and though the description given by Grasset could have easily fitted Harry, one odd little detail assured Finn that it hadn't been him. In the couple of years they'd spent together in Northern Europe, Harry had never once complained about the cold—the colder it got, the happier he became—but he'd never been able to stand the heat.

Finn was as uncertain of most things as Grasset claimed to be, but he knew with an unwavering conviction that Harry wouldn't have been on vacation in the Caribbean. It only served to back up what he already knew, that if Harry were part of BGS, whatever BGS was, they wouldn't be digging around in the dirt trying to identify Jerry de Borg, because Harry knew already.

Harry was dead, had been dead for six years. Even thinking it brought a reminder of the guilt he'd felt at hearing of his friend's death, because he'd doubted him in those final days, that business about falling for the girl.

But if Harry was dead, that in itself raised another question—could it just be a coincidence, another guy with the same name, or a pseudonym picked out of the hat that just happened to be linked to Sparrowhawk? It seemed unlikely, and certainly less likely than the other explanation . . .

Whoever had given that card to Grasset—or rather, whoever had ordered someone to give that card to him, had calculated that Grasset would in turn give it to Finn, or at least pass on the name. They were goading Finn, perhaps in the hope of bringing about the breakthrough they'd been working toward for at least two years.

He felt sick at the possibility that even Jonas's death and the implied threat against Hailey had been part of that goading. For a few moments he weighed up the possibility, setting it against the other scenario of information paranoia, first one seeming more likely, then the other.

Finally he let it go, realizing that it hardly mattered, that in one way or another Jonas was dead because of him. He'd inadvertently set that death in motion six years ago and had given it traction with every year he'd allowed to slip past, believing that doing nothing and living beneath the radar would be enough.

They had come after him, though, even earlier than he'd realized—at first passively and now actively. And it wouldn't stop unless he made it stop, or gave them whatever it was they wanted.

He reached up and pressed the buzzer. The muffled conversation stopped, there were soft footsteps, and Hailey opened the door.

She smiled and he wanted to tell her that she wasn't to open the door anymore, but he held back as he saw how strained that smile was, and the fragility that lay beneath it.

He smiled back and said, "There are some things I need to discuss with you and your parents."

"Sure, come in. I told them Jonas was killed—is that okay?"

"Of course."

As he walked into their living room, Ethan stood and shook his hand and said, "This is a terrible business, just terrible."

Finn wasn't sure he liked Ethan's tone, but then Debbie settled any doubts about what they were thinking when she said, "You must feel awful."

"Mom!"

Finn said, "I do feel awful. If Jonas and Hailey hadn't spied on Gibson, none of this would've happened. True, six months from now it might have been Adrienne and me who were killed out of the blue, but at least I'd have felt good about myself."

Ethan looked defensive. "Steady, Finn, Debbie didn't mean anything . . ."

Finn shook his head. "You're right, I'm sorry. And the truth is, it does all lead back to me. I'm the common denominator, and I'm trying to fix it, but nothing I do now solves the problem of that boy lying in the morgue."

Hailey made a barely distinguishable sound—a whimper, possibly even a word— and sat down. He looked at her. None of them appeared able to reply, and Ethan gestured for Finn to sit and lowered himself heavily into an armchair.

Still nobody spoke and so Finn said, "And while you're holding that thought, while you're still heading from being grateful for me bringing your daughter back to wishing you'd never met me, there's something else I need to tell you."

They all looked at him, but it was Hailey who said, "It's what Monsieur Grasset wanted to talk to you about, isn't it?"

"Yeah. Apparently last night someone from the same outfit as Gibson was looking around the apartment next door—"

Debbie said, "I knew it, didn't I, Ethan? I swore I heard someone in there."

"Grasset went to investigate, but the guy was asking about Hailey, saying he'd heard she'd disappeared, had they found her, that kind of thing, pretending to be concerned, as you'd expect."

Debbie looked desperate. "But . . . I think I spoke to Mr. Gibson the day he was leaving."

"I don't think you did," said Ethan. "I saw him, but I don't think I spoke to him."

"Even so, he might have heard about Hailey, so it could have been a normal thing for his colleague to ask about her."

"It could have been," said Finn. "But it wasn't. Grasset thinks he saw Gibson driving the car that the guy left in. I think the two of them probably killed Jonas earlier in the evening, then came over here. They might have had other reasons for coming, but I think it's a matter of some concern that they wanted to know about Hailey."

Ethan looked at him accusingly and said, "What are you talking about? Hailey doesn't know anything. They killed Jonas because he was poking his nose in, but there's no reason for them to want to harm Hailey."

"Ethan, there was no reason for them to kill Jonas—these are not reasonable people we're talking about. Now, it's possible I'm being overcautious, but I'd rather be overcautious and assume that Hailey might be at risk than let our guard down."

"You kept telling me I wasn't in danger."

He looked at her and said, "And that's what I believed. It might also still be true, but I'd prefer to play it safe."

Debbie took the development on trust and simply asked, "What do you propose to do?"

Ethan cut in quickly, saying, "We go to the police, that's what we do. Finn, I don't care what you claim to have been in your previous incarnation, but I can't entrust the safety of our daughter to you, not if there are people who actually wish to harm her. That's a job for professionals—we have to go to the police."

Finn was bemused by the rapid development in Ethan's thinking. Already he'd gone from suspecting Finn of having been a spy, to accepting it as fact, and now to doubting it.

"What will you tell them?"

"Excuse me?"

"You heard me, what will you tell them? Let's think . . . your daughter who you previously told them had been abducted, but who had actually run away to live with a guy she met online, is now in danger from the people who murdered her best friend, a murder which the police believe is a suicide—and incidentally, the Frosts aren't challenging that belief—so you think the police should investigate BGS or put protection in place around Hailey. And all of this is based on the word of your neighbor, an historian who may or may not have once worked for British intelligence. Sounds good, I'm sure they'll buy it."

He thought Ethan might respond with anger, and Hailey was looking on slack-jawed, but he actually produced a nervous laugh and said, "Now that you put it like that, I guess we would look like the neighborhood fruit loops." Then he looked more serious again as he said, "So what do we do?"

Debbie said, "Should we go away?"

Finn shook his head. "People are easier to hit in transit. I think the best thing is to be secure—that means, Hailey, no school on Monday, no going out, no answering the door, no being left on your own." He turned to Ethan. "I'll go to Geneva on Monday, so you might only have to act like this for a couple of days."

"Why, what will happen then?"

He sensed Hailey's eyes fixed on him.

"I'll deal with it, and if I don't, I'll let you know."

Debbie looked confused. "I don't understand, Finn. How will we—"

"Mom, it's probably best we don't ask any more questions. I'm sure Finn will tell us what we need to know."

Finn looked at her, acknowledging the intervention, then stood and said, "Just be vigilant, for the next couple of days at least."

Ethan stood, too. "Of course, and we won't ask you any more questions, but please, if your plan . . . What I mean to say is, if there are any setbacks, do let us know."

"Of course," said Finn, knowing what Ethan was really asking, to let them know if the threat became imminent.

He left then, turning over the use of that word, "plan." They would have been even more alarmed if they'd known that he didn't really have one. He'd attempt to track down the people who'd killed Jonas, and he'd need to speak to Naumenko at some point, but beyond that, there was no plan. How could there be, when he didn't even know who these people were or what they wanted?

History

Sofi didn't come back from her parents' place until Thursday night. She looked weary when she walked in the door, emotionally rather than physically.

Immediately, he said, "How are they?"

"It's really upset them." She took her coat off. "I know it seems silly, it was just a burglary, but they've never known anything like this."

"It doesn't seem silly at all." He held her and kissed the top of her head, intoxicated by the scent of her after a couple of days without her. "And I shouldn't have gone there last weekend—I should have thought."

She shook her head. "It wasn't your fault." She looked up at him, a reconciliatory smile, and they kissed, haltingly at first, then deeper, falling into each other. And, almost subconsciously, they started to undress as they kissed, edging at the same time toward the bedroom, a little clumsily, without separating.

As he pulled her sweater over her head he said, "Have you eaten?" She nodded and let the sweater fall to the floor as she pushed him over the threshold and to the bed. And they spoke no more, but it was not as it should have been. They made love, so familiar with their own choreography now that there were no missed steps, but still, it was not as it should have been.

Later, much later when she was already asleep, he lay there looking up into the darkness and thought about it, and reasoned that it had been her. In some subtle way he knew she'd been going through the motions, that a small, isolated part of her brain had been elsewhere, perhaps only thinking of her parents, but perhaps more than that, of whether their future would hold through the end of his job. And sensing that she doubted, he doubted, too, fearing it would no longer be the same.

When he woke the next morning, the small lamp was on and he could hear the shower running. She always had breakfast first, and he could smell the coffee in the kitchen. When she came in, she saw he was awake and smiled and said, "Good morning." She kissed him before retreating across the room, taking her robe off and hanging it on the back of the door.

She started to dress, throwing the occasional smile at him because she knew, and was bemused by the fact, that he found the sight of her dressing even more erotic than that of her undressing. For a moment he wanted to persuade her back to bed, however briefly, but the memory of the previous night stalled him.

He said, "I forgot to tell you, I'm away today, back Sunday morning."

"Oh," she said, looking concerned again. "Not this work you've been doing?"

She knew nothing about what he'd been doing this week, and yet something about it had unsettled her. Maybe it was just having met Louisa.

"No, it's the opposite. They've asked me to attend a meeting. Everyone else is busy."

She didn't look convinced. "That's one thing I won't miss about your job—you go away too much."

He smiled and watched as she finished dressing, then said as it occurred to him, "Is there anything about my job that you *will* miss?"

"I don't know. I'll have to see what you're like without it first." She came over and kissed him quickly. "There's coffee in the kitchen. Travel safely."

"I will. See you Sunday."

"I'll be here, sad and lonely." She laughed and headed out of the door.

A stray thought flitted into his head, that he would never see her again—a thought so powerful that he almost leapt out of bed to follow her. But it was nothing more than a stray thought, he knew that, the kind that people in his profession seemed particularly prone to.

He didn't bother going into the office that day. He had nothing left to do and everyone else had already left for Kaliningrad. Instead, he showered and dressed—casual clothes so he wouldn't look odd traveling with Katerina—and then had a long, lazy breakfast, watching the clock. He'd told Katerina he'd pick her up around four.

At lunchtime his phone rang. It was Louisa, sounding even more like a headmistress over the phone than she did in person.

"Ah, Finn, glad I caught you." He raised his eyebrows, and with anyone else would have pointed out the nature of cell phones.

"Is everything going to plan?" Even as he asked the question, he realized that wasn't why she was calling, that she would no longer see any need to keep him informed on the progress of Sparrowhawk. His part in this operation, and essentially in her organization, was over.

"This is probably nothing, but take a look out of your window and see if there's a black BMW parked in the street."

He walked through the apartment and looked down. It was parked a little way along, but the BMW was there, with two guys just visible inside it.

Finn wasn't unduly concerned but said, "I don't get it—I thought he'd have stuck with the agreement."

"Clearly he doesn't trust you to keep your end. We think he's out here somewhere, but we intercepted a call, which is why we know they're watching the apartment."

It meant he'd have to avoid them when he left, but he didn't think that would be so difficult.

"It's not a problem, is it? I mean, it can't compromise the operation?"

"Not at all, no. It's not that." She sounded unsure of herself, something so strange where Louisa was concerned that Finn felt the first hint of unease. "This really could be nothing, but when his man told him that you hadn't left the apartment, Karasek told him to wait a little longer, and then check out the other place."

"What other place?" He felt sick as the answer came to him even before she'd spoken.

"I've no idea, but I thought, just on the off chance, that you *do* have something or someone they want—that . . ."

He was still looking down at the street, and stared with horror now as the BMW reversed slightly, the front wheels turning, edging forward, reversing again, working slowly out of the tight parking spot.

"Thanks, Louisa. I'll look into it." He hung up before she could respond and tore through the apartment, picking up his coat and backpack as he slammed through the door, hurtling down the stairs.

The car had gone by the time he got out onto the street. He didn't hesitate, sprinting quickly away, making rapid calculations—the route the car would have to take, the few shortcuts he could make on foot, still doubting he could be quick enough.

He veered out onto the street, finding it easier to dodge traffic than pedestrians. A couple of policemen looked at him as he tore toward them, but he laughed and waved, giving the impression of someone terribly late rather than up to no good. They both laughed, and one even waved back as Finn sprinted past.

As he reached the junction with Harry's street, he saw the BMW cruise across in front of him. His lungs were burning now, his legs uncertain—he'd been running full speed in the cold for more than five minutes. He was in pretty good shape, but it had still taken it out of him.

He flew around the corner and saw that the car had carried on past the building, looking for a place to park. If they'd realized there was a pursuit in progress, he guessed one of them would have jumped out while the other parked, but fortunately for Finn there was still a lack of urgency about them.

He slowed to a brisk walk, not wanting to make any movement that might register in the driver's mirrors. Once inside the building, though, he skipped quickly up the stairs, pulling the key from his pocket as he reached the top.

She was sitting on the sofa with a book, but jumped up now, momentarily fearful, then happy, then confused—the emotions playing out in quick succession across her face.

"But you said—"

"I know, but we have to go now. Is your bag ready?"

She nodded, pulling on her Converse, which were next to the sofa, lacing them quickly. There was a desperate, determined look about her that was painful to witness, speaking as it did of what she'd come to expect from life. She stood, picking up her book.

"Okay, where's your bag?"

"In here." She pointed to the bedroom and he followed her in. There was a sports bag on the bed, looking quite bulky for someone who had so few clothes. She opened it and put the book in, and he saw that the other books were also in there. He could hardly deny her that.

He was about to speak again when the doorbell sounded and he froze. She looked at him, seeking an explanation, but he simply put his finger to his lips and closed the bedroom door.

He walked over to the window and looked down. They were on the fourth floor, at the back of the building. He lifted the window. There was a metal fire-escape ladder attached to the outside wall, but it was a couple of windows along, meant to be accessed from the roof rather than inside the apartments.

Some of the apartments at the front had ornate balconies, but there was nothing here, just a narrow decorative ledge running under the windows at floor height. He looked up, too, at the guttering above, but there was no obvious way.

Katerina also leaned out, looking down at the paving below, taking in the options as quickly as Finn had. The bell sounded again, but Finn knew they'd just be checking that Harry wasn't in, and that once they were certain, they'd work the lock and search the place.

Katerina caught his gaze now and pointed to the fire ladder and nodded. Before he could shake his head or whisper a response, she climbed nimbly over the windowsill and started edging along the building, showing no apparent fear.

He stared for a second, awestruck, then mobilized, grabbing her bag. He held it out of the window, but waited until she'd seen him before he dropped it, not wanting to shock her with the sound of it hitting the ground below.

He climbed out after her, and even as he gently lowered the window, he thought he heard the apartment's front door open and then close again. He was shocked by how strong the wind was now that he was on the outside of the building, and while Katerina edged along without difficulty, her feet turned sideways, it felt like only the toes of his boots were on the ledge. His backpack was slung over one shoulder, and that seemed to attract the tug of the wind, too, but he didn't want to drop it now, fearing the noise would be audible from inside the apartment.

He passed the first window. The apartment was empty and a decorator was painting, his back to the window. Katerina had already passed the second window and reached out for the ladder. She made barely any noise as she lowered herself down the rungs.

Finn picked up his pace but wasn't sure about the soundness of the ladder, and waited for her to lower herself from the bottom rung and drop to the ground before he started down himself. By the time he was on the ground, she'd already retrieved her bag. He took it off her and she smiled.

He was still deciding which way to go and what to do when the window opened above. It could have been a lucky guess on the part of Karasek's man, but suddenly, Finn remembered the bedding on the chair in the living room, and wondered if that had played a part in convincing him the girl had to be there.

Finn turned his back to the window and started walking; Katerina followed and only she looked back as the guy called something out in Estonian.

As she faced forward again she said urgently, "I think he has gun."

"He won't use it, but it's time to run."

They moved quickly out onto the street, taking a right, Finn heading instinctively away from where he knew the BMW was parked, and once again calculating—would they be down the stairs yet, out on the street, would one pursue on foot while the other drove?

They ran into a busier street, his knee jarring slightly now from the drop and the weight of the bag on one side, but not bad enough to slow him down. A little farther along, he saw someone getting out of a taxi and he picked up his pace. He didn't give the guy a chance to decide, throwing the bag in the back and handing him a couple of notes as he asked for the ferry terminal.

Katerina laughed excitedly once they were moving, but she kept looking back, making sure they weren't being followed. Finn didn't need to look, not now—no one was that good.

"Are we okay?"

"We're okay," he said.

He was already wondering, though, how they'd known. Perhaps it had just been thoroughness on Karasek's part, following all the leads that Finn's movements had suggested. Maybe two people had tailed him and Harry that day, or maybe they'd picked up on Harry afterward. Either way, Karasek had come impressively close to finding her.

Katerina hardly spoke after their escape, and didn't question the change of plan until they were on the boat and heading out. "We're going to Helsinki?"

He nodded, thinking of the many times he'd been to Helsinki in the last eighteen months, some of the grand times they'd had there. Then he looked at her and realized she wanted an explanation for the change of plan.

"I don't want to wait in Tallinn for the late ferry. We can take another ferry from Helsinki to Stockholm." The boat was out on a choppy slate sea now, the sky mean, the promise of a feisty crossing later tonight.

"But you bought tickets."

"It's okay, I can buy other tickets."

The boat listed gently as it rode the swell, and she looked excited and alarmed, and by way of explanation, said, "I've never been on a ship."

He smiled, impressed by how resilient her innocence was. "Your life will be better now."

"I know it," she said, with a certainty he wished he could muster for his own future.

Chapter Twenty-Nine

He trained the next day and ran farther still, his pace much quicker now, his stamina returning. As he came back from his run he saw Hailey looking down from the window of the Portmans' apartment. He waved at her but didn't go to see them.

On Monday morning, he retrieved a bag from his deposit box, containing his gun, ammunition, cuffs, various other things he'd bought nearly six years ago and barely looked at since. The fact that he'd kept them all this time said something in itself.

He'd bought them early on because at some level he'd believed someone would come after him. After the months had turned into years, he'd begun to relax a little. When the first book had become a success, he'd seen that public persona as offering him a little insulation, had let his guard down further by embarking on what, at the time, had felt like a committed relationship—with Adrienne.

Somewhere along the line, between book tours and research trips and the domestic routine of life with Adrienne, he'd fooled himself—though not her, apparently—into believing that everything had normalized. And yet he'd kept the box and he'd kept the contents, because a faint alarm had continued to sound, transmitting its weak signal no matter how far he traveled from that past. And now this was the day when that precaution paid off.

He took an early afternoon train to Geneva. He checked the building where Gibson was living—if Jonas's information was correct. It was a modern apartment building with no concierge. Then he walked to the building that housed the BGS office. The address was also the base for a dozen other companies with unchallenging names. For all he knew, every one of them was a front for some intelligence service or other. There were no bars or cafés across the street but there was one farther along the block, and as long as Gibson walked home, which he guessed he would, he would have to pass it.

Finn checked his watch, bought a newspaper, and strolled back to the café, sitting with a coffee at one of the stools inside the window, like a man who just wanted to watch the world go by. The place was almost empty, but as the clock moved toward the end of the working day, a crowd steadily grew, a surprising number of them speaking English.

Finn checked his watch. If Gibson hadn't made an appearance by six, he would write it off and head to his apartment. He had no idea if the BGS office was anything more than an address, but Gibson had gone out to work every day when he'd lived beneath Finn, so presumably he'd been going somewhere, perhaps even here.

The street outside the café was becoming busier, too, and when Gibson finally did walk past, Finn didn't spot him until it was almost too late. Gibson glanced in at the window of the café, staring directly at where Finn was sitting, though he showed no sign of having actually seen him.

Finn had probably walked past him many times before, but had never taken much notice. Now he took in everything: the young, featureless face, though he imagined Gibson was in his thirties; the prematurely balding hair masked by the fact that it was almost shaved; not particularly tall, a sinewy build as befitting someone who was a keen cyclist.

Having never paid attention to him before, Finn was surprised at himself, because Gibson had the perfect blend of lean anonymity that should have aroused his suspicions. The only thing Finn had in his defense was that the world seemed to be full of nobodies nowadays—they couldn't all be mounting surveillance operations.

He put his money on the counter, folded his paper and left that, too, then got up and sauntered out. Once on the street, he picked up his pace a little until he could see the back of Gibson's neatly cropped head bobbing among the pedestrians in front.

Finn kept a decent distance behind him, knowing the few turns Gibson would have to make in advance of him reaching them. Only as they got closer to the apartment building, and there were fewer people on the street, did he close in. Usually that would be the time to drop back, but Gibson had no idea he was being followed, and Finn wanted to reach the door with him.

Gibson was wearing a suit, an open raincoat over the top of it, a scarf—that much Finn had seen when he'd looked into the café window—and he was carrying a laptop case. Was he armed? It was impossible to tell from behind, maybe not at all with the loose-fitting beige raincoat.

Finn saw him reach into his pocket and pull out a bunch of keys, sorting through them as he neared the door of the building. It was probably a new apartment for him, so he no doubt had to remind himself each time which key was for which door—the mental effort required provided perfect cover for Finn now that they were essentially alone, the one other man on the street walking away from them on the other side.

Gibson reached the door, put in the key. Finn picked up his pace, breaking into a run as he pulled his gun. He almost barreled into Gibson, pushing him through the door, and Gibson responded at first as if ready to defend against an assault or deal with an accidental collision.

He didn't drop the laptop case, but stumbled and turned and said something, then froze in two stages, the first as he recognized Finn, the second as he saw the gun.

"Keep your hands visible and move backward to the elevator."

"What do you want?" He was a Scot—Ethan had told him that, but the delicate and slightly high-pitched voice came as something of a surprise.

Finn didn't answer and Gibson got the message, moving carefully toward the elevator, reaching up and pressing the button. Finn stepped in behind him, pushed the gun into his back and turned him around. He gave a little shove with the gun then, and Gibson reached up and pressed for the fourth floor.

As the doors closed and the elevator moved, Finn said, "I've only killed two people in my life, and one of them was an accident, so when we get to your floor don't do anything to make me add to that tally. You understand?" Gibson nodded. "If there's anyone about, don't try anything, or I'll kill you and I'll kill them, and I don't want to kill anyone. Understand?"

Gibson nodded again and said, "We can sort this out—"

Another increase of pressure, the metal of the gun pushing up against his spine, was enough to reduce him to silence. And the precautionary talk proved unnecessary, because the corridor was empty and they moved quickly into his apartment, even with Gibson fumbling in his nervousness and his unfamiliarity with the keys.

Once inside, Finn reached and turned on the light. It was a large, open-plan apartment, modern but well decorated. Unlike the shell of a place he'd left behind, the walls here had a handful of generic modern art canvases, as if the place had been put together by a designer rather than someone exploring his or her own taste.

"Put the case on the floor." Gibson crouched and put the case down. "Now drop the raincoat off your shoulders and onto the floor, then step forward." Again, he followed the instructions carefully. "Arms out wide and turn slowly."

Gibson turned, then let his arms drop and said, "If you told me what it is that you want . . ."

"Strip."

Gibson looked at him in consternation.

"What?"

"To your underwear. Strip." Finn gave the gun a little shake in his hand, reminding Gibson that he was hardly in a position to negotiate.

Even still, as Gibson took off his jacket—no shoulder holster—loosened his tie, pulled his shirt free, he said, "Mr. Harrington, I don't know what you want from me or what you think is going on, but I don't think this'll solve your problems, whatever it is you're thinking of doing."

Finn didn't respond and Gibson finished undressing. He stood there in a pair of tight-fitting trunks that once again brought to mind his love of cycling, a pile of clothes at his feet. Finn took the pair of handcuffs from his bag and threw them across.

Gibson caught them, but started shaking his head as he calculated what was coming.

"No, please, Mr. Harrington, if you'll just listen—"

"Relax, Gibson, this isn't how I get my kicks. We have some serious talking to do and I don't want to sit pointing a gun at you the whole time. Now put them on, hands in front."

Gibson stared at him, probably trying to read his thoughts, and reluctantly attached the cuffs to his wrists.

"Now what?"

"Bathroom."

Gibson, his eyes desperately trying to calculate what this meant, turned and walked to the bathroom. Finn pushed him inside, then turned on the light. There was a large tub in one corner.

"Into the bath, lie down, head by the taps."

"What, you're gonna waterboard me? Are you crazy?"

"I wouldn't know how to begin waterboarding someone. If you give me instructions, I'll give it a go."

"How would I know? I just—" Finn gestured with the gun toward the bath, and Gibson stopped talking and climbed in. "On my back or front?"

"On your back—we need to talk, remember."

Gibson crouched, putting his cuffed hands on the side of the bath to help himself into a sitting position, then gingerly laid back, his body twitching against the cold surface.

"Good, now stay there for a minute, make yourself comfortable while I check the apartment. If you're thinking about getting out of the bath once I leave the room, don't, not unless you have a rocket launcher hidden in your medicine cabinet, because I will kill you."

Gibson stared up at the ceiling, not responding, looking humiliated. Finn stepped backward out of the bathroom, and quickly checked the other rooms, backtracking each time to pass the open door and get a glimpse of Gibson's knees just visible in the bath.

There was a bedroom, a guest room that looked unused and had a bed full of cushions, a study lined with bookshelves, a well-equipped kitchen, the same tastefully low-key decor throughout.

When he got back to the bathroom, he found Gibson as he'd left him.

"Okay, let's get started. What's your first name?"

"Steve."

"Who do you work for, Steve?"

"BGS."

"Which stands for?"

"Brac Global Systems."

So far, so compliant, answering questions he knew Finn already had the answers to.

"Private company or government-affiliated?"

"Private. Most of us have a government background, but it's a private company."

"Most of us? How many of you are there at Brac Global Systems?"

This was Gibson's first hesitation, but Finn sensed it was because of ignorance rather than evasion.

"I'm not sure. I've only ever dealt with three or four other people."

"Good. So I'm guessing you answer directly to the boss?" Gibson looked at him, not sure how to respond, perhaps trying to calculate where the questions might be leading. As Finn spoke, he put the gun down and took off his watch. He put one hand on the cuffs to stop Gibson lashing out, then leaned over and put the plug in behind Gibson's head. "What I mean is, if you've only dealt with a few people, you must answer to somebody, and if he answered to somebody else you'd have met him, too. So it's a leap, I know, but I'm guessing you answer directly to the boss of Brac Global Systems. It's good that there's a mixer tap. Let me know if it's too warm or too cold."

"I can't tell you who I answer to."

"Why not? It's a private company, it's not like you're bound by the Act. Remember, let me know if it's too hot or cold." He moved the lever midway and turned on the water, checking it with his hands before letting it fall with a surprisingly full flow onto Gibson's face. Gibson sputtered and moved his head frantically to the side. "That's good, move your head to the side."

Gibson pushed himself up the bath so that his head was squashed uncomfortably into the corner, the water gushing down the side of it. He sounded outraged as he said, "You said you weren't going to waterboard me."

"I don't think this is waterboarding. I think your face has to be covered for waterboarding, and you have to be held under the flow of water, you know, so it simulates drowning. I'm not sure of the technique, but then I don't need to know because I said I'm not gonna waterboard you and I mean what I say."

Gibson still didn't believe him and, in his oddly cowering position, said, "Then what's the idea?"

"The idea, Steve, is that you tell me what I need to know or I'll drown you. It's not torture, it's more all or nothing than that." Gibson looked at him, measuring the seriousness of his intent, fear taking shape behind his eyes for the first time. "Who do you answer to?"

"Ed Perry."

That answer, delivered in haste, made immediate sense. He could imagine a hundred different reasons why Perry might have decided to come after him, not least that Finn had ruined Perry's career as well as ending his own with a black mark against it.

"And it's Ed Perry's company?" Gibson gave a compliant nod. "Why have you been watching me—what's that all about?"

"For a client."

Finn nodded. "The client's name?"

"I don't know." Finn leaned into the flow of water and splashed some of it over Gibson's face. "Karasek."

Perry and Karasek, still working together after all this time. Somehow, it gave Finn a little more confidence, increasing his chances from potentially suicidal to dangerous—and perhaps even beyond that, to merely foolhardy. And if he were to succeed, there wouldn't be just satisfaction, but also a line drawn under his past, albeit a dotted one.

"And what's the purpose of it? A two-year surveillance operation is a pretty serious commitment."

Gibson looked confused. "But it's only been a year."

"Two. BGS had a woman there for a year before you."

Gibson shook his head. "I don't even know any women who work for BGS."

Finn shrugged and said, "Why was I being watched?"

"I don't know. We were only ever told on a need to know. Half the stuff your friend's daughter intercepted was notes I'd written to myself, trying to work out what exactly was going on."

"Had you come to any conclusions?" Gibson shook his head and Finn leaned over. Gibson flinched and then relaxed a little as Finn turned off the flow of water. "What's the next part of the plan?"

"I don't know that, either. First there was the hack, then the girl disappeared. Perry got rattled, told us to stand down until he decided on the next move."

That was believable, and Finn realized that in Gibson he had someone keen to stay helpful and alive.

"Okay, you have a colleague and he gave Monsieur Grasset a business card with the name Harry Simons on it."

"That was Perry's idea. He said Simons was someone you betrayed." That rankled but he let it go. "Look, if it helps, I think a lot of Perry's determination to go after you, it was about revenge, maybe for Simons or for . . . I don't know, something that happened between you guys in the past."

"Was Perry here?"

"He flew out yesterday morning. I don't know where to."

"Where does he live?"

"He keeps a place in London, but I don't think he's there very much."

"So your colleague, the one who visited Grasset—what's his real name?"

"Liam Taylor."

"And it was Liam who went with you to kill the boy?"

Gibson looked panicked. "What are you talking about? I'm a surveillance expert, that's all, I don't—"

"So you're saying Liam did it on his own?" Gibson stared at him, wide-eyed, unable to formulate an answer. "Because I don't believe that. Jonas—that's the boy's name—Jonas was tall and physically fit, so I think two people would need to be involved in faking his suicide. Liam must have been one, maybe he did most of the work, but you helped him, I'm certain of it."

Gibson was shaking his head rapidly, recalculating everything, finally saying, "You're gonna kill me, aren't you?"

"Yeah, I'm gonna kill you, Steve, not least because he was a good kid, an amazing kid, but you know what, even if he'd been miserable and boring he wouldn't have deserved that."

"I didn't want to. I didn't kill him, I didn't even want to help. I can't stop thinking about it." He started to cry, not out of self-pity, it seemed to Finn, but because the urgency of his own predicament had allowed him to express whatever emotions the murder had left him with. Finn felt a little sorry for him. "Please . . ." His eyes caught Finn's and he stopped, realizing the pointlessness of it, then he panicked, kicking out, bucking his body, trying to get out of the bath, hindered by the buoyancy of the water, gently pushed back into place by Finn whenever he did make any progress.

Finn waited for him to wear himself out, then said, "Where does Liam Taylor live?"

"Why should I tell you now? You're gonna kill me anyway."

"That's a good point." He was angry with himself, for not asking for Taylor's address before moving on to the subject of Jonas.

He thought through his options, and then he thought about the apartment he was in, about how different it seemed when compared with the apartment in Lausanne where not even a picture had been hung, and he thought about the books lining the study. Was this

Taylor's apartment, he wondered, doubting it only because the guest room had looked unlived in. "Who lives here with you, Steve?"

"No one."

Finn thought back to the specific wording of Jonas's note: *APARTMENT WHERE GIBSON IS STAYING*. It made more sense now—not a BGS apartment, but the place where Gibson was staying, an apartment that belonged to someone else. How on earth had Jonas found that information?

"Okay, I'll just wait until no one comes home. I'm in no hurry."

Urgently, Gibson said, "My partner. I live here with my partner."

Finn thought of the unused guest room, discounting the idea of a business partner, and said, "Female, male?"

"Male."

"You don't want me to hurt him?"

Gibson shook his head. "Please, whatever you do to me, don't hurt—" He stopped, a protective instinct preventing him from saying the name.

"Taylor's address."

"32, rue Cayenne, but you won't find him there. He's in Lausanne. He went back this morning. I don't know where. He said he'd book into a hotel when he got there."

"Lausanne? You have got to be kidding me—he's gone back for Hailey? What do you people honestly think a couple of fifteen-year-olds were gonna do with that information? And, Jesus, it's not like he can stage a second suicide."

"We're just following our orders, but Taylor . . . Look, all I know is he was told to go to Lausanne and await instructions. It might be nothing to do with the girl."

Finn suspected it was everything to do with the girl. This sounded like Ed's idea of total war, the two kids unwittingly making themselves part of the enemy army. It was just as likely that

Perry had targeted them because he'd sensed it would undermine Finn in some way.

With guilty relief, Finn was glad that Adrienne had left, but then Perry wouldn't have targeted her. The aim of this, as well as Ed's paranoid views on security, was to unsettle Finn into making a mistake, not antagonize him into retaliation. It was unlucky for Ed that Finn had found his soul this last week.

"You shouldn't have killed the boy, Steve."

"I didn't kill him, I just . . . I would never . . ."

"Then you should have stopped Taylor killing him, or you should have refused to be a part of it. You knew it was wrong."

Gibson had tears running down his face, or perhaps it was just water from his recent outburst.

"Please, I'm not a bad person."

"That makes it worse."

Finn grabbed the cuffs with one hand, pushing Gibson's arms down against his body, grabbed his throat with the other, and pushed his head under the water. Gibson cried out, the words lost and turning into splutters and bubbles. He kicked out ineffectually, tried to raise his head, twisted his body as if trying to escape from a straitjacket. And all the time, he stared up at Finn and Finn kept staring back at him until the fight had gone out of him and the gaze had become meaningless.

He went into the bedroom and looked in the drawers of the bedside tables. One was full of sex toys, some of them exotic enough that Finn couldn't even work out how they might be used. He took a couple of the more obvious ones and dropped them into the bath, together with the key from the cuffs.

He went into the kitchen and found a plastic bag, which he put over Gibson's head, tearing a piece of the plastic free and placing it in one of his cuffed hands. Finn doubted the police would be encouraged to come looking for a killer, and certainly not for him, but this at least gave them an easy scenario—the sex game that had gone wrong.

He washed his hands, put his watch back on, and before leaving he did one more sweep of the apartment. He found Gibson's phone among his clothes; there were only a couple of names in the contacts—one was probably the boyfriend, the other his parents— and he'd been scrupulous in keeping the phone clean.

He finished up in the study, searching for an address book before discovering Gibson's one lapse, a scrap of paper with *LT* and a UK cell number written on it—so maybe Taylor was new to Gibson, flying in specifically for this current operation. Finn put the piece of paper in his pocket.

He noticed a picture on one of the shelves then, of Gibson and his partner, smiling broadly, somewhere up on the ski slopes by the look of it. They looked a happy couple, and looked, in the way a photograph could sometimes reveal, like good people.

But that good man had, at the very least, helped in coercing a fifteen-year-old boy into a basement, in attaching a rope to a beam, had perhaps helped hold the boy's arms by his sides as Taylor kicked the stool away. Where had his goodness been then?

Chapter Thirty

He took a taxi back to the station and called the Portmans on the way. Debbie answered, and Finn said, "Debbie, it's Finn. Are you all at home?"

"Yes, of course. Is something wrong?"

"No, I don't think so, but I want you all to stay inside until I get back, and don't open the door to anyone."

"Finn, you're scaring me."

"I'm not intending to, Debbie, I'm sorry. I don't want to say too much on the phone, but I'll be back in an hour or so. Just do as I ask until then."

He ended the call and looked out at the evening streets, wondering whether Gibson's partner was one of those people heading home, blithely unaware that his world was about to implode almost as comprehensively as it had for the Frost family.

And as it still might for the Portman family. It was a nonsense to kill Hailey Portman, but it wouldn't be the most ludicrous decision he'd ever been privy to, and without the constraints of government sanction, with only Perry and Karasek as guiding hands, it was all too believable.

Either Gibson had been replaced or, more likely, their plan for Hailey could be carried out solo. An outright murder was unlikely—they'd gone to great lengths to avoid the attention of the police until now, so they were hardly likely to throw the advantage away at this late stage.

He assumed they'd try to engineer an accident, which would probably involve waiting for Hailey to leave the apartment. An explosion within the building was possible, it was true, but he doubted even Perry would go to such extreme lengths to silence a schoolgirl.

His thoughts ran aground again, unable to make sense of the need to silence two teenagers in the first place. He'd thought Jonas's death had been a response to his continued prying, but if they were targeting Hailey too, it was more fundamental than that. It begged the question of what Perry thought they'd stumbled across on Gibson's network.

Finn thought back to the memory stick and its contents. The only thing he could think of that might give them reason to be nervous was the mention of Naumenko and those numbered bank accounts, but even Finn had only understood the significance of those numbers because his own account was among them.

More likely, there was something even more sensitive amidst the vast amount of coded material Jonas and Hailey had found, and in their paranoia, Perry and friends had feared the encryption being hacked. But then, from the little Finn had known of Jonas, maybe that hadn't been such a paranoid notion.

As had often been the case back in the days when this had been his job, the possible explanations were less important than the very real situation he faced in the present. Despite all his assurances, he now had to assume that Hailey's life was in danger, and keeping her alive took priority over explaining the reasons for that threat.

Ironically, all he knew for sure was that she'd have been safer if they'd left her in Uppsala.

When he arrived back in Lausanne, he had the taxi drop him at the end of the street and walked casually toward his building, taking in the cars that were parked here and there. None had an occupant that he could see.

Once inside, he went down to the parking garage beneath the building. There was his own car under its dust sheet—he hadn't driven it in six months. Nothing else looked out of place. The boiler room was locked, but now that he thought about the position, an explosion there would take out the back of the building, not the front, so he could probably discount the total war option.

He took the elevator back up and called the Portmans' number from the corridor outside their apartment.

He heard Ethan say, "Hello?" both through the phone and beyond the door.

"Ethan, it's Finn. I'm outside your front door."

"Do you want to come in?"

Finn couldn't help but be amused, hoping it didn't show in his voice as he said, "Yes, I'm calling because I told Debbie not to answer the door to anyone."

"Of course."

A few moments later, he was back in their living room. It was just him and the parents to begin with, but then Hailey came through and sat on the arm of the sofa next to her mother, putting an arm around her, looking for all the world like the protective parent rather than the endangered child.

Finn looked at Hailey as he said, "I've told you repeatedly that you're not in danger. I spoke to someone in Geneva earlier this evening, and I no longer think that's true."

He noticed Hailey respond to the mention of his meeting more than to the change in her status, sensing that she wanted to ask who he'd met, whether it had been one of the people who'd killed Jonas, whether that person was himself still alive. Finn continued to meet her gaze but gave nothing away.

"How can you be so sure?"

It was Ethan, and Finn turned to him and said, "One of the people who killed Jonas returned to Lausanne this morning. If it weren't for the two people behind this whole business I wouldn't be sure, I'd think it nonsensical, but the people concerned are dangerous and ruthless and they seem to think that Jonas and Hailey, in hacking Gibson's network, got hold of incredibly sensitive information."

Hailey said, "But we didn't." She laughed. "It was all garbage."

"I'm inclined to agree. I've looked through it, and some of it makes sense to me, but I still don't know what they're about or why any of it would be worth killing for."

Except for the mention of Naumenko, he thought. He'd considered it earlier and put it aside, but Naumenko was one of those people whose power and ruthlessness disturbed the trajectory of anything that came too close. Was Naumenko their target, and fear of him the reason they were overreacting now?

Of course, Finn's trajectory had been pulled into Naumenko's orbit, too. There had been a genuine bond between them, fostered by their mutual interest in history, but it was the nature of Naumenko the man that even his friendship could be destructive, and so it had proved for Finn.

Debbie looked up at her daughter and said dolefully, "Honey, see what you've done?"

Hailey nodded, suggesting she was all too aware of the unintended consequences of the deception she'd set in place that day when she'd asked Jonas about hacking networks.

Finn said, "Debbie, what Hailey did was wrong for a lot of different reasons, but nobody in their right mind could have foreseen this. The important thing now is to deal with the situation at hand."

Ethan sounded dismissive as he said, "And how do you propose to do that? You sit here and tell us that one of the people who killed Jonas has come back to kill Hailey, but presumably you have no idea how or when he'll try to do it. So what's the plan, Finn?"

"I'll stay here tonight, that's the first thing. I'll sleep on the sofa."

"Stay in the guest room," said Debbie.

"No, thanks all the same. I don't want to be too comfortable."

Ethan looked at his wife in consternation, and then back to Finn. "I've said it before and you talked me out of it, but the situation has changed, Finn, you have to admit that. I think we should go to the police."

"And tell them what?"

"About this conversation you had, for one thing. You know, before there was no evidence, but now they can speak to this person, whoever he is, and get the information from him."

Hailey had looked remarkably relaxed considering her safety and possible attempted murder were under discussion, but as her father spoke she became more uncomfortable, her eyes skittering between him and Finn. She did not want it to be true, and Finn was touched in some way that she had that emotional investment in him as a person—but she knew it to be true nevertheless.

"Dad, I think maybe the person Finn spoke to this evening—well, I don't think he'll be speaking to the police, or to anyone else."

Finn avoided making eye contact with her, staring at Ethan instead as confusion washed over him and finally ebbed away.

"What? You mean you—"

Finn brushed it aside, interrupting Ethan, saying, "Look, even if we could give the police the addresses of the two people who are behind this, it wouldn't do any good. These are not the kind of people who get arrested and brought to trial."

"So you're saying Hailey's always going to be in danger?"

Calmly, Finn said, "No, because I'm dealing with the situation. I'll deal with the two people behind this, but the imminent threat comes first."

Hailey was relaxed again as she said, "What if he doesn't come tonight? I can't stay in the apartment forever. You know, I have to go back to school at some point."

Finn smiled, thinking how far school had been from her mind during her brief stay in Sweden.

"He probably won't come tonight, and I don't know what his plan of attack is, only that he'll almost certainly try to make it look like an accident."

"Or another suicide," said Hailey. And before Finn could counter she said, "You know, they run in clusters—one friend does it, then others follow suit."

Debbie was horrified, looking up at her daughter to ask if that was true. Hailey nodded nonchalantly.

Finn said, "It's possible, but I don't want you to worry. Chances are, nothing will happen tonight, but I'll be here anyway. Tomorrow, I'll go looking for him." He thought about the phone number in his pocket, acknowledging to himself that it wasn't much to go on.

Once again, on the subject of Hailey's safety Ethan ceded control to Finn, saying, "I guess we have to put our trust in you, Finn. I only hope it's well placed."

"I haven't let you down yet." Ethan acknowledged the fact, even as Finn countered in his own mind that he couldn't say the same for Jonas. He checked his watch and said, "I'll just go back up to my apartment. I'll be back in half an hour or so."

"We're not going anywhere," Debbie said, and produced a brittle laugh that seemed to surprise her.

Finn left, and made a point of turning on the lights in his apartment when he got inside. If Taylor was out there somewhere, Finn wanted him to know he was home.

He checked his answering machine, disappointed that Adrienne hadn't called, unsure what he expected from her, feeling a brief wave of despair at the possibility of her never coming back. Until now, he'd still seen it as temporary, something that would be overcome, a wake-up call for him to change, but perhaps, far from being in a state of flux, it was already settled.

For all he knew, their one-night stop in Paris had been a final unexpected and unwelcome meeting for Adrienne, and she'd breathed a sigh of relief as he'd walked out the door. He went into the bedroom and looked again at her clothes, trying in vain to see some sign in what had been left there.

He'd promised to call her. *Do what you have to do first*, she'd said. It wasn't much to hold on to, but it wasn't a closed door. And he was doing what he had to do, and was glad that she wasn't here now, just as a part of him wished that Hailey wasn't here, that he'd failed to find her at Domtrappkällaren.

He walked through the apartment and turned off the living room light, then after a few moments, edged back into the darkened living room and toward the window. It brought back a bittersweet memory of first seeing the lovelorn Jonas on his lonely vigil.

This time there was no one on the street, no new cars parked below. He tried to think, desperate to see how this threat would manifest itself. And as he stared down at the streetlights and the shadows between the streetlights, he had a terrible sense that he'd missed something, that he'd been missing something all along.

He headed back downstairs and found the Portmans preparing for bed. Hailey was already in her room. Debbie brought him a duvet and a pillow, asked him if he needed anything else, then left him alone.

He put the bedding to one side, arranged things on the coffee table in front of the sofa, took his boots off, and lay back. It reminded him of the night spent on the sofa in Mathieu's apartment, something that already seemed a distant memory, and one that was surprisingly happy.

The only light on in the room was a small lamp on a table behind his head. He was just about to reach back and turn it off when he heard movement and Hailey came in, wearing her pajamas.

He sat up. "You should try to sleep—everything's okay."

"I know," she said, and was distracted then, looking at the gun sitting on the coffee table, a density about it that pulled her thoughts away from her. "You have a gun."

"This is Switzerland—a lot of people have guns. I haven't used it in a very long time, and I'm sure I won't use it anytime soon."

She nodded, finally pulling her eyes away and back to him, and then remembering why she'd come in she said, "I just wanted to say, about earlier. I don't need to know the details, I don't want to know them, but I'm glad you did what you did. If it was one of the men who hurt Jonas . . ." Her throat tightened up, as if she'd been wanting to say this for the last hour or so and yet was still surprised by the emotion of it. After a brief pause, she said, "I'm just glad, that's all."

"Thank you. That means a lot." It was a stock response, nothing more, but no sooner had he said it than he realized it was true—it did mean a lot to Finn that she thought no less of him for killing a man.

She went back to bed and Finn lay down, and after a few minutes he turned off the lamp. He stared up into the darkness, lying awake for a long time, thinking of Jonas and Hailey and what they'd lost without ever knowing they'd had it; thinking of Adrienne, thinking of Mathieu's happy and chaotic household.

He slept then. He woke once when a car drove past on the street, and slept again. He woke a second time, and wasn't sure how long he'd slept or what had woken him. He lay for a second, not moving, and then he felt his body tense, an automatic response that seemed a step ahead of his senses and thoughts, operating at a purely instinctive level.

He wasn't aware of having heard anything, and still now the apartment was silent. Yet his body was ready, pumping with adrenaline, his muscles tightly coiled—he didn't know how he knew, but he knew without doubt that someone else was in the apartment.

Chapter Thirty-One

Finn swung his legs off the sofa, picked up his gun, stepped over his boots, and moved between the furniture shadows toward the door. He could hear the deep breaths of sleep coming from Ethan and Debbie's room, but even in the dark he could see that Hailey's door was open.

He didn't know what Taylor had in mind, and didn't know how long he'd been in the apartment. Finn could only hope that the gentle click of the front door had filtered through to his sleep, that Taylor was only a step ahead of him. He sacrificed stealth now, moving quickly to Hailey's door, pushing it open, reaching in with one hand to turn on the light.

Immediately through the glare he saw a figure near the bed—crouching or sitting, he couldn't be sure—and aimed his gun, blinking through the light-blindness, knowing at least that Taylor would be doing the same.

A second crept by, he heard a muffled cry from Hailey, saw the guy's head, the dark hair, the tan mentioned by Grasset.

Finn kept his voice calm and low as he said, "Keep very still or I pull the trigger."

"No, you keep very still or I'll ram this right into her neck." He had a vague London accent, and at first Finn struggled to understand his meaning. He saw the one hand over Hailey's mouth, her alarmed eyes, her own terrified stillness, and then he saw the reason for it and he understood what Taylor had meant.

With his other hand, Taylor was holding a syringe against the side of Hailey's neck, the point of the needle touching the skin, his thumb on the plunger. Finn looked at Hailey's eyes, and for a moment he considered pulling the trigger anyway, confident at this range of hitting Taylor clean in the head.

But he had no idea what was in the syringe, and for all he knew, the shock of being hit could be enough in itself for him to puncture her flesh, to drive the needle in. Taylor knew that, too, and smiled. Finn could see immediately how this guy would have relished killing Jonas, and as desperate as he was to put a bullet in Taylor's head, he lowered his gun.

"Your plan's blown, Liam."

Finn heard movement in the apartment behind him, as Ethan and Debbie woke, realized something was wrong, clambered out of bed.

Taylor looked derisive and said, "Who are you calling Liam? You've got a very short time to learn some lessons, like you're Harrington and I'm Mr. Taylor. Or you can call me sir."

"I like Mr. Taylor. My family used to have a greengrocer called Taylor."

"Finn?" It was Debbie emerging from their room.

Then he heard, "Oh God, stay here," as Ethan followed her and realized immediately that something was very wrong.

Taylor didn't hear them, still busy being unimpressed by Finn's joke. He turned and smiled at Hailey, and removed his hand from her mouth like a magician producing a bunch of flowers from his sleeve. She gasped, but remained still and silent.

Taylor reached inside his jacket with his free hand and pulled a gun. He waved it at Finn as he said, "Put the piece down, Harrington."

"The piece?" Finn didn't wait for a reply, but nor did he put the gun down. "What's your plan, Mr. Taylor? Whatever's in that syringe, there's no making it look like an accident now, and I doubt Perry or Karasek would be too well-disposed if you ended up murdering her, me, her parents. The whole point is to keep the police out of it."

Finn could sense that Ethan and Debbie had appeared in the doorway behind him, and Taylor's eyes briefly leapt over his shoulders before settling back on Finn.

"My plan's simple, Harrington—you do what I say or I'm gonna drive this needle into her neck and then I'm gonna kill you, her parents, and the neighbors too, police or no police. You understand me now? Put. The gun. Down."

Behind him, Ethan said, "Don't do it, Finn."

"It's okay, Ethan. I'm sure Liam Taylor of Brac Global Systems knows what he's doing, and I'm sure his boss, Ed Perry, knows what he's doing, too."

Taylor looked nervous, confused by the way Finn was speaking, and said, "What are you playing at? What are you up to?" He looked around the room, worried perhaps that it was bugged. "Just put the gun on the chest of drawers over there."

"Whatever you say." Finn moved cautiously and placed the gun on the chest of drawers, and Taylor gestured for him to move back to the doorway. Taylor nodded then, satisfied, and removed the needle from the side of Hailey's neck. She sighed with relief and closed her eyes, but still didn't move.

Taylor stood and said, "You two, back away, against that wall." Finn heard the rustle of Ethan and Debbie's nightclothes as they stepped backward. Taylor looked at Finn. "Move that way, to the side."

Finn moved, and Taylor started to edge toward the doorway, covering all his angles, even Hailey behind him, the syringe still in one hand, the gun in the other.

Finn waited until he was almost at the door and said, "This is your plan? To just leave? What kind of operative are you, Liam? The police are involved now—we'll call them as soon as you've gone. They'll link you from here to Jonas's death. Then you'll talk, implicate Perry and Karasek."

Taylor knew Finn was baiting him but couldn't resist saying, "Talk—me? There's no police force in the world could make me do that."

"Yeah, Liam, I think you and I both know there probably is. You'll talk. Perry and Karasek will still get off the hook, but they'll come after you, whichever prison you're in. No, there's only one professional solution to this situation—you have to kill all of us."

He heard some garbled words from Ethan.

Taylor laughed, making clear he could see through what Finn was doing, but he still said, "Who do you think you are?"

"I'm nobody. I'm just telling you that if you were at all professional, you'd kill every one of us. Of course, if you were at all professional we wouldn't be having this conversation."

Taylor gave another little dismissive laugh and shook his head, then looked as if he was ready to walk away, a moment of theatricality that was meant to take Finn by surprise but was too easy to read. As Taylor turned sharply back, Finn was ready for him.

The only thing Finn didn't know was whether he'd strike him with the gun or go for him with the syringe. It should have been no contest, but Taylor seemed briefly torn, readying his thumb on the syringe before realizing there was only one option. He produced a quick punching backhand, but even then, seemed undecided as to whether he should swipe Finn's face with the whole gun or plant the butt into his cheek.

It didn't matter. Finn saw the hand fly in toward him, grabbed it, spun him around. Taylor was muscular, solid, but there was no strength in him, either because he was disoriented or because the bulk had come through steroids.

Finn was behind him now, holding the gun hand pointing toward the ceiling. Taylor's finger was still on the trigger but he didn't even have the sense to fire a round—maybe he was still wedded to the idea of stealth. Instead, he thrust the other arm backward, trying to hit Finn with the syringe.

Finn edged away from the first thrust, then as he tried to swing again Finn grabbed that hand and drove the syringe into Taylor's thigh, putting his hand over Taylor's thumb and driving the plunger home.

Taylor let out a small squeal and started to kick and flail. Finn drove him forward, smashing him into the doorframe, Taylor's gun arm slamming awkwardly into the woodwork, and Finn's fingers, too. For just a moment, Finn let go, and Taylor's arm recoiled across his body. Finn slammed him forward again and turned him. He pulled the gun free and pushed it flat against Taylor's abdomen, pressing it into the soft flesh of his belly until the barrel was pointing up at the inside of his ribcage.

Taylor's face contorted, a moment of total fear as he understood what was about to happen. Finn pressed the trigger, the gun kicking a bruise across the surface of the flesh, the muffled bang still shattering the air, Taylor's body going into a strange visceral spasm as the bullet spun off bone and through the tissues of his chest cavity.

Finn caught the body as it crumpled, lowering it to the floor, Taylor's startled face looking as if he was still trying to work out what had just happened inside his chest. Finn couldn't see or feel an exit wound, and only a little blood trickled slowly out of Taylor's mouth. The bullet had stayed inside him, which would make him easier to transport.

He took the gun, wiping it clean on his shirt before pressing it back into Taylor's hand, and only now did he realize that Ethan and Debbie were both talking, mild but shocked expletives, talking about the noise, wondering if the neighbors had heard, wondering above all what they were meant to do now.

Finn didn't look at them but at Hailey. She sat up, throwing the duvet back, put her hand to her neck where the needle had been. She glanced at the body, but only briefly, and then up at Finn.

Finn moved toward her and said, "Did it break the skin?"

"I don't know. I don't think so. Will you look?"

She tilted her head to the side and grimaced, as if dreading what he might find there. He looked at the smooth flesh of her neck, his fingers gently probing to find a telltale red pinprick, relieved that there was none. Her neck was hot, like a child who'd been suffering a fever, and he was fearful after the fact now, realizing how easily he could have come in here and found that skin cold and unyielding.

"You're okay."

"Thanks." She looked up at him and smiled, trying to show him how all-encompassing that single word was meant to be.

He nodded, and then noticed a plastic bag on the floor next to the bed. As he picked it up, Ethan and Debbie rushed forward—a delayed reaction—throwing themselves at Hailey, bombarding her with affection and assurances.

The bag was full of junkie paraphernalia. It was crude, but he guessed the syringe that was still lodged in Taylor's leg contained heroin, and given Hailey's recent history, maybe that would have been enough for the police to dismiss the Portmans as the ultimately delusional parents.

Ethan saw the bag and said, "Is that heroin?" Finn nodded. "What are we gonna do? I mean, about him?"

Finn checked his watch. "For the next hour we do nothing. If any of the neighbors have called the police, we'll know by then, and we'll tell them the truth, that he broke in, tried to kill Hailey, I intercepted him and killed him in self-defense."

Ethan shook his head. "No, I killed him. It'd be odd explaining why you were staying in our apartment."

Finn accepted the point but said, "It shouldn't come to that. It's good that nobody screamed. A single gunshot's a funny thing—was it a gunshot, wasn't it? It's hard to tell."

"And if the police don't come?"

"I'll get rid of the body and we never talk about this again."

Debbie said, "You just killed a man. There's a dead man lying right here in front of us." She stared at Taylor now, in compulsion and horror.

Ethan said, "Debbie, don't look at it. Finn did what he had to do to save Hailey." He looked at Finn, a tacit acknowledgment that his words had only been half true, that it had been a preemptive strike as much as an immediate life or death intervention. "I only wish I could've killed him myself."

"Just be glad he's dead."

Finn went over to the body and patted it down. There were no car keys, which seemed strange. Then he found a door key and suddenly realized what he'd been missing the whole time as he'd looked out onto the street. Taylor hadn't been out on the street, he hadn't been booked into a hotel—he'd been in the empty BGS apartment.

"I'll be back in a minute."

He crossed the corridor and opened the door into Gibson's old apartment. The light was on in the kitchen, and it was soon clear that Taylor had pretty much limited himself to that room. His car keys were on the table, as was a plastic bag with various items of food and drink bought from a convenience store. Whatever he'd eaten or drunk, he'd put the remainders and the wrapping back into the bag. The rest of the apartment was empty.

Finn took the bag and the keys back to the Portmans' apartment, and found the tableau of the family exactly as he'd left it. They looked at him expectantly.

"You all realize this is something you can never speak of again. In a day or two this will make the news, and you have to be as shocked and appalled as everyone else." He got three assenting nods. "Okay. I'll use his keys to locate his car. There's a quiet spot I know on the lakeshore. I'll drive him there, leave the drugs in the car, drop his body at the water's edge. He'll have taken heroin and then shot himself. There'll be no good reason for looking too hard for other explanations. Ethan, you'll follow me five minutes later in your car, pick me up and bring me back."

Ethan nodded.

"And as soon as I can in the morning, I'll be flying to London."

That unsettled Hailey, and she stood and said, "How long will you be away?"

"A couple of days, maybe. Look, I'll be straight with you, this isn't done yet, and you still need to be vigilant. I don't think they'll come for you again, but I need to speak to some people and put BGS out of business—it's the only way I'll be convinced you're safe."

"And you?"

He smiled. "If they'd wanted me dead it would've been a lot easier. But you're right, I need to find out what they want from me, then maybe we can all get on with living our lives."

He looked down at Taylor, his face tanned and healthy, peacefully reposed except for the syringe in his thigh, the trickle of blood from his mouth. He wasn't sure how any of the Portmans could get on with their lives after this, how any of them could go back to where they'd been two weeks ago.

For his part, turning the clock back by two weeks wouldn't be enough. He needed to rebuild from much farther back in his own history, and he wouldn't be able to do that as long as this remained unfinished.

Even if she wanted to return, how could he ever think of having Adrienne back? Because there would be other Gibsons, other Taylors, and he could keep killing them but unless he went to the source, to Karasek and Perry, he'd never be certain of being free from that past. The choice had finally been made for him and, one way or another, he was determined this would be ended.

History

He got them a good cabin on the overnight ferry to Stockholm, and left her only to go to the onboard shop to buy something to eat. He didn't want to risk taking her to the restaurant. It was unlikely any of Karasek's people would have joined enough dots to follow them this far, but he also knew how many operations fell through as a result of last-minute complacency.

The boat rolled a little, kneading the waves, but she was used to it now, and sat cross-legged on the bed, eating, happy. When she'd finished she said, "Thank you."

"You're welcome."

"Harry said you will leave your job." He nodded. "What will you do?"

He shrugged. "I like history. I might write a history book."

She smiled broadly and said, "I like history, too."

"Well, who knows, maybe it'll be translated into Russian."

"No, I learn English." He nodded again, not doubting it, still amazed by how she'd come on in this last week.

"What happened to your parents?"

"My father died when I was very small. I don't remember. And my mother, three years ago. She was hit by a car." She relayed the information blankly, as if recounting the plot of a novel.

"I'm sorry to hear that. And you didn't have any other relatives?"

"My mother's, er . . . mother and father?"

"Your grandparents?"

"Yes, they were dead. And my other grandparents, from my father, they didn't want to take me. They're old." Again, there was no self-pity, no search for sympathy, just a basic relation of the facts.

"Aren't you curious, about what will happen to you now, about the man I'm taking you to?"

She smiled. "You said he's a good man."

"He is," said Finn, though he couldn't tell her much more than that because he didn't know how Alex would choose to help, whether by placing her with someone back in Russia or sending her to a boarding school. There would be no more orphanages, that was all he knew. "His name is Aleksandr Naumenko."

She looked wide-eyed for a moment and laughed, saying, "I've . . . I know from the TV, from the news."

"Yes, that's him."

"He's very rich."

"And very powerful. The man who took you from Russia, he won't be able to harm you now."

Finn looked at his watch, calculating how many hours it would be until Karasek was ambushed in Kaliningrad. And yet instinctively, he couldn't help but imagine that Karasek would walk away from Sparrowhawk, the way he'd so far walked away from every other attempt to bring him down. If that were the case, then Katerina really would need to rely on Alex's protection, at least for a while.

"May I read to you?" He looked at her, puzzled. "Harry said it's good for practice my pronunciation."

"Okay, what are you reading?"

"An English crime story. It's very good." She reached into her bag and pulled the book free.

Finn looked at the cover and said, "*Murder on the Orient Express.*" It was oddly appropriate, but he had to wonder if Harry had picked it up somewhere specifically for Katerina, or if it had been in his own collection. He'd ask him about it when he got back.

"Do you know it?"

"I read it a long time ago, but I'd like to hear you read it."

She read to him for about an hour, occasionally asking for guidance on how to pronounce some word or other. Occasionally he corrected her, too, but for the most part he just listened, enjoying the lilting delivery, the nostalgia of a story so long-known that it seemed to speak of his own childhood.

When she went to bed, changing in the bathroom into a pair of pajamas Harry had bought for her, he kept on only the light by the desk. And for hours, he kept reading the book from where she'd left off, sinking back into the story, lulled by the rolling of the ship, the occasional strained clanks from down on the vehicle deck.

He stayed in the chair all night, dozing for short periods but never really sleeping. Once or twice, Katerina seemed troubled in her sleep, acting out bad dreams, but she didn't wake.

Despite the early promise of a rough crossing, the sea settled as the night wore on, and by the time dawn seeped across the horizon, the sea was flat and the sky cloudless. He showered and dressed, and when he came out of the bathroom he saw that she was awake.

She smiled. "The sea made me sleep."

"Good," he said, understanding what she meant. "I'll go and get us some breakfast."

By the time he came back, she was in the bathroom. She came out dressed but with her hair still damp.

"Do you want to dry your hair?"

"It's okay." She looked bedraggled and childlike again.

After breakfast she looked out of the window. The sun was in the sky now, and the first of the islands were appearing in the distance. She looked back at Finn, her eyes full of excitement.

"May we go outside?"

He weighed the very slight risk of Karasek having someone aboard against the fact that they were now on the long approach into Stockholm, within reach of safety.

"Okay, but you need to put more clothes on—it'll be cold."

She laughed, even as she went into her bag for another sweater, and said, "I'm from Russia."

She had a point.

He took her up onto the large open deck on the top of the boat, and despite the sharp wind pummeling it, there were plenty of other passengers who'd been tempted out. Finn scanned their faces, but there was no one to raise his suspicions.

Katerina was mesmerized by the procession of small islands—some within shouting distance of the boat—with their brightly painted wooden houses and jetties, and the blue and yellow of Swedish flags fluttering. A couple of times, he asked her if she was warm enough, but it appeared she didn't feel the cold, so wrapped up was she in the beauty of this bright new country.

Only as the boat came alongside the dock did she turn away from the railing and look at him, accepting that the time had come to go back to the cabin. Other passengers were already massing near the exits, and he decided it was better for them to let the crowds disperse a little.

So they sat for a while when they got back to the cabin, and Katerina said to him, "I'm . . ." She couldn't think of the word, and demonstrated by holding her hand out and shaking it as if trembling.

"Nervous?"

"Nervous," she said, trying out the word. Then she nodded. "Yes. A little."

After all she had been through.

"That's natural. This is something new, and you'll have a new life, but you'll soon get used to it."

"Will I see you again?"

"I don't know. Maybe not."

She nodded, accepting the fact for what it was, and he was hardly surprised, given the losses she'd known and the stoicism with which she'd faced them.

Once the boat had docked and they'd disembarked, they took a taxi to the Vasa Museum. It was a large, modern warehouse of a building from the outside, and though Finn had heard of it, he'd never quite taken onboard what it was. He knew its only exhibit was a salvaged ship, the *Vasa*, but no more than that.

As they stepped into the vast hall, he stopped, awestruck by the sight of the seventeenth-century warship housed there, its masts rising up into the subdued light, people on the tiered floors that surrounded it, looking at the ship from different levels. It was one of the most beautiful things he'd ever seen.

Katerina seemed equally stunned, and spoke in Russian before saying, "It's wonderful."

Finn nodded, then saw Valentin from the corner of his eye, standing guard near the doors. He was smiling, waiting for Finn to notice him, and Finn walked over now and shook his hand.

"Good to see you, Valentin."

"You too, Mr. Harrington. It's amazing, no?"

"Stunning." Valentin nodded toward where Alex was standing, looking up at the towering, dark hull. Finn nodded, too, and said, "I'll leave the bags with you."

"Of course."

He returned to Katerina then and said, "You can look around if you want to. I'll be talking to that man over there."

She looked in Alex's direction and said, "That's him?" She was peering, wanting to match the man she could see with the man she'd seen on television. The pale-gray suit and open-necked shirt, the short hair, the slight tan—all were familiar enough. Finn thought he always looked more trim and physically fitter in person than he did on TV.

"That's him." He pointed. "Look, there are different floors. You can go down and look underneath the ship or go all the way to the top."

She said, "I can go?"

"Yes." She nodded and walked away—unsure at first, then swept up in the drama of the ship itself.

Finn approached Alex, who turned before he got there and embraced him, saying, "Finn, isn't this the most extraordinary thing you've seen?"

Finn looked up the vertiginous side of the ship and said, "It's quite overwhelming."

Alex held his arms out as if displaying something he'd just bought. "Sank on her maiden voyage in 1628 and lay undisturbed on the bottom of Stockholm harbor until 1961. One man believed it was there, found it, salvaged it intact. Such an inspiring story."

"Incredible," said Finn, and he knew now that his earlier comment to Katerina had been the truth—he would write a history book, whether it was published or not.

"So, let's talk," said Alex. "That was the girl, you just came in with?"

"Yeah, her name's Katerina. She's thirteen. She's an orphan. Karasek trafficked her to Tallinn—you probably heard what happened after that."

"Will she need to see a doctor?"

"No. Luckily for her, Karasek wanted her for himself, so she hasn't been raped."

Alex shook his head in disbelief. For all the things he'd done in his life, there were still things that filled him with as much horror as anyone else.

Then he smiled and waved his hand at the room as he said, "My daughter is in here somewhere—she's fourteen now . . ."

"Really? I remember her being so small."

Alex laughed. "Wait until you have your own children, Finn—it's an even bigger shock. But it's good, they can be companions until we decide what to do with the girl."

"Thank you for doing this, Alex."

"This was nothing. What you did was something. Now, do you want to know what happens to her? Is it wise for you to know, if Karasek wants the girl so much?"

Finn immediately saw how important it was that this be the end of it, that the girl had to be able to move on with her life, that there had to be no thread leading back through the maze to him and to Karasek and to everything else that had happened in Tallinn.

"Karasek himself might not be a problem, but you're right, it's probably best we never speak of this again. I know you'll do the right thing for her, that's all that matters to me."

Alex nodded, deep in thought for a moment before he said, "Karasek *could* still be a problem. I hear something happened in Kaliningrad last night, and it didn't go well. People were killed, but Karasek wasn't there."

Finn wondered what that would mean for him, not least the alarming possibility that he wouldn't be able to go back to Tallinn, not for any length of time. And he was probably marked as a traitor now, which made it worse, particularly if the operation had failed totally and claimed casualties in the process.

"Do you know who was killed?"

"Not names. Some of our people, for sure." He studied Finn's face. "This news is bad news for you?"

"You could say that."

Alex seemed grave with concern himself, but then he looked over Finn's shoulder and smiled. Katerina was walking slowly toward them, looking up at the ship. She saw Finn and he smiled, and she looked questioningly, asking if it was okay for her to approach.

Finn introduced her to Alex, who smiled broadly and spoke to her in Russian. Whatever he said, she answered with enthusiasm, and after a moment Finn realized they were talking about the museum.

Alex's daughter came over, also now on the verge of becoming a beautiful young woman, no trace of the child Finn remembered. She clearly didn't remember him at all but greeted him politely and then, after an introduction, entered into an excitable conversation with Katerina in Russian.

Alex smiled indulgently but then said something to Katerina, who turned to Finn in response, her smile fading as she said, "You're leaving?"

He nodded. "Mr. Naumenko will look after you, make sure you're okay."

She looked surprised, as if she hadn't expected him to leave immediately. Urgently, she said, "Thank you, for everything, all the . . ." She looked about her, unable to find the words, her eyes glistening. She put her arms around him, hugging him so tightly that he feared she might not let go again.

When she did loosen her arms, he took her by the shoulders and looked her in the face, then wiped away her tears and said, "Katerina, saving you last week, killing that man, it's the best thing I've ever done." She smiled, nodding, still sad. "Now, remember to look out for my book."

She laughed a little, and he stepped back and shook Alex's hand. "Thanks, Alex, for everything. I'll be in touch."

"I'll walk with you to the door."

Finn nodded and said, "Bye, Katerina."

"Goodbye, Finn."

They left the girls together and walked toward the door. Finn tried not to look back, but when he did, he was relieved to see the girls heading for the steps up to the next floor, arm in arm.

Then Alex said, "When do you plan to go back?"

"Tonight's ferry."

"I think you should go sooner. Go to the airport, get the first available flight." Something in his tone made Finn stop walking. Alex looked at him. "It could be nothing, but . . ."

"What is it, Alex?"

"Your girlfriend."

Finn felt his heart lurch. "What's happened to her?"

"Nothing, it's not that. A faction in Moscow likes to make life difficult for me—it's not a problem because my influence and power is one level higher. But your girlfriend, Finn, she was the source of the story about us."

"But she didn't even know I was in business with you."

As he said it, he thought of Louisa talking about her, thought of the CIA following them, claiming it was Sofi's colleague they were interested in, thought of everything about the way she'd behaved in the weeks since he'd announced he was quitting.

He felt violently hollow, as if he might crumple inward, because he immediately knew it to be true. He'd been duped, emotionally as well as intellectually, and it was worse because he loved her and had believed that she loved him. But she hadn't, and Alex wouldn't have told him this if he weren't certain of it being true.

"You need to go home, Finn. Confront her. There may be an explanation." Finn nodded, knowing there could be no explanation plausible enough to mend the sickness he felt inside. Alex took Finn's hand in his and said, "I'm so sorry, my friend."

"Thanks, and thanks for telling me." He glanced back into the museum, but the girls were nowhere to be seen. He was glad of that, in a way, because he didn't want the memory of Katerina mixed up with how he felt right now. "Look after her, Alex."

"I will. And if there's anything you need. I mean anything . . ."

"I appreciate it."

Finn shook hands again and left, stopping only to get his backpack from Valentin. He felt as if the world had tilted on its axis, as if nothing made sense anymore, as if his whole life had added up to nothing.

And a part of him was still clinging stubbornly to the belief that Sofi wouldn't do this to him, that she loved him as he loved her, and that Alex, even with all his resources, had to be mistaken. Whether or not, Finn had to get back to Tallinn, urgently. He had to get back, no matter what the truth that awaited him there.

Chapter Thirty-Two

The last time he'd flown into Heathrow, he'd sworn he would never do it again. He'd taken the train and the Eurostar on every subsequent trip back to England, but here he was again passing through the seven circles of hell. It at least served the purpose of reminding him why he loved history so much.

He'd called Alex before booking his flight, making sure he was in London, but when he got to the hotel the concierge said, "There's a message for you, Mr. Harrington."

It was from Alex, giving him an address in Mayfair. Finn stowed his bag in his room and jumped in a cab.

It was a fine-sized townhouse, but from the outside at least, it looked a lot smaller than the place in Kensington. He rang the bell, and almost immediately a young guy in a suit, looking for all the world like a member of staff in a trendy design hotel, opened the door.

Finn didn't recognize him, but the young guy spoke in a faint Russian accent, saying, "Good afternoon, Mr. Harrington. Mr. Naumenko is expecting you."

He was taken through to a living room, furnished entirely in white, where Alex was sitting watching the BBC news channel on a wall-mounted TV. At the sight of Finn, he hurried to turn it off and jumped up, coming over and hugging him as he said, "Finn, great to see you!" He stood back, smiling. "You're looking very well indeed." His English had always been good, but now there was almost no Russian lilt at all.

Alex was tanned, lean, and fit as ever, more relaxed than Finn had ever seen him. Last time they'd met, his hair had been graying, but now it was a uniform natural-looking brown.

Was he still dangerous? Did he even need to be anymore? Of course, Finn had never seen him like that anyway—their friendship had always been too good, their business partnership even better.

"You're looking pretty good, too, Alex. The new girlfriend?"

"Not so new anymore. Three years now, and yes, we're very happy." The guy who'd opened the door was still standing, awaiting instructions, and Alex turned to him now and said, "Champagne, I think. We'll take it in the study."

The guy nodded and disappeared.

Finn followed Alex out of the room and said, "What brought about the move? I thought you loved the place in Kensington."

"It's being remodeled. I bought this place so we don't have to be around all the noise and disturbance. I should have told you—I imagine you're at The Halkin."

Finn nodded.

"I should have thought, I'm sorry."

"Don't worry, it's not far."

They reached the study, and Alex stepped aside for Finn to go in first.

"As a matter of fact, you're lucky to catch me—we're flying out tomorrow. Can we give you a ride anywhere?"

"I doubt it, not unless you're going to Helsinki."

"Intriguing," said Alex, smiling, trying to guess what Finn might be up to. "But no, wrong direction. Okay, we'll talk business after the champagne comes, but for now I need you to do something for me." He walked over to one of the bookshelves and took down Finn's three published books in hardback. "It's very good of your publisher to send them to me, but please, you must sign them."

As it happened, Finn had never told his publishers about Alex, knowing it was a friendship they would have wanted to exploit for its publicity value. Finn had sent the books himself on his various visits to London.

"Of course." Alex placed them on the desk and handed him a pen. As Finn signed, he said, "Did you enjoy them?"

"Very much. I knew I would. What are you working on now?"

"Well, as it happens, I haven't done very much work on it this last week or so, but I'm writing a book about the Cathars, focusing on the siege of Béziers."

Alex smiled and nodded his approval. "Yes, I know a little about it. They destroyed the whole town for refusing to give up a handful of heretics."

"That's the one. I'm glad to see you're still interested in history."

"A man needs a hobby, Finn, and all the best football teams have been taken."

The young guy came in with the champagne in an ice bucket and a couple of glasses on a silver tray. He opened the bottle, poured them both a glass, and left.

Alex raised his glass. "To old times."

"To old times," said Finn.

"Come, please." He gestured across the room to two large sofas facing each other. As they sat down, he said, "And last time we met you also had a new girlfriend. Adrienne?"

"Yeah, we're still together."

"Good." He sipped at his champagne. "What's troubling you, Finn?"

"Ed Perry—and Karasek." The second name caught Alex's attention. Finn quickly explained the events of the last week, including the contents of the memory stick. Alex listened intently but without judgment. Finn ended by saying, "Naturally, I need to find out what they're after, and I need to deal with it."

"And you want revenge." Finn offered him a puzzled expression, asking what it was he needed revenge for. "The boy was a friend of yours, no?"

It seemed odd to say it, because he'd met him just a few times, but Finn said, "Yeah, I suppose he was. I'll be honest, killing Perry and Karasek seems like the only way of guaranteeing I'll be left alone, but you're right, they deserve to die for what they've done this week."

"As a rule, I think one only ever needs one good reason for killing a man, but if having two eases your conscience, so be it."

"Aren't you concerned about your name appearing there—the numbered accounts?"

Alex smiled. "Karasek is a bitter man and I've had several successes which he might have believed were at his expense. He'd be afraid to challenge me directly, but if he could find something, anything to discredit me, he would."

"You don't seem unduly concerned."

"You remember we had a great conversation once, you and I, about how the Russian oligarchs were no different to the American robber barons of the nineteenth century, making money in dangerous times. We took risks, and you took some of those risks with me, for which I will always be grateful, but now we are no longer robber barons, we are part of the establishment. Karasek can do nothing to harm me."

Alex was flattering Finn, both in the part he'd played in his robber-baron past, and in the extent to which he was now part of the establishment. But the real difference between them was that

Perry and Karasek didn't fear Finn, and they could hurt more than his reputation if they decided to do so.

Alex got up and crossed the room to the champagne, bringing the bottle over to top up their glasses, then taking it back to the ice bucket.

"Paranoia is a possibility," said Alex. "I heard Karasek was working on something, I don't know what, but a comeback of some sort, and he's a paranoid man. They would have known about your involvement with Sparrowhawk . . ."

"But Sparrowhawk failed—okay, it ruined Perry's career, but if anything, it left Karasek even stronger."

"It doesn't matter. They knew the intent, and you know, there have been many rumors in the last six years, suggesting you never left."

Finn smiled. "If I hadn't left I'd be putting in a call to Louisa Whitman, because that's who I'd like to see right now, but I don't have those contacts anymore."

"You want to meet Louisa? Let me see what I can do." In response to Finn's bemused expression, Alex added, "As I said, I'm part of the establishment now."

He walked to the door, called a name, and had a brief conversation with someone in Russian. He came back into the room then and said, "There is another possibility, of course."

"You think he's still bitter about the girl?"

"No, that hadn't occurred to me, but you could be right."

There was a pause as Alex sipped at his champagne, and Finn said, "About Katerina . . ."

Alex smiled. "We said we'd never talk of her again. You want to know what happened to her now, of all times?"

"No, you're right." It was a complication he didn't need, that was certainly true. "You've thought of another motive?"

"Yes, the numbered accounts. Maybe it's all about the money."

"You think they'd go to all this trouble for that? And Karasek, why would he need—"

Alex wagged his finger, a playful admonishment, as he said, "Karasek's finances were never as strong as they appeared. He's an Estonian—he never had access to the commodities and natural resources that were available to us. I understand much of his wealth was leveraged, built on debt, and during the credit crisis many of those debts were called in. It's one of the reasons he had to leave Tallinn and move to . . . Of course, Helsinki."

"So that's it—you think all this could be about money."

"Isn't everything?" He shrugged. "Karasek and Perry probably have some idea of the business we did together—it could be a combined operation, ostensibly investigating my concerns, trying to undermine me, but finding the means to refinance in the process."

A suited guy knocked and came in, not the same one who'd opened the door to Finn earlier. He handed Alex a piece of paper, gave a small bow of the head to Finn, and left.

Alex looked at the paper and said, "She's having an early dinner at the Berkeley hotel, Marcus Wareing's restaurant. The table name is Adams. If you go there about eight thirty, she'll see you."

"That's impressive."

"Money opens doors, and trust me, whatever other motives they have, Perry and Karasek are chasing the money—yours, mine, and all the money in those other accounts."

Finn shook his head. "I don't believe it. It just seems too crazy."

"You don't want to believe it, because you don't want to believe that people could carry out such crimes for any amount of money, but you and I both know of people who've carried out far worse for loose change."

"True enough. I could use a number for Karasek if you have one."

"I'm sure you could. I'll get it and send it to you."

"Thanks. I'll use it wisely."

Alex nodded, but said, "Isn't there a famous phrase about Béziers—something about killing them all?"

Finn had met a few other Russian oligarchs in his time, and he bought Alex's robber-baron analogy because they were smart people as a rule, and serious, but Aleksandr Naumenko was still the only one he could imagine showing this level of interest in thirteenth-century history.

"That's it. The Abbot of Cîteaux was asked how they'd recognize the two hundred heretics among twenty thousand townspeople. He's said to have answered, 'Kill them all, God will know his own.'"

Alex smiled appreciatively, absorbing words that had managed to maintain their power over eight hundred years—their power and their perverse wisdom and all their compelling horror. It was a ruthlessness of the kind he'd often used in his own life, and Alex's message seemed to be clear, that the real wisdom for Finn now would be to show a little bit of that ruthlessness himself.

Chapter Thirty-Three

Finn arrived at The Berkeley a little after eight, sat in the bar and had a drink, checking out who else was in there, out of habit rather than because he believed Louisa would respond to his sudden appearance by putting people on the ground. She was too relaxed for those games, too in control.

At eight thirty he ordered another drink, but then went to the front desk and said, "I have an important message for someone dining in the Marcus Wareing restaurant, sitting at a table in the name of Adams. She's a Miss Whitman. Could you let her know that her nephew has arrived and is in the bar?"

The concierge had been scribbling on a notepad the whole time he'd been speaking, and he smiled now and said, "Of course, sir, I'll do that right away."

Finn strolled back to the bar and sat down. A moment later, his second drink arrived. He was looking forward to seeing Louisa again, and oddly, he found himself nervous, too, as if he were about to face an appraisal. It took some effort to remind himself that he no longer answered to Louisa, nor to anyone else.

He waited ten minutes. If she'd been mid-course, she wasn't the kind of person to stop just so that she could come out and chat with him. It summed up one of the things he'd always liked about her, that she'd never allowed a job that could be socially cauterizing to limit her enjoyment of life.

When she did appear, it took him by surprise. Someone left the bar, briefly distracting him, and when he turned back Louisa was almost on him. She looked younger than he remembered her, less matronly, a lot less matronly.

He imagined she was only in her mid-fifties, an age gap that had seemed huge when he'd been in his twenties but was now marginal, as if he'd grown older but she hadn't. What he saw in front of him was a bookish, attractive woman in clothes that could pass either for business or for "ladies who lunch."

He stood and she said, "Oh, do sit down, Finn. How lovely to see you." She kissed him on the cheek. "Nephew! Younger brother would have been more appropriate."

The barman started to head over as she sat down, but she whisked him away again with a hand gesture that managed somehow to be both authoritative and friendly.

"Thanks for agreeing to see me, Louisa." He thought of mentioning the irony of Aleksandr Naumenko being able to set up a meeting with her whilst Finn didn't even have her number, but he saw how that conversation would go, how the world had changed, how Naumenko was now a useful ally. "I'll get straight to the point. There's a company called BGS—Brac Global Systems—and for the last two years it's had me under surveillance. I know from my own sources that it's also very interested in the events surrounding Sparrowhawk. I know that Ed Perry heads this organization and that Karasek is, at the very least, a client."

There was a pause but no facial reaction, and then she said, "Is there anything else you want to tell me?"

"Okay, how about this—last week, two employees of BGS put a noose around the neck of a fifteen-year-old boy and hanged him in the basement of his building in Lausanne. The police still think it's a suicide. One of those same employees last night tried to shoot an overdose of heroin into a schoolgirl, but failed. The boy and the girl were best friends, and what they did wrong was accidentally hack into a BGS network and download information."

Her expression became grave, and though no one else in the bar would have spotted it, he knew he'd shocked her.

"They were the sources you mentioned?"

"Yeah, and if it hadn't been for something else, I might never have found out and the boy might still be alive." She nodded, deep in thought, and he said, "That wasn't what you were thinking of, was it, when you asked if I had anything else to tell you?"

As if telling him something that no longer mattered, she sounded distracted as she said, "I was going to ask if you knew anything about the deaths of the two men you've just mentioned, the second of whom was found floating in Lake Geneva late this morning. I presume they *are* the two men you've just mentioned?"

"Tell me about BGS, Louisa."

"It's about to be wound up."

He felt a numb horror as the meaning of those words sunk in. "You mean it's yours? Gibson told me it was private."

"Gibson." She sighed wearily. "It is a private company—almost everyone who works for it believes that to be the case and it can't be traced back to us. It's Perry's baby, and for a while it looked like a good way of keeping him occupied."

Perry. The horror turned to anger. The one thing he'd been assured of six years ago was that, although they'd failed to take down Karasek, they'd harvested enough intelligence to end Perry's career. Only now did he fully appreciate how untrue that had been. Maybe Perry's desire for revenge had been personal, but it seemed he'd been directing it from within the safety of the government's tent.

"Perry's still in? Do you not remember the last conversation we ever had?"

"I do, and I believed it to be the case at the time, but Ed had powerful friends and favors to call in. It's not what many of us would have wanted."

"Most especially Harry Simons," said Finn. "Harry *is* dead, isn't he?"

"Of course he is! And look, Ed Perry's position was seriously weakened after Sparrowhawk—even if we weren't able to end his career, we were able to fence it in."

"By giving him free rein over his own little fiefdom?"

"Not entirely. Gibson was ostensibly ex-GCHQ and had quit to join BGS. In fact, he'd transferred to us and was working for us from within." Finn remembered something Gibson had said, how most of the notes on the memory stick had related to his attempts to make sense of things. Was that why he'd had a network in the first place? "Of course, that makes it all the more regrettable that you and he had a little run-in."

"He killed a schoolboy." Louisa nodded, accepting the point. "What about Taylor, was he one of yours?"

She shook her head. "Former SBS."

"No he wasn't!" She looked askance. "Louisa, I can handle myself, but if I'd run up against special forces last night, it'd be me floating in Lake Geneva."

"Former SBS is what he claimed, and as far as BGS is concerned, that's what he was. Ed might be having his doubts now, of course." She smiled. "I believe in reality he spent two rather unremarkable years in an infantry regiment, nine months in prison, and four years as a freelance bodyguard in Iraq."

As she was in an expansive mood, he said, "What's BGS about, Louisa—what was its purpose, what are they doing coming after me?"

"Finn, do you believe for one moment that I'm about to discuss operational matters with you? As to the latter question, I'm not sure, frankly—we'll look into it, we'll get to the bottom of it, and you'll never be any the wiser." She looked at her watch. "I should go back in. Is there anything else I can help you with?"

That was typical Louisa, to ask a question like that when she hadn't actually helped at all yet. But he also knew that the help could be forthcoming, down the line, if she thought it appropriate.

"You could tell me where Ed Perry is."

"Indeed, I could, but I won't. And what are your plans? Back to work on another book? I bought one, by the way—haven't got around to reading it yet, but I will, perhaps this summer."

"When I was leaving six years ago, you offered me an opportunity to go out in style, with Sparrowhawk—I'd be considered a traitor by many, I'd leave under a veneer of disgrace that only a select few would know to be unjustified, but the prize was the downfall of Karasek and the exposure of Ed Perry as someone who'd been working against this country's interests."

"Not every operation succeeds, Finn. If it had, it would've been a great achievement, and I wish it hadn't failed in quite the way it did and at quite the cost, but that wasn't your fault, either."

"You're missing the point, Louisa." She looked mockingly intrigued. "It's too late in many respects—clearly the world's moved on—but I'm flying to Helsinki early in the morning, where I intend to pay Karasek a visit and finish what should have been finished six years ago."

She raised her eyebrows, still smiling a little. "So those are your plans. I could stop you doing that, of course."

"Indeed, you could, but you won't. The question you have to ask yourself is whether you want to help me or not. Give it some thought."

"No, and I won't condone such stupidity, in either a personal or professional capacity. Not that anything I say will stop you going." She stood up and moved around her chair, then looked at him again. She sounded more conciliatory as she said, "It's been a while since I was in Helsinki. Will you stay at the Kämp?"

"Yes, for old times' sake. Harry and I had some riotous nights in the bar of the Kämp."

"I can imagine."

"Where's Perry, Louisa?"

"You're a fool even to ask."

"I don't think my foolishness has ever been in doubt." She smiled. "Just do me one favor—do a check on Jonas Frost. He was the boy they killed, and I only just met him but he was one of the best people I've ever known. Do a check, and see the real cost of our failure to fence Perry in."

She gave a little nod. "Okay, I'll do that much. And do be careful, Finn. One day very soon, you and I will sit down and have a proper conversation."

She turned and walked purposefully out of the bar. He could imagine her going back to the table, and depending on the identity of her fellow guests, dismissing the interruption and the reasons for it as gracefully and succinctly as she'd dismissed the barman a short while before.

Finn was left wondering what he'd come to London for. He'd found out the galling truth of Perry's survival, and something of what BGS was about. But he still had nothing more than Gibson's talk of revenge or Alex's speculation about money to explain why they'd come after Finn, or what they wanted from him.

He'd laid down a marker with Louisa Whitman, letting her know what had really happened in Switzerland. He'd also let her know what he intended to do, gambling that she wouldn't put obstacles in his way. And he'd received Karasek's contact details from Alex, but all together these things hardly justified the trip.

Perhaps nostalgia had brought him here, a desire to meet Alex and Louisa again, to immerse himself once more in the world of information. But above all, he suspected it was uncertainty that had propelled him. He had no idea what would happen in the next few days or whether his luck would hold, and he wanted someone—even someone who would never talk about it—to know what his purpose had been.

He'd made it clear to Louisa that he was going to finish what should have been finished six years ago, or at least his part in it. Because for all that time, without even realizing it, he'd been living on edge, pushing away the people closest to him, and he wouldn't live like that anymore—the cost was far too high.

History

He got a flight after lunch. From the moment he'd left the museum until after takeoff, his mind sifted again and again through the things Alex had said about Sofi and what it meant, searching for innocent explanations or mitigating factors. The best he could hope for was that she'd betrayed him and loved him at the same time, and that was his final defensive line, the belief that she could not have faked what they'd shared this last year.

Only as the plane flew high above the Baltic did he think of Kaliningrad and all the things he'd feared until a few hours before, things which now seemed like a sideshow because he no longer had much of a future left to lose.

But he would lose it all the same, because if Karasek had survived, and if the subsequent investigation also failed to produce enough concrete evidence to end Perry's career, then the only thing to really come out of it would be proof that Finn had handed sensitive documents to a known gangster.

If that was the case, it all depended on how Louisa had constructed the operation, and how willing she would be to hang Finn out to dry in exchange for the promise of getting the scalps she'd sought further down the line. He'd jumped so readily at the chance of Sparrowhawk, so relieved had he been that they didn't know about him and Naumenko, that he'd ignored the ramifications of it going wrong.

And now, he realized it was just as well he was getting out, because he'd prided himself on his skill, on his expertise, if not his professionalism. Yet in truth, he'd allowed himself to be set up as a scapegoat, and had perhaps been played by a foreign agent for the last twelve months—he'd never seen his business with Naumenko as real corruption, but this was certainly looking like real incompetence.

He took a taxi from the airport, and by the time it got close to the apartment, the streets were already filling up with stag weekenders, some of them dressed outlandishly, providing a boost to the local economy and tarnishing the reputation of the British all at once. Still, he thought, each of these interchangeable groups spilling along the street at least represented a future wedding—there was that to be said for them, if nothing else.

He took the stairs, and even as he pushed his key into the lock he could hear Sofi talking. He made an effort to be quiet opening the door, even though it seemed that she was on the phone. But as he closed it gently behind him, his caution paid off, because a man said a few words, the sound cutting Finn to the bone, and then Sofi continued.

Finn stood for a moment, not sure what to do. They were in the living room, but should he just go in there and confront them? He saw his summer coat hanging on the rack and remembered the gun he'd dropped into the pocket, grateful that he'd forgotten to remove it subsequently. He took it now, and stepped quietly into the living room.

They both had their backs to him. Sofi was standing, talking into the phone as he'd first suspected. A guy with dark, cropped hair and a fitted black sweater was sitting on the sofa, hunched over a laptop on the coffee table. It was Finn's laptop.

It was the guy who spotted him first, perhaps sensing that someone was standing there. He turned, saw Finn, then said something to Sofi. She turned, jumped– unmistakably a jump . . . had she always been secretly afraid of him?—then ended the call and said, "Finn! What are you doing back?"

"I finished early. What's going on?"

"It's really embarrassing—promise you won't be mad at me. My computer went down and I tried to use yours but I think I did something maybe wrong. This is Peter, our tech guy from the newspaper. He can fix it, I promise." It was the intonation, the look on her face—if it hadn't been for what Alex had told him, he would have believed her, as implausible as the story was.

"That's a relief." She smiled, the edges collapsing away as Finn continued: "So he's not trying to hack into my laptop and you're not a Russian agent who's been screwing me for the last year in every way, and I didn't fall in love with someone who pretended to be in love with me when she actually cared nothing."

"That's not true!"

"Are you in love with me?"

"Yes," she said, but there seemed no conviction in it, and the lie leeched the blood and the energy out of him. He felt an odd disconnect at the sight of this woman who was so familiar and yet simultaneously a stranger, too. Because he knew now, in her eyes and her lips and the tremor in her voice, that she had never loved him.

"Were you ever even attracted to me? If you weren't, then you should consider a career as an actress because you had me completely fooled."

"Finn, it's not what you think."

"Yeah, I've been hearing that a lot lately—seems I got everyone wrong."

"I cared for you," she said, and in those four words the betrayal seemed complete. She'd cared for him, she had come to care for him, but not to love him. He struggled even to think of an appropriate response.

But he didn't get the chance to speak again. Sofi couldn't see the gun from where she was standing, but the guy could see it hanging by Finn's side and had probably guessed how this would end. Suddenly, he leapt from the chair, barreling low across the room. He pushed past Finn and out into the hallway, heading for the front door.

Finn raised the gun, aimed at his back and said, "Open that door and I'll shoot." The guy froze, his hand on the latch, as if trying to judge how serious the threat might be.

And then, too late, Finn caught some movement from the corner of his eye and felt something hard crash and splinter into the back of his head. It knocked him forward, a percussive pain sounding through his skull. He thought he'd fired the gun for a moment, but it was the impact of the blow or the door slamming shut as the guy made his escape.

She'd hit him hard with something. He tried to stand upright, struggling to get his bearings. Was the gun still in his hand? For a moment, he wasn't even sure. And then he saw something again, or heard it, felt the disturbance in the air as she swung a second time. He threw himself back into the blow and knocked her backward, too, and heard the clatter and a visceral crack as he crashed to the floor.

He was up quickly this time, onto his haunches, and the gun was still in his hand, he felt it now, but immediately he stopped and stayed very still. It was the laptop, that was what she'd hit him with, and only as he looked at it on the floor did he feel the trickle of blood, warm in his hair.

Sofi looked unharmed. She'd fallen to the floor, too, her head against the side of the sofa, and it could not have been a heavy fall. She didn't look damaged in any way, except for the strange angle at which her head was positioned in relation to her body.

He didn't move for several seconds, still expecting her to groan, to free herself from that awkward resting place, because people didn't die so easily. Finally, he put the gun in his pocket and moved cautiously toward her, reaching out to the warmth of her neck, searching for a pulse he would not find.

And when he finally accepted that no harm could be done by moving her, he pulled her free and rested her head properly on the floor. He touched her lips, brushed his fingers over the softness of her cheek, stroked her hair, trying to understand that she was dead, that he had killed her, that perhaps she had tried to kill him.

He sat next to her and held her hand, and wanted to cry but could not, perhaps because of the shock, or because he didn't know what those tears would be for. He was angry, too, that this had denied him a full explanation, that he was left with only the lies and not the hope that some part of her had been true.

He didn't know how long he sat there. Her hand was still warm when he eventually let it go, though he didn't know if that was residual or the heat from his own hand warming hers. He looked at her face again, at the beauty that had so easily fooled him, and he knew for sure now that he'd lost everything.

He took out his phone, but was hit with a fresh realization, that until the mess of Sparrowhawk was sorted out he couldn't even phone Harry, let alone anyone else from the office. But he needed someone to help him through this, and he had only one contact left, so without even thinking, numb and empty, he put in a call to Louisa, and waited.

Chapter Thirty-Four

His plane took off into a clear blue sky, and it remained like that over the whole of Northern Europe. The snow that had fallen across Scandinavia the week before was still evident, the landscape of Sweden white and clearly defined. But the sea was free of ice now, suggesting this had been winter's parting shot.

It was the same as the plane descended along the Finnish coast into Helsinki. There was still plenty of snow on the ground, but it glistened in the sunlight and he could easily imagine coming back here a week from now to find it all gone. He thought of Harry Simons, and about how depressed he would have been by the thought of the cold weather's imminent retreat.

Once he got to the hotel, he checked into his room and called Karasek's number. It rang a couple of times before someone answered. Finn didn't understand the words but recognized Karasek's voice instantly—he hadn't anticipated that Alex might have given him Karasek's personal cell number.

"Mr. Karasek, it's Finn Harrington."

There was a pause before Karasek said, "Who are you and how did you get this number?"

His accent had improved since they'd last spoken. It wasn't the near-faultless standard of Alex's English, but a vast improvement on where it had been.

"You know who I am, Mr. Karasek, but let's speed things up. I got this number because Aleksandr Naumenko gave it to me. We have some matters that we need to discuss with you."

Finn knew he wouldn't refuse, the unease of having any dealings with Alex being tempered by the presence of an apparent middleman, a meeting certainly preferable to what might happen if he did refuse.

Once again there was a pause before he said, "Then you ought to come over, Mr. Harrington."

"No. We meet in a neutral location and I want a private conversation, none of your guys around. How about the bar of the Hotel Kämp?"

"I'll get back to you." The line went dead.

It was fifteen minutes before he called back. Finn had no doubt that he'd called Perry during that time. Unless Karasek had outworn his usefulness, Perry would have warned him that Finn might well try to kill him.

"Finn Harrington."

"The Ateljee Bar on the fourteenth floor of the Hotel Sokos Torni, two p.m. Don't bring a gun. My men will search you and then leave us alone—we can talk of what we want."

Finn scribbled it down and said, "I'll see you then."

He arrived just before two, and shared the small elevator with a handful of people who were well dressed and in high spirits. They reached the top regular floor of the hotel, and stepped out into a small lobby. The other visitors piled through the door to a metal spiral staircase that climbed up to the bar itself, perched like a crow's nest on top of the building.

Two heavy-set guys, in suits but quite distinct from the small joyous crowd, were standing in the lobby as if waiting to take the elevator down, but as soon as they saw Finn they gestured for him to come to one side. He smiled, waited until the others had set off, clanging up the stairs to what sounded like a party above, and then held his hands out wide.

One stood a little way distant, vigilant, while the other patted him down, clearly looking for either a weapon or a wire. Like Alex had said, Karasek was a paranoid man, and perhaps with good reason—it seemed the world had moved on and left him behind, just as it had with Khodorkovsky and countless others, all in different ways and for different reasons, the one common factor being that they had once seemed to be rewriting history but were now mere footnotes.

Once the bodyguard was satisfied, he stood back and gestured toward the stairs up to the bar.

Finn smiled and said, "I won't keep you long."

The guy looked back noncommittally, giving Finn the impression that he didn't speak English. They were smarter and sleeker than the guys who'd worked for Karasek back in Tallinn, and in better shape than the old crowd, too.

Finn took the stairs, the laughter and voices above him joyous enough that he doubted Karasek was part of it. And as he emerged into the small, crowded bar, he quickly realized it was a wedding party. They were filling the internal bar area and had spilled out onto the large viewing deck on the north side.

Finn turned to look the other way. The southern viewing deck was occupied by just two people, one guarding the door, the other sitting at one of the tables, with what looked like a gin and tonic in front of him—Karasek, looking oddly defiant.

As Finn approached the door, the bodyguard appeared disinclined to move, but Karasek looked over, said something, and the guy opened the door and allowed Finn to step out. Finn smiled at him, then looked at the view and felt the biting wind sting his face.

The bodyguard stepped through the door and closed it, staring out at them rather than at the party within. Finn could see every aspect of Karasek's decision to meet here. It was a controlled environment: out of range of sniper fire or passers-by, plenty of witnesses should Finn want to try anything. The viewing platforms had once been protected only by handrails, but reinforced glass had been placed inside of them now, reaching up to chest height. Despite the appeal of being fourteen floors up, the opportunities for killing Karasek here would be slight.

Kill him he would, though—if not now, then certainly on this trip. Karasek ignored Finn, instead picking up his drink and sucking through the straws. Finn looked at him, smiling, because drinking his gin and tonic through straws was exactly the kind of decision that made Karasek look like a precocious schoolboy in his father's suit.

Finn paid him no more attention, looking out at the view across the city to the blue of the sea and the small flat islands.

After a while, Finn said, "I bet you like it up here. On a good day you can probably see all the way across to Tallinn. I don't think you're really welcome in Tallinn, though, not anymore. I'm surprised they put up with you here. Give them time, I suppose."

"What do you want?"

Finn sat down opposite him, then looked at the door. "I don't like him looking at me."

"What of it? He's inside. He can't hear."

"Okay, sorry to have wasted your time." Finn stood. "I told Naumenko it was better if he spoke to you himself."

Finn walked toward the door, a couple of steps, and was reaching for the handle when Karasek said, "Relax, Mr. Harrington. You seem to have lost your *cool* since the last time we met."

Finn looked back at him. Karasek gestured casually, and the bodyguard nodded and headed for the spiral staircase. Finn gave a look of being contrite, as if he realized he'd been petty. He came back and sat down.

"So, what is so important that Naumenko must discuss with me?"

"Actually, he couldn't care less what you're up to. He knows you're working with BGS to try to bring him down, but he also knows you'll fail to do that. I think he's concerned that his name is mentioned in connection with some numbered bank accounts that you and BGS are trying to access."

"I don't know what you're talking about."

He seemed genuinely mystified, so maybe Karasek wasn't chasing the money after all, but had some other motive.

"Nor do we, if I'm honest, but we'll find out. See, we intercepted the BGS network. We know you're working with them, and we know that in some way you're trying to use me to get to Naumenko. Once we've joined those dots, I think you'll find Aleksandr Naumenko will be very interested."

That was enough for Karasek to look a little rattled, suggesting Finn was in the right neighborhood.

"I have no connection with this BGS. I tell you what I think . . . I think somebody is using BGS to get to me, not Aleksandr Naumenko."

Finn nodded, smiling in a way that made Karasek even more jumpy.

"I imagine you spoke to Perry after I called you. Did he tell you Gibson is dead? I killed him. I killed Taylor, too. They're both dead, but Gibson talked first, so I know exactly how involved you are with BGS, and so does Alex. But here's the good news—the person we really want is Perry, so tell us what you know about what Perry's up to, and we won't have a problem with you."

Karasek smiled, trying to look superior but appearing priggish, then stabbed the air with his finger and said, "Join the dots."

Finn looked out over the city. A small plane was crossing the sky, pulling a long banner behind it. For a moment, he tried to read what it said, forgetting it would be in Finnish.

"You know they killed a fifteen-year-old boy last week, and they tried to kill a girl, too?"

Karasek shrugged, clearly unaware of Jonas's death, but equally unconcerned by it. The death of a boy was nothing to Karasek, but as much as Finn wanted it to be otherwise, it seemed the crimes against Jonas and Hailey had been entirely Perry's doing, not Karasek's.

The small plane crossed into his line of vision over Karasek's shoulder, and Finn realized now that it was circling the tower at a distance. He looked inside and saw the whole wedding party crushing toward the other viewing platform. It seemed the banner was a message for the newlyweds.

He looked back at Karasek and said, "Sparrowhawk—it was meant to destroy you and destroy Perry."

"It failed."

"True." He could hear the plane, but it was out of sight now, on the other side of the tower. "And it's so rare in my business that you get a second chance."

Karasek shook his head, baffled and mocking. Finn heard a spontaneous cheer from the bar and glanced inside, the banner now in sight to those on the other platform, everyone in the bar facing north.

Finn lunged across the table, punching Karasek hard in the face. It wasn't enough to knock him out, but fierce enough to leave him shaken, groggy. Finn jumped up, pulled him to his feet. Karasek mumbled something in Estonian. Finn threw him against the reinforced glass, adrenaline pumping, the cheers and claps still coming from within the bar. He grabbed Karasek by the chest and crotch, and thrust him upward, just managing to get his center of gravity over the lip of the glass, tipping him over.

Karasek realized what was happening and cried out, his voice lost against the party and the wind licking around the tower. He thrust out with his arms, then grabbed wildly as he fell down the other side of the glass, his feet finding the narrow ledge, one hand finding the railing, then the other.

"Stop, Harrington! Wait!" He was breathing rapidly, as if his heart might fail him. "It was Perry who wanted you. He knew Sparrowhawk was a trick, that you were trying to catch him. That's what he was doing. He wants to prove you worked with Naumenko, that you were . . ."

"Corrupt?"

"Yes, yes—corrupt."

"Why did you help? What was *your* reason for getting involved?"

"For everything . . . for Kaliningrad, for Katerina, but . . . it wasn't . . ."

Finn nodded and said, "I know." He punched over the top of the glass, one hard swing downward into Karasek's face. Karasek fell silently—probably stunned by the punch—which Finn thought a shame.

Finn turned and walked off the terrace. As he did so, the first of the wedding party turned away from the other terrace and the view of the plane that now flew on toward the west. Still none of them looked at him or out to the other terrace, let alone wondered if there had not been another man out there.

He caught a glimpse of the bride and groom as he headed down the stairs—not a particularly young couple, perhaps around his own age or Adrienne's. And as he reached the bottom of the spiral staircase, another small group of partygoers was just coming out of the elevator.

The three bodyguards stood alert at the sight of Finn, but he simply smiled and stepped into the recently vacated elevator car. One of the guards, the one who'd been sent down, tried to go back up but found himself stuck behind the late guests on the stairs.

As he left the hotel, Finn noticed a small crowd off to one side—mostly workers from the hotel by the look of them. One of them came running back into the hotel, a look of horror and distress on his face, and in the gap that had briefly opened up Finn saw Karasek's smashed body, which fittingly had landed in the gutter. The crowd and the surrounding street were surprisingly subdued—no screams, no shouts, no alarm.

Finn strolled back to his hotel. He had an answer, one as anticlimactic as had always seemed to be the case—it had all been about revenge, fueled no doubt by Perry's increasing realization that his newfound autonomy was actually a form of sidelining, and perhaps fueled further by Finn's new career. It wouldn't have surprised him if Perry's plan dated back to the first time he'd seen one of Finn's books in an airport bookstore.

Somehow, Finn wasn't even shocked by the pettiness of it. A boy had been murdered, a girl almost killed, families destroyed, and all because one corrupt civil servant had objected to the part another corrupt civil servant had played in his partial downfall. It should have been shocking, but Finn's passion was history, a subject that was littered with trivial horrors.

The snow had been cleared from the esplanade, and people were sitting at tables outside the cafés, enjoying the sun, protected from the cold by blankets. It made him realize how much he'd missed this city, and the north in general.

As he walked, he was still determined that he would kill Perry, that he had no choice anyway if he wanted his life back. But he desperately wanted his life to return to normal now—or a new normal.

He wanted to sink back into his books, into Béziers, but he also wanted Adrienne there with him.

He walked into the hotel and headed across the lobby, making for the elevators. One of the concierges was talking to a young businessman in a suit and heavy coat, but when he saw Finn he stopped and called out, "Mr. Harrington."

Finn turned, and the concierge gestured toward him and said, "This is Mr. Harrington." He looked back to Finn then, smiling as he said, "We just tried your room—this gentleman has called to see you."

"Thanks," said Finn, and looked at the young guy standing there, smooth-faced, pale in a healthy way, his hair about as bedhead as he could get away with whilst wearing a suit—he looked like a Burberry model. Finn gestured toward the middle of the lobby and they moved over there. The guy was carrying a briefcase, which he was holding a little too tightly. They stood for a second and then Finn said, "Well?"

"Right, of course. Is there somewhere we could talk in private, Mr. Harrington?"

"I'm staying here, so there's my room, but before we go anywhere that isn't a public place, how about telling me who you are, who sent you, how you knew I was here, and above all, what's in the briefcase."

"Right, of course. My name's Robin Forrester, I'm from the British embassy, and the briefcase is for you. I can't tell you who sent me."

"Then you can take your briefcase back to the British embassy and leave me to enjoy my little holiday."

Forrester looked impressed in some way, and said, "I was told you'd say something like that. I was also told to tell you that I'd been sent by your friend from the Berkeley hotel."

"Okay, let's go." They walked toward the elevators, and stepped into the first available car and stood in silence as it started to move.

Finn found himself amused by this turn of events. In that final exchange with Karasek, he'd accidentally talked about "my business," forgetting it hadn't been his business for six years. Now it seemed he wasn't alone in forgetting that. He stood there as the elevator ascended, a courier of sorts standing next to him, and it all had a sense of terrible familiarity, as if he'd never left this hotel, as if everything that had happened in the last six years had melted away.

Chapter Thirty-Five

Once they got to Finn's room, Forrester put the briefcase on the desk and finally released his grip on the handle. Finn looked at him, studying the way he was dressed before saying, "You're not at the embassy, are you? You flew in this morning. Were you on the same flight as me?"

"I think so. I was in economy, though. How did you know?"

"You're not wearing a scarf. There don't appear to be any gloves in your coat pockets. You're just not dressed the way you would be if you were based here. You flew out from London, where the weather is balmy, and you still can't quite take in how cold it is here."

Forrester grimaced. "It is a little colder than I'd anticipated, but I'll be flying back this afternoon."

"Okay, let's see what's in this case." Finn walked over to the desk, but Forrester immediately looked uneasy.

"Then I should go, Mr. Harrington. It's not for me to know what's in the case."

"No, you can stay." He went to the far side of the desk and turned the case so that Forrester wouldn't see the contents, then beckoned him closer. "It's not a bomb, is it? Because if it is, we both go together."

"Of course it's not a bomb."

"How do you know? You don't know what's in it."

"Because that's not the . . ." He stopped, realizing Finn was toying with him. "Sorry, I'm a bit slow today—that early flight and—"

"Don't worry about it, Robin." Finn flipped the catches, opening the briefcase and looking inside. A gun in a shoulder holster, spare magazines, a map, and a few sheets of paper. The top sheet had the details of Ed Perry's location. A separate printout showed how to get to it—the place was out in the sticks. "So, Perry's here in Finland." Forrester didn't respond.

He wondered at Louisa's change of heart, but then noticed a small envelope and opened it. There was a single sheet of notepaper inside on which Louisa had written, *I'm so sorry about your friend.* He nodded to himself, and put it back in the envelope.

He took the map out now, studied it, then checked his watch. Even allowing for the weather, it was probably a ninety-minute drive, which would leave him with an hour of daylight if he left soon.

He looked at Forrester and said, "Is there anything else, Robin?"

"Two things. Firstly, there's a car for you in the hotel garage. If you ask the concierge, it'll be brought round for you."

"Good, although I won't need it until tomorrow." He looked at his watch again and added, "Looking at the map, I wouldn't get there in time today."

Once again, Forrester looked slightly uneasy, not wanting to hear anything more than he needed to. That unease probably prevented him from seeing that Finn was feeding him a line, just in case word got back to Perry.

"The other thing is a message from the person who sent you the case. She said, and I quote, 'The foreign national should be left alone.'"

Finn nodded and said, "Any idea who the foreign national is?"

Forrester shook his head, lying reasonably well. "I presumed you would know who she was talking about."

"I do, but unfortunately the foreign national in question jumped from the top of a fourteen-story building about half an hour ago."

Rather than looking troubled or questioning whether he'd really jumped, Forrester frowned and said, "I didn't think there were any fourteen-story buildings in Helsinki—it's quite low-rise."

"When a man's determined to kill himself, he'll find one." Finn smiled, letting Forrester know they were done here. "Thanks for the case. Don't miss your flight."

"Of course. Thank you." He leaned forward and shook Finn's hand, then turned and walked to the door. Just before he closed it behind him, he raised his hand in a wave.

Finn emptied the contents of the briefcase onto the desk and studied the map in more detail, checking his watch to make sure he wasn't wasting too much time. He was determined to keep the initiative, and that meant getting there this afternoon.

There were two printouts, not one; the second, which he hadn't seen at first, was a satellite image of the property. It was a summerhouse set on a small lake, surrounded by forest. From both the photograph and the map, it looked like a private estate, with nothing resembling a village or settlement anywhere close.

Possibly it was Perry's own place—from what little he could determine from a picture of the roof and a small wooden jetty protruding into the lake, it didn't look grand enough for Karasek's tastes. What Finn couldn't understand was why Perry would go there now, with the country still in the grip of winter.

Was it the most simple explanation—that he'd gone there because he knew Finn was coming after him? In that regard he'd chosen well: a place that was remote, where Perry would have the advantage over anyone who didn't know the terrain.

Finn put on the holster, gathered up everything else, and headed back down to the lobby. The same concierge smiled as Finn approached him.

"I understand I have a car in the hotel garage—could you have someone bring it around?"

"Of course, right away, sir."

"Thanks." He strolled away from the desk, thinking through this apparent change of heart from Louisa.

In some intangible way, it seemed too reminiscent of Sparrowhawk, an operation that had been hastily yet intricately planned, in which so many players had been unaware of the total truth, and yet from which Perry and Karasek had walked away unscathed. And now here she was using Finn a second time to try to bring Perry down.

For a moment, he even wondered if Louisa was setting him up—handing him the gun, the car, the directions, luring him into a trap in the middle of nowhere, the perfect place to dispose of a body, allowing them all to go on as they had been before.

It was nonsense, of course—a touch of paranoia to go with all the other reminders of his old life. Louisa Whitman had wanted to eliminate Perry for a long time. And perhaps she'd been moved by Jonas Frost's death, but she wasn't doing this because Finn had proved the moral case, but because it was expedient, an easy way of erasing one of their own without getting their hands dirty. No wonder Forrester had wanted no knowledge of what was in that case.

He saw a jeep pull up outside and a valet jump out of it. He walked forward, took the keys, and got in. He was about to arrange the maps on the passenger seat when he noticed the satnav on the dash. He turned it on and saw that there was only one route programmed into it: the Hotel Kämp to Perry's place on the lake. And he smiled—even if they were setting him up, at least they were doing it in style.

Chapter Thirty-Six

The farther he got from Helsinki, the more fiercely winter seemed to be still holding on. For the first three-quarters of an hour, he'd made such good time that he thought he'd been overcautious in judging how long it would take him. But then he turned onto back roads, and his progress almost came to a halt.

The snow looked like a solid crust over the earth, particularly where the trees opened out into sweeping meadows that stretched flat and white to isolated farmhouses. The sun was falling away to the south and west behind him, but now that he was away from the city, it seemed harder to believe that a few glorious days would be enough to allow a thaw to set in.

By the time he reached a turn off the road, finding a gate in the deer fence and a track beyond it, he reckoned he only had half an hour of daylight left. In among the trees, the snow was already taking on its own shadowy darkness.

He closed the gate behind him and drove on, slowly, keeping the jeep as quiet as possible on the final approach, relieved that they'd chosen petrol for him rather than diesel. He drove for ten minutes more, then saw what at first he thought to be a clearing up in front and the house off to the right-hand side.

The clearing was the lake, and out here the ice had not melted. The house was bigger than he'd imagined, wooden and brightly painted in yellow and green. There was a single light showing in one of the rooms.

Finn stopped the car, sat for a moment with the engine idling, then turned it off. And all the time he watched the window with the light on, glancing now and then at the other windows, too, looking for movement and seeing none.

With the engine off, the silence was overpowering, and he realized his attempt to drive slowly along the track had been pointless. Perry would have heard him even before he'd reached the gate, and he certainly would have heard him in the thirty seconds he'd sat with the engine idling.

Yet he hadn't looked out. That meant one of two things, either that Perry wasn't curious because he knew who his visitor was, or that he wasn't in the house. Finn checked his mirrors, the forest behind him now looking as if evening had already arrived. He turned casually from side to side too, but if Perry was outside, he wasn't anywhere close.

Finn stepped out, leaving the door open, the jeep itself between him and the house. He strolled to the back as if checking for something, looking out into the woods behind the house. Then he turned and walked the other way, finally stepping to the front of the car, giving up his partial cover.

As had always been the case in the past, his senses tricked him with what followed. Did he hear the distant hammer crack first, or the whistling firework sound that told him the bullet had missed? The whistle of the bullet had been close, creating the illusion that he'd felt the air moving, and then it had splintered into one of the trees beyond, snow falling in a hushed shower from the branches.

Finn dropped to the floor and scuttled behind the jeep, placing himself behind the front tire. A little snow was still toppling down from the tree that had been hit, and he drew an imaginary line from the contact site, through where he'd been standing, projecting onward to give an idea of Perry's direction. It had been a rifle shot, but with so much tree cover he guessed Perry could only be a couple of hundred yards away.

Another shot rang out through the still winter air, the round hitting the side of the jeep, but not at the front, where Perry knew Finn was taking cover. The shot had hit near the back, then another. Finn knew what Perry was up to, and now he regretted that they'd given him petrol instead of diesel.

A fourth shot came as Finn sprang away from the jeep toward the trees. He heard and felt the dull roar of the petrol tank going up before he'd come to a stop. He didn't hesitate now, scrambling quickly to his feet and darting away from the burning vehicle, back along the track he'd driven down, cutting into the trees, putting on speed even in the snow.

He heard another shot ring out, but it was blind, nowhere close to where Finn was running. Perry had lost him, and now Finn was deep into the trees. He stopped, keeping a tree between him and the area where he assumed Perry must be hiding. He took his gun from its holster, dropped to his knee, and looked out from the cover of the tree, completely motionless.

He stared for a few seconds, seeing nothing. Then he spotted a disturbance in the air—Perry's breath billowing out into the cold. He was obscured by a tree, but there was the hunting rifle leaning against that same tree. Perry was probably looking through binoculars, scanning the deepening woods for signs of Finn, no doubt becoming more nervous with each failed scan of the terrain.

Perry and the gun were about thirty yards away. Finn looked at the snowy path between him and his target, scanning the gentle undulations for signs that there were obstacles over which he might trip or stumble. It looked clear. He checked his pockets, making sure he had quick access to the spare magazines.

Finn started running, fast, covering ten yards before Perry realized something was amiss. Even when Perry's senses kicked in, he probably didn't know where Finn was, only that there was the sound of movement. He reached down for the gun, but Finn was ready.

He fired off a couple of rounds, deafening in the chill stillness of the woods, one getting lucky and hitting the stock of the gun, knocking it to the floor. Perry recoiled and set off, darting away through the trees. As Finn reached the abandoned hunting rifle, three of four shots sounded in quick succession, blind. It was covering fire from Perry even as he continued to run, inadvertently letting Finn know that he also had a handgun.

Finn stepped out from behind the tree, studied Perry as he weaved desperately away, then fired a single shot down the central line along which Perry was moving. Occasionally, a shot like that proved lucky, but it wasn't what Finn was expecting and it wasn't what he got. He stepped behind the tree as Perry responded with another desperate volley of shots.

Perry was running away from the house, and Finn wondered where he was heading. It didn't look like a strategy, more like a panicked escape, but if that was the case he was surely heading in the wrong direction, unless he intended to run all the way around the lake and back again.

Finn sprinted after him, waiting thirty seconds before firing off another round. The same volley came back. Finn wondered what he was carrying, how many bullets in a magazine, whether he had spares—possibly not if the gun had been only a backup for the hunting rifle.

He repeated the same actions: sprinting, a single round, taking cover. A shot came back, the closest yet, clattering through the snow-covered branches to the left of where Finn stood, but it came alone. As the thunderclap of the first shot faded, Finn heard the failed click of the next.

He looked out and saw Perry running, a sudden change of direction, toward the lake. If he'd had another magazine, he would have stayed out of sight until he'd reloaded, or he'd have run on, changing it in flight. Perry was out of ammunition, and if Finn had read him right, he was trying to cut back along the lakeshore to the house.

Finn fired a shot off to his left, aiming about twenty yards in front of the line Perry was taking, then set off after the bullet. Perry, sensing that he was about to be intercepted, made what seemed like a calamitous decision; Finn listened in amazement as he heard Perry's hard footfall stamping across the ice.

Finn ran faster, spotting him a few paces before reaching the open shore. Perry was about ten yards out on the ice, just about to cross Finn's line of sight. And Finn could see his reasoning, at least, because it was a shortcut back toward the house, but no less ill-judged for that.

Finn fired a shot into the ice in Perry's path, and watched as he came to a stumbling halt, staring down at his own feet for thirty seconds, getting his breath before slowly turning to where Finn stood at the edge of the lake.

Two bullets, thought Finn, he had two bullets left in this magazine and he had to make them count, because changing the magazine at this point wasn't an option.

Perry was wearing a heavy parka but no hat, suggesting he'd left the house in a hurry once he'd heard the car. But he'd known in advance that Finn was coming, that was certain, and he looked back at Finn as if he'd expected nothing less.

"How did you know I was coming, Ed?" Perry didn't look inclined to answer. "What—you just guessed that if I killed Gibson and Taylor, I'd probably want to come after you and Karasek?"

"Gibson!" It was obvious he'd known that Gibson had been playing both sides. "You know, Louisa isn't the only one with undercover sources—and mine know what they're doing."

"Hasn't helped you, though." Again, Perry didn't seem inclined to respond. "Why couldn't you just leave me alone, Ed? I left six years ago. You should have just left me alone."

Ed nodded, glancing to his right, and Finn wondered if he was judging the distance, working out if he could make a run for it.

"I didn't set out to come after you, Finn. Karasek was the one who was obsessed, the sick bastard, even after all this time. But imagine how I felt when I found out you'd been in business with Naumenko all along. Finn Harrington, falling on his sword to try to expose me, letting people think he was a traitor, the ultimate double-bluff . . ."

"I was never a traitor, Ed. I was corrupt."

"And there's a difference?"

"I thought so." Across the lake the ice cracked, splintering and grinding against itself. Finn looked toward the noise, then back at Perry. "It's a long time since you were in the field, Ed, and that was a poor decision, going out on the ice."

Ed was dismissive as he said, "That cracking doesn't mean a thing—I know this lake, I know how strong the ice is."

"That wasn't what I meant. I'm sure the ice is strong enough, but it still doesn't give you any cover."

Perry looked down at the ice before meeting Finn's gaze again.

"I'm asking you not to do this, Finn. I'm not asking for myself. I have a wife now, I have . . ." His throat seemed to snag. "I have a baby girl."

Finn found himself wondering how old Perry was—mid-forties, he guessed—and said only, "I didn't know that."

"She'll be two in June." He shook his head and looked across the ice to the house, stubbornly out of reach. He sounded emotional as he said, "It's all I was trying to do, Finn. When I found out about the money, I . . . It wasn't about you, it was about my little girl, security for her, her future."

Finn felt sorry for him suddenly. He looked small and vulnerable standing out there on the ice, a man desperate to be with his young family. And thinking back to the way he'd been in Tallinn, the care and concern he'd shown for his people, Finn could imagine him making an indulgent father. If only that had extended to the children of other families.

Perhaps Perry sensed that Finn's resolve was weakening, because he said now, "We can end this here, Finn. We've both made mistakes, but . . . I'm just asking you to show some compassion, that's all. Show some compassion."

Finn nodded and thought back to Tallinn again. He thought of Katerina and wished he'd asked Alex after all. He wanted to know that something good had come of her, that maybe she was the one person in the world who was still grateful that he had walked into her life.

He raised his gun, took aim, and shot Perry in the chest. Perry staggered back a little, then fell to his knees. Finn stepped onto the ice and walked toward him. He looked down at him. His eyes were looking as if at someone lying on the shore, his mouth moving through a silent attempt at final words.

Finn could think of some final words of his own, of the many things he'd wanted to say to Perry but hadn't. But what was the point of final words between them? What had been the point of any of it?

He raised his gun and shot Perry in the head. The wound didn't produce much blood and the body crumpled sideways onto the ice. Finn stood looking down at it for a moment or two, then across the lake. The woods looked lost in night now, and even the sky was falling away into a deeper blue.

He turned and walked back to the shore, and along the shore to the house. There was a Volvo in an open garage to the side of it. Finn went inside the house and checked the kitchen first, then the other rooms, looking for the keys. He went back outside and found them in the ignition of the car.

He drove back to Helsinki, taking it easy in the darkness, stopping a couple of times to off-load the gun and then the unused magazines. He left the car on a side street and walked the final leg back through the city center to the hotel.

He hesitated in the lobby, looking through to the bar, which was lively as ever, but he didn't go in—it would only remind him of Harry and the days when this had all seemed like fun. It was time to go home. He booked a seat on the early flight to Geneva the next morning. In every sense, it was time to go home.

Chapter Thirty-Seven

The plane arrived on time the next morning, just after ten, the weather once again benevolent. He walked through the arrivals gate, saw the people standing there waiting for passengers, and almost walked past the suited driver holding a card with his name on it.

It wouldn't have mattered because the guy had spotted him.

As Finn stopped, he said, "Good morning, Mr. Harrington, I'm your driver—I'll be taking you to Lausanne."

"Will you now?" Finn walked on and the driver fell in with him. "Don't suppose my publisher sent you?"

"Funny you should say that, sir, I'd like to read one of your books. History." He said no more, as if that word was enough in itself, which Finn supposed it was.

He showed Finn to a black Mercedes with tinted windows, opening the rear door for him. Finn smiled at him, then crouched down and looked inside before committing himself.

When he saw her, he said, "I'll walk."

Louisa laughed. "Do get in, Finn." Finn handed his bag to the driver and climbed in, and she added, "Actually, I almost didn't catch you this morning. I thought you'd still be in Finland."

"My business there was finished more quickly than I'd anticipated."

"So it seems." The driver got in and pulled away. "Satisfied?"

"Can we talk candidly?"

She looked at the driver. "In front of Jim? Of course—he's not a chauffeur!"

Jim looked in the rearview mirror and smiled.

"It wasn't about satisfaction."

"I know. It was about finishing what we started six years ago."

"Something like that." He looked out at a car alongside them, the driver staring quizzically at their tinted windows. Then he turned back to Louisa. "I don't know how much of this'll be news to you—you didn't seem unduly surprised at Alex setting up our meeting at The Berkeley, so perhaps none of it. But there's something I want you to know about Sparrowhawk, something about why I accepted the role of the fall guy."

She smiled, looking quite touched, and said, "Oh, Finn, why do you think we chose you? We knew you wouldn't say no, because we knew about you and Naumenko. It was an issue at the time, but we're quite relaxed about it now, as we are about the fact that you profited very handsomely from those business dealings. Of course, best not tell me how much you profited or we might change our minds, these being austere times."

Did they know about him and Naumenko? Some of it, maybe, but if they'd known everything he couldn't imagine them being relaxed about it even now. It didn't make sense for them to be relaxed at all.

"I don't get it, why would you be relaxed about what I did back then?"

She thought about it for a moment and then said, "The answer's complex. Firstly, you were never cut out for this line of work—you were too much the kind of maverick we try not to recruit anymore.

Your actions, and I don't mean to suggest we knew about them all along, only near the end, but your actions were those of the thrill-seeker. Perry was driven by greed, and a natural treachery that saw him sacrificing colleagues and his country's interests. You never were, and although I don't approve of what you did, you never put lives or our national interests in jeopardy, and you may even have accidentally enhanced the latter."

"Perry knew I was coming yesterday. He implied the information had come from one of your people." She smiled, sanguine. "Do you have any idea why he went out to his summerhouse?"

"It wasn't a bad place to wait for you, I suppose. He knew you'd come after him, source or no source, and I suspect he wanted you to find him at his summer home, not his apartment in Helsinki. He had a wife and a young daughter."

"He told me that." Again, he felt a flash of sympathy for Perry, thinking of him out there on that cold, gray lake.

"Yes, the cost of our line of work's always higher than we imagine it will be. You know that as well as anyone."

He looked at her and nodded, the briefest acknowledgment of another part of their shared history, when Louisa alone had helped him pick up the pieces of a life that had seemed irreparably damaged. But he had no desire to dwell on that past, and he knew she wouldn't want to either.

"So, I take it we can draw a line under all of this now?"

"We don't want you back, if that's what you mean, but no, you shouldn't be bothered again."

Finn smiled and said, "I've quite enjoyed parts of the last few days, but trust me, Louisa, I wouldn't come back. Besides, I have a book to write."

She faced forward, looking content with the way things had panned out, and they continued in silence for a while. After a few minutes, without looking at him, she spoke again.

"There is one last thing you could explain to me, Finn."

"If I can."

"Not about Sparrowhawk as such, more . . ." She looked at him and said, "Jerry de Borg."

"Is Harry Simons dead?"

"Of course he is! That's the second time you've asked me that."

"I know, because Jerry de Borg was mentioned on Gibson's network, and only Harry could have leaked that name."

"Harry's dead." She stared at him for a second or two. "But he didn't die that night on the dock. He lived another couple of days. At one point we thought he might even pull through."

Finn felt a searing anger. "So why wasn't I told?"

"Oh, do be sensible." She paused for a moment. "He was conscious for a while, so lucid I was convinced he'd recover. Perry was there, and Perry told him that you'd betrayed him, that you'd been working with Karasek. Harry wouldn't have it. He was adamant. Perry told him it couldn't have been anyone else and Harry shook his head and said, 'It was Jerry de Borg.' Those were the last words he spoke—to us, anyway."

Finn smiled, his throat tightening with emotion.

He imagined Harry saying it, and laughed at the wild goose chase he'd sent them on. "Imperative to identify Jerry de Borg."

"Who is he, Finn?"

"He's nobody. It's a joke." She looked more confused than he'd ever seen her. "Look, I went home one weekend for an old friend's wedding. I sat next to a guy called Jerry de Borg—nice guy, in a band, beautiful girlfriend, we had some laughs. When I got back I was telling Harry about this guy and he says, 'Jerry de Borg sounds like someone in a spy novel.' After that it became a running joke, if anything went wrong, if anything happened that we couldn't make sense of . . ."

"It was Jerry de Borg!"

"Exactly. If you'd asked me six years ago, I would've told you."

Louisa nodded, deep in thought for a while before saying, "Well, that's one more thing we can cross off the list. And I can't say for sure, but I think we might have had an innocent musician under surveillance for the last six years."

She looked at him and smiled. She was joking—or at least, he thought she was.

And a mystery of his own was solved, too. He realized a part of him had relished the thought that he'd meet Harry again, even if he'd been recast as an adversary. But there was no mystery there, and no way back to that past.

Chapter Thirty-Eight

Finn had them drop him along the street from the Frosts' apartment building.

He climbed out, and as he waited for Jim to get his bag, he leaned back into the car and said, "By the way, thanks, for helping me yesterday."

She smiled. "No, thank you, Finn. For the second time, it seems our disparate interests have dovetailed rather nicely."

"I'm sure they did, hopefully for the last time."

"Oh, you never know. Remember what I said, Finn—one of these days you and I will sit down and have a proper conversation."

"You don't want me back, so I'm not sure what we'd have to talk about." He waited a beat and added, "Or are you writing a book, too?"

She laughed, but he didn't wait for a response, just took the bag from Jim and set off along the street.

When he got to the apartment it was Sam Frost who opened the door. He stared at Finn for a moment as if he didn't recognize him, then said, "Finn, sorry, come in. Come through to the living room."

Finn left his bag in the hallway and followed him through. Maria was there, and a woman he presumed was her mother, looking through some brochures.

Maria looked up and said, "Hello, Finn."

"Hello." He waited to be introduced to the older woman, but it seemed to slip everyone's mind.

Maria said, "One never expects to plan a child's funeral."

"No."

The older woman stood and said, "I'm making coffee—would you like some?"

"No, thank you, I won't be staying." She nodded and left the room.

Sam said, "Please, sit down."

"No, I won't. As I said, I can't stay. I just wanted to tell you, it's done."

"Oh God," said Sam, a mixture of emotions playing out across his face.

Maria only looked up and asked, "Did they suffer?"

"Not as much as you, and I don't expect it to provide much solace, but I feel better for knowing those people aren't in the world anymore. I just wish . . ." He ground to a halt, seeing the pointlessness of it all.

Maria said, "We'd like you to come to the funeral, if you would like to."

"I'd like that very much. Take care." He turned, and Sam took that as his cue to show him back to the door.

Finn picked his bag up, but then Hailey emerged around the corner of the L-shaped hall.

"I thought I heard your voice! How . . . I mean . . ."

"It's done," said Sam, repeating Finn's words.

Hailey nodded. She looked unsure whether to kiss him on the cheek or hug him, a new shyness and uncertainty around him that had emerged in the days he'd been away. He was glad of that.

"Good," she said. Then, as if explaining her presence, she said, "I came over to spend some time with Alice—just because, you know . . ."

Sam said, "She's been a great help."

As they spoke, Alice herself came around the corner but kept her distance. As with her brother, the two unremarkable parents had produced a child of striking beauty. She smiled awkwardly at him, then turned and disappeared again.

Finn said his goodbyes, and found a cab to take him home. And as he got there, he saw Grasset standing outside, as he had been a couple of weeks before, admiring what felt like a summer morning.

"Bonjour, Monsieur Harrington."

"Bonjour, Monsieur Grasset. Another beautiful day."

"It is beautiful." Finn was ready to walk past him, but Grasset said, "Monsieur Harrington, your wife, she came back. Yesterday."

Finn felt a weight sliding away from him, a relief that was almost frightening. He couldn't help but smile, yet he still managed to say, "She isn't my wife."

"*Oui, mais*, er . . ."

Finn went in and pressed for the elevator, then went up the stairs rather than wait for it. He heard a voice as soon as he opened the door, and walked into the kitchen to find Adrienne sitting talking to Debbie, coffee cups in front of them.

"Hello."

Debbie jumped up and said, "Oh my goodness, I'll leave you two alone."

Adrienne looked up and smiled at Finn, a smile that was still measured. "You don't have to leave, Debbie."

Debbie laughed nervously and said, "Oh, but I do." Then she looked at Finn. "Hailey went back to school today. I know you said about being vigilant, but she was insistent, and . . ."

He was impressed, and wasn't sure why, that Hailey was maintaining her secretive habits. Certainly, he wasn't about to reveal her deception by telling Debbie she wasn't at school.

"That's good. She's safe now, anyway."

"It's taken care of?" He nodded and she mouthed a silent *thank you* to him.

Adrienne stood, and gave Debbie a brief hug before she left. She turned to Finn then and kissed him on both cheeks, but offered no hug.

"We need to talk," she said.

"Okay." He sat in the chair vacated by Debbie. Adrienne sat down again. She looked more beautiful than he'd ever seen her, a glow about her that was probably nothing more than the glow of enforced separation. She looked a little more curvy, too— the healthiness of the diet in her brother's house. "Are you back?"

"I don't know." She frowned, and then gave a little noncommittal smile. "I want to be. I've missed you, and yes, the last few days have been . . . a revelation. But things have to change, Finn. Most of all, I need you to be completely open with me, completely honest."

"Things will change. And I'll tell you whatever you want to know."

"Were you a spy?"

That was clever, starting with something they'd already covered.

"For want of a better word, yes. I left six years ago, and I can't talk about a lot of what I did."

"Did you ever kill anybody?"

He was surprised by the question. Unless Adrienne was bluffing him, Debbie hadn't mentioned what had happened in their apartment. He'd have to let her know that it was okay to tell Adrienne—in his experience, most people needed one confidante.

"I killed two people, one of them by accident, one of them . . ." He stopped. He would have to tell her about Sofi in time, but not now, not yet. "That was years ago, but in the last week I've killed four more."

Her mouth fell open.

"You've killed four people this week!"

He nodded, surprised at how lightly he carried those deaths, certainly more lightly than Sofi's, or even the guy in the church.

"Two of them were the people who killed Jonas, and one of those was trying to kill Hailey when I intercepted him—I killed him in their apartment."

Adrienne looked more shocked by that revelation. "But Debbie didn't say anything . . ."

"I told them to forget about it, not to tell anyone. I also killed the two people who ordered Jonas's death and who would never have left me alone if I hadn't killed them."

As if it was the one revelation she hadn't expected, she said, "You're a killer."

"Hardly. I've killed people, that's not the same."

"Would you kill again?"

"If I had to, and so would you. It's what we do to protect ourselves and the people we care about." She smiled, finding something worthwhile in that comment. "There's something else I need to tell you, about my past—"

As if trying to head him off at the pass, or perhaps because his previous comment had rendered her incapable of keeping quiet, she said, "I'm pregnant." He became immediately concerned about his face, fearing that he could not make the expected expression fight its way through the shock. This was why she looked so good, so curvy, so fecund—it was obvious to him now. He tried to speak, but she said urgently, "I'm having it, so don't even think about it."

He was taken over by a different kind of shock, and said, "What makes you think I would wanna get rid of it?"

"You kept saying you didn't want a family."

"Yet! All men say that, and . . . I had other reasons, but . . . How long have you known?"

"The last time we spoke, when you were in Béziers. I tried to tell you, but I didn't get the opportunity." He shook his head, already ashamed of the persona he'd maintained and even become in the last six years. Then, as if to drive home that the change would not be as immediate as he imagined, she said, "I thought you might have noticed at Mathieu's, that I drank no wine."

Her hands were clasped on the table and he reached across, separating them, holding them, feeling the warm smoothness of her skin.

"I'm amazed you've stayed with me these last four years, but I'm glad you did, Adrienne, because I love you and I want us to be married, and the thought of having a child with you is . . . it's the best thing that ever happened to me."

She smiled and squeezed his hands, but then the smile straightened out again and she said, "What did you want to tell me about your past?"

Finn nodded, accepting that it was the one thing he had to tell her, that there could be no future together unless he did tell her.

"Okay. It's about my old job, the reason I thought it would come back to haunt me. See, I was corrupt. I used my contacts and my position to forward the business interests of someone I befriended in the course of my work. All these years, I thought my former superiors knew nothing about it, but they knew all along. The person I worked with—and I worked with him, not for him—was Aleksandr Naumenko."

"Aleksandr Naumenko? The oligarch? The multibillionaire? You're friends with Aleksandr Naumenko?"

"Well, kind of. I saw him last week, but before that I hadn't seen him in three years, maybe four." He didn't wait for her consternation to subside, but carried on, saying, "The business was incredibly lucrative and I made a lot of money. I mean a *lot* of money."

Now she looked baffled. "What happened to it? We live okay, yeah, you make good profits from your books and I have my own money, but . . ."

"I'm being open, remember." She looked expectant. "For six years I haven't touched it. Like I said, I thought it would all come back to haunt me. As of today, I found out that it won't. The money's been sitting in a numbered account here in Switzerland for all that time. It's actually the main reason I moved here."

"Even though you've never touched it." He nodded. "How much?"

"Give or take, a hundred and eighty million dollars."

She stared at him and laughed involuntarily, stopped herself, then laughed again. Finn laughed, too, as if for the first time he'd realized how extraordinary it was, how it summed up the desiccation of his life that he had been able to sit on that fortune all this time.

She found a frown and said, "This doesn't change anything." He shook his head, accepting the point. "But it means we can move, right?"

"Anywhere you like."

She offered him another smile, seductive, as she said, "So . . . how about we move into the bedroom? It's traditional, no, after a separation?"

"It is, yeah, and I'd love to—but, you know, I do have a book to write."

He kept a straight face long enough to leave her doubting for a moment.

Then she saw through it and said, "So you should get to work."

"I will."

Slowly, he stood, but he continued to hold on to her hands, bringing her to her feet. He kissed her, but she pulled back a little, curious again as she said, "A hundred and eighty million dollars? What did you do to make—"

He put his finger to her lips and said, "All in good time."

She weighed up his response and, to his surprise, nodded and smiled. It was true, there were other things he needed to tell her, so many other things, but they could wait, at least for a little while, at least until she came to know him for who he hoped he really was.

History—the present

Sergei saw her come out of the building and walk toward him across the quad, and he knew the intelligence was good and that this trip up to Harvard hadn't been in vain.

He studied her as she walked—it was obvious the girl didn't have a clue about what the future might hold for her. She was dressed casually but expensively for the late fall in New England, she was tall and fair and beautiful, with the telltale cheekbones, but this was not where she belonged.

He looked briefly at the other people traversing the quad, in and out of the college buildings, but his eyes quickly darted back to her. She was almost on him now.

The key would be in the first contact—he had to pitch it just right. He knew her name of course, but wondered whether he should use it or begin by calling her "Miss." No, that would show him up as a creep, and calling her Katerina would at least grab her attention, stall her long enough for him to strike.

She was only a few paces away now, and he stood and reached inside his jacket. She spotted the movement and looked at him, smiling—in his head he repeated his earlier observation, that she didn't have a clue.

"Hi, hello, it's Katerina, isn't it?"

She stopped, puzzled, but looked relaxed and didn't clutch her bag any more tightly, as some people did. All those books, thought Sergei, and yet she carried it effortlessly.

"Do I know you?"

"No, Katerina, but I know you." He brought his hand back out of his jacket and handed her the card. "My name's Sergei Baum and I work with Stein Model Agency in New York City. I'm sure you've heard of us."

She nodded and laughed, finding some amusement in the card or in him, he wasn't sure which. Maybe she was just nervous.

"Katerina, you're tall, you're beautiful, and most importantly, you have *it*. I have an instinct for these things, one that's never let me down yet, and I know we can make a star of you at Stein. How would you like to be a model?"

"I'm flattered, Mr. Baum, but—"

"No, you'd be perfect, just perfect, and it needn't interfere with your studies, not at all. A lot of our girls study at the same time as launching very successful careers." He thought he could see her wavering and said, "I'll even make a wager with you, Katerina, and you don't have to decide right now—call me once you've had a think about it—but I'll make a wager that you'll be on the cover of *Vogue* within one year. One year! I guarantee it."

She smiled, looking genuinely flattered, but just as he was beginning to think he'd reeled her in, she handed the card back, so decisively that he found himself taking it.

"Thank you so much, Mr. Baum, but no thank you."

With that she moved gracefully on, walking away from him with such poise, such effortless beauty, that he couldn't resist one last desperate gambit.

"I can make you a supermodel, Katerina!"

She stopped long enough to turn back with another bright laugh as she said, "But I don't want to be a supermodel—I'm going to be a historian." Her eyes seemed completely alive to the absurdity of it, but he saw now that there would be no persuading her.

And with that she was gone, disappearing among her fellow students. His phone buzzed in his pocket. He took it out and glanced at it—the office—then looked up again, feeling the pressure he was under, thinking it wouldn't hurt to try one more time. But she had vanished, slipping seamlessly back into her own life.

And as hard as he stared at the sea of students moving purposefully about the campus, as striking as she was, still he could not see her. Her name was Katerina, and he'd spoken to her just moments before, but already her disappearance seemed total, almost as if she had never been there at all.

Acknowledgments

Thanks to Deborah Schneider and her team at Gelfman Schneider/ICM. Thanks to Emilie Marneur, Victoria Pepe, and all at Thomas & Mercer. And finally, thanks to Juri Nummelin and Harto Pasonen, who took me for a drink and inadvertently helped me to plan a killing—just another day in Helsinki . . .

About the Author

© 2015

Kevin Wignall is a British writer, born in Brussels in 1967. He spent many years as an army child in different parts of Europe, and went on to study politics and international relations at Lancaster University. He became a full-time writer after the publication of his first book, *People Die* (2001). His other novels are *Among the Dead* (2002), *Who is Conrad Hirst?* (2007), shortlisted for the Edgar Award and the Barry Award, *Dark Flag* (2010), and *A Death in Sweden* (2016). His novel *The Hunter's Prayer*, originally published as *For the Dogs* in 2004, has been made into a film directed by Jonathan Mostow and starring Sam Worthington and Odeya Rush.